SONS OF YOCAHU

A Saga of the Tainos' Devastation on Hispaniola

Gloria Bond

S&S PRESS

To the late Dr. Alfred A. Levy, whose unwavering
confidence taught me integrity and honor.

Contents

Forward

Sons of Yocahu: A Saga of the Tainos' Devastation on Hispaniola takes place on the Caribbean island of Quisqueya, which is known today as Hispaniola, where Haiti and the Dominican Republic are located. It is created to symbolize — not only what happened to the Tainos who once dominated this island — but also the catastrophe that befell all other Native Americans, who experienced the removal of both their lands and cultures. For too long the foreign settlers of the Americas and their descendants failed to recognize the wonderful and fascinating cultures these people had, which were in many ways superior to theirs. Instead, these settlers came with attitudes of superiority and viewed the Native Americans as inferior, primitive, and barbaric, which led to the condoning of genocide and other great crimes. As a result of this predicament, it is taking the Native Americans generations to overcome the trauma of their past and to regain the status that they lost. Sadly, when the settlers came, they failed to see that to the Native Americans, the land belonged to everyone and was to be shared. To the settlers, the land was to be owned, and they should acquire it for themselves. And the people they found living on it, were to be *pacified*, or brought under control.

I chose the island of Hispaniola as the setting for my story, because its history is easy to tell, since its devastation occurred within only one generation. Further, Columbus indicated in his journal that this island was superior to the previous ones he visited, for he was impressed by the sophistication, wealth, and friendliness of its people and thought that they were strikingly beautiful. When he claimed Quisqueya for Spain, he named it *La Isla Española*. Little did he realize that the Quisqueyans thought that he and his men were gods, for they had been waiting for generations for their highest *zemie* (or god) Yocahu, who once lived with their ancestors, to return to them to bring them a higher form of living. Even the 16th century *padre*, Bartholomé de Las Casas, observed that in the beginning, the Indians believed that the Europeans were angels from heaven.

When Columbus first arrived on Quisqueya, he also did not realize that it was divided into five major kingdoms, with a total of about 80 smaller *cacicazgos*, or minor kingdoms, within them. The five major kingdoms are illustrated below:

Because some of my readers had trouble remembering the Indian names and confused them, I re-named the major kingdoms as follows:

Quisqueya
(Hispaniola)

Indeed, when Columbus arrived, Magua, or the Fertile Kingdom, was an extremely fertile area. A very old queen named Higuanamá ruled Higuey, or the Kingdom of the Great Old Lady. Maguana, or the Kingdom of the Mines, was an area that contained mines of ore. Xaragua, or the Mother Kingdom, was a place where the mother tongue was spoken, a place of high culture, and a place where a school existed in the royal courts of Queen Anacoana for the education of the royal children of Quisqueya and the surrounding islands. And Marién, or the Kingdom of Marién, was a significant place, because here, King Guacanagarí came to the Santa Maria to greet Columbus and his men to invite them to the first of many feasts. It was in Marién that Columbus later built Fort Navidad out of the ruins of the Santa Maria after it sank, and it was here, where Columbus left his men when he returned to Spain. In addition, to avoid further confusion, I found it necessary to change the names of two kings: Cahoba to *Cahoba the Great* and Canaobo to *Canaobo the Fierce*.

My biggest challenge was to create compelling adventures from scanty material. Since the Quisqueyans were totally destroyed and had no written records, I recreated their culture by extracting information from the journal of Columbus, the writings of Bartholomé de Las Casas, the works of anthropologists, records of historians, the Internet, and other sources. Some events in this book may sound so incredible that readers may think that I made them up, but they were based on actual studies, records, and reports. Most of the happenings in this book occurred on Quisqueya, but a couple of them occurred on other islands or in South America. I am told that King Cahoba's vision is recorded in history books on Hispaniola today. Since the Tainos are believed to originate from the Arawaks, Anacoana's wedding is based on an anthropologist's report on weddings in Arawak tribes. Gonzalo Fernández de Oviedo y Valdés, a 16th century historian, also mentioned observing a similar type of wedding ritual among the Tainos of *Española*. The Carib attack is also fashioned after an event in the autobiography of a daughter of a modern day anthropologist, who was captured in the jungles of South America. Even the vision that Neef received represents the mysticism of Native Americans and their closeness to their ancestral spirits. Its events refer to actual happenings. And the pacification of Cuba was moved up in time to fit my story.

Since Columbus was so impressed with *Española*, I took occasional liberties to build up its grandeur. According to the late Swedish anthropologist, Sven Lovén, there actually was a canal that the people of Xaragua (the Mother Kingdom) built to save them from having to journey around the Guayacarima Peninsula. I also slightly altered the Taino class structure on this island. Within the traditional Taino society, there existed *caciques*, or kings, who were at the top of the social scale; below them, came *Nytainos* and priests (*bohutios*), who made up the upper-class; and last, the

Naborians were at the bottom of the class structure and served as servants to the *caciques* and *Nytainos*. However, in my book, I divided up the lower class into two groups: the *Naborian* servants and the commoners. The *Naborian* servants were those who were captured on other islands and sold as slaves on Quisqueya, and the commoners were humble people of this lowest social rank, who were free to come and go as they pleased. In addition, I made a *behique* to be, not a priest, as some experts often refer them to be, but a female, whom the anthropologist, Sven Lovén, identified as *a wise old woman with a vast knowledge of herbal cures*. In indigenous cultures, this type of woman plays an important role in society. In my story, she is represented by the kind hearted, Lida. Today, herbal cures, such as hers, are often recognized for their scientific basis, and modern pharmaceutical companies are now sending people to these cultures to study about them.

In addition, since nobody can document who killed the people at Fort Navidad, and it appears to be out of character for the gentle Tainos to have committed this massacre, I felt that I could make up my own explanation of who the culprits were, whom my readers can find out about in this book. Because I mentioned a Bible that was written in Spanish in *Sons of Yocahu*, religious scholars may argue that there was no such translation at the time of Columbus, but I believe that anything could be possible, particularly in Spain. For while most of Europe prevailed in illiteracy and darkness during the Middle Ages, literacy and high intellectual achievements thrived in the Iberian Peninsula. Thus, the existence of a Bible that was translated into the dominant language of its country could have been most feasible in Spain, even if at that time, the Inquisition was particularly strong and caused people to keep their accomplishments hidden out of fear of being condemned as heretics. Further, if there were to be a Spanish translation of the Bible, Columbus would have been one of the most likely people to own such a copy, for he was extremely progressive for his time and thought much like a person of the twentieth and twenty-first centuries.

Many asked, "Why publish such a story now, when we already celebrated the Quincentennial for the discovery of America years before? That issue is over."

Despite those comments, we must realize that many Native Americans do not even observe Columbus Day, because of the injurious effects this discovery had (and still has) upon them. If this book were to be published only for the Quincentennial, it would be an insult to these people. So let us designate the Quincentennial period to be only for those who wish to honor that European discovery, but let this book be published to honor the Native Americans, for the need for a book, such as this one, is just as urgent *now* as it was during the Quincentennial. As long as the Native Americans are still subjects of injustice, their predicament is never over. The urgency to recognize their worth should never be seasonal, such as every five hundred years, for their problem continues and cannot be solved with land grants or a few added liberties. Rather, *at all times,* should greater steps be taken to recognize these people, so they can someday become significant nations. In fact, the need to create books to awaken the world of the worth of the Native Americans should be ongoing and forever, if it takes us that long to solve the problems that we settlers created.

And now, please come with me to Quisqueya, for a fascinating adventure!

Gloria Bond
Author

Sons of Yocahu

A Saga of the Tainos' Devastation on Hispaniola

Prologue

The Fertile Kingdom, 1465
Island of Quisqueya, Caribbean

 Within the cave, Guarionex sat captivated, as his father built up a sacrificial fire. While the tentacled flames stretched ceilingward and reflected off the green nephrites on Father's crown, entrails of parrots shriveled, hissed, and curled upon the altar, spreading the smell of meat into the air.

"Oh, *zemies* of the heaven and earth," Father chanted. "I, King Cahoba, chief *cacique* of Quisqueya, come again for my yearly vision. I plead for your guidance and wisdom."

Guarionex did not mind his big brother's head resting upon his shoulder as he slept, for he was more interested in Father's ritual. For years, he had waited for this day, when he turned ten years old — the proper age to be clothed in a loincloth. It meant that he was old enough to accompany his father and brother into the Fertile Valley to receive the annual vision. Since Father was the highest king of Quisqueya, it was his privilege to receive instructions from the *zemies* for the entire island.

Although Guarionex had been fasting for two days now, he had grown past hunger and thirst, and his head was filled with the warnings his brother, whom he called Eldest-Son-of-My-Father's-First-Wife, told him — that this excursion to the wilderness was going to be boring. But now as his older brother slept, Guarionex remained alert, for contrary to his brother's opinion, he found Father's religious ritual fascinating.

It didn't take him long to realize that this year was different, for when they first entered this cave, Father said that he was not going to take any herbs or powders for his vision, as he did every year. And now as Father's voice droned into the night, Guarionex felt his head nod. Soon, like his brother, he too, was fast asleep.

Suddenly a cry echoed in the chamber. Guarionex jerked awake. Father was trembling violently, with fear overpowering his eyes. The flames leapt ten times taller than they had been, and as they curled upward, an amorphous image was forming within them, eerily shaping and reshaping itself. Guarionex saw that Eldest-Son-of-My-Father's-First-Wife was now standing in front of him, with knees pounding at each other. When he turned and fled, Guarionex jumped up to run after him, but Cahoba the Great called out.

"Stay, my sons. Stay. Princes should never allow fear to conquer them."

Guarionex stopped. Slowly, he turned his head and forced himself to focus upon the object on the altar. It had grown tall. Two feet formed; a bottom of a robe appeared; next, came arms, shoulders, a neck, and last, a head. Soon, he saw a human-like form, with flesh as white as a breast of a shark, hovering above the altar. Unlike Father, it had no tattoos on its skin. As its face grew distinct, a pair of deep-set eyes and a narrow nose appeared, with hair falling past its shoulders and hair even growing from its chin. It wore a robe, which came to its ankles that consisted of a delicate substance, beneath which Guarionex discerned a muscular physique.

As Father fell to his knees with his jaw frozen open, the image began to speak.

"Cahoba, my son, fear not. I am thy friend."

Its voice came as rushing winds, love and forgiveness, thousands of fragrances of flowers, falling cascades, and other beauty — too great for words. It soothed away the apprehension that paralyzed Guarionex, and he heard his father's rapid breathing return to normal.

"Who are you, O Great One?" Father said.

"I am Yocahu, the *zemie* from the heavens. It was I, who spake to thy mind to abstain from any hallucinating aids, for thou needest neither incantations nor herbs to call upon me. And it was I, who visited thine ancient fathers and promised them that I would return some day."

"Ah, so you've come back to us, at last."

"Not yet, my son. I come only to give thee a warning."

Gurarionex saw love, warmer than the flames, emanating from Yocahu's eyes.

"Cahoba, as long as thou reignest, peace shall prevail, but after thou passeth through death to rest in *Coaibai*, thy son will only rule a short while. Then foreigners, wearing many clothes, will arrive from the East. They will cause great destruction among thy people."

"Nay, nay, that cannot be so..."

"With fierceness, they shall rule over all of the five major kingdoms of this island and will cause hardships, murders, and terrible starvation."

"Nay! Nay! Nay! Then, what will become of my sons?"

The image began to fade.

"Do not go yet, my Lord, tell me about my sons..."

The image disappeared altogether.

"Come back, my Lord. Please, please. Come back."

The image re-appeared, with love still emanating from its face.

"If thy people become perfect in keeping the promises their ancient fathers made with me, I will return and will make them the greatest people on earth—even before those foreigners arrive, so no harm can ever befall them."

When the image left again, blackness surrounded Guarionex and his father, excepting for a steady shimmer from the moon that glowed through the cave entrance. Guarionex slowly made his way toward Father, and when he reached him and the king did not acknowledge his presence, he turned and extended an arm toward the altar. Its stones felt cool and void of soot, as if no fire was ever there.

"Do you always see Yocahu every year during your vision, Father?"

"No one has, my son. Not since the day he left our ancient fathers. I always see laughing *zemies,* who bring good omens."

The king's voice broke. As he sobbed and his mighty shoulders heaved, Guarionex threw his arms around him. Just then, Guarionex saw Eldest-Son-of-My-Father's-First-Wife returning through the entrance of the cave. His brother had missed the vision altogether.

As Guarionex felt his father's arms encircle him, a thought hit him.

"Father, my days with a loincloth will be much more troubled than the days without them, won't they?"

Cahoba tightened his hold around him, as he said, "My son, I see that you have already grown much wiser, since you began wearing your loincloth."

As Guarionex watched his brother approach, he longed for the times, when he could run free and naked again, but he knew that those days were gone forever.

Book One

1

The Fertile Kingdom, 1484

When the old *cacique* died, drums reverberated this news throughout the villages, and all Quisqueya wept. People came in scores to view the hollowed out body of Cahoba the Great, as it hung to dry above a fire in the central plaza. Some came with their heads sprinkled with ashes; others came dressed in clothes of mourning; but most came the way they always dressed: naked, loin clothed, or wearing a simple dress, called a *nagua*. Many arrived after traveling over miles of muddy, windy, paths. But no matter from whence they came, or in what shape or form they arrived, they appeared with tears streaming down their faces. When they sat in silence, listening to the *bohutios*, or priests, addressing chants heavenward in wavering voices, while drums beat to sonorous sounding instruments, many of them wondered, *What will happen to us, now?*

For years these Quisqueyans had known about the Vision of Yocahu, which their old king had received that told that they would be destroyed soon after he died. They also remembered that if they continued in their tradition of the *Yocahuan love* and developed it to perfection, Yocahu might arrive before any menacing foreigners could ever reach them and would then keep them from harm. And everyone said that the only foreigners they knew who were ferocious enough to destroy them, were the Caribs, for those cannibals were always roaming the sea and invading islands to capture people for food.

The people particularly loved Cahoba the Great for what he did for them, for as soon as he received his memorable vision, he took immediate measures to protect them from any invaders. The first step he made was to hire a warrior named Canaobo the Fierce, whose armies were feared throughout the land.

As the funeral ritual proceeded, a five-year-old boy sat alone upon a fallen log. He had not a stitch of clothing on, since he was too young to wear a loincloth. His thin body slouched forward and hiccupped in sobs.

"Grandfather, please come back to me."

No one paid any attention to him. Nor did they look at his shriveled legs that dangled in front of him or his two crutches that leaned against the log.

17

Neef wiped his large, dark eyes with the back of his palm, smearing mud and tears across his face. The sight of his grandfather's lifeless body was hard to bear. He thought of how he used to crawl into Grandfather Cahoba's lap each night, as the villagers gathered around a fire to tell tales and sing *areitas*. He wished that he could feel Grandfather's strong arms again. He wished that he could hear his deep voice chanting the histories and genealogies. Whenever he sang them, he made their stories so real that Neef could almost see and touch their characters and events.

As Neef wiped his eyes again, although the adults were unaware of him, he was sensitive to everyone around. Some of them were strangers, but he recognized several *undercaciques* from the lesser kingdoms, for they often came to Grandfather Cahoba for advice. He saw the village women, who sat each morning singing in the shade of palm trees, scraping freshly harvested manioc. And he saw the town children, whom he could not play with, because he was unable to run and jump, as they could.

Soon the priests announced that the spirit of their king was entering into the land of *Coaibai*. The music then turned high-pitched, to the point that its wails hurt Neef's ears. At the same time, it drowned out a voice of another child close by.

"Why are they singing about the king going to *Coaibai*? Where is that place, anyway? How can our king be there, if he is lying in front of us?"

Neef turned and saw that the child who spoke was about his age. Since he had never seen that boy before, he assumed that he must have come from a far away kingdom. Unlike that boy, Neef already knew the answers to his questions. In fact, he knew many answers, which older children often wondered about. As far back as he could remember, he had always understood that *Coaibai* was a place located somewhere on this island, where the spirits of good people went to rest after they died. But bad people were not permitted there, and their spirits had to wander the earth, to torment mortals, instead.

The music grew softer now, until it was a little louder than a whisper.

The boy spoke again, "Where's the basket, where they'll put the king's bones?"

Since the music had toned down, the boy's voice could be heard distinctly this time. His father turned crimson and looked around to see if anyone had heard his son. When the adults did not appear to notice, he leaned close to the boy.

"Hush. Not so loud."

"But you said that after our kings die, their bones are put in baskets and are hung from the ceiling of the palace. Where is that basket?"

"Shhhh, I'll tell you later," the father whispered.

"Tell me NOW."

The father sighed, leaned close to the boy, and whispered in his ear.

Neef wiped his eyes and watched the boy. To him, that boy did not appear to be at all sad that his Grandfather Cahoba was now dead.

As hired mourners started new wails, Neef suddenly wanted to be away from this place, for all the weeping in the world could not bring Grandfather back to life. He wished the chanting and drums would stop. But instead, the priests picked up shakers whose vibrations added to the volume of the music.

When someone tossed new kindling into the central fire, causing its flames to leap higher, Neef reached for his crutches. He didn't know where he should go, but then, the beach came to his mind, because that was where he and Grandfather always loved to be. As he hobbled past mourners and wailing people, not a head turned toward him. Soon he reached the familiar shore and felt its cool sand beneath his feet. Its ebbing waves were a soothing sight, for they reminded him of the countless times he and Grandfather had strolled together here, as they looked out into the sea.

"How was the ocean made, Grandfather?" Neef recalled saying many times.

"It started from a fight, Neef. Long ago, a father and son had a big argument, and the son became so angry that he tried to murder his father, but his father murdered him first. Then the father put his son's bones into a calabash, and his bones turned into fish, which burst the calabash. Then all of the water flowed out of the broken gourd and formed the ocean."

"If we are on one side of that ocean, then what is on the other side?"

"Many, many islands. But none are as great, or as advanced, as Quisqueya."

Sometimes during their walks, Grandfather wept over Neef's physical handicap.

"I am sorry that the *zemies* made you crippled, Grandson. But they have blessed you with a keen mind, to make up for it."

Neef still remembered a certain day, when he was three years old, as he and Grandfather walked along this beach. For the first time, he had recited, not only the names of the five major kingdoms of this island and their *caciques*, but also the names of all 80 of the lesser kingdoms and their rulers that were governed by the five greater kingdoms. When he was done, Grandfather laughed, cheered, and clapped. He said that he knew of no other three-year-old, who was as smart as he was.

Only two weeks before as he and Cahoba the Great walked upon this same path, he noticed that his grandfather was not as lively as he usually was. His breathing was laborious, and he preferred to walk away from the water to keep his feet dry. So Neef stayed close to him and watched the waves from a distance, puzzled that his grandfather was different that day. As he watched Cahoba hunch forward, inching along and coughing, Neef had no idea that he had been ill for a long time, for no one told him about it.

As they strolled hand in hand, Grandfather finally said, "Neef, no matter what happens to Quisqueya, those waves will always wash upon that shore."

"What do you mean?"

"They will always continue to be there, ebbing back and forth, just as they had for centuries, even when trouble came. It won't be long now until I die, and when..."

"Grandfather, you must not say that. You'll never die. You'll always be here."

"Nay, Neef. I am now an old man, and soon the kingdom must be turned over to my son."

"You mean ... to my uncle?"

Neef was referring to whom his father Guarionex called Eldest-Son-of-My-Father's-First-Wife. He had heard people talking much about him lately.

"Everyone says that Eldest-Son-of-My-Father's-First-Wife and his friends drink too much *chicha*, Grandfather. I've heard many people say that they don't want him to become the next king."

Grandfather Cahoba sighed.

"When the time comes and my son is given the responsibility for the kingdom, he will do a good job. You will see. I taught him well, and he knows what he must do to keep our people safe."

Neef listened, with his five-year-old mind trusting Cahoba the Great's judgment.

"I have already prepared the work that is required of him," Grandfather said. "All he needs to do is to continue what I started. Years before you were ever born when I received The Vision of Yocahu, I searched the island for the best fighters, who could protect our people. And I found Canaobo the Fierce in the Kingdom of the Mines. At that time, he and his armies had just moved from far up north to Quisqueya. Ever since I hired him, the Carib attacks have been minimized."

"Grandfather, why couldn't you form your own armies, instead of paying someone else to fight for us?"

"Oh, we could never fight. You see, we *Tainos* of Quisqueya are Yocahu's special people. We are the *People of Peace*. You must always remember that."

"But why can Canaobo the Fierce fight, and we can't?"

"Sometimes I forget that you are just a little boy and do not understand many things, because you are always asking questions that are beyond your age. Listen carefully to what I am going to tell you, my son."

At that moment, Grandfather went through a series of coughs, so he stopped and lowered his body to the ground. Neef squatted next to him, waiting for him to recover. When the coughing subsided, Grandfather absent-mindedly stared into space, while plunging his hands into the sand and bringing them up with heaping piles of granules falling through his fingers. When he sifted out a small piece of black coral, Neef recalled his grandfather's words of, *you don't usually find black coral around here*, and watched as Grandfather turned that rock over in his palm and ran a finger over its porous surface, with the faraway look still in his eyes.

"Neef, we don't fight, because long, ago, the great Yocahu came down from the heavens to our ancient fathers. In those days, our ancestors lived like savages. But with love, Yocahu raised their standard of living to great heights. Within that atmosphere, our fathers began to flourish in every area of learning. They developed great works in fine arts and literature. Their technology multiplied, as they created inventions they never knew were possible. They discovered cures in medicine, beyond anything we know today. As our fathers grew strong under the influence of Yocahu, there was no fighting among them, but only a great love that bonded them in ways that no other people on earth have ever experienced. And after they lived on this level for a long time, one day, Yocahu said that he had to leave.

"Our fathers begged for him to remain with them, and after much pleading, he finally promised that he would return some day.

"Yocahu told them, *You must always keep the love I have taught you, for when I return, if you have preserved it, I will make you the greatest people on the earth.*

"Because of Yocahu's promise to us, we *Tainos* do not fight. We must keep *the love*. If we begin to battle, we will learn to hate, as the people on the other islands do. And then, we can no longer be Yocahu's special people."

"But Grandfather, you didn't answer my question," said Neef. "Why can Canaobo the Fierce fight, when we can't?"

"Neef, Canaobo the Fierce may fight, because he is a foreigner. He and his men came from the Lucanyan Islands. Lucanyans do not know of *the love*. They made no promises with Yocahu, as the Quisqueyans did, so they need not love, as we love."

"But Grandfather, is it right for the Lucanyans to fight, if it is not right for us?"

Grandfather suddenly grew impatient with Neef's questions. He clenched his fists and threw the black piece of coral into a bush in the distance.

"Aye! It is right for Canaobo the Fierce to go to war for the *People of Peace!*"

His sudden outburst came as a surprise to Neef, and Neef said nothing more.

As Neef walked alone, allowing the waves to bathe his feet and drench the bottom of his crutches, clumps of seaweed became tangled between his toes. But he pulled them away and tossed them back into the sea. He passed a fenced corral, in which the townsfolk stored their living food supplies. It enclosed several varieties of fish and two swimming turtles. As he hobbled along, his crutches left deep impressions in the wet sand that quickly filled with water.

Suddenly he heard laughter in the distance. It was coming from a hut that was set on higher ground, away from the village. Curious, he hobbled toward that *bohio* to investigate. As he hid in nearby bushes, Neef peered through leaves into the hut. He saw that it was filled with people. He counted twelve men in it, and they were behaving merrily, as if they were at a party. And then he saw his uncle, Eldest-Son-of-My-Father's-First-Wife, sitting among them. Although their voices were loud, they were too far away from the funeral to be heard. The men were holding gourds of some kind of drink, which caused their faces to glow with red.

One man then lifted his gourd toward Eldest-Son-of-My-Father's-First-Wife.

"Here's to our new king! May you rule long and well."

When his uncle arose, Neef saw that he was unsteady on his feet.

"I promise all of you, the first thing I will do, is to dispel that silly superstition about Yocahu talking to my father. I was there when he claimed it happened. I can tell you, there was no such vision."

"Above all, you must stop the rise of taxes, so our people can enjoy life!" one of the men shouted.

"Get rid of Canaobo the Fierce," another said. "He's draining our economy."

"Aye, out with that Lucanyan! We don't need him. Push him out of our island, altogether. Everybody knows that we are too great and powerful to be destroyed."

As Neef stared into the hut, he couldn't believe what he heard. Suddenly he dropped one of his crutches, and it hit the ground with a loud thud. The noise caused the men in the hut to turn in his direction.

"Well, look who's here. Hey, there's your little, crippled nephew."

When Eldest-Son-of-My-Father's-First-Wife turned toward Neef, his eyes were unfocused and glazed.

"Come in, come in. Join us in our celebration. Please sit down. Can someone pour some *chicha* in a gourd for my nephew?"

Neef backed away. He knew drunken men when he saw them. Grandfather had told him to always avoid them, for they had no control over their faculties.

"Excuse me, Uncle, but I must go back to the funeral."

Eldest-Son-of-My-Father's-First-Wife started toward him. He was wobbly on his feet.

"Funeral?" His words were slurred. "It is not a time to be sad and crying. It is a time for joy, for you will soon be liberated from old ideas that have weighted down our island for too long."

Neef could not run, but he was quick with his crutches, and soon he found himself fleeing across the sand. When he glanced over his shoulder, he saw that his uncle and friends were not pursuing him, but he could still hear their laughter coming from the hut. After he sped over the sand for some time, he finally slowed down. He could now hear the drums and instruments from the funeral again. As he panted to catch his breath, he saw in the bushes, a tiny black object. As he hobbled slowly to the spot where the object lay, he recognized that it was the same piece of coral that Grandfather had thrown two weeks before, in a fit of anger. He shut his eyes and heard Grandfather's voice echoing in his head: *Aye! It is all right for Canaobo the Fierce to go to war for the People of Peace!* Neef stooped down and picked up the black rock. As he closed his fingers around it, he knew that it was all that he had to remember his grandfather by.

"Neef! Neef!"

Neef turned in the direction of the voice that called and saw his sister Sabila running toward him, Her long, glossy, black hair flew outward behind her.

"I've been looking all over for you. Hurry. Father wants us both to be with him, right away."

"Where is he?"

From the look on Sabila's face, Neef knew that she had no time to reply. Instead, she motioned for him to follow her, and she turned abruptly and flew in the direction of the village. Although Neef was quick with his crutches, he could not catch up with her, but he was close behind. Soon they came to the hut of the chief *bohutio*. Neef had never been in it before, but he understood that many sacred ceremonies transpired here. Several priests were now lined up in front of it, as if they were acting as guards. They were not the same priests, whom Neef saw participating earlier in the funeral ceremony.

Neef finally caught up to his sister.

"What's happening, Sabila?"

Sabila still did not answer and walked past the priests, who were guards. They nodded at both of the children approvingly and allowed them to enter their hut. Inside, Neef strained his eyes to adjust to its dimness. After he blinked several times, his eyes focused on the silhouettes of several *zemies* placed on low tables, and as his eyes adjusted further, he saw that they were carved out of either wood or stone, and some of them were adorned with charms and shell necklaces. Smoke from burning incense filled the room and smarted his eyes. Then he saw his father across the room. Father arose and walked toward him and Sabila.

"You two have taken long enough to get here."

He seemed impatient and somewhat irritable, as if he had been waiting for them a long time. He then walked to the center of the floor and knelt in front of a *bohutio*, whom Neef recognized to be the head priest of the entire island. Father motioned for the children to sit in a far corner, next to their mother. As Neef obediently hobbled to the place pointed out to him, he could hear the wailing and chanting outside, as the funeral rituals proceeded. He wondered whether anyone out there was aware that he and his family were now in this hut.

"Children, I want absolute quiet," Father said. His voice was calmer now.

The head *bohutio* then laid his hands upon Father's head and closed his eyes.

"Oh, wise Guarionex, son of Cahoba the Great, I give you all rights, all privileges, all powers, and all authority to be King of Quisqueya, so that you can rule as the highest *cacique* over all the land. May you reign well over the five major kingdoms as your father had — especially over your own land, the Fertile Kingdom. I exhort you to always remember the needs of, not only your own kingdom, but also those of the other kingdoms, namely, the Kingdom of the Great Old Lady, the Kingdom of the Mines, the Kingdom of Marién, and the Mother Kingdom; for if you do, each of them will share with you their strength, support, and wisdom. Remember to rule with the *Love of Yocahu*, for it teaches that no kingdom is greater than the other, but they all stand as equals, because they were each created to have strength in their own uniqueness. I grant you dominion over the 80 lesser kingdoms that function beneath the five great ones. Always be mindful of each kingdom, no matter how small it is, for each is mighty in the eyes of Yocahu.

"Remember, remember. Continue the work that your father Cahoba the Great had begun. Quisqueya needs protection from foreigners, who may try to hurt it and destroy its greatness. Remember that if the Quisqueyans keep their promises and Yocahu returns before any aggressive foreigners arrive, then this entire island will be saved and will be raised to a state that the world has never known. Inspire your people constantly with *the love*, and inspire them *to love*. Show them how to keep the promises of Yocahu, in ways that they can still enjoy life.

"Never forget the strength of the *Tainos* of Quisqueya, for we are the only people on earth, who know the power of *the love*. We must be examples for the rest of the world to become as we are, and as great as Yocahu is. And now, I grant you health and strength, so you can function as an even greater king, than your father Cahoba the Great had ever been."

The chief *bohutio* then removed his hands from Guarionex's head. He walked over to a table, reached behind a large *zemie,* and pulled out a crown of gold from beneath a beaded piece of cloth. Neef recognized that it was the same crown that Grandfather wore during formal occasions, for he knew well the stones of nephrites that were embedded in it. The priest came over to Guarionex and placed it upon his head. Once Father was crowned, no one said anything for a long time.

Finally, Neef could not stand the silence any longer and said, "Father, were you just made the new king?"

Guarionex had a far away look in his eyes and did not answer, so the chief *bohutio* intervened.

"Children, please understand that your father is still in shock, for it was only during the funeral, when I informed him that he was to become the next king, and he needed to be crowned right away."

Then he walked over to Neef and Sabila and knelt in front of them.

"My dear children of Guarionex, before your Grandfather died, the *zemies* communicated many times with me and the other *bohutios* that your father should be made the next king. Your uncle has made many choices that made the gods unhappy, and they took away his privilege."

"But I just saw my uncle," said Neef. "He thinks he is already king."

"Nobody is a king, until he is crowned. I realize that both of you are not old enough to understand why your father was put into your uncle's place, but someday, you will."

Neef thought of the scene he had recently observed of his uncle drinking *chicha* with his friends and remembered what those men were saying. They had said that everything Grandfather had stood for was false.

"I am old enough to understand," he said.

"I am, too," Sabila added. "We are both old enough to know what is happening."

"Is this how a person becomes king — hidden away from all the people?" Neef asked.

"Nay, my son. A coronation is never performed in secret. It usually involves everybody. It is always a time of grand celebration and feasting. But this time, the circumstances are different."

Neef thought of the frequent drunken brawls, in which Eldest-Son-of-My-Father's-First-Wife often got involved. He thought of the whisperings he often heard about him, and how the townspeople used a word that he did not understand to describe him. They called his uncle *incompetent*. He turned to his father.

"Father, now that you are king, does it mean that I will someday be king also?"

Guarionex turned and stared at Neef, as if he was withdrawing from his trance.

"My son, the people may not want a cripple to rule over them," he finally said.

His words stung, but Neef tried to be brave and bit his lip, to keep from crying. In a small voice, he said, "So who will become king, after you?"

Guarionex shrugged.

"We will take one step at a time. Maybe our people will vote for a new king, as they do on the other islands."

Neef looked at the *bohutio*, and then at his father.

"Isn't Eldest-Son-of-My-Father's-First-Wife going to be angry with you for being crowned king, without him knowing about it?"

Guarionex arose.

"That is why I said *one step at a time*, my son."

Again, a silence hovered in the hut. Neef was bewildered, for too many events had happened that day, and he barely heard his father, as he spoke again.

"My son, from now on, everyday when I hold meetings in the royal house, I want you to come with me. You may not be safe alone, anymore."

And when Neef heard his father's words, he was more confused than ever.

2

Blooooooooooooooooooooooooooooooooooooot!

A conch shell trumpeted from an approaching canoe. As its blast swept across the water toward the Fertile Kingdom, it reached the royal *bohio*, where King Guarionex and his advisors sat in a solemn assembly. Since the king and his men were concentrating on serious matters, they ignored the conch. However, Neef, who sat alone in the back of this room away from the men, was aware of every sound that came from outside.

Ever since Guarionex was made king, Neef had to go everywhere with him, because his father was afraid that someone might try to hurt him, particularly his uncle, Eldest-Son-of-My-Father's-First-Wife. As Neef obediently accompanied his father, he was thrilled to ride in a litter with him, as they traveled throughout the Fertile Kingdom, overseeing what people were producing for trade. Father insisted that he personally checked up on the quality and quantities of fishnets made of palm fibers, and that the cotton hammocks were kept up to par. He constantly reminded the carvers that Quisqueya was famous for its wooden bowls and carved furniture, so they must keep up their good work. Although on Quisqueya, *guanine*, or gold, was not as desirable as its nephrites, articles of both types of jewelry that were created on this island traded well elsewhere. Neef also learned that the women of Cuba sometimes preferred the cloth goods of Quisqueya to what they, themselves, produced, because the Quisqueyan women often thought of ingenious and creative ideas with their beads to sew into their cloths. Even the baskets made from *hava* leaves were of the highest quality, for not only could the Quisqueyans weave them so tightly that they could hold water, but the designs they wove into them were superb.

These travels throughout the kingdom kept Neef entranced, but lately, they began to occur less frequently, for King Guarionex was becoming more occupied in meetings, which stretched on for hours. So Neef had to sit in a corner of the royal hut and listen to the men talk about subjects that did not interest him. From what he heard, he gathered that they were upset that Canaobo the Fierce had increased his fees for their protection, because the Carib attacks had become more numerous and their armies were growing. Day after day as Neef sat quietly at these meetings, he eventually discovered a spot in the floor, where the hava mat did not fully cover the ground and exposed a patch of dirt. In that patch, he drew swirls, squares, and triangles, with the tiny piece of black coral that Grandfather had thrown. He loved to make up stories with the shapes he created to represent animals, trees and people.

Blooooooooooooooooooooooooooooooooot!

When the conch blew again, Neef glanced up and instinctively reached for his crutches, but stopped, because he remembered that he was not supposed to be going anywhere. He then returned to his drawing. Father had become so strict with him, since he was made king and insisted that Neef remained quiet during these meetings, and not even whisper.

"Manioc grows easily in the kingdom of Siba, and even if it is only a minor kingdom, it produces so much of it, that its people could stand to triple their contributions," Neef heard one of the men say.

"And the communities in the forests could also increase their wood products," said another.

Father told Neef that the men in this room were carefully chosen. All of them were related to him in some way. Some were *undercaciques*; some were priests of various ranks; while others, were men of influence of the *Nytaino* upper class. They were uncles, cousins, or distant cousins to him. Neef did not always know their names, since his parents taught him to address them by how they were related to him, such as *Third-Son-Of-My-Father's-Brother'-Fifth-Wife*, *My-Mother's-Father's-Second-Brother*, *My-Mother's-Youngest-Brother*, and *My-Father's-Second-Brother's-Third-Wife's-Second-Son*. When Grandfather was king, Guarionex's older brother, Eldest-Son-of-My-Father's-First-Wife, was always present at these meetings, but since his father was inaugurated, Neef had not seen him anywhere.

Blooooooooooooooooooooooooooooooooot!

There went the conch again. This time, Neef heard the voices of children joining in a chant outside.

"Come sit a welcome! Come sit a welcome! The traders are here!"

Neef yearned to peek outside, just for a second, and when he looked over at King Guarionex, he was surprised that his father was looking right back at him, as if he understood what he desired.

"Son, you have my permission to go and see who is approaching."

After Neef went to the doorway of the royal *bohío*, he looked down the hill and saw townsfolk rushing to the beach far below. They were waving at an approaching canoe and began sitting welcomes on the sand. Some of them even swam out to the vessel, while others joined the children in their chant.

"Come sit a welcome! Come sit a welcome!"

"Oh, ho!" said Neef, laughing. "Basamanaco and his traders are arriving."

"If you wish, my son, you may also go to sit and welcome those traders."

Neef was so ecstatic to be granted such freedom, because it had been a long time since he was permitted to be outside alone, that he hobbled out of the *bohio*, without looking back.

"Neef?"

Neef returned, somewhat annoyed to be called away from the freedom that he missed so badly.

"When you meet Basamanaco, invite him up here, will you?"

Neef nodded and hobbled toward a path that led down to the beach. As he struggled downhill with his crutches, he could hear the traders panting far below, as they paddled to shore. From the side of this hill, Neef could see their muscles bulging, whenever they dug their oars into the water. It wasn't easy for him to descend hills, but he had no choice, because the royal *bohio* was set somewhat above the sea. As he proceeded downward, using one hand to hang on to his crutches and the other to grab at branches, he moved slowly from branch to branch.

Suddenly he saw a figure emerge on the trail, just above him. As he looked upward, he found himself staring into the face of Eldest-Son-of-My-Father's-First-Wife. He was surprised that his uncle's countenance had changed greatly, since he last saw him on the day of Grandfather's funeral. His eyes were now hard and cold. Neef smiled, anyway.

"Hello, Uncle! I haven't seen you in a long time."

"So, you little brat. You think you're going to be king some day, don't you?"

The chill in his uncle's voice was such an abrupt change from before, that it startled Neef, and he backed away. Because he was not proficient with moving backwards with crutches, he tripped over a rock and tumbled on his back. But Neef was used to such spills and quickly sat up, brushing the dirt off his legs. As he wordlessly stared up at Eldest-Son-of-My-Father's-First-Wife, he saw a strange gleam in his uncle's eyes. Neef swallowed and laughed apologetically.

"I'm not good at climbing down hills, Uncle."

Neef pulled himself to his feet, with the help of his crutches.

Eldest-Son-of-My-Father's-First-Wife threw his head back and guffawed.

As his uncle wiped tears from his eyes because he was laughing so hard, he said, "Just a little bit farther, Nephew, and you would have gone tumbling, head over heels, down to the bottom of that hill. If that happened, what would your father do, with a broken, crippled, heir-to-the-throne? It wouldn't have taken much to get rid of you, would it?"

And then, Eldest-Son-of-My-Father's-First-Wife was gone, as suddenly as he had appeared.

When Neef finally reached the beach, he could see sweat streaming down the traders' faces and backs, as their canoe hit the sand. Townsfolk immediately rallied around them, shouting welcomes as they helped the men out of their vessel. Neef searched for their leader, Basamanaco, and he soon saw him rising to his feet. When Basamanaco reached his full height, his muscular body stood well over a head taller, than the rest of the traders, and he did not appear as worn-out as they were. Then Neef saw Basamanaco turn toward him, break into a smile, and extend his arms outward. The next thing Neef knew, he was being swooped up into the air and flipped onto Basamanaco's shoulders. Basamanaco appeared to be as strong as ten men, to him. Upon those shoulders, he felt that he had gained a unique status, and it caused him to forget that he was unable to walk, like other children.

Neef leaned forward and whispered into Basamanaco's ear, "Did you know that my father is now the king?"

"Who doesn't? The whole island knows it, my boy."

"He won't let me out of his sight, anymore. Won't you come up to say *hello* to our new king?"

When Basamanaco ran up the hill with Neef still on his shoulders, the town children ran laughing after them. Finally they stood in front of the royal hut, where the other children knew that it was time for them to leave, for they were trained that the king's hut was a place that they should never disturb or enter. Basamanaco lifted a knocker that hung from an outside beam and struck a post several times. After Basamanaco was invited into the hut, he lowered Neef to the floor, slipped to his knees, and bowed humbly before King Guarionex. Neef did the same.

When Neef looked up at his father, for the first time in his life, he saw — not his father — but a king sitting upon a *dohu*, or a throne that stood close to the ground. He never realized before that his father had such a handsome face, and that he was the only man in the room, who wore a crown of gold. Father's *undercaciques* just wore crowns with feathers in them. Like the rest of the *Nytaino* elite, his father had his hair styled in elegant tufts, which his servants arranged carefully every morning. Tattoos of black, blue, and an occasional red, decorated his body, legs and face. Neef was told that the swirls in those tattoos represented his father's various levels of accomplishments that he had acquired during his years in the Mother Kingdom, when he attended the School of the Princes. The snake-like figures meant that he had memorized the sacred *areitas* to perfection, which were reserved just for *caciques* to know. The crosses symbolized the tree of life that connected him with the world of *Coaibai,* where the spirits of good people dwelled. The ornaments hanging from his earlobes, neck, and ankles, were indications of his power, position and wealth. Yet Neef was told that among Guarionex's most significant trinkets, was his *zemie*, which hung from a simple piece of string from his neck, for it gave him constant protection from the evil spirits, known as *mapoyas.*

"*Tayno*, Basamanaco," King Guarionex said to the trader. "Peace be with you."

"And *tayno* to you, your majesty."

The king frowned, as he studied Basamanaco.

"Those wounds. They look fresh. Did you have to fight off Caribs?"

Basamanaco looked down at his chest.

"These scratches? I never noticed them before. They must have happened, when I was trying to keep our canoe from turning over in strong winds out at sea. But such is the life of a trader. Out at sea, we get the worst of all kinds of weather."

"I am glad that you and your men are safe."

Basamanaco bowed again. With each breath he took, Neef noticed his keloid scars rising and falling on his leathery skin. Unlike the king, he had neither tattoo nor charm to adorn his body or to show any accomplishment. Nor did *cibas* of gold encircle his forearms. Not a single tuft nestled in his hair, but instead, he tied his long, straight, black hair behind his neck. And the only jewelry he wore was his small *zemie* that hung from his neck for protection.

"Your majesty, Neef said that you wanted to see me."

The king nodded, and then he turned to his men and waved, as a sign that he wished to dismiss them. After they left, when Neef, Basamanaco, and the king were alone in the royal hut, King Guarionex finally spoke.

"Basamanaco, I hear that your wife is a marvelous *behique.* I've heard all about how she can cure people with herbs, when no one else can."

"Aye, my lord. Lida has a special gift."

"Can she make my son walk, without the help of crutches?"

Color drained from Basamanaco's cheeks.

"Ah, nay, nay, your majesty. That is asking for too much. I've never seen her make a crippled person whole. I don't believe she has such herbs to do it."

"Then she must try many times to make my son well, until she succeeds."

"What are you saying, your majesty?"

"If you take my son to live with you for several months, or even a year or two, do you think your wife could eventually find a proper cure for him, if she experimented with concoctions long enough?"

Basamanaco began to tremble, and Neef realized that he was afraid of his father, of what he could do to him, if he refused to accept this request.

"What…what…will h-h-happen to Lida, if she can't make your son whole?"

When Guarionex did not answer, Basamanaco continued.

"I cannot make promises for Lida. And I do not think she can make such promises for herself, either, your majesty."

Neef was surprised that Basamanaco, who was much larger than everyone else on this island, could be so afraid of his father. He often heard people mentioning the word *power*, when they spoke of his father, and that word was also used when they spoke of Grandfather, when he was alive. Neef always wondered what *power* meant, but now, he was beginning to understand.

"I am sure that Lida would love to have Neef in our home," Basamanaco continued. "But unfortunately, I was not planning to go there right away. This is not a good time to take your son with me, your majesty. Perhaps I can take him, during another trip. After I am through with trading at your kingdom, I plan to head south to the Kingdom of the Great Old Lady. Then I will travel to the Kingdom of the Mines to trade. And last, I will go to the Mother Kingdom, before I finally head north to my home in the Kingdom of Marién."

When Guarionex arose, Neef saw determination in his face.

"I want you to take Neef and his sister away from here, as soon as possible. I want you to leave with them tonight."

"What? But I will be gone over a *uinal*, before I reach my home, your majesty."

"Then your men must complete your plans, without you. I am giving you an assignment that you MUST carry out, right away."

"Your majesty? Did I hear you correctly?"

"Basamanaco, I will give you a canoe for your own use, and tonight after dark, you are to take both of my children away in it."

When Basamanaco began to protest, the king held out his hand for silence.

"Instead of circling our island as you have planned, you must travel another route that will lose anybody, who may be pursuing you. And eventually, you must head south to the Mother Kingdom. After you do the business that I will ask you to do there, then you are to take my son back to your home in the Kingdom of Marién."

The king leaned forward, and Neef saw that his countenance had changed, and now, love filled his eyes.

"Basamanaco, I have known you all of my life. Ever since I was a boy, like my own son, Neef, I and the other children enjoyed going to the beach to sit a welcome for you. All of us grew up loving you, and we looked forward to your arrival, because whenever you came, not only did you have a treat for each of us, but we knew that we could trust you, for we sensed that you were filled with only good, and nothing else. Can I now depend upon you to care for the well being of my own children?"

"Of course, your majesty, but, but, but I do not understand."

"You, Basamanaco, are always first to hear about what's happenings on this island. I am sure that you know the circumstances, under which I was made king."

Basamanaco nodded and said, "I've heard that you were crowned in secret."

"My brother Eldest-Son-of-My-Father's-First-Wife is planning an insurrection to overthrow me. But you and I know that he was never fit to be king, and this island must continue to be protected from any invasions from foreigners. My children are no longer safe here, and I need someone to take them away. Will you do it for me?"

Basamanaco nodded again.

"Let me explain the plan. Basamanaco, nobody else knows this island, as well as you do, for you have traveled to all of its major and minor kingdoms many times, along many rivers and paths. That is why I am asking you to take my children away along secret routes, so no one can find you.

"I intend to give you full responsibility of my children. Although my daughter Sabila is only 10 years old, I would like for you to take her to the Mother Kingdom and enroll her in the School of the Princes there. I realize that a child must be at least 12 years old to be admitted to The School, but I want you to approach King Beheccio and ask him for special permission for her to begin her education early. If you explain to him the political situation that we face here, he will understand."

"Your majesty, wait. Haven't you heard the latest development in the Mother Kingdom?"

"No one has mentioned anything out of the ordinary to me, lately."

"Ah, so your brother and his followers must have stopped the messenger with this news. You see, an important wedding will soon occur there. King Beheccio's sister, Princess Anacoana, will be married. Once she is made queen, she will be given full charge of the School of the Princes, so it will be she, whom I will need to ask permission for Sabila to attend The School early, instead of her brother. Once she is married, she will become Queen Anacoana and will rule the Mother Kingdom equally with her brother."

"To whom is she marrying?"

"The Lucanyan, Canaobo the Fierce."

"What? The man whom I pay to protect us from the Caribs? Why, he is not even a king, but only a warrior!"

"He certainly is a king, your majesty. Did your brother block this news also? With the Carib invasions becoming more massive and powerful, when they attacked the Kingdom of the Mines recently where Canaobo the Fierce lives, their king was killed, but Canaobo the Fierce appeared with his armies, slaughtered most of the Caribs, and pushed the rest of them out of the land. The people were so overjoyed with this victory, that they voted for him to be their next king. As soon as he became king, he asked for Anacoana's hand, and her brother accepted immediately."

"Canaobo the Fierce is to marry Anacoana? I cannot believe that! He is not even a Quisqueyan. How can he carry on with *the love*?"

"This marriage will unite the Mother Kingdom with the Kingdom of the Mines, your majesty. It will greatly strengthen Quisqueya."

King Guarionex arose and paced the floor.

"So the gentle Anacoana is matched up to that vicious Lucanyan," he muttered to himself. "Does Beheccio know what he is doing? How could he ever wed his own sister to that barbarian?"

The king's eyes turned distant.

"When I began attending the School of the Princes in the Mother Kingdom, Anacoana was still in her days without a loincloth. She was a charming, wonderful child, who won over everybody's heart."

The king walked to the doorway and looked out into the sea for a long time and spoke to himself.

"Even if the women of the Mother Kingdom are considered to be the most beautiful in the world, I hear that Anacoana has become the most striking of them all."

As Guarionex continued to mumble beneath his breath, Neef found his mind wandering to thoughts about the Mother Kingdom. He had heard people saying that this kingdom had preserved the mother tongue, or the dialect that was spoken when Yocahu lived on Quisqueya with the ancient fathers. They also said that this kingdom was considered to be the epitome of refinement and culture, and the School of the Princes was formed in its royal courts, where kings of the surrounding islands sent their children to be educated. Everyone said that while Anacoana was attending the School of the Princes, she became an exceptionally accomplished poet and musician. So today, when women throughout the island sat in the shade of palm trees scraping manioc, they always sang the *areitas* she composed.

Finally Guarionex returned to his *dohu* and sat down.

"Could you get my children to the Mother Kingdom in time for the royal wedding?"

"Certainly, your majesty."

"Then let us start, as soon as possible. Please do not tell anyone about your mission."

"And my traders, your majesty? What do I tell them?"

"Tonight you will instruct your men that early tomorrow morning, they must set off on their trip, without you. Tell them you've had a sudden change of plans, that you must return home — or any other excuse you can think up. I will buy up all the goods that you were planning to trade in my kingdom, so you and your men can leave right away. And in the canoe that I will give you, I will also place gifts for you to bring to the wedding."

"Your majesty, when I bring Neef home with me, how long must I keep him?"

"Until your wife gets him well. Nay — until I call for him, when it is safe."

"And if Lida does not get him well?"

Guarionex stared at Basamanaco for a long time, before he finally spoke.

"Basamanaco, I would never punish you, for I know that you and your wife will try your best to do all you can for Neef."

Basamanaco bowed.

"Even if Lida can't make Neef well, we will always treat him, as if he were a prince in our home, your majesty."

Gurarionex then turned to Neef.

"The Mother Kingdom is a land that is considered to be the greatest in all the world, my son. It is a place of much *ayiti.*"

"What does *ayiti* mean, Father?"

"It is a word that means *finding your higher self.*"

"I do not understand."

"In time, you will, my son. But for now, just enjoy the Mother Kingdom when you are there. You will see that it is much more progressed in both modern advances and the ancient arts, than anywhere else. That is why people everywhere look up to it, and the *caciques* trust The School to educate their princes and princesses."

As Guarionex described the Mother Kingdom to Neef, Neef's mind began to wander again. He thought of how he would soon be seeing Canaobo the Fierce. Everyone knew that, unlike the Quisqueyans, that warrior was afraid of nothing, and no one. And he loved to fight in wars. By contrast, the Quisqueyans did not own a single weapon, not even a *macaba*, or club, which everyone on the other islands kept for protection in their homes. Further, the Quisqueyans were proud of the skill they developed in running away from their attackers. Unlike them, Canaobo the Fierce never ran away from anyone, but faced his enemy. And secretly, Neef admired him for facing his enemy.

Neef then glanced through the open doorway and saw the familiar ocean below. For the first time, he understood Grandfather Cahoba's words that no matter what happened on this island, the waves would always wash upon that beach. And then he looked back at the corner, where he sat earlier that morning. The piece of black coral was still lying in the patch of dirt, where he left it. Quickly, he hobbled back to snatch up that precious rock, to take along with him.

3

As a lone canoe approached a waterway of the Mother Kingdom, Neef sat in the back of that vessel, plunging a paddle into the water, as he attempted to synchronize his strokes with Basamanaco's. He was enjoying a new freedom, for when he was in the Fertile Kingdom, he was never allowed to paddle any canoe. He looked at Basamanaco, who sat up front, and called out to him.

"If I can handle a canoe by myself for an entire month, will you take me to Cuba with you, when you go on a trading trip?"

"Maybe."

Neef did not like that answer, because it made him feel that Basamanaco did not have faith in him. He wanted to learn how to paddle as well as a trader, for they were strong men, who did not tire easily and were accustomed to traveling long distances. He could always recognize traders in town by their well-developed biceps. Neef pushed aside the disappointment Basamanaco's answer caused him and called out to his sister.

"Want to try paddling, Sabila?"

Sabila sat with sulky eyes in the center of the canoe, among the gifts for the wedding. She did not answer Neef, but turned to Basamanaco, instead.

"I don't want to go away to school. Why can't I stay at home?"

"We're not safe there anymore, remember?" Neef said, answering for Basamanaco.

As Sabila still faced Basamanaco, she said, "Is our uncle really causing that much trouble for Father?"

Basamanaco looked uncomfortable, as if he did not want to say anything negative to the children about their uncle, Eldest-Son-of-My-Father's-First-Wife.

"Sabila, it is a great honor to attend the School of the Princes," Basamanaco said. "Always remember that you were born a princess, and only people who have ancestors who originated from the *Cave Cacibagiuagua*, like you, are allowed to attend that school. Someday when you are made a queen, it will be your responsibility to be an example to your people, and The School will teach you how to be that example. In fact, there are many things that you must first learn about, before you can become that queen."

"Father said that I must remain at The School for two extra years, because I am beginning two years early. That means that I must stay there for eight years altogether, so I can finish with other students my age. It is not fair that I must be forced to stay at that place for so long."

"Sabila, when you are done with your schooling, just think how much better educated you will be than the rest of the princes and princesses. And you may even end up being much more cultured and refined than all of them also."

Sabila ignored him and slunk into a deeper depression.

"Did you hear me, Sabila?" Neef called from his end of the canoe. "I asked you before, why don't you try paddling? It's fun, and it will make you happier."

Sabila glared at Neef.

"Quiet, Neef. Basamanaco, do they teach girls to paddle canoes at the school?"

"I don't believe so. When you attend the School of the Princes, I am pretty sure that they will teach you how to behave, act, and think like a queen."

"Why can't we have a school of our own in the Fertile Kingdom?"

As Neef paddled in the back of the canoe, he sighed, for his sister had been sulky, ever since they left home. Unlike Sabila, he found this trip to be fascinating. As they passed small canoes that lined the banks of the river, he saw fishermen broadcasting *baygua* powder across the surface of the water. He heard that *baygua* stunned the fish below and caused them to float to the top, which enabled the fishermen to pluck them off the surface. The canoe glided past people, who waved enthusiastically, and Neef returned their greetings, while Sabila continued to sulk. Soon they saw women slapping laundry against rocks, and when their tiny children ran after their vessel, laughing and screaming, the women called out to older children to retrieve them.

Neef wondered about the many waterways that branched out from the one they traveled in. He stared down streams, to see if he could figure out to where they flowed. He also wondered about the walls made of stone that stood on either side of the river, in which they traveled.

As if Basamanaco heard Neef's silent questions, he called out to him and said, "Long ago, the ancient fathers of the Mother Kingdom constructed those walls. We are in one of the canals they built. It cuts directly southward through the center of the Mother Kingdom and saves us a couple of days' journey, if we were to go around the Guayacarima Peninsula. This canal was constructed to help farmers irrigate their

32

crops. It is fed by the River Camin that originates from those mountains in the distance."

Neef looked at where Basamanaco pointed. The mountains appeared far away to him. They made him think of the Canta Mountains, which he often heard the elders of his village discussing, where the two famous caves were located that were believed to be where the first humans originated.

"Are those the sacred Canta Mountains?"

"Not those mountains, Neef. I've never seen the Cantas. They are located somewhere else on this island."

"I wish Grandfather were here, so he could tell me the story about the Cantas again."

Basamanaco dug deep, smooth, even strokes into the water, while his eyes turned inward. Finally he broke his silence, by singing in his base voice.

> Oh, mighty Cantas of Quisqueya
> Majestic towers rising to the sky
> Rising to the sky,
> Rising to the sky.
>
> With twin caves nestling in her bowels,
> *Amaiuaba* enclosing common man
> Enclosing common man
> Enclosing common man
>
> And *Cacibagiuagua*, the other cave,
> Embracing *caciques* and the sun,
> *Caciques* and the sun
> *Caciques* and the sun.

Neef could not help but stare at Basamanaco.

"How did you ever learn that *areita* about the Canta Mountains? I thought that it was reserved, only for the *caciques* to know."

"I was never formally taught that song, Neef, but when I brought princes and princesses back home from The School to their islands in my canoe, they sang many *areitas* that they were taught. I could not help but learn them."

And in a singsong chant, Basamanaco proceeded to recite the long story about how humans came forth from the Canta Mountains. Neef was impressed that he sang with as much expression as Grandfather Cahoba had. As Basamanaco continued, Sabila withdrew from her moodiness, and Neef joined in with the singing, for unlike other children his age, his quick mind had enabled him to memorize this long poem to perfection, merely from listening to Grandfather. He also had learned many other areitas perfectly from Grandfather. Soon he found himself singing about Marocael, the *zemie* who was left in charge of the two caves.

> Oh, son of the great *Zemie*
> Son of the great Maroca,
> Mischievous, careless, forgetful Marocael
> Childish, forgetful, Marocael
> Childish, forgetful, Marocael

Neef began to sing about when the earth was young, when the *Zemie* Maroca gave his son, Marocael, charge of two caves. The common humans were kept in a cave called *Amaiuaba*, and the *caciques* and the sun were kept in *Cacibagiuagua*.

Neef sang about how Marocael was instructed to never let the people out of those caves, because humans beings were so curious, that once they saw the earth, they would never want to return to the dark caves again. He sang of how one day, Marocael forgot to seal up the doors of the caves, after feeding the people inside.

And within the *Cave Cacibagiuagua*, the sun was first to notice that the opening of the cave was not sealed. After the sun rolled the rock that covered the entrance aside, he went outside into the world to explore, and the *caciques* timidly followed him. And when they found the *Cave Amaiuaba* nearby, they also rolled away its stone and invited the common people inside to step out and join them. As Neef continued to sing with Basamanaco, for the first time, he felt a thrill fill his body, for he began to vicariously experience how it must have been for the first people, during their initial discovery of the earth, as they exclaimed,

> So clear the streams!
> So green the greens!
> How soft, how awesome,
> The nodding blossoms!
> Come, pick this thing and taste its sweet
> And suck its sweet
> And suck its sweet.

As Neef sang, he began to understand why Grandfather used to express this song with so much feeling, for he now found himself immersed within a conglomeration of shifting moods. From deep within him, he experienced the joy that Marocael must had felt, as he played in the field below, as any boy would, and then, when he glanced over his shoulder and noticed the rays of the sun emanating from the mountainside near the caves, he was suddenly seized with horror, for he realized that the humans were out. Sweat began to ooze from Neef's pores, as he saw himself, as Marocael, running in panic up the hill toward the caves, yelling as loud as he could,

> Go back, go back, you naughty people
> Forget the smells, forget the sights
> Think not the joy of cries of birds,
> Revert you back to dark of caves,
> To dark of minds,
> To dark of minds.

At this point, Neef wept, just as Grandfather always had wept, as he teetered back and forth between the feelings of urgency Marocael was experiencing and the exhilaration the first humans felt, during their enlightenment and discovery. And then Neef sang about how Marocael turned a corner in the mountain path and suddenly found himself for the first time, face to face with the sun. When this happened, Neef saw a blinding flash in front of him, as Marocael suddenly turned to stone. The *areita* then ended, with its final lines telling of how Marocael's stone image still stands in the Canta Mountains before the Caves *Cacibagiuagua* and *Amaiuaba*, as their guardian.

After the *areita* ended, Neef felt an exhaustion that he never before experienced. He must had been singing extremely hard and with much feeling, because he was now hoarse. So he paddled in silence and reviewed the scenes he just experienced in his mind, amazed at what the *areita* had done to him. After a while, he called out to Basamanaco in a raspy voice.

"I felt different when I sang that *areita.*"

"Aye, Neef. I know you did."

"Is this what Father meant about reaching one's *ayiti*?"

"You were at the beginning of finding your higher self, Neef."

Neef pondered over Basamanaco's comment. His arms now ached, for he was paddling for a long time. Finally he spoke again.

"Basamanaco, do you believe that the story of the two ever caves happened?"

"It is what the Quisqueyans believe. My people are not from this island, for they lived on the mainland of *Guanine*. There are many people living on *Guanine*, and each group of people has its own set of stories that often differ from each other."

"Then how do your people believe the first people came about?"

"I believe as my fathers did, that the first family came from across the great waters on a boat."

"On a boat? Really? And Yocahu? Do you think as the Quisqueyans do, that he descended from the sky long ago to visit the ancient fathers?"

"Neef, that story of Yocahu is similar to what many other people believe, but every tribe has its own version of it. Aye, I believe that he will return to bring more knowledge to many people in this world, just as he promised."

"But Basamanaco, he is supposed to only come to us, the Quisqueyans, because we are *Yocahu's Special People*."

Basamanaco did not reply.

"Did your people fight?"

"Aye, Neef. We did much fighting."

"How could your people believe that he would come to them, if they fought?"

"My people did not believe in *the love* as the Quisqueyans do, that it would bring them the highest status with Yocahu. Fighting was important to them. Anyway, my people are gone now."

"Where are they?"

"Killed."

Basamanaco looked extremely uneasy, so Neef decided to refrain from asking any further questions about his people for a while.

But finally Neef said, "Do you think the prediction in Grandfather's vision will ever happen? Do you think that strangers will someday come to destroy us?"

"I don't know, Neef. I think maybe your Grandfather had drunk too much hallucinating herbs during that vision."

"That's not right, Basamanaco. Both my father and Grandfather said that that vision was different, because Grandfather consumed nothing to make it happen."

"Are you sure? Kings and *bohutios* always need to drink, eat, or inhale something, to help them get in touch with the world of spirits."

"I am certain of it. Anyway, why aren't you sure strangers will come to kill us?"

"As a trader, I have traveled to many places, and nowhere else on earth, have I seen any land as astounding as Quisqueya. How can the kingdoms of this island possibly be destroyed? Even when the Caribs attack, they kill and capture only a few of us, but they never take all of our people. And no one is stronger than a Carib. When we arrive at the Mother Kingdom, you will see its mightiness. Its language and culture of the ancient fathers are hundreds of years old. But at the same time, it is extremely progressive, modern, and advanced. Such a kingdom can only exist on Quisqueya, and because of the greatness of the Mother Kingdom, as well as the greatness of Quisqueya's other kingdoms, I cannot see how anybody could be strong enough to kill us all."

"But my father and his advisors say that the Caribs are getting more powerful."

"You must realize that the people of Quisqueya have a weapon greater than what any enemy owns."

"But we have no weapons. We don't even fight."

"The weapon we have is love and peace, my son. Because of *the love*, the *zemies* have protected us and have made this island stronger than other lands."

"Then you believe our destruction will never happen?"

"How can I?"

Neef thought of the conversations that transpired in the royal *bohio* in the Fertile Kingdom, when he sat in meetings with his father and his advisers.

"So that means you think Yocahu will be here soon, to make us the greatest people on earth, and to give us protection from any foreigners," he said.

Before Basamanaco could reply, the canoe arrived at a fork in the waterway, and Basamanaco steered to the right, where the sights around them suddenly changed and caused Neef to forget what he had said. They glided pass huge *bohios* of thatch, towering above stone foundations. Compared to the small, round, huts of the Fertile Kingdom, these buildings were far more magnificent than anything Neef had ever seen. Male voices, singing in harmony, floated down from one of those structures, and Neef recognized that they were singing one of his favorite *areitas*.

"Neef, that song is one of many that Princess Anacoana composed that now circulates our island."

Neef nodded, for he already knew all about Princess Anacoana's compositions.

"Who are singing?"

"The young men, who attend the School of the Princes. Many of them have come from far away places, even from islands that take many days to reach."

"Will I learn to write such music some day?" Sabila asked.

This was the first time in a long while that Sabila had said anything.

"Of course, you will, my daughter. And you will also learn how to play several musical instruments."

The canoe passed another large *bohio*. This time, female voices came from it.

"Those are the princesses," said Basamanaco. "The school keeps the princes and princesses separated."

"What else do the students learn?"

"Many subjects, Sabila. The stars, moon phases, history, hunting for the princes, and sewing for the princesses, I suppose. I've never been there but have only heard people talking about them. I'm only a trader, you know. But I've heard plenty of singing and poetry from the students, when I take them home in my canoe. In them, they speak of love, forgiveness, and of things that are far too marvelous to repeat."

"Will I be able to attend the School of the Princes someday?" Neef said.

"Why shouldn't you? You're a prince, aren't you?"

"Father said that our people would probably not want a crippled person to rule over them, so I thought that maybe I wouldn't be able to attend The School. Did you ever know anybody crippled who went there?"

When Basamanaco did not answer, Neef turned his attention back to shore. He saw young men and women, who were older than Sabila, strolling about. They were separated in groups, according to sex. Their beauty amazed him, for they were extremely finely clothed, and the young women were especially gorgeous in their dresses of many colors, with their hair in elaborate styles. Neef couldn't help pointing at them.

"Are those the princes and princesses of The School?"

Before Basamanaco could answer, they passed buildings of thatch that were much larger than the previous ones. Basamanaco lifted a hand toward them.

"The storehouses of King Beheccio and Princess Anacoana. You should see the fine goods they contain. There are pottery that are made into shapes of intricate figures, cotton hammocks of amazing quality, and bales of cotton that are so large that they require several men to carry."

"I've been to many places throughout the Fertile Kingdom with Father," said Neef. "Father likes to check to see if our people are doing a good job with the items they make, so their goods will trade well. Are the products of the Mother Kingdom better than ours?"

"I wouldn't say they are better, Neef, but they are certainly of the best quality."

They passed canoes lining the banks that were packed close together. Neef immediately recognized them to belong to traders, because goods from many lands were heaped upon them. They resembled Basamanaco's canoe. And far in the distance, he heard the beats of a truncus drum as a *bohutio* chanted with it.

At that moment, Basamanaco pointed ahead.

"There is the dock, where we will land."

4

The Mother Kingdom

When Princess Anacoana heard the *Naborian* servants enter her hut, she shut her eyes and pretended to sleep. As the servants approached her hammock, she heard Nila say, "Hush, now. The princess needeth her rest, for *the struggle* during her wedding today will take all of her strength from her."

Anacoana shuddered, when she heard Nila mention *the struggle*. She hoped her servants did not notice her trembling because of it, but the *Naborians* said nothing, as they straightened up her hut. With eyes still closed, Anacoana thought of Nila's constant reminding of how gloriously happy she should be, because today, she would be married. But instead, anger screamed within her at her brother, *Beheccio, how dare thee match me up with Canaobo the Fierce!* Although Anacoana would soon be crowned queen of the Mother Kingdom, she felt that instead, she was to be made a slave to her people. It wasn't her idea to unite her kingdom with the Kingdom of the Mines, but the whole world was excited over this union, because everybody wanted to increase the strength of Quisqueya.

And now on her wedding day, she must face her greatest fear of all: *the struggle.* Nila often assured her that this struggle was only a game and was just another part of the wedding ceremony to prove her integrity. She said that the men, whom she would be facing in *the struggle,* were instructed to not hurt her and to allow her to win the match.

Through slightly parted slits, Anacoana watched her servants hobble toward the doorway, while Nila trailed behind them with her rotund body sighing with every step. When the servants shuffled their way outside, disappeared behind the caney walls, and only Nila remained in sight, Anacoana sat up.

"Nila! Thou must not leave me alone."

Nila paused.

"Didst thou call, Princess?"

"I need thee."

Nila wiped her hands upon her *nagua,* as she always did when Anacoana wanted her, and then she painfully moved back toward the princess, dragging her calloused feet across the dirt floor. Like the other *Naborians,* she walked with difficulty, because when slave traders captured her, they broke her arches so she could not run away. When Anacoana's parents purchased her, it was too soon for anyone to know that Nila's captors, who had repeatedly raped her, had impregnated her. Fortunately, when her baby was a stillborn, Anacoana was born the following day, and the queen handed her the princess to nurse. From then on, an intense bond formed between Nila and Anacoana, and since then, Nila's faithfulness proved that there was never a need for anyone to break her arches.

When the king and queen later died of a strange disease, Anacoana was just ten years old. It was Nila, who then held her for many days afterward. And it was Nila, who came to her at night, when she was afraid, and Nila, who cheered when she accomplished anything new. And now, even when the princess was 21 years old, Nila was again ready to hold her, as if she were still a child.

"Nila, at all the royal weddings I have attended, every bride looked so haggard, after her struggle. Their beautiful dresses were always torn to shreds. Art thou certain that those men will not hurt me?"

"That is what they say, Princess."

"And, hui, I still wish not to marry Canaobo the Fierce, for I know nothing about him. In fact, I know not anything about any man. From the time I entered the School of the Princes, I was kept apart from men and was only taught by women. And what did they teach me? Thou knowest what they were — the flow and emotions in poetry, how to invent powerful stories, and how to create catchy rhythms and build their ecstasy into *areitas.* With my hands, too, I've learned how to create designs of intrigue and sew them with tiny stitches and small beads into fine cloth. I even was considered to be the best in my astronomy class, and my teachers always told me that I knew just as much about the stars, as the best male students; but I believed them not, because I knew not any male student, with whom I could compare myself. Ah, and my worst subject was how to be a good wife. And since my teachers, themselves, were women, how would they know what men want from women?"

"Princess, Princess. Thou must confuse not thy mind on thy wedding day."

"Hui, I wish I were still a child without a loincloth, so I could run freely anywhere, without anything upon my body. At least, I would be permitted to mingle in the courts, among both men and women, with not a single worry about how I looked, walked, or behaved, or whether I should be married."

"Princess, thou must go back to sleep, now. All will be well, I tell thee, for in a little while, thy wedding will be over."

"But I wish not to go through with it, I tell thee. Why should I give myself to a strange man, who knoweth not about *the love?*"

Nila gently pushed Anacoana back into the hammock, pulled the covers over her, kissed her forehead, and quickly hobbled out of the hut, without saying a word.

As Anacoana lay back in her bed, the years that she spent at the School of the Princes spun before her. It was a period when she was forbidden to mingle with the opposite sex, or she would be punished. Sometimes when no one knew it, she watched the princes of The School at a distance. Their deep voices fascinated her. They sported and wrestled with each other, the way puppies played. And often she saw Semola staring back at her. She heard that he was a prince from a far off island called Guanahaní. He stood a head taller than the other young men, and his stares made her blush. But she was not afraid to stare back at him. People said that his mind was quicker than the others, and The School was considering of making him one of its instructors some day. But when Semola finished his education, he was never made an instructor, and after he went home to his island, she never saw him again.

Soon after she completed her education at the age of eighteen, kings and princes began to send messengers to ask for her hand. She never knew who they were, for her brother, King Beheccio, interfered and turned them all down.

"None of them are good enough for thee, Anacoana," he said. "Their kingdoms are too insignificant."

And when he said nothing more, it caused her to despise him, for as her legal guardian, he made too many decisions for her and informed her of too little. As the proposals continued, Anacoana only heard about them through Nila. Nila told her that among those proposals, she received an offer from Cahoba the Great of the Fertile Kingdom, who was the highest king of Quisqueya. King Guacanagarí of the Kingdom of Marién had also requested for her. Even if both of those kings reigned over major kingdoms of Quisqueya, Nila said that they, too, were not satisfactory to Beheccio.

"Thy brother said that thou must be a *first* and legal wife," Nila told her. "Those kings want thee to be their fourth or seventh wife, but not their first." And to comfort her, Nila would put her arms around her and would add, "Thy brother Beheccio only wisheth for the best for thee. And once thou becomest queen of the Mother Kingdom, he understandeth that thou wilt then be granted just as much power, as he hath."

"When I am queen, will Beheccio treat me with more respect?"

"Oh, Princess, thy brother respecteth thee to no end, even now. He loveth thee so much that he desireth to protect thee."

And then one day, when Anacoana had given up hope that she would ever be wed, Nila came to her with excitement in her eyes.

"Canaobo the Fierce was just made *cacique* of the Kingdom of the Mines. He hath asked to marry thee, Anacoana. And thy brother accepted."

"He what? Beheccio matched me up to that man, without even consulting me, Nila?"

As Anacoana lay back on her hammock, she shed many tears. Even if she had never known a man, soon after she was wed, not only would she need to become a lover to Canaobo the Fierce, but because she was his wife, it would be his privilege to offer her to any male guest he pleased, as a symbol of hospitality. At this point, she did not want to be a lover to anyone. And every time she tried to discuss her fears with Nila, Nila would push her concerns aside and assured her that there was nothing to be afraid of, and what she feared, were actually special privileges reserved just for queens.

"Beheccio, how could you do this to me?" Anacoana wept.

Of all the men on Quisqueya, Canaobo the Fierce frightened her the most. By now, he must be an old man, for when he first came to Quisqueya with his armies, it was during her days without a loincloth. Back then, Father was still alive, and the stories he told about Canaobo the Fierce absolutely frightened her. She couldn't understand why Father, who stood for *the love*, was held spellbound, whenever he heard about the tactics of war that Canaobo the Fierce practiced.

Besides teaching her about *the love*, her parents also taught her other powerful lessons. When she was still a little girl without a loincloth, she heard of a princess and prince from The School, who were secretly slipping out into the night together. When their relationship was discovered, and they confessed to being intimacy with each other, the entire town was in an uproar. The common people were then allowed to storm into the palace, to drag that princess and prince to the main plaza. Anacoana could never forget the fear she saw in the faces of the prince and princess.

When Anacoana looked up at her mother, she saw fire in her eyes, as the queen pointed after the crowd.

"Follow them, Anacoana. Thou, and the other children, must see the kind of punishment they deserve."

Anacoana obeyed and ran to the town plaza, as the mob shoved all around her. She didn't understand why the townsfolk waved pointed sticks and yelled, "Whores! We trusted you to be our leaders, and you have let us down and defiled yourselves!"

As the prince and princess struggled to get away, people pushed in front of Anacoana, until the crowd around her became so thick that she could no longer see the couple. All she saw were waistlines and loincloths. And she heard words shouted that she did not understand, but assumed from their tones that they were cruel and cutting.

Finally when they were in the middle of the plaza, Anacoana saw the crowd beginning to raise their sharp sticks, and when they plunged them downward, she heard a piercing shriek above all the commotion. It came from the princess. Her cry rang so loud that Anacoana plugged her ears and shut her eyes. When she took her hands away and opened her eyes, she saw more people in front of her, raising their arms into the air again and again, and then over and over, they plunged their arms downward. She heard thuds, as both the prince and princess screamed. Finally, their voices grew softer. Then all went quiet, and the crowd filed away.

Anacoana ran forward, to see what had happened. She reached a clearing and gasped, for in front of her, were two limp and lifeless forms lying over pools of blood. She could tell that something had gone out of the prince and princess. As small as she was, Anacoana understood that they had both committed a serious crime. Their kind of crime meant a violent death. It meant people spat at you and called you bad names. It meant that nobody loved you, anymore.

When Anacoana entered The School, this experience bore so deeply into her, that she was afraid to speak to any of the princes. It also made her extremely aware of Semola's stares. And now on her wedding day, she could not see how she could ever adjust to speaking to any man, particularly Canaobo the Fierce, let alone submitting to his will.

When the *Naborians* entered the hut again, Anacoana heard them pouring water into her basin. A sweet aroma filled the room.

"Princess...Princess. Thou hast slept long enough. Wake up. We must prepare thee for thy wedding."

Reluctantly, Anacoana opened her eyes. She saw Nila spreading out a *nagua* made of soft cotton, upon which tiny beads were sewn into geometric designs. Another *Naborian* squatted on the floor over a wooden tray, arranging combs and strings of shells that would adorn her hair. Thin cords of palm fiber, which would be used to tie her tresses, lay next to them.

"Princess, we must get ready for the first ceremony."

Anacoana was not afraid of this first ceremony, for during this time, Nila said that she would be introduced to her guests. Many of them came from distant lands. It was only the last ceremony, *the struggle* — the one in which she must wrestle with strange men — that she feared.

Anacoana sat up.

"Nila, who will be in *the struggle* with me?"

Nila smoothed down the *nagua* that lay in front of her.

"No one but thy brother knoweth, Princess. He hath made all the arrangements. But I hear that they will be the most desirable of the unmarried men in all the lands. Thou must not be afraid of them, for I told thee many times already, that they were instructed to not hurt thee."

Anacoana allowed the women to remove her robes and raised her arms, so Nila could scrub her body with a sudsy plant. When a servant added more powder to the bath, the fragrance in the room intensified.

"Nila, I have heard that Canaobo the Fierce has a lust for women."

"Princess, Princess. Thou must remember that the greater a king, the more wives he will want."

"Will he have a lust for me?"

"Of course, thou art a beautiful woman. In fact, thou art considered to be the most beautiful on all of Quisqueya. And in the future when Canaobo the Fierce chooseth other wives, thou must always remember that among all of them, thou wilt be his highest wife of all. Remember also that thou wilt be a unique queen, for thou shalt bear heirs for two kingdoms — for both the Mother Kingdom and the Kingdom of the Mines. And what other queen on this island will ever have that privilege?"

"But I will have an uneducated husband."

"If thou meanest being educated in a school, how could he be? He was neither born a prince, nor do the Lucanyans have a school like ours on their islands. Yet I have heard that he hath educated himself beyond the wisdom of other kings. Thou must worry no more, for thy brother hath matched thee up well. Today, all of Quisqueya rejoiceth to have both kingdoms united."

"He must be coarse, like all other barbarians."

"Oh, but he is cultured, Princess. I have observed him, when he came to visit thy brother one day. Some people need no schooling to become refined, and he is one of them. And I heard thy brother and his advisors say that he is a genius in many ways, and he hath out-witted the largest and most powerful enemies many times. When thou seest him, thou wilt agree with me that he is, indeed, clever and refined. In time, thou shalt see that he hath truly earned his position as ruler of the Kingdom of the Mines, for more than just his brave deeds."

"I heard that he is also quick to anger."

"Princess, Princess. It is a good match, I tell thee. The priests confirmed many times that the *zemies* have approved of thy union with him."

"Nila, I cannot go through with it."

Nila embraced Anacoana and kissed her.

"Remember, soon thou wilt have full charge over the School of the Princes."

But as she spoke, Anacoana saw tears on Nila's cheeks.

"Nila, thou art crying."

"Nay, I weep not, Princess. It is nothing to worry about."

Anacoana thought it was strange for Nila to have tears in her eyes, after all the encouragement and glowing repetitions that she was giving her.

The *Naborian* women then fitted the *nagua* over Anacoana's slender body. As the princess sat upright upon a low stool, they carefully arranged her hair into tufts and intertwined them with shells.

"After my struggle, this dress shall be torn, and my hair shall be..."

"Princess, Princess...thou must not worry so. Come. The litter waiteth outside to bring thee to the first ceremony."

After Anacoana stepped into the litter, hefty *Naborian* men lifted her up and carried her in the direction of the royal hut, while servant ladies hobbled behind them. As the party approached the main plaza, Anacoana saw people pressing along the walks and waving at her as she passed by. She waved back. The *Naborian* men carried her past a long hut, where through its open sides, she could see the preparations for her wedding feast. Food was heaped high on wooden dishes; and the faint scent of *chicha* drink carried over to her from large pottery urns. She saw that three low thrones, or *dohus,* were now standing side-by-side where she, Beheccio, and Canaobo the Fierce would sit during the feast after *the struggle.* In front of those *dohus,* stood three drinking vessels that were imported from the Kingdom of the Great Old Lady. They were shaped as female figures.

Wrinkled, gray, and bent women sat near a communal hut in the shade of palm trees, gossiping in whispers as they suckled at their breasts, the infants of the *Naborian* women, who were busy with the preparations. Anacoana marveled at those old ladies, for they knew secrets the *Naborians* and the noble people did not know, such as how to produce milk for babies, long after their child-bearing years.

The *Naborians* carried Anacoana past musicians, practicing their performances for the wedding feast, as dancers leaped in time to their mellow drums and castanets.

The air was bursting with perfumes from flowered wreaths both men and women wore, as well as from garlands that decorated walkways. Cooking smells, too, came from large fish turning on spits, pepper pot stews bubbling in ceramic wares, and iguanas simmering in thick broths. Among these aromas, the scent of baking tortillas told everyone that the Kingdom of the Great Old Lady had sent its cooks to specially prepare their famous, delicate dishes, just for the wedding.

As the litter traveled closer to the royal building, Anacoana spotted a small group of foreigners in the distance, climbing up a windy path toward the town square. Even from afar, she could tell that these men were much more muscular than anyone else she had seen. They wore feathered hats that hung over their broad shoulders and large chests, and they held wooden shields in their solid-looking, bulging arms. Anacoana turned around to the *Naborian* women, who trailed behind her litter and saw Nila among them.

"Nila, who are those men down there?"

"Hath no one told thee that they were coming, Princess? They are the warriors of Canaobo the Fierce. They have especially prepared themselves for the gladiator fights that they will be participating in today."

"Gladiator fights?"

"Aye, they are part of the celebrations, Princess. Instead of the ball games in the arena that we usually hold, Canaobo the Fierce hath requested that we have gladiator fights today instead, just for his marriage celebration."

"What do the gladiators do?"

Nila seemed reluctant to answer, but finally said, "Two men at a time enter the field in the ball park and shoot at each other with arrows."

Anacoana gasped.

"You mean, they try to kill each other?"

"I hear that they have been practicing much for this event. They are considered to be the best fighters in their land."

"But why?"

"In the land that Canaobo the Fierce originally came from, it is an honor for a man to die for his king, Princess."

"And whom will they die for today?"

"For thee, of course, your majesty. Canaobo the Fierce insisted upon it."

Blood rushed to Anacoana's head.

"For me? I wish not for anyone to die for me. Didst thou not say that this day should be a happy one? Surely, my people will not come to watch these horrible games, to make themselves happy."

"If thou wishest not to attend them, thou mayest not do so, Princess."

"I have no desire to watch them, Nila."

Anacoana tried to lean back upon her pillows, but she found that she was now too tense to relax. When Father was alive, he used to bring her and Beheccio to ball games that took place in that same arena, where the gladiator fights would soon be held. The audience always rose, when she and her family entered. During those games, Father used to tell her that on the mainland of *Guanine*, the captains of the winning teams were killed, because the people there believed that it was the greatest honor to die such a death, for it enabled a person to obtain the highest position in the afterlife. But Father was proud that on Quisqueya, particularly in the Mother

Kingdom, the winning teams were given fine gifts, instead, for the Quisqueyans saw no honor in being killed for any victory.

As Anacoana thought of the gladiator fights again, her blood began to boil.

It is my arena, she thought. *It is also my people's arena. How dare Canaobo the Fierce bring this bloodshed into my country!*

She could no longer contain herself. Suddenly, she snatched up a pillow and positioned to throw it out of the litter, but when she raised it above her head, she beheld the joyous faces of her people through her window, pressing together along the walks, as they waved madly at her. Slowly, she dropped the pillow and smiled back at them.

As she fumed inwardly, she thought she heard her father's voice.

*Anacoana, Anacoana...be not angry. With anger, thou canst not rule with **the** love.*

With tears stinging her eyes, she felt Father come near.

Thou must influence thy husband with love and peace.

Anacoana pondered over Father's words and began to feel her inner turmoil recede. Just at that point, the *Naborian* men stopped in front of the royal hut and lowered her litter.

As the first ceremony began, Anacoana looked over at Beheccio, but he did not return her glance and only stared straight ahead. She wanted him to explain to her about this ceremony, which was about to begin. Thus far, he kept her in the dark, and most of what she knew that was going to happen today, was through Nila.

Soon the Master-of-the-House stepped forward and announced to the guests that as he called their names, they must come up and present their gifts to the princess. The people cheered, and Anacoana smiled and nodded at them.

The Master-of-the-House then cleared his throat, and in a loud voice said, "Your majesty, as representatives of Queen Higuanamá of the Kingdom of the Great Old Lady, I present to you the queen's grandson and her great, grandchildren. Behold, the Family Guayema of the Kingdom of the Great Old Lady."

The crowd clapped, and a man with six small daughters approached Anacoana. Behind them came *Naborians*, carrying gifts. Anacoana arose and greeted them. As her eyes fell upon the eldest girl, she saw that the child was intent upon watching her younger sisters, as if she previously had rehearsed this approach with them many times. One of the younger girls had frightened eyes and avoided looking at Anacoana. However, the youngest child flashed a smile at the princess. As the family turned to leave, Anacoana felt drawn to those girls, for something suddenly hit her. She realized that some day, she would be responsible for all of those children, as each of them grew old enough to attend the School of the Princes, over which she would soon be given charge. A sense of serenity flooded her, and the fear that had plagued her all morning began to dissipate.

As other families were called, and each of them came forward, Anacoana searched to see if they brought any children, and she listened carefully to hear from where they had come, so she would know whether or not those children would eventually attend her school. There were families from the major and minor kingdoms of Quisqueya. Some came from other islands. Others came from places on the mainland of *Guanine* that she never knew existed. And the Master-of-the-House addressed each of them.

"From the great land of *Guanine*, the first family of Nehualpa, who traveled all the way from the land of Texcoco, in the World of the Lakes..."

Anacoana was honored to meet this family. And next, the Master-of-the-House announced only one person.

"Your majesty, as representative of the Fertile Kingdom, the Princess Sabila."

Anacoana then saw a beautiful, round-eyed girl appear. As her long braids hung past her shoulders, she looked down at her feet as she approached. She did not look old enough to enter the school, and Anacoana was surprised that this child was alone, particularly since she represented the highest kingdom of the island. And then, Anacoana saw trailing some distance behind that girl, a small boy, hobbling with crutches. She wondered who he was, for his name had not been mentioned. Not far behind that boy, came a tall man, dressed as a commoner. His arms were filled with gifts for her. She stared at that man, for she was certain that she had seen him before, but could not recall who he was. Perhaps he was one of the many people who occasionally visited her palace, such as a trader, ambassador, or professional trickster. She turned back to the Princess Sabila, who continued to stare at her feet, and when she reached Anacoana and bowed gracefully, the crippled boy caught up with her. Anacoana noticed that his legs were shriveled. In silence, she watched him struggle to also bow before her, next to the girl. When both children turned to leave the royal hut, Anacoana felt a boldness suddenly surging through her body. She started after them, just as the Master-of-the-House began to announce the name of the next family.

"Your Majesty, the family of..."

Anacoana held up her hand.

"Wait!"

The boy and girl froze in front of her.

She turned to the tall man, who was dressed as a commoner, who held the gifts.

"Is this boy thy son?"

The man suddenly looked uncomfortable.

"Is something wrong, your majesty?"

"Who is he? Is he a prince? If he is, will he attend The School when he becometh of age?"

"Your majesty, the boy is certainly bright enough, but..."

As Anacoana studied the boy, he looked straight back at her. His eyes were curious and had no fear in them. She could not help but experience a love flowing through her for him, which she never felt before.

Without taking her eyes off the boy, she said, "Let not thy physical condition interfere with thy plans to attend my school someday."

She did not know why she had said that, for she did not even know who that boy was, whether he was of royal blood, or a commoner. Then she walked over to him and took both of his hands into hers, and when she did, she felt the presence of her father again. He was standing next to her and began to speak.

I am proud of thee. Thou art learning how to apply **the love**.

At that moment, Anacoana could see the worth of this little, lame boy.

She heard herself saying in front of everyone, "This child hath the potential of becoming a great prince, or even a mighty king, someday."

And then she kissed Neef on both cheeks.

As Anacoana returned to her *dohu* to wait for the Master-of-the-House to announce the next family of guests, she finally understood the wisdom of the first ceremony. The ancients had designed it to teach insights she and other rulers needed. It taught her of *the love*, and for the first time, she felt ready to become a sovereign over two kingdoms, and maybe, to even become the wife of Canaobo the Fierce. She even found herself looking forward to *the struggle*, for she realized that it, too, would provide lessons for her, as long as she had *the love* with her. And strangely, her fears were no more.

5

Even if Anacoana was no longer afraid, her hands were clammy. As she sat in her *bohio* waiting for *the struggle* to begin, the noises from outside made her nervous. When an occasional voice became too loud, she heard someone say, *Hush, hush. The princess is resting.*

After she returned from the first ceremony, while she lay in her hammock, she could not sleep, for the shouts from the arena carried from across the town and kept her awake. The yells, *shooooot, shoooot* from the gladiator fights offended her, particularly when the crowd cheered after a man screamed in agony, as if an arrow had pierced him. How could such an uncouth game transform her peaceful people into such barbarians? Even after Father came to her today, she still experienced bursts of anger from time to time, whenever she was reminded of the outlandish behavior Canaobo the Fierce had introduced to her people, and even angrier at Beheccio, for matching her up with him.

Later, when her *Naborians* came to take away her footstool, her basin, her gourd of water, and other belongings in the hut to reduce the chances of her tripping over anything during *the struggle*, she protested, as they carried out those items. But they assured her that it was for her own safety. After they left, Nila entered to fasten her hammock to its post. As she tied it higher than it had ever been tied, Anacoana saw that her hands were shaking.

"Why, Nila, thou fearest for me."

Nila's voice was trembling, as she wrinkled her forehead and spoke.

"Nay, nay, Princess, of course not. I am happy that today, thou shalt be a woman. When thou art married, thou must remember thy responsibilities toward thy husband, and if thou seest him doing anything unwisely, thou must forget not that he should be taught correct principles with *the love*. As a woman, thou hast powers to help him."

"Nila, be honest with me. Art thou afraid for me?"

Nila's eyes filled with tears.

"Aye, Princess."

She then embraced Anacoana and left quickly with Anacoana's pillows.

And now, with the gladiator fights still fresh in her mind, Anacoana stood upright and waiting. Suddenly a conch shell blew. Its blast caused her to jump, even if she was anticipating it, for it meant that *the struggle* was about to begin. Anacoana stood tall, brushed out the creases in her *nagua,* and walked to the door. When the crowd saw her, they cheered. As she studied the audience outside, she saw guests from local and foreign lands, of kings, queens, princes, princesses, *bohutios,* and representatives of kings and their families. She saw the crippled boy among them, and again for a brief moment, she wondered who he was. She avoided looking in the direction of the musicians, for close to them, was where they had placed the *dohu* for Canaobo the Fierce, and she knew that he would be seated there. Then she heard the Master-of-the-House announcing that *the struggle* was to begin, and it was time for her to enter her *bohío* again. And once she returned to her *bohío*, she heard the musicians begin to blow their *mayohavau* instruments, accompanied by the beat of drums, while castanets clicked in the background. Then there was a silence, and the Master-of-the-House stood at the doorway. In a loud voice so all outside could hear, he announced her first challenger, the Prince Yucama, from the Island of Babeque. Anacoana heard the crowd cheer again, and the Master-of-the-House left.

The next thing Anacoana knew, she was face to face with a man with black paints covering his cheeks, neck, and chest. Behind his paints, his dark eyes flashed at her. The sight of him caused her to cringe, but she remembered that this was only a game, which she was supposed to win, and she positioned herself to fight off this stranger. As the prince bent forward, with his arms held to his side like claws, looking as if he was going to pounce on her, he moved in close. She jumped out of his way. He was so close that she could feel his breath upon her face. And then, with a sudden swipe, he swung his arms around her. She struggled to free herself, kicking, scratching, and thrashing, but his arms were as immovable as the trunk of a palm tree. Several tufts in her hair, which her servants had carefully arranged, unfastened and tumbled past her shoulders. No matter how hard she tried, she could not free herself from his grip. He pushed his mouth close to hers. In panic, she brought her teeth down upon his shoulder and dug them into his flesh. When he cried in pain, she heard the crowd outside laughing, but he still did not release her. So she sunk her teeth even deeper. The next thing Anacoana knew, the Master-of-the-House was standing nearby to separate them. Dejected, the Prince from the Island of Babeque left the hut, with his head hanging low. And the audience outside cheered.

Anacoana could feel the anger, which she already had experienced before *the struggle*, expanding within her, because the Prince from Babeque had broken the rules and had hurt her. Before she could think more about it, she found herself facing her next opponent. She vaguely heard the Master-of-the-House say that he was a king from a town on Quisqueya, called Jacmel. Because her body was weakened from the previous struggle, she stood panting, as her next opponent faced her. In a flash, the king from Jacmel jumped forward, and she crumpled to the ground beneath his weight. She could not move, not even to thrash her arms or bite him. His teeth gleamed in front of her eyes against his brown skin, as his mouth broke into a smile. She could hardly breathe, but with all her strength, she managed a scream. And then, the Master-of-the-House was there once more, jerking the man off from her. And with reluctance, this king was forced to leave her *bohío*.

Anacoana was so exhausted after the second round that she did not think that she could withstand five more, for she had no strength left. But somehow, she survived the third, fourth, fifth, and sixth rounds, and when the Master-of-the-House announced the seventh and last man, she did not hear his words.

Anacoana stood panting, as she leaned against a post with her back facing the doorway, unaware that her last opponent had entered. When she heard a cough, she immediately spun around, and then she saw him, less than an arm's length away. There stood Semola before her, tall and lean, with high cheekbones, just as she remembered him. Her mouth fell open in surprise, and her old feelings began welling up inside of her again. He stood staring directly at her, as he often did when they were both students at The School, but now, he was only a few feet away. She saw that tattoos now covered his body, as indications that he had accomplished much at the School of the Princes.

"Do not be afraid," Semola whispered. "I promise that I will not hurt you."

Unlike the other men, she saw gentleness in his eyes. He did not even try to wrestle with her, but kept his distance, as he stared into her face.

"Oh, Anacoana. You are even more beautiful up close."

He did not speak the mother dialect, as the people of the Mother Kingdom did, but she liked his accent, for it sounded exotic to her. She felt her heart begin to pound, and she wished that he would never stop looking at her in that manner. She did not want him to go away, as she did the others. He came forward and reached out to her, and she let him touch her chin and lift her face up to his. The thrill of his hands entranced her, and she could not pull away from them.

"Anacoana..."

At first, she was at loss for words, but when she finally began to speak, she was surprised at what tumbled out of her mouth.

"Semola, hast thou ever asked for my hand?"

"Five times, Anacoana, but your brother always turned me down. He said that my island of Guanahaní is too insignificant and too far away."

"I was hoping that thou wouldst ask for me."

"Shhhh, if we are quiet, the Master-of-the-House will not interfere, for he only comes to protect you, when he hears noises that indicate that you are being hurt."

Semola took his hands away from her face and slid them down to her shoulders. She felt her shoulders tingle. She wanted to reach out to him also, but did not.

"I know you also love me, Anacoana. I always knew it. Listen, I have a plan. Tonight Canaobo the Fierce will be too drunk from the feast to even know if you slip away. I will then have my men ready, so they can help me take you away to my island. They will be waiting and on guard, in places nobody will think of going."

"Oh, Semola..."

"My island is not like Quisqueya, for on Guanahaní, my people are allowed to choose whomever they wish to marry. Please allow me to take you there, when everyone is asleep."

She let him draw her close, and as he pressed her body against his and caressed her back, she responded with sighs. She had no idea that she could experience such thrills with a man. As she buried her face into his neck, breathing the sweet scents that he had used to wash himself, she allowed him to squeeze her tighter, as he kissed her hair. His breathing grew rapid, and soon she felt the wild pounding of his heart against her chest. She did not want him to stop his caresses, and when he brought his hands to her face again, she saw that his eyes were moist.

"Anacoana, I want you to be my queen. I want you to be my lover."

Her head began to spin, as he drew his face close to hers. She parted her lips, but did not know why she did. It seemed such a natural thing to do. But just as Semola was bringing his mouth close to hers, she suddenly heard a shriek. It made her stiffen and pull away.

"What is the matter, Anacoana?"

"Someone screamed."

She backed away from him.

"Why, why are you...what do you mean?"

"I heard it. I heard a scream."

Semola tried to approach her again, but she stepped even farther away.

"Nay. Please stay away from me. I cannot. This is wrong."

"What? What we feel for each other is right."

Tears smarted Anacoana's eyes, but she blinked them back.

"I recognize that scream, now."

Semola stepped toward her.

"Semola, nay, I say. Thou must hold me not, anymore. That scream. It was the princess I heard screaming, Semola."

"Princess? What princess?"

"The princess, whom the crowd dragged into the plaza, when I was a little girl. The people killed her and her lover with their sticks. They called her a..."

"Please, let me hold you, just one more time..."

"Nay, nay, not even once. I cannot. Thou must leave now. Thou must understand that my people come first. I *must* marry Canaobo the Fierce, Semola. And thou must also understand that, long before I ever marry him, I had been married to my people, since I was born."

"Anacoana, please..."

Semola stepped toward her, but in a loud voice, Anacoana said, "Leave! Thou must leave!"

Her shouts brought the Master-of-the-House into the *bohío*, and through blurry eyes, Anacoana saw him taking Semola by the arm and leading him away, as Semola kept his eyes turned back toward her. As she followed him and the Master-of-the-House out of the *bohío*, she became aware that her hair was frazzled, and her *nagua* was torn in places. By the time she stepped outside, her tears were gone and her vision had cleared. *The struggle* was finally over. She heard the crowd cheer, as she held herself high in front of them. With her face aglow, she waved both of her arms in the air, cheering with the people. She remembered well the final words of this struggle, for she had rehearsed them many times, and now she found that they were part of her. And with all her heart, she called out, so all the world could hear.

"I have overcome! I have overcome! The greatest and most desirable men of all the lands have tempted me, but I have resisted them all! I have overcome!"

The people cheered again and again.

Then Anacoana turned in the direction of the musicians, and for the first time that day, she laid eyes upon Canaobo the Fierce. She saw him rise. He was as tall and muscular as his gladiators. He had no tattoos upon his face, chest, and arms. And when he walked over to her, she saw the war scars across his body. He took both of her hands into his, and with great care, he looked into her face. When she looked back at him, she saw wisdom and experience. And she saw tenderness, which she did not know warriors could have. She realized then, that Nila was right, that he *was* a good match for her, that not only was she to teach him correct principles with *the love*, but he would do the same with her. And at that moment, she forgot about the fights in the arena that had angered her. When he kissed both of her hands, the crowd cheered. His kisses brought no thrill, as Semola's had. But she knew that she would soon learn to love him, even deeper than the emotional infatuation she felt for Semola. And as she and Canaobo the Fierce hooked arms, their eyes linked.

While the musicians started their songs again, Anacoana's *Naborians* came to her, arranged her hair into tufts, and placed new ornaments in them. They draped a robe over her tattered *nagua* and fitted a girdle around her hips, from which hung a mask that was covered with tiny, thin, tiles of gold. When Anacoana was properly dressed, she and Canaobo looped their arms into each other's again, as a royal couple. After their blood was allowed to flow together at the wrists, they both drank from the same wooden bowl.

And thus, Princess Anacoana became Queen Anacoana, queen over both the Kingdom of the Mines and the Mother Kingdom, and she pledged herself and loyalty to Canaobo the Fierce.

6

While winds whipped against his vessel and dark clouds gathered up ahead, Basamanaco paddled in silence, as he headed up north toward the Kingdom of Marién. As the events of the past two weeks circulated through his brain, he briefly glanced over to the other end of the canoe to check on Neef, who lay curled up in a deep sleep.

The memory of Sabila still haunted him, as she stood on the banks of the Mother Kingdom, weeping bitterly while their canoe pulled away. Basamanaco thought of how, when each time kings asked him and his traders to bring their princes or princesses to the School of the Princes in the Mother Kingdom, his heart went out to those young people, whenever he left them behind; for without fail, they wept and begged to be brought back home. And now, he felt especially badly for Sabila, because throughout the years, he had grown to love her deeply. Ever since she was a babe, carried around and suckled by a *Naborian* wet nurse, he was secretly charmed by her beauty. When she began toddling, he always saw her on the beach among the townspeople, sitting a welcome for him and his traders as they approached in their canoe. Even back then, she was the prettiest child he had ever seen, and as he handed out treats to the outstretched hands of children, he often pressed an extra piece into her palm, because he adored the sparkle in her huge, dark eyes. And when he pinched her cheeks that surrounded her tiny mouth, they felt as delicate as the petals of flowers. And now, she was about to be instructed in the ways of a true princess. It meant that eight years from now, when it was time for her to come home after her education was complete, she would be wed to either a prince or a king.

As Basamanaco glanced again at Neef who was lying where some of the wedding presents once were placed, he saw dirt smeared across his cheeks. He loved him also. He was not as beautiful a child as his sister, but the deep questions in his eyes intrigued him, even if Neef were only a five-year-old boy. Neef's eyes always emanated an understanding beyond his years. For this reason, it drove him, Basamanaco, to make special efforts to be Neef's friend, whenever he arrived at his village. He loved the way Neef thirsted after the stories of his travels, and he loved to share them. Yet as mature as Neef appeared to be, he was still a small boy.

As Basamanaco thus pondered, he thought of how in a few days, he would see Lida again. As usual, she would be waiting for him, as he approached the beach of his town of *Guarica*. She often stood apart from the rest of the crowd, among her favorite cluster of palm trees, whenever he and his men arrived. Always, she had no child close by or in her arms; always, she looked barren, with loneliness in her eyes; yet, always, she stood faithfully, waiting for him in the shadows.

Her time to bear children had passed long before other women, and her body sagged in places, as those bodies of women whose time had passed. Yet she stood faithfully, faithfully, with her hair drooping to her shoulders and her lower jaw slightly protruding. She never came to the canoe to meet him, as some of the other wives did with their husbands, but instead, she always stood apart from everyone. Still, he could feel her eyes welcoming him. And when he was almost to shore, she would disappear. And when he finally reached his hut, he always found waiting for him, two bowls of baked fish, still hot off the spit; and near them, three different kinds of cassava breads, wrapped in husks of maize, which were placed neatly on two small, woven mats. The hut was always spotless, with their few belongings stacked neatly in a corner, their two hammocks tied against their posts, and Lida's loom in its usual corner. Only the food awaited him, and not even Lida would be present. But as soon as he sat to eat alone, she would suddenly appear. Then he would arise, and towering over her, he would take her hands into his; and then they would sit and eat together, grateful to be united again. Each day of his arrival, it was understood that they ate alone, and not with the other families in the communal hut. And as they unwrapped the maize husks from the cassava breads, he would see emptiness in her eyes. Although she never complained, he thought he knew why it was there; for he knew how she grieved each time he returned, because she saw how the children ran up to him, and how he tossed them in the air and ruffled their hair. He also handed them each a treat. Although Basamanaco enjoyed these children, he was aware that these scenes made Lida keenly sensitive that she had not borne any of them for him. And he knew how much she wanted a child.

She was a woman who frequently forgot herself. As the town *behique*, she gathered herbs from the forests, dried them in the sun for brews and concoctions, and used them to cure the sick. She was always willing to drop everything she was doing, to help those in need. But when he returned, she put him first, and the townsfolk second, so the two of them could share a meal alone in their *bohió*.

As they thus sat and ate in silence, she would finally say, "Did the trading go well?"

He would nod.

"And how did things go here?"

"Arira had a hard labor, but she brought a healthy man child into the world. She would have died without my help, I think."

And after a pause, she would continue to relate events of how she helped others in the town.

"I stayed five days with Sheema to nurse three of her children with high fevers. The brews cured two of them, but the youngest one died."

Every time she spoke of a death, especially of a child, her protruding lower lip quivered. She never mentioned her barrenness, but he knew it ate at her. He knew that, year after year, she wished that someone would give her one of those babies, whom she nursed back to health. He knew that a child, or maybe even three of them, would help fill that gap in her life, when he was away. He dared not even hope for six children, like most of the town women had. Just one would be enough. Just one child would give Lida the special status that she needed in the community, as she and the other women would sit in the plaza and brag of their offspring, while suckling babies at their breasts.

Lida was not really barren, though, for she had conceived many times, but those pregnancies always ended too soon for the babies to survive. And after those babies were lost, he often awoke in the middle of the night and heard her sniffling in the dark, for she had no herbs to cure herself of her curse.

At one time, though, she actually did carry a baby in her belly until it was old enough to live. Never before, did Basamanaco see such joy in Lida's face, as she paraded it around the plaza and sat with it among the other women to suckle, as they suckled theirs. The babe was a little girl, and to Basamanaco, she was extremely beautiful; but she had an odd color, and she never grew fat, like the other babies. And one morning, they found her dead in her little hammock. From then on, the emptiness returned to Lida's eyes, but now, it was even deeper than before the child ever came. Even after she bore this baby and it died, the townsfolk still considered Lida to be barren, because she was left with no child. As Basamanaco sensed her aching, he could not take away her reproach, although he loved her, even more.

The townsfolk always remained insensitive, not only to Lida's needs, but also to Basamanaco's. They never realized that during Basamanaco's travels, the voices of those little ones calling, *Come sit a welcome, come sit a welcome*, whenever he and his traders came to shore, was worth more than all the nephrites, amulets, or gold he ever traded for. And their welcomes caused Basamanaco's yearning for children to grow even deeper.

"Your trips take you away so often, how do you expect to have time to teach a child your genealogies, your histories, or your *areitas*?" the townsfolk would say.

But it was those genealogies, histories, and *areitas* that Basamanaco wanted to teach a son, for his roots were different from those of the people of Quisqueya. He wished for them to be preserved. His histories did not tell of two separate caves from which the people originated, like the Quisqueyans believed. Instead, they taught that all men came from one common set of parents; that all men were brothers; and that the people of *Guanine* and the surrounding areas all came from a single, ancient family, who once sailed across the ocean on a boat long ago.

As Basamanaco repeatedly plunged his paddle into the water, he heard Neef stirring behind him, and when he glanced over his shoulder, he saw that Neef's eyes were now wide open and were staring straight at him. Basamanaco smiled, as he continued to paddle.

After a while, Neef said in a sleepy voice, "Why are you so tall and big?"

Basamanaco chuckled.

"I am not a *Taino*, as you are, Neef. My ancestors are big people from Guanine."

"Are our people small, compared to the people of Guanine?"

"Oh, the Quisqueyans are normal sized people, but my ancestors are also much larger than most of the people of *Guanine*. Long ago when my people were plentiful, they were known as *the giants*. But all of them are dead, now."

"If they are dead, how did you get here?"

"My Great, Great Grandfather, Xem, came from Guanine a long time ago. His father was king of a great nation there, where there were buildings that reached up to the sky, and the streets were made of gold."

"Xem's father was a king? Then why did he leave?"

52

"When he was a boy, the throne was robbed from the giants, and Xem saw murderers behead his father. When they sought to kill the rest of his family, Xem disguised himself in commoner's clothes and snuck out into a land, where the giants did not dwell and where nobody recognized him, since everyone was looking for someone extremely large. You see, Xem was only a boy, so he was the same size as the adults around him. He hid himself so well that his enemies never located him. But when he learned that all in his family were dead, he escaped to the forests, where he came across traders, who took him to the safety of Quisqueya. Those were during the days before the Caribs moved to their islands, and it was safe to roam the sea."

"Did you say that traders brought Xem to this island?"

"Aye, when he was only about ten years old."

"Then why are you not a king or prince, as your ancestors were?"

"The people of Quisqueya were kind to Xem, but they only accepted him as a commoner. Because he was safe here, he made it his home. In time, though, he grew restless and wished to leave, so he eventually became a trader, like the friends who brought him here. You see, the excitement of traveling helped him get rid of his restlessness, as well as helped him forget about the inheritance that he lost."

"Is that why you are a trader?"

Basamanaco nodded.

"My father was a trader, his father was a trader, and Xem also. And each of them went back to *Guanine* to the land of the giants, to get themselves wives."

"Is your wife a giant?"

"Nay. Lida is a *Taino*. I did not want a giant for a wife, but even if I did, I hear that they are now all killed. When my father went back to Guanine, my mother was one of the last giants left."

Satisfied for the moment, Neef sat up.

"May I help paddle the canoe now, Basamanaco?"

"Of course. You know where you are supposed to sit, when you do."

Basamanaco and Neef then adjusted positions, so Neef could also paddle. After a while, Neef began asking questions again.

"Basamanaco, at the School of the Princes, will they soon begin to teach the students how to fight and be good warriors? I heard that Canaobo the Fierce has already started to teach the children in his kingdom how to be soldiers."

"That will never happen in the Mother Kingdom, Neef. It is against the teachings of Yocahu."

"But Canaobo the Fierce and Queen Anacoana are now married, so wouldn't they do identical things in both of their kingdoms?"

"You are asking questions I cannot answer. But I do know that in Guanine, in some places, they teach children to fight in their schools.

"Where?"

"In more places than I can tell you. As soon as their boy babies are born, they are given little bows and arrows to play with. Certain people even believe that a man can attain the highest honor by being a good warrior, and dying in battle is considered to be the best way to die."

"Why would they believe that?"

"Ah, Neef, Guanine has many hard things for a boy, like you, to understand — or even for an adult on Quisqueya to understand."

"Tell me about those hard to understand things, anyway, Basamanaco."

Basamanaco rowed silently for a while, as if he was thinking about what to say next, and then he said, "Well, on Guanine in some places, human beings are used as sacrifices to gods. To be thus killed is only another way to die with the highest honor. Sometimes if a soldier is not killed in battle and he is taken captive, rather than remain a prisoner, he often asks to be sacrificed to gods, so he can receive the highest honor in the next life."

Neef did not say anything for a long time. Finally he said, "I understand."

But Basamanaco was not certain that Neef actually understood. He also did not want to tell Neef anything more about his people, for he did not want Neef to be afraid of him, as the people of Quisqueya feared the Caribs. He definitely couldn't tell him that, when the intruders had killed his ancestors, they used them as human sacrifices, and Xem witnessed their hearts torn out of their bodies and fed to gods of stone. And most important, Basamanaco would never tell Neef that his own ancestors, the giants, also practiced human sacrifice before they were captured.

As the canoe traveled up the western shore in the Windward Pass, the ocean breeze hit them full force. Winds whistled around the canoe, and waves slapped its sides. The dark clouds in the distance were heavier now, and the water, choppier. But Basamanaco continued to paddle tirelessly.

"Rain up ahead," Neef called out.

If he were with his traders, Basamanaco would have continued traveling, anyway, but because Neef lacked experience with the canoe, he said, "There is a landing place in Cahay, where the villagers provide shelter for travelers. Let us stop there."

Then he steered the canoe toward shore. As they approached land, the people of Cahay gathered on the beach to sit their welcomes. They also came with provisions. Even as thunder rumbled in the distance, children's voices chimed above it.

"Come sit a welcome. Come sit a welcome."

Basamanaco's heart swelled, when he heard them. As the canoe hit the sand, thunder rolled again. This time, it was closer.

The people led them to a roofed structure with no sides. There, Basamanaco saw a stack of firewood for guests to use. When the thunder clapped a third time, it was louder than before. Then lightning lit up the sky, and rain began pelting upon the thatched roof. When a fire finally crackled beneath the shelter, Neef sat shivering, close to it, as he clutched both of his crutches to his thin body. After Basamanaco threw a cloak on, he came over to Neef and lifted up one side of it to cover Neef's shoulders. Neef snuggled up to him, as his teeth chattered.

The rain hit the roof harder now, followed by more thunder and lightning. Basamanaco felt Neef's shivering subside next to him. Then Neef lifted his mouth close to Basamanaco's ear.

"Were you ever swept out to sea in a storm, such as this one?"

"This is no storm, Neef. This is only rain."

"Isn't it a storm? Then it must have been raining much harder than this, when you were swept out to sea in some of the stories you told me about."

"Much harder. I was carried into the sea many times. But I always came back home."

When thunder resounded again, Neef buried his face in his knees and plugged his ears. When he finally looked up, he again brought his mouth to Basamanaco's ear.

54

"Do I paddle well enough, for you to bring me along to Cuba on a trading trip?" Basamanaco smiled.

"You need much, much more practice, Neef."

Neef snuggled closer to Basamanaco.

"I love you, Basamanaco. You are the best trader in the entire world. I am glad that you were not swallowed up into the sea."

But Basamanaco could not reply, for there was a lump in his throat. Children never told him that they loved him, and all he could think of was that soon he would be bringing Neef home to Lida, and when he did, they would finally have a son.

7

The Kingdom of Marién

Five years had passed, since Neef arrived at the town of Guarica to live with Basamanaco and Lida in the Kingdom of Marién, and now he was ten years old and was wearing a loincloth. Although he was homesick, he loved living with Basamanaco and Lida, for they were always kind to him. He often thought of his sister Sabila, who was still at the School of the Princes, and he looked forward to the day, when both of them could return home to the Fertile Kingdom to live with their family again. From time to time, a messenger arrived with news that Eldest-Son-of-My-Father's-First-Wife was stirring up a rebellion back home, but they were only minor ones that were quickly put down. And equally important, most of the people back home supported Neef's father, King Gurarionex.

Neef often yearned to accompany Basamanaco whenever he went away on his trading trips, particularly when he left for the other islands that took him away for days, such as when he traveled to Borinquen, Cuba, Guanahaní, or Beheque. Whenever Basamanaco was gone for a long time, Neef experienced great restlessness, for even if Lida gave him much attention and fed him one type of herb after another — which never strengthened his legs — that restlessness increased by the day, as he dutifully accompanied Lida into the forest to help her gather herbs that cured the illnesses of the village folk. It wasn't that he did not like learning how to recognize which plants were poisonous, which were not, which were used for rashes, which were needed for the rapid healing of broken bones, or which could cut high fevers; but there was something else that gnawed at Neef. *He was bothered that he had never taken a solo trip.*

Although Basamanaco taught him the genealogies and areitas that he always wanted to teach a son, he had never prepared Neef to take a canoe trip alone. Other boys, younger than he was, took such trips into the inland streams. From the time they could walk, their fathers began training them to survive in the wilderness, so they could take their solos at the age of eight and be away for a week. And to those boys, their solos were more important than reaching the proper age to wear a loincloth.

Neef always felt that it was his physical handicap that kept Basamanaco from teaching him the necessary skills for a solo. So whenever an eight-year-old boy paddled inland on his canoe for a week, while the rest of the town people cheered and wished him well, Neef was always there watching after him, intensely jealous and angry.

When a boy solos, sometimes he did not last the entire week, because a storm arose, or his canoe sprung a leak. Maybe he injured an arm, or experienced some other kind of accident. Neef saw boys come home early, because something scary from the world of spirits had frightened them. He knew all about those unseen beings, which Grandfather had said belonged to a real world that consisted of both good and evil forces. The *zemies,* whom the Quisqueyans worshipped, and the *opias,* which did not possess belly buttons, both belonged to the good side. But the *mapoyas,* which were the spirits that sought to destroy all humankind, belonged to the evil side. Grandfather always said that the Quisqueyans were peaceful and loving, because they placed themselves under the protection of the goodly *zemies* and *opias,* but because the Caribs and other ferocious tribes placed their trust in the *mapoyas,* they loved bloodshed. And it was mostly the *mapoyas* that sometimes frightened the boys in the wilderness.

If a boy failed to return at the end of a week, the village formed a search party for him, and under those circumstances, he was usually found disoriented and lost; but in rare instances, he was never found at all. Then the townsfolk assumed that perhaps he encountered the Caribs in the woods, who ate him.

Years before, when Neef used to attend the solemn assemblies with his father Gurarionex and his men, he began to understand the power of the *mapoyas.* During those long meetings, the *bohutios* used their priestly charms, chants, and hallucinating powders to communicate with the *zemies* and *opias* for guidance in how to govern the people. On many occasions, though, the evil *mapoyas* intervened, and the priests had to cast them away. Sometimes they even gave them offerings to appease them. Although he never saw those spirits, Neef definitely felt their presence and power.

Yet Neef was not afraid of *mapoyas, opias* or *zemies;* nor was he afraid of a solo trip. At ten years old, he felt that he was more than ripe to prove himself to be a man by completing a solo. And if no one were willing to teach him the art of survival, he would have to acquire those skills, himself. So when Lida did not need him in the forest, he spent those hours in preparation.

It did not take him long to figure out how to prepare *baygua* powder for fishing, for he had watched other boys make it many times. And one day, he approached an elderly gentleman to ask him if he could borrow his canoe. It was only large enough for a single passenger and his fishing gear, but it was sufficient for Neef.

"Take it and keep it," the old man said. "I am too old to use it, anymore."

After he acquired that vessel, for weeks Neef practiced paddling up and down streams, until his arms gave out. Then he pushed himself, even more. When his canoe first overturned, he remained calm. He found that, even without the use of his legs, the water buoyed him up, and he could swim. In fact, the water gave him greater freedom, and when his body was submerged, he felt himself kick his legs slightly. Almost immediately, he mastered the art of righting his canoe and slipping back into it, even in swift currents. The constant paddling made him strong, and sometimes he paddled so intensely for so long, that his arms kept him awake at night, as they throbbed from the shoulders to the fingertips, but he never complained.

Finally the day arrived when Neef felt that he was ready for his solo, and he approached Basamanaco and Lida to tell them of this news. But even after he demonstrated his competence with the canoe to them, apprehension filled their faces.

"I cannot let you go," said Basamanaco. "Don't you see? I am responsible for you, and you are a king's son, who I must some day return home safely."

"Basamanaco, you don't understand. Just because I'm a crippled prince, does not mean that I shouldn't accomplish any physical feats. I've been asking you for a long time to take me with you to Cuba when you go trading, but you never helped me gain the skills I needed. And now that I have prepared myself to take a solo, I am not asking you for permission anymore, but I am *telling you* that I am going."

The fear increased in Basamanaco's eyes.

"What will I tell your father, if you never return?"

"Just tell him it was all my idea. But don't worry. I'll return."

When the day of Neef's departure arrived, curious villagers gathered to watch him off. None of them ever knew that he was the son of the famous King Guarionex, because to keep Neef safe from his uncle, Basamanaco always hid his identity. Instead, the villagers believed Basamanaco's lie that he had found Neef abandoned and alone in his travels, with neither family nor home. And since they knew that Basamanaco always wanted a child, they thought nothing more of it. So the villagers called Neef, *Basamanaco's Crippled Boy.*

As Neef steered his vessel away, he glanced back at the people, crowding along the shore. Unlike when other boys left on their solos, there was no one who wished him well. Instead, all he saw were countenances filled with worry. And then he saw Basamanaco running up with a long coil of rope made of palm fibers.

"Whenever you travel, you should always bring rope with you. You'll never know when you'll need it."

"Come home, if there is a storm," Lida said. She was weeping.

After Neef took the rope, he turned completely away from the sad faces and did not look back. As he paddled upstream, he came to parts of the island, where he had never been before. He remembered what Basamanaco said about the wilds of Guanine, that sometimes they were not safe, because within them, large, wild cats and other huge animals lurked in the vegetation. Sometimes they even attacked people. But here in the wilderness of Quisqueya it was safe, because only creatures no larger than iguanas, small rodents or exotic birds existed.

As Neef paddled deeper into the jungle, the vegetation often became so thick that it extended toward the middle of the stream and brushed against him. Sometimes branches from either side stretched outward so low that they intertwined, and then, he was forced to bend forward to pass under them. When he came to tributaries, he followed them, while taking mental notes of the direction he took. He heard calls from both large and small fowl, and he saw their brilliant colors flashing through the trees. Although some of the bird cries were new to him, he found that he could already imitate many of them. He projected birdcalls, and then waited for responses. Often they came.

As he pushed upstream and water rushed against his canoe, he inhaled the clean, humid air, and the newness of this experience caused him to laugh out loud. For the first time, he was truly alone, truly independent, truly a real boy, and maybe, even truly a man.

When he finally arrived at a cove where the water was still, he paddled into it to rest. As he looked around, he realized that it was a good place to try out the *baygua* powder that he had prepared, so he took out a pouch of rat skin that he had sewn himself, reached into it, and broadcast the poison across the water. As the bodies of fish floated to the surface, there were so many of them, that it soon became apparent that he had a food supply that would last at least a week, if he smoked the fish. He gathered up his catch and placed them in a basket that he had woven himself out of *hava* leaves. It was lopsided and crudely made, and its workmanship did not compare to the fine results the women of Guarica obtained.

As the day continued, Neef journeyed farther upstream. And finally, he felt that he must pull toward shore to begin preparing his fish so it could last the rest of the week. Soon he saw large rocks ahead of him. Although the bank was not as smooth as the shores in the Kingdom of Marién, he was not going to allow its roughness to interfere with his landing. After he used his paddle to pull his canoe toward land, he grabbed at bushes to bring him closer to shore. When his canoe finally bumped a large rock, he rolled his body onto it, and then dragged his boat over a bed of pebbles, so it would not drift away. And when his canoe was well settled upon the rocks, he tried to rise with his crutches, but the surface was too uneven to allow him to stand, so he had to crawl, instead. After he dragged his useless legs across that rocky bed, halfway over those rocks, he remembered that he forgot the gear that he was planning to use. He also needed the fish he had caught, but they, too, were still in the canoe. So he crawled back across the rocks, retrieved what he needed, and returned, dragging his body the way he came.

Once on better land, as he ignored the stings from his newly acquired abrasions, he scrounged what he needed to start a fire. After he cooked enough fish to eat right away, he set to work upon slicing the remaining supply into thin strips, so he could smoke them slowly to make jerky. He knew that this process would take days. And true to his previous calculations, he still felt that he had enough food to last at least a week, especially if he ate sparingly.

As the fish smoked, the position of the sun told him that it was only mid-afternoon. Since there were still several hours of daylight remaining, he arose on his crutches and swung his body along a path that led into the forest.

Soon the chatter of parrots surrounded him. It was especially intense in this part of the woods. Although the Quisqueyans often served those birds as delicacies and *undercaciques* used their feathers for crowns, when Neef looked up at them, he couldn't help but admire their beauty and intelligence. Ever since he was a tiny tot, he longed to have one of those birds for a pet, to teach it to talk, and for it to become his friend. He used to watch older boys shinny up trees, and when they were high in the branches and hidden among the leaves, they imitated calls to attract the birds.

When one came near, they often captured it for a pet. Sometimes, though, a boy grabbed a parrot to make it squawk, and when the other parrots around heard that commotion, because they were naturally curious, they flew over to see what was happening. As soon as they came near, the boy worked quickly and grabbed as many parrots as he could, wringing their necks until they snapped. And then, he dropped those birds to the ground, until there was a mass of beautiful feathers at the foot of the tree. When he finally completed his kill, the boy shinnied down the tree, tied the birds' feet together, and took them home, so the entire village could enjoy a feast.

But Neef did not want to ruin those beautiful birds. He only wanted one of them as a friend. So he cupped his hands to his mouth and called.

"Awwwkeeee! Awwwwk! Awwwwk!"

He saw the birds up high perch at attention and cock their heads.

"Awwwkeeee!"

As Neef stared upward, tears filled his eyes, because those birds were too far up, and he could not climb, like other boys. As the tears flowed down his cheeks, all the hard work he went through to prepare himself for this trip, flooded his mind, when suddenly, something flashed through him. *Come on, you didn't come here to cry. If you want a bird, you have to be smart about it.*

It jolted Neef out of his hopelessness. He quickly dried his eyes and began to think of solutions. The coil of rope that Basamanaco gave him came to mind, and he retraced his steps to the canoe again, crawled over the rocks, and this time, returned with the rope. With the rope in hand, he studied the trees, calculating.

Maybe I could climb up this rope, if I knotted it at even intervals. Then, if I tied one end of it to an arrow, shot it with a strong bow or catapult-like object, so that the rope would loop around a branch high up there...

His thoughts deepened, while he glanced around for materials to make a bow and arrow, or any invention he could create.

When the sun finally went down, Neef had only skinned the bark off a medium sized piece of wood for a large bow, and he was hungry. The fish he was drying for jerky was still wet, but he took one of the strips and ate it raw. Although he was alone, his mind had shifted to fill itself with goals that he never dreamed he could ever have. Even when darkness fell and thickened, a sense of exhilaration filled him, for he now existed in a world of plans that excited him.

It took Neef a week to finally figure out how he could climb a tree with his useless legs, and another two days to catch his bird. He named his parrot Tira. By then, the skin on his hands was rubbed off in many places, and pus oozed from scratches all over his arms. Although a week had past, he did not feel that he was ready to return home, for since his first landing, he had not traveled far. And then, he looked at his food supply and laughed.

"Tira, look!" he said. "We have enough to eat for another week!"

When his bird only looked at him, he continued.

"Let's set off to discover new places, won't we?"

Tira responded, by nuzzling her beak against his nose.

As Neef and Tira traveled upstream, Neef marveled at the exquisiteness of the land, the mightiness of its mountains, the thick vegetation, the various bird cries, the clear, clean water, and the subtle perfumes emanating from tropical blossoms. Everything seemed to fit so well together, and they all caused him to think of *Makanaima*, or the Great Spirit and Creator of heaven and earth, who dwelled in the heavens, long before people were ever placed into their caves. Although the Quisqueyans never worshipped *Makanaima*, but only gave this creator respect and reverence, Neef now worshipped that spirit, anyway. He did not care one bit, if anyone considered his prayers to *Makanaima* to be blasphemous. As he paddled with Tira on a perch close to him, he began to sing silly, nonsensical thoughts that came to his mind.

> Who is greater, greater, greater
> A man who finishes his solo, solo, solo,
> Or a man who feels the power, power, power
> Of Maka-maka-naima,
> Maka-maka-naima,
> Maka-maka-naima?

"You know what, Tira?" Neef finally said. "For a long time I did not want to be a king, like Father or Grandfather Cahoba. I preferred to become a warrior some day, such as Canaobo the Fierce. Do you know why? I didn't want to run away when the Caribs came, like Grandfather and Father would, because I wanted to be just as brave, as Canaobo the Fierce is. I wanted to fight to the end. But now that I am out here, I realize that I don't want to be a warrior, after all. Instead, when I grow up, I want to become a trader, such as Basamanaco. You see, Basamanaco also fights off the Caribs when they attack, but he is constantly traveling to different lands. When he does, sometimes he must travel through wilderness, and I would love to be surrounded by this much beauty all of the time."

Tira squawked.

"And you know what? Basamanaco is just as brave as Canaobo the Fierce, but he doesn't ever have to boss people around or attend long meetings, like a king does.

"Out here, I feel equal to all the creations of Makanaima."

When he nuzzled up to Tira and felt her smooth feathers against his cheek, he added, "I even feel equal to you."

Neef then looked up at the sun.

"It's time to go to shore for the night again."

As he started toward shore, he heard a thundering sound in the distance. He had no idea how far he had traveled that day, and it was too late to venture off to see what was causing that rumbling. So as soon as he hit land, he began to prepare his shelter for the night.

When morning came, Neef awoke to the distant and steady rumbling that he had heard the day before. Since it was dim by the time he came to shore the previous evening, he had not realized that he was close to the bottom of mountains. Before he set off to investigate the source of the thundering sounds, he left Tira tied to a low branch, so she would not be in the way, if he had to do any climbing.

"I'll be back, Tira," he said.

Soon he found himself standing at a river, and not too far off, he discovered the cause of the thundering noise. For the first time in his life, he beheld water tumbling straight down from a cliff. Basamanaco had told him about such things. He called them *waterfalls*. But this waterfall was much more fantastic than any of Basamanaco's descriptions. And as Neef stared at this newfound beauty, he began to yearn to climb to its top, even if it may sometimes involve not using his crutches.

After Neef climbed for some time, he stopped to rest near a small stream that trickled downhill. He drank his fill and gazed upward, chewing upon a piece of jerky and spotted an opening of a cave in the distance near the edge of a cliff.

Before he could study the cave much further, snapping sounds came from behind him, as if an animal was running through brush close by. And then, a man suddenly jumped out into the clearing. He appeared so unexpectedly, that Neef cried out. As Neef stared at that man, he looked familiar to him, but he could not recall where he had seen him before. As the man stared steadily back at Neef, a smile swept across his face.

"Hui! So, you've been hiding here all this time, have you?"

"Do I know you?"

"That doesn't matter. I know who *you* are. You're Guarionex's brat, aren't you? So what are you doing, out here in these woods?"

"Are you from the village of Guarica? I don't remember seeing you there. Are you part of a search party that's looking for me?"

The man laughed a wicked sort of laugh. And then he reached to his side and pulled out a knife that was chiseled out of obsidian. Neef gasped, when he saw it.

"I've been looking for you for a long time, crippled boy."

The menacing look on that man's face, with his knife in hand, flashed on instincts that screamed inside of Neef.

In an instant, Neef was speeding toward a path that was previously formed by animals. At 10 years old, he now was quicker with his crutches, than ever before. In addition, he had acquired new skills in these wilds that helped increase his mobility. Before he knew it, he had left that man far behind and could no longer hear or see him. He then remembered the cave he previously saw near the cliff and decided to hide there. It would mean ascending farther up the mountain. He was not sure how fast he could climb, but if he made it there, it would give him extra protection.

As Neef started his climb, the terrain grew steeper. He clawed at the mountainside, grasped at branches, and pulled his body upward, hand over hand. Finally he was at the mouth of the cave and slipped into its entrance. The cavern was shallow, and a large rock stood in its center. He made his way behind the rock and crouched down, so he would remain unseen. He did not know how long he would need to stay here, but he was glad that he did not have Tira with him, for her screeches would have given away his whereabouts, long before.

As Neef remained behind that rock, he finally recalled where he had seen that man. It was five years before in a hut near the beach, on the day of Grandfather's funeral. He was one of Eldest-Son-of-My-Father's-First-Wife's rebels, but because he now was no longer wearing a feathered hat, finely tailored clothes, or tufts in his hair, his appearance had greatly changed, so Neef did not recognize him. Neef thought further and remembered more. That man's name was Jama.

So Father's fears are well founded, Neef thought. *Eldest-Son-of-My-Father's-First-Wife actually does want to hurt me, to prevent me from becoming the next king. But does he know that Father doesn't want me to be any kind of king, whatsoever?*

Neef remained in hiding for a long time, but Jama did not appear. Finally when he thought it was safe to do so, he arose from behind the rock and hobbled to the cave entrance. But just before he reached that entrance, he suddenly heard noises of someone approaching, and before he could return behind the rock, Jama was standing at the doorway of the cave, squinting to adjust his eyes to the dimness.

"There you are, you brat! You won't get away, this time!"

Neef froze. In panic, he dropped one of his crutches, but held on tightly to the one still in his hand. As Jama came closer, Neef saw his knife in one hand. As he approached, he did not leave Neef much room to move about, except for backwards, and Neef knew that he was not good at backing up. Now that he had only one crutch, his handicap was even greater. So he remained as still as possible, as he held his remaining crutch in front of him for protection.

"Got you cornered at last, you crippled weakling."

Jama had a sneer on his face, as he showed his yellow, decaying, teeth. He was now so close that Neef could smell the foul odor of his breath. As Jama raised his knife upward, Neef also raised his crutch, to defend himself. Jama suddenly lunged, but Neef dodged out of his way, and with all his might, he swung his crutch. He heard a whack, and Jama's shouts echoed in the cave, as he grasped at one of his hands, as if it were in pain. Then Neef saw the knife flying through the air, out of the cave entrance, and down, over the edge of the cliff.

"Damn that crutch! So, you're putting up a fight, are you? Didn't your father teach you about *the love*, brat? Nobody on this island fights, remember?"

Neef moved as fast as he could toward the cave entrance. He was not sure how well, or how quickly, he could escape with one crutch and descend the side of the hill, but he knew that if he remained here any longer, he would not be able to hold off his enemy. And just as he turned past the opening of the cave, he felt a jerk, for Jama had grabbed hold of his crutch and was yanking at it. Neef's mind went wild.

"Let go!"

If Jama took his crutch away, he wouldn't be able to escape, at all. Neef hung on, wrapping his arms around his only means of mobility, but Jama was stronger, as he twisted, wrenched, and shook, to free the crutch out of Neef's grasp.

"Nay! You can't have my crutch!"

Neef fell to the ground, still hanging on. Jama yanked, and then kicked Neef in the face, but Neef still clung to the crutch, as blood spurted from his nose. Then Jama started dragging him across the cave floor, over small rocks that cut into his skin. When Neef neared the entrance, he reached out to the side of the cave and grabbed at a large, jagged rock. With one arm, he forced himself to his feet. Because Jama could no longer drag Neef's body, he came forward and shoved the crutch into Neef's crotch, which caused Neef to stagger backwards. To prevent himself from falling flat on his back, Neef overcompensated by pushing his body forward. As he fell forwards, he crashed, smack into Jama. Since Neef no longer had any means to keep his balance, he clung to his opponent, who was taken by surprise by this impact, and tottered backwards. Before Neef knew it, he heard Jama screaming again, as both of them staggered toward the edge of the cliff. Jama then tripped over a rock behind him, and as they both fell past a bush toward the mountain edge, Neef grabbed for that bush, to break from his opponent. But Jama continued to fall backwards, and soon, Neef found himself flat on his belly, still clinging to a branch from the bush, as he stared into open space. He then saw his attacker, tumbling through midair below, screaming a long, loud, scream. Neef dragged himself on his belly to have a better look at his pursuer. He saw Jama land on a ledge below, bounce off of it, and then proceeded farther down.

"I didn't mean to kill him," Neef said to himself.

But then, another thought came to him.

Are there other men nearby looking for me?

When Neef finally reached his campsite, he immediately took Tira and his belongings and left on his canoe, cautiously looking around him for any other intruders. He saw no one. Although it was a temptation to head straight for home, he chose to continue his journey upstream, for to him, his trip had just begun. But now that he had killed a man, he no longer felt equal to the trees, or to the rest of nature.

When the day finally arrived when Neef felt that he was ready to head for home, he reflected upon his solo trip and realized how much it had changed him. He turned to Tira.

"You know what? I'm not angry with the other boys anymore, because they can do things I can't. I can now paddle a canoe, just as well as any of them. I can climb trees, as they can. And my solo lasted twice as long, as any of theirs."

But with regret, Neef could not forget that he had also killed a man, which all of the other boys had never done. And when he thought of Lida and Basamanaco, he no longer minded their lack of confidence in him, because now, he had confidence in himself, which he, alone, had built. He also remembered his sister Sabila, who was at the School of the Princes, and wondered if she had grown as much as he did.

When Neef's canoe finally approached the inland pier of Guarica, because the sun was now low, shadows spread across the land. As soon as the village folk spotted Neef, they began to shout. Shortly, a cheering crowd lined the banks and sat welcomes. Unlike his departure, the faces that now greeted him were joyful.

"Look! Basamanaco's Crippled Boy returned!"

Those words turned Neef cold. Out in the wilderness, he forgot that he was crippled.

"Welcome home!" Neef heard Basamanaco shout.

"You were gone so long, that we all thought you had perished," someone said.

"Where were you?" someone else shouted. "We sent people looking for you many times, but nobody could ever find you."

When the canoe reached the dock, someone took Tira from her perch, while others lifted Neef to carry upon their shoulders.

"Hurrah! Basamanaco's Crippled Boy is home!"

And high above everyone, Neef thought in his heart: *I was never a crippled boy, nor will I ever be one. It's these people who are crippled, for they can only see my outward appearance, but not how well I can think, or what I can do.*

Although none of the other boys ever received such a welcome, Neef knew that this rejoicing was occurring, because he had accomplished a feat that no one, but he, ever believed he could perform. And as the people scampered about with him, he saw from far off, a litter carried by eight men coming near. He could not see who was in it, but he knew that only kings and members of royalty were transported in them, so he assumed that perhaps the famous King Guacanagarí of the Kingdom of Marién was approaching. He had never met him before.

Since the people were so engrossed with their commotion, they did not notice that their leader was coming. When the litter finally arrived, the people suddenly stopped shouting, put Neef down, and fell prostrate to the ground.

And then, King Guacanagarí stepped out into the open. When Neef started to bow also, the king held out his hand for him to remain standing with his crutches.

"My boy," he said. "What an amazing accomplishment, especially for someone with your...uh..condition. I was just about to have my fourth meal, when news of your arrival reached me. Won't you join me, so we can eat and celebrate together?"

Neef could not believe what he heard. He was looking forward to spending a meal alone with Basamanaco and Lida, but he accepted this invitation, anyway. He liked this king, for he reminded him of his father, with his soft mannerism, gold crown, tufts in his hair, tattoos, and fine clothes.

Later, as Neef sat across from King Guacanagarí over the day's fourth meal, he found himself reciting the names of the *caciques* of all 80 minor and major kingdoms of the island, along with the entertainers, as they chanted these names in an *areita*. Here in this palace, he couldn't help doing that, for it reminded him too much of his old home. And he even sang other *areitas* verbatim, as the musicians played their tunes. And then, he noticed King Guacanagarí looking at him strangely.

"Where did you learn all of this, my boy?"

Neef did not realize that he was being carried away, and Basamanaco's warnings came back to him that he should never let anyone know of his true identity, because news could reach Eldest-Son-of-My-Father's-First-Wife that he was here in the Kingdom of Marién.

"It all comes naturally with me, your majesty."

"My boy, if all of this comes naturally with you, you must visit me often, so we can get to know each other. I am sure that there will be many other things in this palace that will come naturally to you."

"Your majesty, I would love to come to see you."

Here in King Guacanagarí's palace, Neef felt that he had come home to the Fertile Kingdom. Yet even if he returned to his home now, he knew that conditions would never be as they used to be, because now, a deep sorrow lingered inside of him, for he could not forget that he had killed a man, and *a Taino of Quisqueya should never kill*. And he felt that not even a trip to Cuba with Basamanaco could take that sadness away.

8

Blaaaaaaaaaaaaat!

A conch blasted in the bay. Its bold trumpeting was unlike any other conch that Neef had ever heard. Since it was barely dawn, it had jostled him out of a deep slumber, and he sat up, rubbing his eyes. He couldn't understand it, for those sounds forced his mind into frenzy, and it had troubling effects upon something that came from deep within him.

Soon he heard footsteps running outside, and people began shouting.

"Caribs! Caribs! Caribs!"

Neef saw Basamanaco jump out of his hammock, and before he ran out of the hut, he said, "Lida, get Neef out of here."

As soon as Basamanaco was outside, Neef heard him shouting to warn the rest of the town.

"Wake up, everybody! The cannibals are attacking Guarica! They're sounding their war cry! Quick, everybody, run to the hills! Hide! Hide!"

The conch sounded again. This time, its blast was louder and closer. When Neef snatched up his crutches, Lida was already at his side. Soon he was on his feet and hobbling as fast as he could, close to Lida. Once outside, townsfolk passed him. Although people were in panic, they suddenly quieted down, for they had trained themselves to run in silence. Neef looked for Basamanaco, for he wanted to ask him what was the best thing to do, during these attacks. But before he knew it, Basamanaco was behind him. He swept Neef up, swung him over his shoulders, and began speeding toward the hills.

"Basamanaco! Put me down! I am eleven years old. I can move faster than most people can. Besides, I'm staying back to fight the Caribs with you."

But Basamanaco ignored him and surged forward.

"You don't run fast enough," he said.

"Basamanaco, I want to fight the Caribs with you and your men, I said!"

"Nay, Neef. When they attack a village, they come too well equipped, and they bring too many warriors with them. No one will stand a chance to survive. So my men and I will need to also hide."

"Well, put me down, anyway."

They reached the palisade gates, and once through them, they turned toward the hills, and continued to the forest. Helpless in Basamanaco's grasp, Neef glanced back and saw three, no, four...no, six...ten...canoes approaching in the bay. They were about the size of Basamanaco's vessel, but instead of eighty men, only about fifty were in each of them. He could not see the faces of the Caribs, for they were too far away, but many of them wore feathered hats, which were not like the colorful, feathered crowns the *undercaciques* he knew wore. Instead, they consisted of dark plumes that bobbed in front of their faces. As he hung on to Basamanaco's neck, Neef watched in awe, as the vessels skimmed across the waves, in a mad race to shore.

The Quisqueyans continued to flee around them. Although they did not fight, they knew how to run quickly in silence, to hide in ways that their pursuers would not know their whereabouts. As Basamanaco sped on, Neef watched, as they left men and women far behind. Many of them carried one or two babies. Occasionally in the shuffle, small children became lost, and as they stood alone, bawling, people in the crowd would notice them, and even if they were not close friends or relatives, they would snatch up those little ones, while hushing them, and then, they ran with them toward safety.

Upon Basamanaco's mighty shoulders, as Neef looked back toward Guarica, he saw that someone had set fire to its signal tower to warn the other villages. As its torch burned high above the town, within minutes, smoke also rose from other signal towers, throughout the countryside.

Soon Neef and Basamanaco reached the forest, far ahead of everyone else. As they came to the hills and began winding up a path, twigs snapped beneath Basamanaco's feet. They climbed higher, and after Basamanaco turned off the trail and crashed through bushes, he finally reached a large rock at the side of a hill, and stopped. He lowered Neef to the ground and placed him into the cavity, between the rock and hill. Neef said nothing, while Basamanaco broke off nearby branches and covered him up with them.

"When the Caribs come, don't you dare move or make any noise."

Basamanaco turned to leave, but then, he returned for a second and whispered, "I must go and help others to safety."

And then he was gone.

As Neef crouched within the cavity, he heard the conch blast again. It seemed to come from on land, this time. The cannibals must have reached Guarica, and maybe, they were even searching its *bohios*, or huts. Neef suddenly remembered Tira. He had left her on her perch, outside the hut. But then, he reminded hmself that Caribs didn't invade towns for birds, but for people, and his mind became at rest.

Within seconds, he heard people approaching around him, and through cracks between leaves, he saw them running pass him, as they sought hiding places. He was amazed at how quietly they scurried about and disappeared. Then after what seemed forever, thuds began to vibrate the ground. They came from footsteps that were considerably heavier than the people of Guarica's. As they neared, they thundered, louder and louder.

Then Neef saw them, with their devilish headpieces, bobbing feathers, and painted faces. As the Caribs scattered throughout the forest, they looked in all directions and sniffed the air, as if they were dogs. Their tattoos were, not at all, like the ones engraved into the flesh of the kings Neef knew. Neef heard that their tattoos represented allegiances with the *mapoyas*, or the dark powers. And now as they ran, hither and thither, holding their spears, bows, and clubs called *macabas* tightly in their fists, they pulled brush aside and kicked away rocks and pieces of wood.

A warrior paused in front of Neef, appearing to stare directly at him. Neef held his breath. The man stalked closer toward him and ruffled the leaves in front of him and over him, while sniffing the air. Then he turned away and walked to a clump of bushes, a few feet over. Suddenly, with one muscled hand, the Carib reached into the vegetation and yanked out a woman, who was clinging to two small babies. She screamed, and her voice reverberated throughout the forest. Both of her babies started to bawl, as if they knew that their lives were in danger. Neef bit his lips to keep from crying out, for he recognized that woman to be one of Lida's close friends. Lida often visited her, when her children were ill. The Carib slapped her over and over again, until she fell backwards, as she still clung to her children. As she lay bleeding from the mouth, he jerked the smaller child from her arms, and with one sweep of his *macaba*, he clobbered its tiny head and shattered it to bits. After blood and brain tissue splattered across the trees, he tossed the small carcass aside. The woman tried to stand so she could run to her baby, but fainted. When the second child screamed, the *macaba* thumped again. And its cries ceased.

From then on, the Caribs pulled adults and children from bushes. Victims screamed and thrashed until their strength gave out, and after they were subdued, some were dragged, bawling, down the hillside to the beach. Arrows that whizzed through branches were often followed by shrieks, which caused Neef to shudder. The sounds of arms breaking, of fists pounding flesh, as well as of *macabas* slamming upon bodies, left a sickening flavor in the forest. Night came, and the search for people persisted in the dark, with twigs cracking when the warriors stepped on them in the moonlight. Occasionally, a human wail pierced the air, when someone was found.

Neef sat, wide-eyed. The night was too thick to see the Caribs now, but he could tell that they were passing a gourd of water around among themselves, for he heard their gulps, as they filled their mouths. It made him realize that his mouth was also dry, and his stomach ached from not eating, since early morning. But he remained motionless, as he felt the leaves around him vibrating every time a Carib brushed by. Neef pressed closer to his rock, alert to the *crack cracking* of heavy footsteps. Several times he dozed off, only to be awakened by the Caribs yelling. Although he did not understand their language, some of their words were similar to his own, and he could tell that they were calling out vulgarities, to insult the Guaricans. The coolness of the air caused him to shiver, but he bit his teeth tightly together, to keep them from chattering, so no one would hear any noise coming from his direction. Something touched his foot, and he jumped, but it was only a small rodent, wandering about in search for food. As its bright eyes stared briefly up at him, they glistened in the dark. And then it ran off.

Finally, streaks of dawn pushed faintly through the leaves. Neef saw the muscular figure of a Carib with tattoos on his brown skin, standing only about a foot in front of him. He was holding a crutch. Then Neef realized that his crutches were not next to him, and he must have dropped them, before Basamanaco had placed him in his hiding place. His hands grew clammy.

Another Carib approached the man with the crutch. They both examined it, and the first man shrugged, as if he was puzzled by it. He dropped the crutch and forgot about it. Neef had heard that among the Caribs, when a child was born handicapped, it was strangled, because they had no need for it, especially if it were a boy, for to them, boys were supposed to become warriors.

Suddenly, a conch blew. As its sound filled the forest, it left a ring in Neef's ears and lingered in the air. It must had been a signal for the Caribs to evacuate, for those warriors brought their search to a halt. Soon, they gathered their prisoners, whom they had tied together in groups during the night, and they began to drag them, hollering and weeping, to the main paths. The people stumbled over the mangled bodies of those who had resisted and fought to their death. The prisoners wailed in a chorus that was deafening, but their cries grew softer, as they were led away down the hillside, to the awaiting canoes on the beach.

Neef thought of Basamanaco, Lida, even King Guacanagarí, and the other people of Guarica. He wondered who was safe. He also thought of what Basamanaco constantly told him about the Caribs.

Once the Caribs bring their prisoners to their homeland, they immediately castrate the men, so their flesh will be tender and succulent, when it is time to eat them. The Caribs especially love the tender and juicy flesh of babies, and if the women prisoners have babies with them, they will roast the infants on spits in front of their mothers in a grand feast, to put the mothers in agony. They also will fight over the women they capture, whom they will use as concubines. They want only healthy women with strong bodies, who look as though they can bear strong sons, for as soon as their sons are weaned from their mothers' breasts, they will take them away to another island, where they, alone, will train to become warriors.

Neef heard the conch again, and this time, its sounds came from the sea.

A villager soon came running through the woods, calling, "The Caribs are gone! It is safe to come out of hiding!"

But even after that man ran past him, Neef still dared not move. Instead, he waited and watched other people through the leaves, as they stepped out into the open in front of him. Finally when more of them came out of hiding, he pulled himself to his feet and shook the stiffness out of his body. A sense of relief surged through him, as he glanced around at the survivors. And when he saw Basamanaco and Lida among them, he could not help but laugh with joy. Soon Basamanaco came toward him, holding the crutch that the Carib once handled.

Throughout the woods, survivors began calling out names of loved ones, and they waited with anxiety, when there were no responses. Many were found maimed and groaning, and when some were discovered to be dead, people wept.

"Amita, Amita, oh my daughter..."

"Maluka...Maluka..."

As the day rolled on, the weeping grew louder. And finally the elderly man, who had previously given Neef his canoe, called out to everyone.

"My friends, do not mourn so much. Remember, someday we will be rewarded for all of our suffering. We have remained a virtuous and peaceful people, for hundreds of years. We have not participated in any kind of fighting, even when under attack. Just wait and see. When Yocahu returns and finds us faithful to *the love*, he will elevate us to be the greatest people in the world, so that we will stand higher and stronger than even the Caribs, or any of the nations of Guanine. He will feed us greater knowledge than any of the other nations ever had, or will have, and no one will be able to surpass us."

The people ignored this old man, as they went about their business.

Amid the lamentation, Neef looked out into the bay. He could see the Carib canoes retreating, and now they were tiny dots in the horizon. Neef thought of the captives from Guarica, whom he would never see again.

And then, he heard the elderly man say, "Remember, my friends. This time, the Caribs did not conquer and destroy us all, as Canaobo the Great's prophecy said they would. That is a good sign. That means that, sooner or later, Yocahu will come to save us, before any other foreigners can get here."

As the solemn faced people still ignored him, they carried the dead and maimed down the hill.

"We're having a grand funeral today," someone said. "Our loved ones need to have proper burials, so their *opias* can rest in *Coaibai*."

Neef looked at the injured, as they were lifted downhill. Some of them did not look like as though they were going to live much longer.

And then, he remembered Tira again. He climbed down the hill and went quickly to his hut. She was not perched upon her stand, where he had left her, but he found a heap of crumpled feathers, mingled with blood, beneath it. As he blinked back tears, he hobbled quickly away and went through the palisade gates. As he looked out into the horizon once more, the silvery reflection of the sea came into focus, and he saw that the Carib canoes were now gone altogether. But then, he noticed another black dot far away. It appeared to be a canoe coming toward Guarica.

His body stiffened, and he searched for Basamanaco.

When he found him, he said, "The Caribs are returning. I can see one of their canoes out there."

He saw panic sweep across the faces of those who heard him, but Basamanaco calmly looked out to sea. Everyone knew that his eyes were much better than theirs, because during his travels, he trained them to see far off

"I see no Caribs, Neef," he said. And then he chuckled. "Neef, do you know who is coming? It is your sister, Sabila!"

With the aid of his one crutch, Neef started toward the beach, but Basamanaco caught hold of his arm.

"Neef," he said. "I want to tell you something important. You are now old enough to understand about the cycles of life."

Neef paused.

"Neef, when tragedy strikes, that event is only a part of many cycles. Our town has just suffered a great loss, but in that cycle, we will soon experience an equal gain. Maybe your sister's return will represent that gain that should soon happen. I don't know why she is coming here, for I thought that she still had one more year left of schooling. But we will soon find out. Anyway, your sister should be a great lady by now, with all her training The School gave her. Maybe, as part of that cycle, she will be replacing the loss of Tira, or the losses that have just occurred in our village."

"I don't understand what you are talking about."

"Don't you see, Neef? Life is a cycle that keeps repeating itself. When we experience a loss, we later experience an equal gain. These patterns continue, year after year."

Neef shrugged, because he did not know how to reply to Basamanaco. As he hobbled toward the shore, he was still trying to figure out what Basamanaco meant about cycles. Then he thought of two events, which could fit into the patterns of those cycles. If Yocahu returned now and made the Quisqueyans the greatest people on earth, he would be making up for the loss they had just experienced. But then Neef began wondering beyond those two events. Once Yocahu made the Quisqueyans the greatest on the earth, then after he left again, an equally intense tragedy would need to occur. Neef then pushed his thoughts aside.

As Sabila's canoe grew nearer, Neef saw that *Naborian* servants maneuvered it. Since everyone in Guarica was now recovering from a devastating tragedy, no one else, but him, was at the beach to sit a welcome. Once the canoe landed, Sabila climbed out of it and ran to him. When he arose to greet her, he was surprised that she no longer towered over him, and he was almost as tall as she was. And he also saw that Basamanaco was correct, for she indeed had grown into a beautiful, young lady.

"Neef! You've grown so much!"

After Sabila embraced him, she said, "The school is giving us a break, and we're allowed two weeks to go home to visit our families. But when I reached our home in the Fertile Kingdom, I could not even visit our parents. I don't know what is happening there, but there was fighting going on, and no one would let me set foot on ground. One of the *bohutios* told me that I would find you here in the Kingdom of Marién."

"How does he know I'm here? Nobody should know that."

Sabila did not respond to Neef's question and embraced him again.

"Oh, my little brother. You don't know how good it is to see you again, especially since I won't be able to see our parents, for a long while."

Just then, Neef recalled something.

"Sabila, when you were at The School, did you discover your *ayiti*?

"My what?"

"Your *ayiti*. You know, your higher self."

"Oh, that? My teachers are always mentioning that word *ayiti*, but they often talk about the strangest things that I either can't stand to hear about, or to try to figure out."

"You mean, you never felt it?"

"What is there to feel?"

"Sabila, after all these years at the School of the Princes, you still don't understand how it is to experience your *ayiti*? The School is supposed to help you find it. Remember when we were traveling to the Mother Kingdom six years ago, and Basamanaco and I sang about the two caves? I began to discover my *ayiti*, starting from that time, and when I took my solo last year, I discovered another form of it."

"Come on, Neef. Let's talk about something else. I've had so many subjects drummed into me at The School, that I'm tired of hearing about them. We haven't seen each other in such a long time, and I have so much to tell you."

As Sabila chattered about her friends and all the fun she was having, she looked extremely attractive in her beautiful *nagua*, with her hair styled in fashionable tufts. And now that she had a body of a woman, she was the most stunning princess Neef ever saw. As he quietly listened to his sister's chatter, he realized that they were both two opposite people, for she would never understand Basamanaco's previous discussion on the cycles of life, and he knew that, as far as she was concerned, one's *ayiti* did not exist.

Book Two

9

Salty sprays cuffed the deck of the Santa Maria and cast a mist upon a thin figure, struggling beneath the weight of a tray. A boy, bent forward and barefoot, slid a foot or two over the moist planks. His small-boned frame made him appear younger than twelve years old. As the caravel gave a sudden jolt, a piece of salted pork tumbled over the edge of the tray, but the boy caught it, just before it hit the floor, and as he did, his arm knocked against a mug of wine, splattering its contents across a pile of biscuits.

"*Vija, mío!* Capitán Colón will refuse to eat this food."

As Mateo approached the captain's cabin, where he knew that Colón now hunched over papers, he glanced toward the horizon. It had been thirty-one days, since he and the crew had set sail from Spain to cross the Western Ocean, and still, there was no sight of the Indies. For weeks now, everyone had stopped talking about the reward of 10,000 *maravediés* that the queen had offered to the first person who sighted land. At this point, Mateo did not care about any kind of money. He only wished to be back in Spain.

To him, it was hard to believe that just a month before, while he lived in a monastery in Palos, Castile, he had yearned to sail to find new lands. Whenever Capitán Colón came to visit Juan Perez, his good friend who was a friar at the monastery, Mateo could not help but follow Colón around, for he brought fascinating stories with him about his travels and dreams of finding a new route to the Indies.

And when Mateo asked Colón a question or two, the captain would place a hand on his shoulder and say, "*Mi híjo,* I used to wonder about th' same things as ye do, when I was yer age. As a boy, every day I would stand at th' docks 'n watch th' ships come 'n go. Even back then, I knew I belonged to th' sea."

When the queen finally was able to give Señor Colón permission to sail, and he obtained three ships for his journey, he came to the monastery and told everyone this good news. While Juan Perez broke open wine in high spirits, Colón turned to Mateo.

"I realize ye're two years younger than I was when I first went to sea, but I need another cabin boy, 'n I think ye'll make a good one."

Mateo knew that Colón favored him, because of his blond hair and blue eyes, for the people in the part of Spain where they were, tended to have darker features. And he also knew that Colón felt akin to him, because they both were easily enchanted by stories about the sea. But only a few days after the onset of this journey, Mateo learned the truth about himself. He wasn't at all like Colón, because the ocean immediately taught him that he actually hated it. And as he worked among the crew, he realized that he and those men were also not alike, for unlike him, they easily allowed the views of others and various external influences to change their perceptions and personalities, as well as to lose sight of goals. Even if many of them were not the usual hardened sailors, the sea had turned them sour, vulgar and crude. They were men of dignity and accomplishment, who were nobles of the king's court, doctors, a chalkier, a merchant, a tailor, a lawyer, and even a linguist. And of course, a couple of them were toughened sailors. Strangely, though, when the ships set sail, even the hardened sailors wept, for everyone wondered whether they would ever see Spain again.

During this journey, the weather went well, but after many days and no land was sighted, the crew began to gather in angry whispers. Quietly, Mateo listened to the stink of mutiny, as foul talk of the captain grew into unbelievable proportions. Even those men on the other two caravels of the fleet, the Pinta and the Niña, had lost faith in Colón — particularly Pinzón, the captain and owner of the Pinta. Maybe it was because Pinzón's ship was the swiftest of the fleet that made his head swell. Or, maybe it was because he had also contributed to a third of the cost of this trip. But to Mateo, that man growled too much and forgot too quickly about who was supposed to be in charge of this journey.

Once when Pinzón came aboard the Santa Maria, he whispered to its crew, "We've been all fooled by Colón's hallucinations. I should've known all along that he was inept. Now I've wasted my money!"

"Then let's cast him overboard 'n return to Castile," someone said. "We'll tell th' queen that he fell into th' ocean 'n drowned."

"Nahhh, she wouldn't believe that story from us."

"Then maybe we should tell her that he was leanin' over too far on th' railin' with his quadrant, when he fell into th' ocean."

Only yesterday, the crew confronted Captain Colón, as they attempted to take control of the ship.

After they grabbed hold of him and bound him to a post, they shouted, "*Señor*, we're turnin' back to Castile!"

But when Colón spoke to them, Mateo realized that their behavior was no surprise to him. He wasn't even concerned that their food supplies were low and would barely be enough to last a return trip home, and that the ships had sprung serious leaks.

"Give me two days," Colón said, with calmness and confidence in his eyes. "If we don't reach land in two days, I promise ye, we'll turn back."

What seemed funny to Mateo was that during this rebellion, the wind suddenly stopped blowing, and the ship would not travel any farther, until the men agreed to let Colón go. And as soon as they did, the sea began pumping waves into itself, and the caravels started to move again. Then squalls of clouds, driftwood, birds, weed grass, and other signs of land appeared.

When Mateo reached the door of the captain's cabin, he braced himself as he balanced the tray of food, knocked, and waited. When he heard nothing, he pressed his ear against the door. When it continued to be silent inside, he finally pushed the door open. Sure enough, Captain Colón was seated at his desk as usual, but this time, he was bent over a map.

"Good evenin', Señor Capitán. Yer dinner."

Colón remained intent in his work, as if Mateo was not even there.

"*Señor*, ye should've seen th' large fish this mornin'. They were swimmin' close to th' ship, 'n we almost caught one, but he got away."

When the captain still did not respond, Mateo became aware of the squeak of an oil lamp that hung from the ceiling. To the right of Colón's desk, he saw shelves that were too small to accommodate the library that the captain had brought along, so books were crammed into them. More books also stood in a stack in a corner of the room, behind a chair that slid back and forth across the floor to the swaying of the ship. Upon that chair lay a Bible. It was printed in Spanish and was not in the usual Greek or Latin. Mateo had promised the captain many times that he would never tell

74

anyone about this Bible, because Capitán Colón said that if anybody found out about it, the Inquisition may burn him at the stake. Right now, its wrinkled pages lay open to *Saint Mark*. Yesterday, it was open to *The Acts*.

Mateo tiptoed to a small table and placed the tray upon it. He hoped that Colón would not notice the condition of the food, with wine splattered all over it. Then he turned in the direction of the door to leave. As he passed Colón, he timidly peered over his shoulder to see what he was doing.

At the center of the map that spread before the captain, Mateo saw the Western Ocean, with Europe to the right of it, and the Indies at its left. He saw the islands of Cipango and the land of Cathay within the Indies. As Mateo stared at the details of the map, he felt that he could spend days in this cabin, if he were allowed to, for Colón owned such curious objects that nobody else ever had.

Colón ran his hand through his white hair and looked into space. His reddish face was haggard, but determination emanated from his eyes. Mateo knew that some nights, he never, ever slept. On his friendlier days, the captain had pointed out this map to him many times and told him that the route they were taking, would eventually bring them to an eastward approach of the Ganges River in India. He was positive that this route also covered the remaining third of the globe, which he said was yet undiscovered. He said that God was inspiring him to take this trip, and he was not only to find a new route to the Indies, but he was also to bring Christianity to the heathen nations.

When the captain continued to ignore him, Mateo moved to the stairs and slowly climbed them. Just as he reached the top and placed his hand on the doorknob, Colón suddenly called out.

"Mateo?"

Mateo spun around.

"Ye told me that yer father knew people who traded in th' Indies."

"*Sí, señor*. He was not really my father, though. He adopted me after my family was killed."

"What did he say about them?"

"About whom, *señor*?"

"About th' people in th' Indies. Th' ones in Cathay."

"'He said that their eyes are different 'n very mysterious, *señor*. He said that they drive hard bargains when tradin' their goods." Mateo thought for a minute and then added. "Their wives also don't spend as much money as th' women of Europe."

The captain looked into space for a moment.

"*Gracias, mi hijo.* Ye may leave now."

As soon as Mateo stepped outside, a breeze from the ocean blasted him in the face. Birds pressed together upon the ship's railings, mizzenmast, and mainmast as they prepared themselves for a night's rest. Although the sky was still light, an occasional star winked among streaks of orange and red. Mildly disappointed that the captain did not speak much to him today, Mateo inhaled the fresh, salty air. He wanted to hear more about the Indies. He wanted the captain to tell him about the heathen nations and about Cathay and Cipango, with their gold and precious stones, marble palaces and marvelous bridges. He wished to hear about the Great Kahn and Marco Polo again; and of how two hundred years back, a descendant of the Kahn, who had heard about Marco Polo's visit to his ancestor emperor, had sent a messenger to Europe to ask for someone to come to Cathay to teach his people about Christianity. And also, Mateo wished for the captain to tell him again about how he had obtained his Bible that was written in Spanish.

Prior to this journey, Mateo had never seen such a Bible. The captain had told him that it was a gift from a very special and learned friend, who had obtained it from someone else. But Colón's friend feared that if anyone found out that he owned such a Bible, it would be destroyed, and he would be tried and punished for being a heretic, just for owning it. Because Colón was curious about that Bible, his friend gave it to him. And Mateo sensed that the captain was not afraid to own that Bible, just as he was not afraid to have his other possessions of curiosity, or to take this trip across the unknown sea to find the Indies, as well as to form opinions that were extremely foreign from everyone else's.

That night, Mateo awoke to find that a fever was raging through his body. His muscles ached, and his lips were parched. As he lay on the deck, someone nearby was snoring, and another person muttered in his sleep.

"Margarita...Margarita..."

Whenever Mateo awoke at night, the rocking of the ship usually lulled him back to sleep, but now as he lay tormented by a high temperature, the movement of the crew on deck kept him awake. His feverish eyes made the stars appear brilliant, even if they were already exceptionally beautiful at sea. As a wave hit the prow of the Santa Maria, they created a succession of booms, resembling giant drums. Water swept across the fo'c'sle on the other end of the ship. Mateo sat up, with his head spinning, feeling extremely nauseous. He arose, staggered to the railing, hooked his arms around it, and braced himself to keep his balance. While his head swirled, the night breeze soothed his hot body, as it blew through his clothes.

A man walked up to an ampoletta close by, turned it upside down, rang the bells close to it, and sang a verse to announce to the crew that it was now the hour before midnight. As waves crashed against the ship, Mateo hugged the railing and stared into nothingness. While still standing, he dozed off. The boat gave a jolt. He opened his eyes, heard the bells ring once more and heard the ampoletta-turner sing that it was midnight. With sleep heavy in his eyes, Mateo still clung to the railing, too exhausted to return to his place on deck, too afraid that if he did, lying on the deck there would bring back a greater nausea. He dozed. Again, a jerk roused him. Half awake, he rubbed his eyes. Although the bells had not yet rung, he estimated that it must be close to two in the morning. Then he noticed that his fever was not as intense as it used to be.

As Mateo gazed absent-mindedly into the ebony depths, he saw a light far away flicker on for a second, and then, it blinked off. He disregarded it, for he thought that his fever was causing him to hallucinate. His eyelids grew heavy again and began to close, but before they were completely shut, the light in the distance came on again. Instantly, Mateo grew alert and squinted into the dark. The light remained on longer, this time. He could not tell how far away it was, but it was bobbing up and down — flickering and flickering — and then it disappeared.

The ampoletta-turner rang the bells twice. Then he sang his song. It was finally two o' clock in the morning.

Mateo leaned forward. When he saw the light again, he grew excited and forgot all about his fever. He turned and dashed toward the captain's cabin.

"Capitán Colón! I saw a light out there!"

When Mateo entered Colón's room, the captain was awake, bent over his desk beneath the oil lamp. Without a word, Colón followed Mateo outside, with his telescope in hand. At the railing of the ship, he peered through his glass in the direction where Mateo pointed.

"I was standin' here lookin' that way, *señor*."

"I see nothin', Mateo."

"But *señor*, there was a light."

The captain studied the darkness again, but saw nothing. Mateo also saw nothing. The light was gone. Slowly, Mateo turned to his place on the deck to finally attempt sleep while lying down, feeling somewhat ridiculous. He threw himself over his covers and turned on his back to watch the stars once more.

Then he heard Colón shouting.

"Señor Guitiérrez! Come quickly! I've somethin' to show ye!"

Mateo jumped up, ignoring his dizziness. He was soon next to the captain.

"Didn't I tell ye that I saw somethin', *señor*?"

But both Guitiérrez and the captain did not hear him, as they held their spyglasses up toward the darkness.

"See that light yonder?"

"I see nothin'."

The men continued staring through their telescopes, unaware that Mateo was close to them. Mateo waited and thought of how weeks before, a crab on weed grass and a simple squall of clouds had caused the crew to believe that they were approaching land, but none appeared. Resigned, Mateo tiptoed back to his sleeping quarters. He noticed that his fever had totally lifted, and the night had grown cool enough, so he could pull the covers over himself. Soon he was fast asleep.

Suddenly, there was an explosion. Mateo awoke. People were scurrying everywhere on board. Not one of the day crew remained asleep near him, and he saw that everyone was crowded along the railing. The smell of cannon smoke drifted from the Pinta, ahead of them.

"*Tierra! Tierra!*"

Mateo jumped up and squeezed into a space at the railing. The clouds had lifted, and in the moonlight, he could see a large, faint silhouette far away. And then he remembered something else Captain Colón had told him. He said that once they reached land, he would no longer be merely called Capitán Colón, but he would have earned a new title — Admiral Don Christóbal Capitán Colón, the Admiral of the Open Seas. And then, he would become governor of all the lands he discovered. Colón's family, too, would be given positions as leaders in these newly discovered places.

Mateo then turned to the person next to him and tapped him on his shoulder.

"*Perdone, señor*," he said. "Who won the 10,000 *maravediés*?"

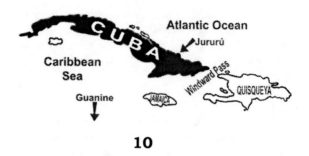

Atlantic Ocean

Jururú

Caribbean
Sea

Guanine

Windward Pass

QUISQUEYA

10

Jururú, Cuba

"Come see the men from heaven! Come see the men from heaven!"

The calls of a messenger awoke Basamanaco. As he glanced around the hut and saw Neef lying on a mat among his traders, he reflected upon the events of the previous day. After trading up the coast of Cuba, he and his men finally arrived at the town of Jururú, where villagers offered them huts for the night. After such a strenuous day, Neef was particularly glad to finally get some rest.

Neef had been begging to come to Cuba for years, and now that he was twelve years old, Basamanaco at last granted him permission to accompany him and his traders on a trading trip to this island, for Neef had grown strong and proficient with the canoe. And when they crossed the Windward Pass three days before, Basamanaco was pleased at how well Neef handled the gusts and demonstrated stamina, almost equal to that of a grown trader, despite his physical handicap.

As Basamanaco quietly watched the messenger through the open doorway of the hut, he saw him shift directions and head uphill toward another cluster of *bohíos*. Basamanaco turned on his side, closed his eyes, and pretended to sleep. Throughout this trading trip, people were telling odd stories about *zemíes* who had descended from the sky, just as Yocahu had appeared to the ancient fathers. But he was not certain whether or not to believe them. And now, this runner was adding to his doubts.

"Come see the men from heaven!"

With his ear pressed to the ground, Basamanaco heard the thumps the messenger created as he ran. He could tell that the messenger was now moving toward the entrance of Jururú and would soon run though its palisade gates to head toward the next town. As the messenger sped into the forest, his voice was crisp and clear, even if he was traveling farther away.

"Come see the men from heaveeeeeen...."

Basamanaco could tell that Neef was beginning to sit up from the way his crutches were scraping the ground. The traders around him also began to stir.

"Is that man telling us that the *zemíes* we've been hearing so much about, are actually here?" he heard Neef say to the others.

"Sounds like it, doesn't it? Let's go to the beach to see if the men from heaven might be there. People have been saying that they travel on water in giant birds."

Basamanaco kept his eyes closed, as he heard the traders in the hut begin to leave. He recognized the voices of his other traders outside, who had slept in neighboring *bohíos*. People from the village were also awake now, and their excited

78

chatter filtered through the doorway and walls of the hut. It appeared as if everyone was heading toward the beach. He heard Neef's crutches hitting the ground again as he rose to his feet, and then, he heard him walking to the doorway. But the thuds suddenly stopped.

"Basamanaco, wake up. Did you hear that messenger?"

Basamanaco lay extremely still, with his back facing Neef. He heard Neef coming toward him.

"Basamanaco..."

"Aye, I heard him making that ruckus. I still need to sleep some more."

"But you're always the first to investigate anything new. What's wrong?"

Basamanaco opened his eyes and turned toward Neef.

"I am somewhat skeptical of all of this."

"I don't understand."

"I don't think the people on Quisqueya have lived a perfect enough life for Yocahu to return to them."

"But we're not on Quisqueya."

"Well, the Cubans are even worse, so why should he come to them? It's not that I don't believe that Yocahu will ever come, it's just that I've heard many wild stories in my travels, and an incredible amount of them have never materialized."

"But Basamanaco, all during this trip, we've heard reliable people say that Yocahu has returned. You've heard the *bohutios* saying that Yocahu even brought his angels with him. Everyone says that they match their descriptions in the *areitas*, because their skins are as white as the breast of a shark. They even have hair growing from their faces, and they cover their bodies with robes. I've heard that many of them have hair as brown as coconuts, and a few even have hair as fair as the rays of the sun."

"Neef, you have no idea how people exaggerate in their rumors. I've heard many such tales in my travels, and they all died, as quickly as they were created. These stories will, too. You'll see."

"Please come to the beach with me, Basamanaco. Let's see for ourselves, whether those rumors are true."

Basamanaco rose reluctantly.

"Very well. I'll go to please you."

"I've heard that Yocahu and his sons are also giving out *turey*."

When Neef mentioned *turey*, he meant *gifts from heaven*.

"Hurry, Basamanaco," he said. "It looks like we're the last ones left in the village."

As Basamanaco stepped through the doorway after Neef, he snapped his fingers, as if he remembered something. He ran back into the hut. When he returned, he had his stone axe tucked into the waistband of his loincloth.

"The villagers didn't leave any *macabas* in this hut for us to use to club any attackers. I guess my stone axe will have to do."

As they headed toward the beach, Basamanaco muttered, "I must admit, that unlike the other times, the rumors this time have become stronger by the day. Just last night, someone told me that those *zemies* are taking people upon their giant birds to bring them back to heaven. He also said that the first island to report the appearance of Yocahu was Guanahaní."

Even before Neef and Basamanaco reached the shore, they saw the tops of strange objects towering above the trees. As they came to a clearing, they saw the giant birds that people had mentioned; they bobbed silently and proudly, reflecting off the morning sun, with their wings expanded high above the water. And coming toward shore with odd, long paddles, were funny, short, fat canoes that held human-like creatures with pale skins, whose bodies were covered with robes of various colors. Some of them even wore robes of shiny, gray material. And true to the words of the *areitas* that described Yocahu, they even had hair on their faces. Basamanaco saw Neef gawking at those creatures, and he couldn't help doing the same.

"In all my travels, I have never seen anyone with hair growing from their faces," Basamanaco said.

"Basamanaco, I can't believe how marvelous and grand those giant birds are. How did those *zemies* ever transport them to the water from heaven?"

But Basamanaco was too entranced to hear Neef. Yet even then, he kept a protective hand on his stone axe, until one of those beings on the strange canoes turned in his direction and smiled, which caused him to relax his hand.

"Hui, they are not acting at all like Caribs, or like any of the other unfriendly tribes I know," he said.

The fat boats hit the beach, and the strangers stepped out. Basamanaco noticed that one of them was carrying a long, stick-like object, wrapped in cloth of green, yellow, and other colors. The stranger took that stick and shoved it into the ground, until it stood by itself. Then he allowed its cloth to unfurl in the breeze. As the cloth flapped about, he knelt on the sand and spoke, with his eyes cast heavenward. When his voice carried across the sand, his words were incomprehensible.

"Do you understand what he is saying, Basamanaco?"

Basamanaco was concentrating so heavily on the new sounds the stranger was speaking, that he did not hear Neef again.

".....claim....land...name ye Juana...Sovereignsofspain."

Other foreigners had knelt on the ground during this ceremony, and they bowed their heads reverently, as they held their hats in their hands. The people of Jururú also knelt on the sand near them and bowed their heads, as they imitated the strangers.

When the ritual was over, the strangers turned to the people and grinned.

Neef whispered, "Look how friendly they are. They don't even have bows and arrows with them, either."

"I am not certain that they are like the Quisqueyans and carry no weapons, Neef. See those long, shiny, flat sticks? You know, those things that are hanging from their waists? Some of them keep their hands on them, like I often do with my stone axe, when I am in strange places. What do you think those sticks are?"

Basamanaco did not mention that he did not like the caution he saw in the strangers' eyes, and those people made him uncomfortable, despite their smiles.

"Look," Neef said as he pointed in the distance. "Who are they?"

Basamanaco stared in the direction of Neef's finger and saw people with darker skins standing apart from the light skinned foreigners. Some had features, similar to the inhabitants of the island of Guanahaní.

"I think those are the people, whom we heard were taken aboard the giant birds for Yocahu to take back to heaven," Basamanaco said. "Wait a moment. I think I recognize one of them."

Basamanaco stared at the person who looked familiar to him. He definitely had features as someone from Guanahaní. Basamanaco noticed that he had a peculiar expression on his face, as if he was in fear. And then, one of the foreigners came over and nudged that man. That man nodded, as if he knew what was expected of him; then he turned to the people of Jururú and projected his voice.

"Do not be afraid of these men. They are your friends. They are Yocahu and his angels, who have come from heaven. They came to my island of Guanahaní about half a *uinal* ago."

The man's voice was unsteady, and his dialect was hard to decipher.

The people of Jururú wept.

"Yocahu, you have come at last! We are your servants! We are ready for you to teach us."

Even Basamanaco's tough traders broke down and bawled as babies.

"You came just in time to save Quisqueya," one of them said.

Basamanaco studied the man from Guanahaní.

Why must he speak for those foreigners, he thought. *If they are Yocahu, shouldn't they already understand and speak all languages? Why does that man look so afraid? If these strangers are from heaven, he should be happy to be with them.*

Just then, Basamanaco remembered where he had seen that man.

It was many years back when I saw him, he thought. *I believe he used to be one of the students at the School of the Princes in the Mother Kingdom. But wasn't there something else about him?* Basamanaco picked his brain. *Wait. Wasn't that man also at Queen Anacoana's wedding? I think he was chosen to be one of the princes in her struggle.*

Basamanaco looked at Neef. Neef did not appear to recognize that man, but he was only a little boy at that time, and now that man had matured and was not as elegantly dressed, as when he was at the wedding.

What did the Speaker-of-the-House say his name was? Semola! That's it. He's Prince Semola from Guanahaní! Could he be King Semola, by now? If so, why would he want to leave his people to be with these strangers?

The people pushed closer to the strangers, while Basamanaco lagged behind, with Neef next to him. As Basamanaco and Neef edged forward, Basamanaco noticed a boy among the foreigners. He looked younger than Neef. His hair was as fair as blossoms on a *guayacan* tree, and his eyes were the color of the sea.

When Mateo looked back at the Indians pressing near him, their teary faces touched him. As he and the Christians traveled through these islands of Cipango, or the Japans, so many of the Indians appeared extremely happy to see them. Although some of them were warlike, most of them were friendly and had much love in their faces. And after many days of visiting various islands, just when he was wondering when they would finally reach the mainland of the Indies, they arrived at this land; and as they traveled along its coast, it was so immense, that Admiral Colón said that he thought that they had reached the mainland. He said that once he went on land, he would name this land Juana. It left Mateo confused, for Admiral Colón had told him that the mainland would be much richer than the other places they had discovered, but Mateo saw no riches here, and the people appeared to be just as poor as those on the other islands. Before they landed on Juana, Mateo could see from the ship that, like the other places, the people here also lived in grass shacks with no furniture, and their possessions were scanty. And they all went around with no clothes. And now that the Christians had reached the mainland, where were the marble palaces, magnificent bridges, or streets of gold that Admiral Colón kept talking about?

Admiral Colón had mentioned that when they reached the mainland, he would send out a search party to find the descendant of the Great Khan. But Mateo was beginning to wonder, *will there also be no Great Khan*?

Mateo turned to Colón.

"Admiral Colón, th' people here are still so very poor."

As Basamanaco concentrated upon what the strangers were saying, he found himself imitating that boy. He always repeated languages that were new to him, whenever he came to strange lands. And as he spoke, the rest of his traders, as well as the people of Jururú, copied what the boy was saying.

"...sssoooo....vurrry.....poooooh...."

When Basamanaco looked out into the water, he saw another short, fat canoe coming from one of the giant birds, with more men on it. It carried several other Guanahaníyanos and a group of pale skinned strangers. When that canoe landed, the man, whom the boy called Admiral Colón, waved to the newly arrived Guanahaníyanos to bring over a large, wooden box from their fat boat. He also instructed other Guanahaníyanos to carry over a large, cloth sack. When the box was placed upon the ground, the man called Admiral Colón unlatched its lock and lifted its lid. Basamanaco walked over to peer in it. The man called Admiral Colón reached in and took out some dried leaves, which Basamanaco could smell, even while he stood at a distance. Their odors were interesting, but unfamiliar.

"Spice!" the man called Admiral Colón said. "Where?"

As the people around Basamanaco imitated the man called Admiral Colón, this time, Basamanaco did not copy him. He watched. The man called Admiral Colón brought out other kinds of dried leaves.

"Where?"

Basamanaco began to understand. He wished that Lida were here, because maybe she might know where to find them. He had never seen those leaves before in all of his travels, not even among the goods that came from Guanine.

Admiral Colón looked exasperated. He turned to Semola.

"Ask these people where we can find these spices," he said. When Semola hesitated, Colón said, "What are ye waitin' for? Did my men not teach ye Spanish well enough?"

Semola finally spoke.

"Yocahu wants to know where he can find these kinds of leaves."

The people then pointed in different directions. One pointed south. Another east. One northeast. Then someone said, *Guanine.*

Basamanaco had never seen those leaves in any of the places the people pointed to, and he wondered what illnesses they cured. He knew that the people were only guessing, where they could be found. He watched as the man called Admiral Colón put the leaves away and start to bring out other objects from that box. Semola also asked where they could be found, but nobody knew anything about them, either. Admiral Colón also showed them items of stone that were shiny bowls and flat, round objects with curious, bright designs painted on them. He referred to them as *china.* He displayed shiny, smooth, colored, fine cloth that he said was *silk.* There were dark, carved objects of strange woods and many other goods that Basamanaco

82

had never seen before. Everyone stared at them in awe, but said nothing. So, like the dried leaves, Admiral Colón put them away, looking puzzled. He finally closed the lid.

The strangers nudged Semola again, and one of them pointed to the large sack that the Guanahaníyanos had carried from the fat boat. It was set on the ground next to the box. Semola nodded and spoke again.

"Yocahu has *turey* to give you."

The people clapped and laughed, while Basamanaco and Neef waited to see the gifts from heaven.

The Guanahaníyanos went over to the sack and dragged it toward the people. The people crowded around it. Basamanaco also inched forward. When he was close to the foreigners, he could smell their bodies. Their odors were different from any of the people he had met. In fact, they smelled as though they never bathed. Even their bone structure did not seem to be the same as his people's. Their noses were thin and high, their faces narrow; their arms and legs appeared to be unusually long; and as they spoke, they used their tongues in strange ways. Basamanaco wanted to touch their cheeks, to feel their arms, to clutch their bodies beneath their robes, so he could see if they felt the same, as his people did. He suppressed the compulsion to run his hand across their robes of various colors, like he always would, when he examined goods he bartered for. He yearned to feel the texture of the shiny, stiff, gray clothes some of them wore. He stepped forward and pretended to accidentally bump into a man with a shiny robe. It felt hard and smooth. The man stiffened and reached for his flat, thin stick, which hung from his waist, but stopped, as if to catch himself. When he relaxed and smiled at Basamanaco, Basamanaco saw wariness in his eyes.

Then Basamanaco saw the light-haired boy walk over to the large sack.

As Mateo pushed his way to the sack, he called to Admiral Colón.

"Please let me give th' Indians th' beads."

He liked these Indians on Juana, for they were kind and smiled often. In some of the places they explored, he and the Christians encountered Indians, who shot at them with arrows and spears, and in those places, the Admiral said that the Christians needed to be heavily armed at all times. But on most of the islands, the people wept and treated them as if they were gods. Sometimes they threw large feasts for them.

Mateo dug into the bag and took out a string of beads. Most of the beads consisted of bright colors, but some of them resembled strings of pearls.

Mateo handed a yellow necklace to a woman.

"Beads," he said.

Basamanaco watched as the woman took the beads and held them up for others to see.

"Look, everybody! Yocahu gave me *turey*!"

"Hui, give me *turey*, too," someone else said.

"And me."

Basamanaco laughed, when he saw the strangers handing out those objects.

"Neef, maybe these men are Yocahu, after all," he said.

"Haven't I been telling you, that they were? Look, Basamanaco, they're giving away some different kinds of gifts, now."

The Yocahu boy was giving out items that reflected images.

"Mirror," he said.

The people looked in the mirror and laughed, when they saw themselves.

The Yocahu boy gave out a silvery object.

"Scissors," he said.

Some of the other strangers gave out objects that they called *glass*, which appeared to be broken pieces of something to Basamanaco, but the people took them, anyway, because they were *turey*. And then someone brought out from the sack the most marvelous item of all. It made music.

"Hawk's bells," the stranger said.

"*Chunque, chunque* hawk's bells," the people said. "Please give us more hawk's bells."

Neef left Basamanaco's side and hobbled forward to receive a *turey* for himself. But Basamanaco continued to stay far away.

If Yocahu is giving away so many gifts to these people, maybe I could give them a gift of my very own, he thought.

He stared at the *tureys* the people were holding. All of them seemed so marvelous and magical. Quickly he turned and dashed toward his canoe. As he ran along the beach, he found himself singing one of his favorite *areitas*.

> One day soon, said fair Yocahu
> He will return to bring us more
> To teach us and to make us stronger
> Then our kingdom rules the world
>
> Soon our kingdom rules the world
> Soon our kingdom rules the world

When Basamanaco reached his canoe, he surveyed his wares. He saw a stack of neatly folded hammocks from the Mother Kingdom, a pile of pottery pots of various shapes from the Kingdom of the Great Old Lady, herbs from the Fertile Valley which cured infections and expelled worms from people's bodies, and tobacco leaves from the Kingdom of Marién. He grabbed a hammock and headed back to the people, but then, he remembered the Yocahu boy and returned to his canoe. As he rummaged beneath his goods, he found a rubber ball from the Kingdom of The Great Old Lady at the bottom of his pile.

Basamanaco approached the crowd on the beach and saw that they were still surrounding the sack. The Yocahu boy was still handing out beads to the people, and one of the other strangers presented a necklace to the village *bohutio*. The *bohutio* grasped the gift and wept. While all of this was happening, Basamanaco saw one of his traders approaching another stranger, who had removed his thin, long stick from its container and was holding it in his hand. As his stick glistened in the sun, his trader was so fascinated by it, that he reached out and touched it. Suddenly he screamed and abruptly withdrew his hand, while blood gushed from his hand and poured down to his elbows.

The owner of the shiny stick turned and saw what had happened.

"No!" he yelled. "Don't touch! Sword!"

When the people saw how easily the sword had cut Basamanaco's trader, they backed away in fear. They had never seen magic like this before.

Basamanaco soon arrived with his cotton hammock. He was awestruck at what the sword had done to his trader. He quickly decided that instead of giving this

84

hammock away as a gift, he was going to trade it for a sword. He perceived that it, alone, had a force and strength greater than all the gifts that the people around him were receiving. He approached the stranger, who held the sword, and pointed to it. Then he held out the hammock.

"Trade," he said.

The stranger's eyes turned hard, and he immediately placed a protective hand over his sword. He shook his head.

"No!"

Since the stranger did not appear to understand, Basamanaco again pointed to the sword. But the stranger called to one of his friends, and when his friend came over, he was holding several gifts from the sack and handed Basamanaco a necklace, a pair of scissors, and two hawks' bells. But Basamanaco shook his head and pushed the objects away.

"It is not a good bargain," he said. "You cannot give me items of so little value for a hammock."

The strangers still did not appear to understand what he wanted, so Basamanaco pointed again at the sword. But the man rattled the goods in front of him, with his face turning red, and his light colored eyes growing cold and hard.

"Take them, ye *majadero!*"

The man dumped the objects in front of Basamanaco and snatched the hammock away. Basamanaco felt a chill in the air around him. If he were dealing with the people of *Guanine,* or anyone else, and especially the people of the kingdoms of Quisqueya, he would be driving hard bargains and would even attempt to squeeze from them as many goods as he could for that hammock. But still in his mind, was the power of that sword and how quickly it drew blood from his trader. It had happened swifter than a blink of an eye. And with meekness, Basamanaco swallowed his disappointment, picked up the items at his feet, and walked away.

As Basamanaco left the crowd, he again remembered the Yocahu boy. By now, that boy was no longer giving out gifts and was standing in front of the trader, who was bleeding. The boy was pressing a piece of cloth against the trader's hand, to stop the blood. Basamanaco approached the boy and held out the rubber ball that was made in the Kingdom of the Great Old Lady. As the Yocahu boy looked up from what he was doing, his clothes were now smeared with blood. He smiled.

"*Gracias, señor.*"

With a free hand, he took the gift.

Basamanaco then motioned for the boy to follow him, and when the man's bleeding had stopped, the boy came. When they both were a good distance away from the people, Basamanaco showed the boy how to hit the ball with his hips, shoulders, and chest, while never using his arms and hands. The boy attempted to hit the ball in this manner, but he often forgot what he was supposed to do and used his hands. The boy laughed and Basamanaco with him. And as they laughed together, Basamanaco saw no hardness in the boy's eyes, as he had observed in the strange men. After awhile, Basamanaco turned away to walk alone on the beach, and the boy went back to the strangers.

As Basamanaco walked along the shore, he saw a son of a *cacique,* staggering in his direction. Basamanaco recognized him to be one of several young men, who were sitting around a fire drinking *chicha* the night before. They were singing so loudly that mothers had dragged their children into their *bohíos* and did not allow them out again. This young man must have slept through the cries of the messenger this morning, and now, he appeared as if he was suffering from a hangover. He looked down the beach and frowned at the people holding their gifts, as if he was trying to comprehend what was happening.

"Uhhh, my aching head," he groaned.

As he shook his head to clear it, he also rattled his gold ring on his nose.

Basamanaco saw that the strangers at the sack had noticed this prince, for they began pointing at him and started whispering among themselves. The strangers stopped their activities, and together, they walked toward the son of the *cacique*. As they neared, the prince stared at them in a daze, and then as if something registered in his brain, he fell to the ground, weeping. While still sobbing, he arose and extended his arms.

"Yocahu, you have come at last. You are most welcome to my father's house. Just ask for whatever you want, and Father will give it to you. Let me run and tell him to prepare a feast for all of you tonight."

The prince did not realize that his father was already on the beach, with the rest of the villagers. And Basamanaco discerned that the strangers did not understand a word the prince had said. Instead, they reached out and gently touched the prince's nose ring.

"Where?"

The people began to gather around the prince and the strangers. And Basamanaco shoved through the crowd to have a better look. There was something odd in the strangers' faces and eyes. They shook the nose ring again.

"GOLD...where?"

Basamanaco understood what they wanted. Those men were asking for *guanine*.

The people around the prince imitated their sounds.

"GOAAD...whea?"

One of the foreigners called for Semola.

"Ask him where we can get gold."

Semola feigned ignorance and said, "These men are your friends. They say they are from heaven."

But someone from the crowd knew better.

"Nay, the foreigners want *guanine*."

"We don't have much *guanine* on Cuba." another said.

"*Hui*, but there is much *guanine* on Quisqueya. Quisqueya is the island next to ours, and it is very rich. We trade our goods for *guanine* that comes from there."

"There is also even more on the mainland of *Guanine*. It's to the west. You'll find much, much more there, than on Quisqueya. You must first cross the waters..."

"But Quisqueya is closer. It lies in that direction. It has five great kingdoms, which are ruled by the most powerful *caciques*."

As the people spoke, Semola remained silent.

Then someone called out, "*Hui*, Basamanaco, you must lead them on your canoe and show them where they can find Quisqueya."

"That is right. Basamanaco knows. Quisqueya is his home. It's his *bohio*."

"Basamanaco, take them to your *bohio*."

This time, it was the foreigners who repeated words, as they tried to figure out their meanings.

"Bohío? Guanine? Quisqueya?"

Basamanaco noticed that Semola's lips were trembling, and his eyes were now filled with tears. Then, he lost control of himself and began to weep.

"Nay. You must not take us to Quisqueya — especially not as captives. There's a rule there that any prisoner who arrives on that island will be made into a *Naborian* servant. If you take us to that island, we will never regain our freedom, and we shall never see our homeland again. Bring us back to Guanahaní. Please, please bring us to our *bohío.*"

As Semola babbled in his tongue, the strangers were baffled by his behavior. But as he sobbed, Basamanaco knew for certain now that he was a prisoner of the foreigners and was no longer a prince or king. He then saw a tattoo upon Semola's arm that indicated that he was now married, so somewhere back on his island, he had a wife, and possibly children. Yet he, Basamanaco, was unable to help him, or even speak to him, for he knew that these strangers would prevent it, and they had come with more power than he had ever seen. And he wondered, too, whether Semola was afraid that he would be disgraced, if Anacoana saw him in his fallen state, if he were brought to Quisqueya, for he recalled now how he used to hear that Semola had asked for her hand many times.

As the strangers pointed into the direction of Quisqueya, repeating the word *bohío*, Basamanaco perceived that they were confused. But at least they understood that it was a place where *guanine* was found.

And still fresh in Basamanaco's mind, was the strange look in the foreigner's eyes when they inquired about *guanine*. It haunted him. He then waved to his traders.

"My men, come with me! We have business to finish."

His traders cast questionable glances at him, for they wished to remain. But they silently followed Basamanaco, anyway, for they sensed that he had something important to tell them, when they were far away.

Other people from the surrounding villages began to appear. By now, they had heard the news from the messenger, and they were bringing gifts. Some of them even had objects made of *guanine* with them. When the foreigners saw these people coming, they ran to their cloth sack to hand out more beads, broken pieces of glass, scraps of metal, fish hooks, and hawk's bells.

As Basamanaco began to lead his men away, he felt a tap on his shoulder. When he turned around, he saw the fair-haired boy standing behind him. He held out a strange, small animal that was carved out of wood.

"Horse," the boy said.

Basamanaco took the wooden animal and ran his fingers over it. The workmanship of this figure was fine and detailed. It must have been carved with an extremely sharp instrument. The boy had made a fair trade, equal to the cost of the ball, even though Basamanaco had not expected anything in return. Basamanaco looked up to thank the Yocahu boy, but he was gone.

"Basamanaco, why don't you want to show Yocahu our island?" one of the traders said.

Basamanaco looked straight at his men.

"What makes you think they are Yocahu? Those strangers give me no indication that they know anything about our land. How could Yocahu ever forget where he once visited the forefathers? Those people are more like men than *zemies*, to me."

"But..."

"They shall find their way to Quisqueya, soon enough. Come, men. We have work to do."

"How can you say..."

"And besides, if they are Yocahu, why would they want *guanine* so badly? Wouldn't they be able to make it themselves? Anyone knows that *guanine* is the excrement of the *zemies*. Why should they want their own poop?"

Soon Basamanaco, Neef, and the traders had packed their belongings to leave. As they pushed their canoe into the water, Basamanaco saw the wives of the *cacique* walking in the direction of the river to bathe themselves. He knew that they were preparing to make themselves attractive, because their husband, the king, would soon offer them to the strangers to make them feel welcome.

"My men, we must return to Quisqueya, before the strangers have a chance to get there," he said.

11

The Windward Pass
On Basamanaco's canoe

"Basamanaco, why must we go back to Quisqueya right now? We hardly saw Cuba."

"Neef, I promise that as soon as I can, I will take you back there again."

"But I've waited for this trip for years, and now, you're cutting it short."

"I told you, it is urgent that we reach Quisqueya, before those strangers do."

"You mean, before Yocahu does?"

"I'm not sure if they're Yocahu, Neef. Once those foreigners reach our island, my men and I may need to help our people. We have much experience in fighting off the Caribs, and our people don't even know how to protect themselves."

"Do you actually believe those strangers would try to harm us? Suppose they are Yocahu, after all? Then you'll be protecting our people from *zemies*."

"Neef, you've been good friends with King Guacanagarí lately, haven't you?"

"He keeps inviting me back to his palace. I don't know why. He says that he likes to talk to me about some of the problems he has in running his country, because he thinks I give good suggestions, for someone my age. But many of the ideas I give him are not even mine, but they're yours, for they are things that you've told me about, especially concerning your travels. He is always surprised at how much I know."

"Ah, Neef. It's also because you learn extremely fast, with whatever I teach you. And you remember everything I say. You didn't tell him that Guarionex is your father, did you?"

"He still thinks that I once was a homeless cripple, and you had found me in your travels. I've told him that I've gained my knowledge from wandering from place to place and listening to people."

"Good. We can't have news reaching the Fertile Kingdom that you are here."

"I'm always careful, Basamanaco."

"When we get back to the Kingdom of Marién, I want you to go immediately to King Guacanagarí to tell him that we have seen Yocahu on Cuba, and he is now coming to our island. But don't let the king know about any of my doubts. Let him decide for himself when he sees those strangers, whether or not, they are gods. And in the meantime, I will have my men stand guard over our people. We must be prepared to protect them, if they need it."

"Why are you so afraid, Basamanaco?"

"Listen, Neef. I think that these men came with weapons that have more power, than anything you and I can ever imagine."

"Weapons? I didn't see any."

"What do you think their swords are for? To cut down coconut trees? And those men have an unusual interest in obtaining riches, especially *guanine.*"

"But they are so friendly, generous, and kind."

"Have you noticed those large, black, funny looking tubes sticking through the sides of their giant birds? I think they are some kind of weapon that are even stronger than their swords. I've been watching those people very carefully."

"I've been watching them, too, and I saw nothing wrong with them."

"I've noticed that they look at us, as if we are wimps, who are greatly inferior to them in intelligence, strength, and fighting power."

"And the Yocahu boy, to whom you gave the rubber ball, Basamanaco? What do you think of him?"

"He is the only one of those foreigners, whom I trust. From the look in his eyes, I can tell that he has a pure heart."

Neef paddled in silence for a long while. Finally, he spoke again.

"So…you said the first thing that you want me to do, when we get back home, is to go to King Guacanagarí to warn him?"

"Don't sound like you're warning him. It will scare everybody. Tell him that we came back early, because we have some good news. Tell him that we saw Yocahu on Cuba, and they are heading toward Quisqueya. Say nothing more. Let the king decide what to do and who those strangers are, when he meets them. He'll make a good judgment, soon enough."

"How about Canaobo the Fierce? Should we send a messenger to tell him about those men?"

"I want to keep him out of this, for awhile. He is too suspicious and resorts to violence, too quickly. With his temper, it may cause disaster, because I don't think he is any match to the strangers."

"What do you mean? Nobody is a better warrior than Canaobo the Fierce."

"Neef, I am telling you, these men came with power."

"And my father? Should we send messengers to warn him?"

"Not yet. He has too many struggles of his own in his kingdom to worry about."

"Basamanaco?"

"Do you understand my instructions, Neef?"

"Aye, but Basamanaco, does this mean that you might need to fight these men, if they prove to not be Yocahu?"

"We will try to avoid it, for we are no match to them, so my men and I may need to guide the people into hiding."

"Well, you see…if we learn that they are not Yocahu, I can also help you fight them."

"Ah, nay, you couldn't…"

"Really, I can, Basamanaco. Two years back when I was taking my solo trip, I accidentally killed a man."

Neef proceeded to tell Basamanaco what had happened with him and Jama.

"My uncle had sent him on a search of the island for me, but I killed him accidentally. I didn't mean to."

"It's just as well that he is dead. Otherwise, once your uncle finds out about your whereabouts, his men would be here, in no time. And there is no telling how many of his other men are out looking for you."

"If I killed a man when I was ten years old, I can also kill more of them, now that I am twelve."

"Nay, Neef, it is all right for my men and me to engage in fighting, to protect ourselves and our people when we are attacked, but it is not right for you to do it."

"Why not? You and your traders fight off dangers, all the time."

"But my men are foreigners, who have decided to live on Quisqueya, because at one time, they fell in love with this island for its richness and high standard of living. When my men grew up in their native lands, they were taught to fight, since the day they were born. And you already know about me, that my ancestors were giants, who were a warlike people. But you, Neef, you are, not at all, like us. You are a *Taino*. You are not any Taino, but a Taino of Quisqueya, who belongs to the *People of Peace*. And most important, you are a son of the highest king of Quisqueya, who must serve as an example to your people and show them how a true Quisqueyan Taino must be. You must never forget that."

"Basamanaco, that's just what Grandfather used to say. But it doesn't matter whether I am a prince, anymore. I no longer live in a palace, and nobody knows who I am."

"But you know who you are, Neef."

Neef withdrew into silence again.

Finally he said, "So, you don't want me to be untrue to the life of a Quisqueyan, the way my uncle, Eldest-Son-of-My-Father's-First Wife, behaves?"

"Aye, Neef. A true prince never is."

"But if those strangers are Yocahu, does that mean that I will be going back home to the Fertile Kingdom soon? Does that mean that peace will soon spread throughout Quisqueya?"

When Basamanaco said nothing, Neef thought he saw sadness in his eyes.

"Basamanaco, you really want me to continue living with you, don't you?"

"You are the son Lida and I have always wanted."

Neef placed his arm around Basamanaco's shoulders.

"You are right, Basamanaco. With all the turmoil in my kingdom, I don't see how we, as a people, can be ready to receive Yocahu."

"Aye, Neef."

"Basamanaco, would you prefer that I remained living with you, more than to have Yocahu return to us?"

"Aye, Neef."

Once Basamanaco was understood, Neef saw the sadness leave his eyes.

And as they paddled with the rest of the traders across the Windward Pass, Neef realized that *the love* was particularly strong with Basamanaco, despite his heritage.

12

It was fifty-four days, since the first landfall occurred on the island of San Salvador, and thirty-eight, from the time the Christians arrived on Juana — or Cuba, as Colón heard the Indians call it. Because of Juana's immensity, Colón was certain he reached the mainland of the Indies, and he even sent a search party to find the Great Khan, or at least, his descendant. But his men returned without finding that emperor. So before they left Juana to discover more places, he and his men signed a declaration for the world to see that they had reached the Asian continent.

And now on 6 December 1492, only two ships sailed across the Windward Pass in search for the island the natives called *Bohío*. As the trade winds hit them from all directions and pushed them onward, Colón had no idea where the Pinta was. When her owner, the scoundrel, Martín Alonso Pinzón, deserted the fleet, he was driven by rumors the Indians on his ship were spreading, about an island called *Babeque* nearby, where quantities of gold could be found. And now without the Pinta, as the Santa Maria and the Niña traveled together with the hour of vespers drawing near, an immense silhouette appeared in the distance.

A sailor waved from the mainmast.

"*Señor!* I see *Bohío* up ahead!"

Since night was falling fast, Colón called to the captain of the ship ahead.

"Vincente, sail as quickly as you can to that island, 'n when daylight comes, find us a harbor!"

Vincente's caravel, the Niña, was smaller and swifter than the Santa Maria, so it pushed easily away, with her sails billowing to full capacity. Colón gazed after her, with emptiness gnawing within him, for since the disappearance of the Pinta 15 days before, he felt as if part of him had become dismembered. Throughout this trip, Pinzón was often insubordinate, believing his judgment to be superior. Colón suspected that he even planned to steal back to Spain with as much gold and riches from the Indies as he could, to obtain the glory of discovering a new route for himself.

Everywhere Colón traveled, he asked Indians whether they had seen the Pinta. Occasionally, he heard stories of someone sighting her, but she never appeared. Yet he had to carry on, to be as thorough with his discovery as possible. He had to keep his head high and remember his devotion to his duties to his God, to whom he had promised to make this journey, and to her majesty Queen Isabella of Spain, who had confidence in him and knew that God was inspiring him.

It didn't help matters, when the natives he captured and locked below gave them problems. Sometimes he wished that he had chains with him, because he did not always feel that he could trust them, but when he looked into their faces and saw such intelligence and humility, he couldn't help feeling a great love for them and was glad that he brought no shackles. Their faces told him that they were creations of God and possessed the mental capacities of learning many subjects, particularly the idea that in the beginning, God created the heaven and earth. Yet these Indians told such odd tales, which he could never believe. For instance, they kept talking about people called the Caribs, whom they said would like to eat everyone on these ships. And when these Indians realized that they were coming closer to *Bohío*, they wailed as babies and pled for us to not go on, that we must skip that island. With gestures, they demonstrated strange stories of how its inhabitants ate people, by first slashing their throats, then drinking their blood, and finally, cutting their bodies into pieces. And they gestured that everyone on board would be killed. What odd tales! At this point, he, Colón, did not believe anything they tried to communicate. Ever since he took them on board his ship and promised that he would bring them to Spain, they had tried numerous tricks to get him to return them to their islands, particularly that tall interpreter from the island of San Salvador. Sometimes when they neared land, a few of them even dove over the railing and escaped.

These Indians were so meek at first, when they stood in front of him and his men, as naked as their mothers bore them, pointing upward, as if they were asking if he and his men came from heaven. They even kissed their feet many times and acted as if they were worshipping them. But not long after they were taken aboard the ships, they appeared to lose faith in him and his men, and they began their antics and silly stories, with their constant pleadings to bring them home. He never was sure exactly what they were trying to say, nor were *they* sure of what he said to *them*. And it distressed him that his linguist, Luis de Torres, who was extremely well trained in the Hebrew, Greek and Chaldean tongues, could never see any correlation in their language to anything he studied. Perhaps Torres and these Indians would finally come to understand each other soon.

The islands of Cipango were so disappointingly poor. And Juana, even if it were the mainland, has no riches worth mentioning. Perhaps he, as well as the rest of Europe, had misunderstood the writings of Marco Polo, for here in Cipango, he saw nobody diving for pearls, although he saw shell heaps, which were indications that natives could have been searching for pearls. And although he never found the Great Khan, when he eventually returns to Juana, he is quite certain that he would find Cathay and other wealthy countries with marble palaces and streets of gold.

As the gales whipped around Colón while he stood upon the stern castle, he cast his eyes across the deck and saw his crew bent against the gusts that forced them to move sideways, as they carried out their chores. A sailor soon edged toward the ampoletta, flipped it, and rang the bell six times to let everyone know that it was the hour of vespers, while he sang the usual song for this time of day that told of Christ being born of Saint Mary and baptized of Saint John.

Since this hour meant that it was time for the crew to exchange places, Colón watched as the night company moved in, while Pedro Gutiérrez approached to replace him. Colón nodded at Gutiérrez and turned toward his cabin beneath the stern castle, with slumber heavy on his eyes. Yet he could see that once he retired to his quarters, he would not sleep, but instead, he would take his quill and enter notes into his journal, as he pondered over the events of the day. Then the night would pass so quickly that soon, it would be time for his watch again.

When Colón finally sat at his desk with quill in hand, as he bent over his journal, his head drooped, and soon, his eyes closed. Within seconds, he found himself within a long forgotten scene. He was back in Genoa, standing at a quay and watching ships coming in and leaving for the sea. Even if he was then a small boy, already he knew that he was a person of destiny, that he and the ocean were partners. He knew that somewhere before, in a place that he could not recall, he made promises with God to cross the Western Ocean and bring Christianity to the heathen nations. In addition, he knew that it was his responsibility to disperse a vast ignorance of the ocean that prevailed over Europe.

And then his mind began focusing upon another scene. He saw another boy, his own son, Diego, who was twelve years old, the same age as the younger cabin boy, Mateo. Diego was standing next to the friar Juan Perez, his friend who consented to care for him during this trip. Through a pair of metal gates, Diego looked as though he was swallowing back tears.

Colón knew that Diego would be in good hands, here at La Rábida in Palos, Spain; yet his son didn't understand that he, his father, was driven by God to find a new route to the Indies. But his friend Juan always knew it, and he accompanied Colón many times to the palace to appeal to Her Majesty Isabella, to convince her of the divine nature of this journey.

"Do ye think that Papa will ever return?" Diego said.

"*Naturalmente, mi hijo.* Ye must have faith. God is with him, ye know."

It was here, at La Rábida, where Colón met Mateo. He was another boy whom Juan Perez cared for, because of family circumstances. From the beginning, Mateo followed Colón constantly with questions about the sea, and Colón recognized his yearning for adventure, which had also driven him when he was young. So after Spain defeated the Moors and began expelling them and the Jews from the land to strengthen the stand of Christianity, Queen Isabella turned her interests to new matters; and finally, she agreed to Colón's journey.

It was then that Colón approached Mateo, to ask him to be a cabin boy. Of course, he would never risk the life of his own son on such a trip, but he believed that he would be doing this orphan boy a favor by taking him along.

As Colón shifted his thoughts back to Diego, he saw his son staring back at him through the gates again. His eyes were exactly like his mother's, Doña Felipe e Moniz, who had passed away only months after he was born. She was such a highly refined, well-bred Portuguese woman, and he ached for her touch and voice again.

And then, his thoughts wandered to his younger son, Fernando, the result of his loneliness. When he plunged into despair over the death of his wife, wondering why God failed him and took his greatest treasure away, he met Beatriz de Arana, a warm peasant girl, who reminded him of her. Her caresses wiled away his misery, and she gave to him the love he yearned for. But when the day arrived when he heard the cries of his bastard son, Fernando, he felt as though lightning struck him. Those lusty cries of this newborn made him realize that he had allowed his human desires and insecurities to cause him to turn inward and grow far from God. They reminded him that he had a unique purpose to fill, god-given promises to meet. And while alone in a room one day, he fell to his knees and wept, for he finally understood that all along, his God never abandoned him, but he had abandoned his God. He realized that Doña Felipa was only taken away for a short while, because God had other plans for him. Colón then resolved to regain what he lost, to again remember the determination he once bore as a boy, to cross the unexplored ocean. Repentant and suffering from the depths of hell, he resolved to make amends with his Creator.

"Wake up, *señor*, it's time for yer dinner."

Colón opened his eyes and saw Mateo standing in front of him. For a moment, he mistook him for his own son Diego and reached out to him, but then caught himself.

"Ye must've had a bad dream, *señor*. Ye were moanin' in yer sleep."

As Mateo placed a tray of food on a small table, the odor of freshly cooked fish filled the room. Ever since they hit the first landfall, they were having meals of fresh food again. In the dimness, Colón saw that Mateo had also brought a bowl filled with guavas and pieces of pineapple. Just looking at it, caused him to salivate.

"*Gracias, mi hijo.*"

As Colón reached for the fish, he turned to Mateo.

"Ye must have learned a lot about th' sea by now, *mi hijo.*"

Mateo's face grew red, and he hung his head.

"*Señor*, ye have said many times, that ye always loved th' sea. But I've decided that once I return to Castile, I shall never sail again."

Colón laughed and placed an arm around Mateo.

"God created us all differently, *mi hijo.* He gave me a special destiny, but He also gave ye a mission of bein' kind to everyone, with that good heart of yers."

"Me, *señor*?"

"*Sí.* Never seen anyone with a kinder one."

When the ships finally arrived at *Bohío*, Colón claimed that island for Spain and named it *La Isla Española.* He calculated that it was twenty degrees north of the equator, and at this time of the year, daylight was 20 ampollettas or ten hours long. And as he traveled along the northern coast of *Española*, he saw that the water was clear, deep, and relatively free from shoals and rocks, and no shallower than seven fathoms deep.

It did not take Colón long to realize that he and the Christians had entered into a land that was superior to anywhere they had ever been before, for everywhere they traveled, the beauty of this island struck them with awe. They beheld mountains of limestone that rose so abruptly, that they were far more impressive than the Confederation of the Swiss. Hundreds of rivers flowed through lush, fertile hills and valleys. Trees, prolifically bearing fruit, hovered in groves. He and the Christians beheld mastics, aloes, pines, and exquisite blossoms that emitted exotic perfumes they never knew existed. Birds of a thousand songs darted through the wilds. Never before, had he and his men come so close to Eden.

For a few days, Colón and the Christians enjoyed good weather, just as they had throughout the trip, but then rain poured and winds whipped the ships, and it became as winter in Castile. But that weather, too, passed, and when warm breezes blew again, it was as though spring had returned.

Then it became time for Colón to send Christians inland to explore once more. His men returned quickly, with stories of the shyness of the Indians, of how they constantly ran away. They said that before they ever reached the villages, the Indians set fires to torches upon towers, to warn other villages that they must flee. So by the time the Christians reached each community, they found them empty, with sometimes over a thousand huts evacuated, which meant that at least 3,000 people had fled. They found curious baskets containing human bones that hung from the beams of the larger huts. Shrines of stone stood within each home. And sometimes, small dogs that could not bark, cowered from them.

Occasionally the Christians caught a glimpse of the Indians of *Española* while they ran away, and they saw that they were an extremely beautiful people. Their skins were considerably fairer than those of the other Indians in the other lands. Some of them were even as white as the women in Spain.

"They are a timid people, who bear no arms, *señor*," a Christian reported to Colón. "'N they appear to be extremely peaceful."

"They are just as naked as th' Indians in th' other lands," another said.

"Their temperaments are so mild that they'd make good servants, *señor* — perfect subjects for her majesty. It'll be easy to clothe 'n teach them Christian customs."

"*Sí*, 'n three of us could kill a thousand of them, without any resistance."

Colón listened to these accounts, greatly pleased. It meant that these people could easily be converted to the true religion.

"If we show these Indians nothin' but kindness 'n shower them with many gifts, word will circulate quickly that we Christians come as friends," he said. "In fact, this news about us will spread as rapidly as th' signal fires upon their towers that warn them to flee."

The next day, Colón also wished to see the villages of this island. So he took his ship and entered the mouth of a river, which he named *Guadaiquivir*, after a river in Spain. Since he could not travel against the currents, he tossed a rope to land, so his men could pull the Santa Maria upstream. As he thus traveled, he observed glorious sights that took his breath away, of mountains, valleys, villages, and houses. Everywhere, he saw that the land was well cultivated and populated. But as soon as the people saw his ship approaching, they set their signal towers afire and fled in silence. Their flight puzzled Colón.

He turned to Pedro Gutiérrez, who stood next to him.

"See how those people are so afraid of us? Don't ye think it's because they are constantly hunted down by aggressors?"

"Or maybe, no one ever comes to their island, *señor*, 'n they are not used to strangers."

Colón thought upon what Gutiérrez just said for a moment.

"No, I think they are always hunted."

At midnight, Colón instructed the Christians to turn back downstream toward the bay, and as they traveled with their sails catching a breeze, he realized that the emptiness that plagued him since the disappearance of the Pinta was no longer with him, and now, a fascination for this island filled that void.

When they reached the bay at dawn, high winds hit the ships and tossed them to and fro. They soon came across an Indian man in a small canoe, battling the gusts. Colón was pleased when his Christians remembered his advice, for they volunteered to rescue that man, and as soon as they took him on board, they loaded him with gifts and brought him to shore. After that event, the two ships continued eastward, along the coast, in the same direction that they had been traveling, before their trip inland.

Not long afterwards, though, they saw a crowd of about five hundred people lining the beach. Unlike their other experiences on *Española*, these people were welcoming them, as they waved their arms and cheered. This was the closest the Admiral and his Christians had ever been to the people of this island.

"Ah ha!" said Colón. "See what I've been tellin' ye'? The Indian we rescued this mornin', must have spread th' good word about us."

As Colón leaned against the railing among the other Christians, he studied the Indian faces. Consistent with the reports of his men, they indeed possessed fair skins and were an extremely handsome people, even if some of them had their bodies and faces covered with tattoos. Their mature women wore simple dresses, while the younger ones wore nothing more than a loincloth over their hips, or sometimes, nothing at all. With joy, they shouted welcomes. Some of them even sat on the beach. And as in previous places, many pointed heavenward. Colón felt his eyes go blurry, as a love for these gentle folk overflowed from his heart. At last, their kindnesses were paying off, and these Indians were no longer afraid of them.

He could see that the people on this island were far from anything the Indians on board described them to be. How could such gentle, warm folk possibly drink the blood of human beings or cut them into pieces to eat? Why, they all had the purity of children emanating from their faces. Some of them even dove into the water to greet them; and with the agility of fish, they glided freely, laughing as they surrounded the ship. None of the Indians elsewhere ever gave them a friendlier reception.

Colón called to Luis de Torres, his linguist, who was hanging over the railing a few feet from him.

"Find out what kind of Indians they are. Ye know, what do they call themselves?"

Torres gestured and called madly, and the Indians responded with smiles.

"*Tayno. Tayno.*"

Torres called back to Colón.

"I think they said that they are th' Tainos."

When Colón later entered his cabin, he found that Mateo had already delivered his morning meal, and the food had since turned cold. Gratefully, he sat to eat, pondering over what he should record in his journal this morning. Just as he took a sip of wine, he heard voices outside his cabin. Then, a loud knock resounded upon his door. Without waiting for an invitation, a sailor entered. His were eyes round with excitement.

"*Señor*, a king from this island wishes to see ye. He brought his men from his court with him."

The sailor had an Indian to act as an interpreter with him, whom he had retrieved from below. Colón noted that this Indian was one who most actively acted out the bizarre stories about the people on this island wanting to eat everyone.

Soon after Colón arose, the Indian king entered. He looked no older than twenty-one years, and he wore a crown studded with green gems. Tattoos covered his face and body, and gold bracelets encircled his forearms. Rings of gold dangled from his nose and ears, and a girdle with tiny, golden tiles hung over his loincloth. Other men in his court entered after him, and they were dressed almost as elegantly as he was, but instead of crowns of gold, they wore gorgeous hats made of feathers of many colors. And within this crowd of dignitaries, a boy was also present. He was clothed only in a simple loincloth, and he walked with the aid of crutches.

When the king and his party were completely in the cabin, he presented to Colón a girdle, much like the one he, himself, was wearing, upon which was mounted a mask, lined with intricate tiles of gold that looked as if they were each tediously pounded flat. He also handed Colón objects of polished green stones, cloths with patterns of tiny beads sewn into them, and woven baskets with amazing designs.

The king bowed, then pointed to himself.

"Guacanagarí. *Cacique* Guacanagarí."

Then he pointed eastward, and gestured as if he were eating.

"Guarica."

Colón turned to the interpreter.

"Says name is Guacanagarí," the interpreter said. "Wants you...come eat tonight...at his town...Guarica. Is east of here."

"Ye say yer town is Guarica?" Colón said.

The king nodded, as if he comprehended.

"Guarica," he repeated.

The king extended his arms outward.

"Kingdom of Marién," he said.

Colón did not understand what Guacanagarí was trying to tell him. And then the king pointed heavenward, and his eyes turned misty.

"Yocahu, Yocahu."

The king began to weep, and he stepped forward and embraced Colón. When the king gained control of himself, he looked around the cabin, examining its walls, the beams in its ceiling, Colón 's chair, his table, and his library crammed on the shelves.

"Please, please, stay 'n share my breakfast with me," Colón said.

He offered his food to the king. The king eyed a biscuit curiously and handed it to his men, who divided it into morsels and shared it among themselves. And then the king walked over to the banner of Castile that was propped, rolled up, in a corner, which Colón used whenever he claimed lands for Spain. Colón walked over to him and unrolled the banner to show him its greens, yellows and whites. Guacanagarí ran his hand over its surface. His eyes misted again.

"Turey."

"This is an emblem of th' king 'n queen of Spain."

"Turey."

There was a quiver in the king's voice.

"Yes, ye're right. We have a marvelous kingdom back in Spain."

The king bowed, and then turned to leave. Then he turned back to Colón.

"*Tayno*," he said. "*Tayno, tayno.*"

And as the royal procession left the cabin and Colón watched after them, he was unaware that down below in his ship, among its cargo, other Indians, whom he had collected from various islands, wept, *Bohío, bohío, bohío. We want to go home to our bohío.*

13

It was not just the beauty of *Española* that caused the Admiral and his men to fall desperately in love with her, but this island was filled with a richness, from which they could not pull away. Its servants, common folk, and aristocracy all spoke in such soft tones, expressing manners of gentleness, love, and kindness. And although the Christians could not find the spices they wanted here, nor could they find the objects of gold, teak, jade, or ivory that they sought, they saw that this island possessed wealth, which came closer to what they expected of the Indies. Almost every one of the *Nytaino* upper class here, and sometimes even the common folk, wore jewelry of gold. And in the town of Guarica, King Guacanagarí was constantly bestowing gifts and favors upon them. With elaborate gestures, he often said, *Whatever you desire, I will grant you.* Not once did he cease to extend his friendship. And he gave them whatever he had, whether it were food, housing, or women.

The feasts King Guacanagarí held to honor the Christians were many, and the Christians never questioned, whether he could afford all of these celebrations. Neither did they suspect that in his elaborate hospitality, Guacanagarí was giving them everything he and his people possessed. And as these feasts lasted late into the night, while the Tainos danced around their fire — their women in one circle and their men in another — they sang along with the mellow sounds of their drums and instruments about their histories, genealogies, and philosophies. The Christians never realized that a queen of a southern kingdom of this island named Anacoana had composed many of those *areitas,* and she was constantly sending her messengers to the various kingdoms throughout the island, to teach everyone her latest pieces.

Although the Christians could not fully adjust to the Indian food, they adapted quickly to their carefree lifestyle, for here upon *Española,* the worries of Castile — especially the burdens of supporting a family back home — slunk away. The tropics bore strange effects upon these men, for it released from them lusts and inhibitions they had squelched all of their lives. And their brains became particularly affected, for even the most intelligent of them began to ignore their abilities to reason and intellectualize. For after being at sea for so long, so in love were these men with this island that they pled with the Admiral daily, *Please let us remain here forever.*

But the Admiral refrained from answering.

On Christmas Eve, another feast was held in their honor. And because it was a special day in Europe, the Admiral allowed Mateo to remain at this celebration later than he normally did. Yet as the Christians laughed and downed gourds of *chicha,* which they said tasted like English beer, Mateo sat gazing into a fire, yearning for the bleak monastery in Palos, Spain he called home, where his adopted father had left him in care of monks. There was much excitement each Christmas at that monastery, for the monks gave gifts to the few children who lived there, that they, themselves, created. Mateo always received something from his Papa, or his adopted father. And last Christmas morning, he found at the foot of his bed, a gift from Bernardo, a monk who always had twinkles in his eyes. Bernardo had whittled out a wooden horse, just for him. Later, Mateo gave that horse away to an Indian in the land of Juana, because he was such a nice man.

Because he was far from home, Mateo was certain that this Christmas would be a lonely one, and there would be no presents for him. And when the fire at which he sat began to hiss, he looked down at the flames and saw that they were sizzling, because his tears were dropping into them. He wondered about Papa, whether he was worried about him at this moment. Like him, Papa had no family, for his wives had disowned him, when he was baptized into Christianity, so he would no longer be identified as a Moor. Papa's family and wives called him an *infidel* and left for Morocco, three years before the mass expulsion of Jews occurred in Spain this year. But Mateo still thought that Papa was a good man, for after a mob stormed into his home when he was five years old and killed his family for helping Jews, Papa came and took him away.

Before Papa brought him to La Rábida, he told Mateo, "Don't ever tell anybody who yer real father was. Ye must learn all ye can about yer Christian religion here, while I go away 'n do my business. I'll visit ye, from time to time. But it is not safe for ye, a boy with blond hair 'n blue eyes, to be seen with a bushy haired, olive-skinned man, like me. Even if I am now a Christian, people still suspect that I am secretly a Muslim."

Although he could barely remember his family, Mateo recalled that his own father said that he had met his mother when he was traveling in Scotland, and because Mateo and his siblings were half Scottish, they were all blond and fair. And in addition, his father also possessed light, Germanic features from his Visigothic heritage.

Mateo's brief sketches of his father were that he was much like Admiral Colón. He was unafraid to believe what he thought he should believe. Every evening his father gathered the family in the sitting room and read out of a Bible that he had obtained when he once lived in England. But like the Bible the Admiral owned that was written in Spanish, that Bible was also not written in Latin or Greek, but in English. That Bible, too, had to be kept hidden. Mateo's father said that he owned one of the few copies that were produced long ago, when an Englishman named John Wycliffe translated the Bible into English, because he felt that people should have Bibles written in their own language, so they could understand them.

While the fire continued to sizzle as his tears dropped into it, Mateo watched after a group of naked children, as they raced across the plaza. One little girl accidentally knocked over a wooden bowl of fruit and sent its contents rolling across the ground. She stared briefly at the mess she made, but when a *Naborian* came to clean it up, she ran off. She was never scolded, nor was the incident ever mentioned. Mateo thought of how in Europe, children would have been reprimanded for such carelessness, and he looked after that child with mixed feelings. As undisciplined as these children appeared to him, he envied them for a freedom he did not have.

He turned to a group of women, who sat chattering upon mats. Occasionally they glanced at a group of men several feet from them, as if they were discussing their husbands. Some of them held babies, who suckled at their breasts. Once in a while, a chorus of giggles rose from them. In the meantime, the Indian men, whom the women were giggling about, grew noisy as they passed around gourds, which caused their skin to turn a deep crimson with each swallow. They laughed easily, as they slapped each other's shoulders.

Mateo yawned. He was unaccustomed to being awake at this hour and wondered how the little children around could remain active for so long. As he looked across the plaza, he saw mats of woven palm leaves lining the ground, with food piled high upon them. He could not understand how these people could have so much to eat all the time. In the middle of the plaza, he saw King Guacanagarí sitting upon a low chair. Admiral Colón squatted next to him on a similar type of chair, but he looked so uncomfortable and unnatural in that position, that it caused Mateo to snicker through his tears. Colón was studying a pile of gifts that he just received. Again, the king gave him another of those girdles with a mask of gold mounted upon it, similar to the one he gave Colón the day he came to the Santa Maria. Mateo wondered why the Indians valued those girdles so much. He saw other gifts surrounding Colón, such as baskets of fruit, dried leaves that the natives called tobacco, red fruit that they called tomatoes, carved wooden bowls, and cloth objects.

As *maracas* clicked to the rich tones of *mayohavaus* and drums, a man wearing many necklaces got up and sang a catchy tune. Mateo remembered that Colón said that this sort of person was an Indian priest, but when he said this, Mateo noted that

99

Colón had contradicted himself, for he also mentioned before that these people had no religion at all — and what priest had no religion?

Soon men and women arose, formed into separate circles and began to dance, with several Christians joining them. Many of the Christians were so tipsy, that they were unsteady on their feet. As Mateo watched both the Christians and Indians, he felt his sleepiness leaving, and a strange yearning overtook him, for suddenly, he wanted to jump up with everyone, to sing along with the Indians and make his feet fly, the way they were stepping. The dances were unlike anything back home, and their music unearthed feelings and instincts he never knew he had. But Mateo fought back his emotions and continued to sit alone by the fire, calmly listening to the swishing of the shells that the Indians wore around their ankles, as they sang with their priest.

As Mateo looked into the shadows, he discerned two figures coming toward him in the distance. He recognized that one of them was a boy on crutches, whom he often saw in the village. He looked similar to another crippled Indian boy, whom he saw on Juana. The boy now was walking with a huge man, who also resembled the Indian on Juana, to whom he had given his wooden horse. The crippled boy came near the fire and looked straight at him, while the man remained at a distance. When the boy spoke, his voice was soft, like the rest of his people's.

"*Tayno.*"

Mateo did not understand him, but he returned his smile.

"*Buenos noches.*"

They sat awkwardly, not knowing what more to say, and when Mateo looked over at the huge man, he saw him talking to a group of Indians, and then, that man and his group spread out and began walking among the people, as if they were watching over them. Mateo wondered why those men were not participating in the festivities.

Just then, King Guacanagarí arose, and the instruments and singing ceased. The *cacique* extended his arms toward the Christians, as he smiled widely and pointed to the shadows behind him. His actions puzzled Mateo, but the other Christians appeared to understand his gestures and acknowledged the king's speech with smiles. Soon a group of women appeared. As the light from the torches reflected off their smooth skin, they slipped, feline-like, through the crowd toward the Christians, with slow, careful, movements. Mateo never saw such women upon this island before, for he was usually on board the ship at this hour. As he watched them, he assumed that they only came out at this hour. Strangely, they aroused sensations in him.

Mateo stared after the women, as they slipped their arms around the Christians, and while the drums began a new beat, more of them pushed forward. When one of them brushed against Mateo, her flesh felt soft, and he liked her exotic aroma. Just then, she turned abruptly toward a Christian near him, and the wreath of flowers that hung from her neck smacked across Mateo's face, taking him by surprise and breaking the spell that had captivated him.

Mateo moved backwards to get out of her way. He searched for Admiral Colón and saw that he was no longer by Guacanagarí's side. He finally found him sitting on the ground, next to another Christian, undaunted by the new changes that were occurring at this feast. Mateo pushed his way toward him.

"I see great potential here," the Christian was saying to Colón. "Did ye see how th' cotton grows wildly along th' hillside? And th' abundance of aloes..."

"*Sí, sí.* A lot of riches can be acquired here besides gold."

Mateo came and sat next to Colón, who did not notice his presence. He saw that Colón's face was more reddish than it usually was. He must have had too much of the Indian drink. Mateo, himself, had discovered that that drink was too strong for him and preferred the taste of the island's water, instead.

As the musicians switched rhythms again and increased the pace of the music, the melody turned erotic. A strange expression swept across the Christian who was speaking to Colón, and he refocused his attention to a woman who was approaching him. This change of atmosphere suddenly caused Mateo to become greatly uncomfortable, and panic swept through him. He grabbed hold of Colón and shook him.

"*Señor...*"

The Admiral took another sip from his gourd, and then turned. Mateo never saw him this tipsy before.

"Oh, *hola*, Mateo. I was lookin' for ye. 'Tis time to return to th' Santa Maria. Before we left Spain, my friend Juan Perez made me promise that I'd take good care of ye durin' this trip, 'n tonight is no exception, even if I did allow ye a little more freedom."

In the torchlight, Colón's face glowed. He was one who seldom drank heavily, but since it was Christmas Eve, he must have drunk more than usual. One of the women approached him and hooked an arm through his, but he gently pushed her away and pointed to Mateo, gesturing that he must take him back to the ship.

The woman nodded and turned to another Christian close by, and then she led him into the darkness, with the Christian stumbling after her, while the drums rumbled.

Mateo noticed for the first time that the naked children were gone and assumed that their mothers probably had them tucked in bed, by now. He also looked for the older children, the ones who wore loincloths. A few of them were still around. As Mateo studied his surroundings, he saw that he and the Admiral were the only Christians left at the feast. Far away, the boy with crutches was still sitting near the fire. Mateo had forgotten all about him, when he left in search for the Admiral.

As Colón arose and led Mateo to the beach, the Indians began a new dance around the fire. When Colón and Mateo reached the rowboats, Mateo turned and waved to the crippled boy. As he did, he noticed a figure in the shadows, in an inconspicuous area. It was a man, tall and well built, with a feathered hat. He was dressed as the Tainan aristocracy, but he was too far away and too deep in the darkness for Mateo to see his face. As Colón pushed their boat into the water, Mateo felt the strange man's eyes boring through him.

When they were rowing toward the Santa Maria, Mateo finally said, "Who were those mysterious women, *señor*?"

"They are th' wives of th' *cacique*, Mateo. When we were on th' other islands, th' *caciques* there also gave their wives to th' Christians. But it usually happened after yer curfew, when ye had already returned to th' ship for th' night."

"Why did ye not go with one of them tonight?"

"They are beautiful, aren't they, *mi hijo*? I have never seen any women as beautiful as these on Española. But I leave them alone, because I have a special destiny, which God has planned for me. If I succumb to these women, I will forget that destiny."

"Why must ye avoid them, when ye have such a destiny?"

"Long ago, when I lived by my desires 'n lusts, I became so engrossed in my passions, that they caused me to forget my promises with God."

"So ye must live a saintly life, as a *padre's, señor*?"

"*Sí, mi hijo.* If I want to remember my godly mission."

"Do ye think that these women are tryin' to gain certain favors from us Christians?"

"What kind of favors, Mateo?"

"I don't know. I just get th' feelin' that they think we're gods, or somethin', 'n maybe they think that if they please us enough, that we will grant them somethin' they want badly."

"Ye mean, they might be usin' us for political gain?"

"Maybe that's it, *señor*."

"Hmmmm. If ye're correct, I wonder what they would want from us? But these lovin' people, Mateo? No, they couldn't possibly. 'N remember, they are heathens, *mi hijo*, 'n th' most important thing we can do for them is to teach them th' gospel."

As Mateo pondered over Colón's last comments, he thought he heard something whiz through the air pass them, and then he heard a soft splash, as if an arrow had hit the surface of the water, similar to the sounds when the Indians on the other islands attacked. Mateo spun around, but saw nothing.

"Good heavens, *señor*. I think we've just been shot at. I thought th' Indians on this island were friendly, 'n none of them owned any weapons."

Colón continued to row.

"I haven't heard anythin' unusual. It's late, Mateo, 'n ye're tired."

Mateo could barely hear the sound of the oars dipping into the water above the music. As he stared back to shore, he saw that the mysterious figure had come out of the shadows and now stood on the beach. It appeared to be holding a bow in its hand, and its feathered hat reflected off the moonlight.

"*Señor*, I tell ye, we've been shot at. There he is, standin' on th' beach."

Colón did not even bother to turn his head.

"These people wouldn't hurt anyone, Mateo."

Mateo stared at Colón in disbelief, for he always told his men that whenever they went to shore, they must use extreme caution and should remain heavily armed at all times. But here on *Española*, he had changed somewhat, because the Indians behaved differently. And perhaps tonight, he had drunk too much.

"I also noticed that some of th' Indians were actin' as if they were guards at th' feast. They were walkin' back 'n forth 'n were not celebratin' with th' people."

"Nonsense, Mateo. I didn't see them, 'n I always notice these things."

Just then, Mateo saw one of the Indians, who acted as a guard, run up to the crippled Indian boy by the fire. He then pointed to the shadowy figure on the beach, and the boy rose abruptly and sped away with his crutches. Mateo was amazed at how fast that boy moved.

"Admiral Colón...there's somethin' goin' on..."

"Mateo, I've heard enough. I don't want to hear any more of yer suspicions."

Mateo never saw Colón behave in this manner before, for he was quite irritable.

"I'm sorry, if I snapped at ye, Mateo, but I'm not feelin' well tonight," Colón finally said. "I guess the Indian food I ate did not agree with me."

After they reached the ship, Mateo immediately crawled beneath his covers on deck, for the weather had turned cool tonight. And Colón retired to his cabin, because he was not feeling well. The two men, who were left in charge of the ship, sat on deck and passed a jug back and forth, as consolation for not being allowed to attend the feast.

As Mateo looked up at the clear sky and listened to the water lapping against the hull, the stars made him think of the first Christmas long ago. Then his thoughts wandered to the exciting Indian music; the perfumed women with smooth, soft skin; the drunken laughter; the Admiral's devotion to his mission; the Indians, who were marching about, who appeared to be protecting the people; and the strange whizzing in the dark, as he and the Admiral rowed back to the ship. He even wondered why the crippled Indian boy ran away, when he saw the shadowy figure with the bow and arrow. And then, his hatred for the sea returned, and he yearned for Spain again. He wished that the excitement of this trip to the Indies had never lured him. And soon, he was asleep.

When the Christians returned to the ship, their clatter awoke Mateo. As the men passed by, they carried the odor of *chicha* with them. Mateo saw that Colón was now awake and was standing next to two other figures.

"Santiago can't watch th' ship tonight, Admiral. He is dead drunk."

"Javier is worse."

"Then who will take watch?" said Colón. "I would do it, if I were feelin' better."

"How about th' cabin boys?"

In the moonlight, Mateo could see Colón's jaw drop.

"Come on, th' older one is just as drunk as ye are."

"Well, th' younger one, then."

"Mateo? Impossible. He is too small 'n has no experience."

"*Señor*, we've shown him often enough how to man this ship, while we were out at sea. Besides, he is in th' best condition of all of us, 'n we all need to sleep."

"No, no...'tis a foolish thing..."

"Capitán Colón, we need a break for just for one night. Come on, it's Christmas mornin'. It won't hurt anyone, if that boy took over."

"Besides..." the other man said. "We are so close to shore, what harm can ever happen?"

From his position on deck, Mateo watched after Colón, as he staggered away, shaking his head and muttering, "No, no."

Mateo could see that Admiral Colón was in terrible shape. Then from a distance, he heard him call over his shoulder.

"All right. Just for tonight."

When the two men bent down and shook Mateo, he smelled the alcohol on their breath and pretended to be asleep.

"Boy, boy, wake up!"

Their voices were slurred.

Mateo gradually opened his eyes and saw their faces close to his. One of them had hair falling over his nose, and both of them had wrinkled, unbuttoned shirts that drooped over their trousers. They shook him again, harder this time.

As Mateo sat up, they said, "Get up to th' steerage! We need ye to guard th' ship."

At the tiller, Mateo felt the waves slapping against the sides of the hull. Here in the bay where the water was usually a dead calm, it was choppy tonight. When the waves hit, it took much of his strength to keep the ship under control. As Mateo struggled at the tiller, all was quiet, as everyone sprawled across the deck in drunken slumber. He turned his head to shore and saw the flicker of a lone torch, similar to the light in the distance the night they first spotted land. Since then, he learned that the Indians burned a certain kind of wax lamp to keep mosquitoes away. He watched the flame gradually die down, and then grow strong again. Mateo yawned. His head nodded and drooped lower and lower.

When a wave crashed against the ship, Mateo awoke. For a moment, he wondered where he was, but before he could gather his wits together, the tiller lurched out of his hands. A deafening sound of ripping wood filled the night. Mateo grabbed for the tiller to regain control of the ship, but when the Santa Maria swerved and leaned to one side, terror seized him.

"Help me! Somethin's wrong with th' ship!"

Colón charged out of his cabin.

"Wake up! We hit a reef!"

The crew turned alive, as everyone suddenly began running in all directions, shouting orders. A group of men jumped into one of the small boats, lowered themselves into the water, and escaped to the Niña.

"Fools!" Colón said, as he looked after them. "They're thinkin' only about savin' their own necks!"

As the rest of the crew scrambled to save the ship, eventually another boat filled with people and left; but this time, that vessel went to shore and returned to pick up others. After it made several trips, Mateo finally climbed into that boat with Colón and others. As they rowed toward shore, Mateo sat in silence, with eyes averting Colón.

"First th' Pinta disappeared," he muttered. "Then, because of me, there is no more Santa Maria, either. Now, only th' Niña is left."

Slowly he became brave enough to face Colón, who by now, had taken over the rowing. The muscles in Colón's neck bulged in the moonlight as he pulled at the oars. He was much more sober than he was earlier tonight. As Mateo turned away, filled with guilt, he saw the Santa Maria sticking up awkwardly from the blackened water.

"I bet th' Indians won't think we're from heaven, now," he muttered.

When Colón spoke soon after that, his voice was surprisingly cheery.

"Men, all is not lost. Much good can come from this disaster, ye shall see."

After rowing in silence again, he continued.

"In fact, what do ye think, if in th' mornin' we tore that old ship apart 'n used its timbers to build a fort for us, eh?"

"A fort, señor?" Mateo said.

He could still smell the Indian drink on Colón's breath, and he was glad that Colón was still somewhat under its influence, for if he were not, he would probably be giving him a tongue-lashing.

"Why not, mi hijo? It'll be th' first European settlement in th' Indies. 'N we'll call it Fort Navidad, because we built it on Christmas Day."

Mateo felt a little encouraged, and timidly, he leaned forward and placed a hand on Admiral Colón's shoulder.

14

Within the cabin of the Niña, Admiral Colón paced the floor, with his eyes turned inward. It was by the grace of God that he and the Christians were led to Española, for nowhere before, had they found greater happiness. It was nearly a month since they arrived on this island, and ever since then, its charm increased by the day, until now, it was so intense and wooing that his men pled constantly to remain here forever. The enchantment of these tropics, the pacifying effects of these gentle and kind people, and the elegance of their culture, all mystified them. And his men were weary of traveling.

As Colón continued in circles, he glanced at his calendar. It was Thursday, 3 January 1493, a little over a week since the Santa Maria had sunk. Although he planned on leaving port today, his schedule was altered to depart on the morrow, for Indians needed him. If all goes well, he would set sail at sunrise.

The Niña would have to return to Spain alone, for only God knew where the Pinta was. Throughout this trip, that blasted, gold-hungry Pinzón manipulated his crew to be constantly angry with him, Colón, who was now the Admiral of the Open Sea. He could no longer search for that infidel, and because there were so many items collected from these Indies — including twenty Indians — with only one ship remaining, it was expedient that he returned to Spain, as soon as possible; but when he does, he must also leave a third of his crew behind.

Colón felt it in his bones that his men would be in good hands, here on Española. He made certain that Fort Navidad was constructed soundly from the ruins of the Santa Maria. And miraculously, God enabled the Christians to complete this structure in just a week. Not only was Colón certain that God was caring for them, but he was also certain that the Tainos would also care for his men. After all, no other people could be friendlier or more generous. How could they give him any fears? These people did not even believe in bearing arms. In fact, they would never know how to use weapons, if they were given any. Only last week, his men demonstrated to these Indians their Christian artillery in a mock fight, showing these people the power of the sword and blunderbuss. And as the Indians watched them in amazement as curious, little children would, as soon as a musket and Lombard fired and a ball penetrated the remains of the Santa Maria in the water, the explosion petrified them so tremendously, that some of them fell to earth, as if they were dead. When the Christians saw how easily these Indians were frightened, they comforted them and assured them that as long as they, the Christians, remained close by, they would protect them from their enemies with their powerful weapons.

However, the Admiral reasoned that, if by any remote chance that these Indians actually did turn against his men while he was gone, a lone Christian, properly armed, could quickly kill a thousand of them. Nevertheless, he instructed his men to always treat these gentle people with the greatest respect and kindness — especially their women, children, and king.

As Colón continued his pacing, he passed his desk and caught sight of his journal, where the names of thirty-five men were listed, whom he planned to leave behind. He glanced down and saw the names of Diego de Arana, the newly appointed captain of Fort Navidad and Pedro Gutiérrez, the fort's new lieutenant. As he skimmed over the page, he saw other names, such as Francisco de Vergura, Gabriél Baraona, Pablo...and (the Admiral winced)...and...there was Mateo Gonzalez, the cabin boy. His heart gave a twinge, but then he shrugged off his sentiments. He already had another cabin boy, who was much more experienced and better qualified than Mateo.

A knock came from the door of the cabin, and Pedro Gutiérrez entered. He soon stood in front of the Admiral, looking tall, lean, young, and impeccably clean-cut. Colón never forgot that Gutiérrez was a representative of the royal household, and that he was the nephew of his good friend the friar, Juan Perez, who was caring for his son, during this trip. On the night of landfall, Gutiérrez also viewed the strange lights in the distance with him. Now, Gutiérrez saluted.

"Ye wished to see me, *señor*."

"*Mí amigo*, since ye are now lieutenant of Fort Navidad, I am dependin' on ye 'n Rodrigo de Escobedo, th' secretary of fleet, to give Captain Diego de Arana yer support, at all times, as he leads th' fort as its master-at-arms."

"Ye have my word, Admiral Colón."

"Do ye need anythin' from me, before I depart?"

"No, *señor*."

"Once I reach Spain, I will be seein' yer uncle. Would ye want me to tell him anythin' for ye?"

"Tell him all is well with me, *señor*. And tell him to tell my parents that I am most happy to be here on this island."

"It is good of yer uncle to care for my son at his monastery."

"He is a good man, *señor*. Yer son could have no better care."

The Admiral nodded. Then he cleared his throat.

"Gutiérrez, please watch over Mateo for me."

"I will care for th' boy, as if he were my very own son, *señor*. I've heard that he went into shock, after he learned that he must remain here. He was never cut out for th' sea, ye know."

When the Admiral did not respond, and a silence followed, the lieutenant turned to leave, but then turned back, to say one more thing.

"All will be well in Navidad, I assure ye."

"*Gracias*."

The lieutenant bowed. As he climbed the short flight of stairs that led up to the deck, the Admiral noticed that one of the hinges at the knees of his armor squeaked, and it reminded him that he was leaving his men in this strange land, lacking many necessities, such as a simple can of oil.

At sunrise, as the Niña weighted her anchors and pulled away from shore, light winds filled her sails. A small crowd of loinclothed Indians waved from the beach, smiling broadly, as their women propped babes upon their hips. Even at this early hour, a few Tainos dove into the water and swam along the ship, and with teary voices, they shouted their farewells.

"*Tayno! Tayno! Tayno!*"

From the shore, one of the Indian men yelled a warning about the Caribs to the Christians, despite his belief that the Christians were their beloved god Yocahu, who could not be harmed or killed. Close to that man was the crippled Indian boy, leaning

106

upon his crutches. With deep sadness, the Admiral watched these people grow smaller, as the Niña pulled farther away. He was finally leaving these loving, peaceful folk, and like his men, he wished to never depart from this paradise.

He stared after the Christians he was leaving, who stood upon the beach among the Tainos. Many of them wept openly. Yet even as they wept, the Admiral perceived contentment on their faces; for he knew how much they now loved this island. Besides, this parting would only be a short while.

As the ship continued to withdraw from shore, the Admiral saw Gutiérrez standing next to the other two officers. Gutiérrez was waving. So were a physician, a silversmith, a lawyer, a chalkier, a gunman, even an Englishman, as well as several sailors. And standing among those Christians, Colón saw Mateo, wiping his eyes with the back of one hand, as he held a book with the other. This book was a gift that he, the Admiral, gave him only moments before. It was his Bible that was written in Spanish, the most valued item that he brought with him. Although Colón still owned another Bible that was written in Latin, he knew that Mateo would understand the one in Spanish. Although its pages were worn and its corners bent, he felt that it, more than anything else, would help sustain that boy until he returned. When he placed that book into Mateo's bony hands, tears streamed down that boy's face as he mumbled a sentence of thanks.

"Read this often, Mateo. It'll give ye strength. Always remember that with it, ye will be able to teach these heathens th' gospel."

Mateo nodded, incapable of speaking.

"When I return, ye'll have all these Indians converted to th' true religion, eh?"

Mateo half smiled and tried to laugh through his tears, but did not succeed, and finally said, "Ye're leavin' me behind, because I sunk th' Santa Maria, aren't ye? Ye won't say it, but I know it."

The Admiral swallowed, and then he placed a hand upon one of Mateo's thin shoulders.

"Mateo, I would bring ye with me, if I could. But ye must remember, I've only enough room to bring back one cabin boy, 'n I had to choose th' one who'd sailed before."

The Admiral secretly hoped that his leaving Mateo on this island would not cause him to hate the sea even more than he already did. And with regret, he realized that his plans to teach Mateo about the exhilaration of adventure and finding new lands had failed.

Mateo's thin body shook, as he said, "Please, please come back from Castile, as fast as ye can."

As the Niña sailed onward, the Admiral ordered a small boat to be sent ahead to clear the ship of the many reefs and shoals. He also made sure that a man remained at the top of the central mast at all times, to be on constant lookout for underwater obstacles. As they headed northwest along the northern coast of *Española*, the Niña took a wider course than when it first approached the island. They passed through countless reef-created channels and steered from other dangers beneath the sea, while they observed white beaches and flat lands that stretched far inland and ended abruptly into towering mountains. Everywhere the Niña sailed, the Admiral saw that the island was well peopled and peppered with thatched huts. And he recorded every detail into his journal and named one of the mountain ranges the *Monti Cristi*.

As the days passed, the Admiral pushed farther for a last look of the Indies. Exhilaration swept the ship, as he and his crew talked about heading homeward, to announce to the world and the Catholic Sovereigns — King Ferdinand and Queen Isabella — that they had succeeded in paving a new and quicker route to the Indies, across the once unknown sea. The Western Ocean was tamed! They had traversed the last third and undiscovered portion of the earth. And now, Spain — not Portugal — led the world in exploration.

Proudly, the Admiral stood upon the deck, inhaling the aromas of the goods of the Indies that drifted up to him from below. As a boy, he always enjoyed exotic smells from faraway lands, but these smells now were new and different. Upon the ship, came the subtle odors of mastic, fine gums, and aloe. There was a blend of scents from giant bundles of cotton and exotic fruit, such as pineapple, guavas, and other produce. Even wooden bowls, ceramics, cotton hammocks, and fishnets of palm fibers emitted subtle smells of their own. And the living cargo of Indian slaves, beneath the deck, gave off their own peculiar human odors. From where the Admiral stood, he could hear their faint cries of *bohío, bohío, bohío,* as all twenty Indians wept as babies from below.

But the most valued products that the Admiral was bringing back were locked securely in the cabin of the ship, and they had little or no smells. They were the precious stones, jewels, gold, amulets made of nephrites, and the girdles with masks that consisted of tiny gold tiles.

After the crew passed through another narrow channel of rocks and shoals, the beauty of Española became so striking, that the Admiral felt compelled to travel even farther, to take in more sights of villages, people, and terrain that took his breath away. Yet he knew that this journey must come to an end, for the ship had developed too many leaks and was in dire need of restoration.

"Admiral, I see a ship ahead!"

The Admiral looked up toward the sailor, who was shouting from the top of the central mast. With a blue kerchief tied around his head to keep the sweat out of his eyes, the sailor was waving madly with his right hand, while he shaded his eyes with his left.

"It's a ship, all right. Why, it's...it's...it's th' Pinta! Th' Pintaaaaaa!"

The Admiral adjusted his eyes into the horizon. He spotted puffy sails far away. Immediately, he held up his telescope. Indeed, there was a ship. As the Santa Maria neared this vessel, the Admiral discerned that it was definitely the Pinta. Soon they were close enough that he could recognize the members of its crew. Through his spyglass, the Admiral searched among those men and found Pinzón.

"There he is," he said. "I can tell by th' way he is holdin' up his shoulders, that he never found his gold. Serves that greedy fool right, for desertin' th' fleet."

But then, the Admiral caught himself and forced his anger out of him.

Does it matter? he thought.

And then he refocused his thoughts upon the two ships, which would now be traveling home together, to represent the glory of Spain.

15

Somewhere in Castile

I cannot march much longer. I am too weary. And it is cold. This cannot be heaven. The Admiral. Why does he make us march on these chilly paths in this land? All I see are strange people, with pale faces, and they only stare at us as we walk by, as if we are goods that traders bring to market.

How could I ever have thought the Admiral was Yocahu, and that he came from heaven? I even thought that his men were his angels. How foolish I was! Long before they took us across the great waters, I, King Semola, realized that these men were not Yocahu, and they were not taking us to heaven. Instead, they were only taking us upon a large, enclosed canoe to their own land. But I was afraid to admit that I was fooled from the start.

I suppose all of you thought the same way as I did, especially once we started across the great waters, when most of us began to die from the strange curses the foreigners brought, which killed us faster than the Caribs slaughter helpless babes. Look at us now. There are no longer twenty of us, but only six of us left. We do not know who will die next.

I don't know why, but even as we crossed those waters, I still hung on to the idea that the Admiral was Yocahu. Even after I stopped believing that lie, I kept telling all of you that he was taking us to heaven, and there would be peace for us after this hard journey. I am sorry that I kept reminding you of that place of rest that our fathers spoke of, where there are many lakes and streams. I kept telling you all that soon we would be eating the delightful food of the *zemies* in the land of Yocahu, which grow on trees and are the size of guavas. But I told you these stories, because I wanted us all to continue to have hope and to stay alive. Yet, I wonder if my efforts were worth it, for tomorrow, there may no longer be six of us.

I cannot give you hope, anymore, for not one of us can believe that this land is heaven. It is too cold. And it is so harsh and unfriendly. Everywhere here, we are forced to march, march, march in this strange parade, and we see nothing but foreign faces. So many foreign faces. And look at how those people all cover their bodies with thick robes to keep themselves warm. But they give us nothing to make us comfortable.

These people cannot be Yocahu, for they do not have any love for us. They do not want us to be a mighty people, as Yocahu wants us to be. I have never been so hungry and cold. These stone paths that wind around the foreigner's *bohios* are cold and hard beneath our feet. These chains that they have put upon us make it hard to move. I cannot deny, anymore, that this land is only the other side of the great waters. Compared to this land, our islands are heaven.

Look at those strange and tall *bohíos*. Many of them look as if they are made of stone. Don't you think it is odd, that the people here do not sit upon the ground, and they always must sit on *dohus*, like the *caciques*, only their *dohus* are built so high that the bottom of their feet touch the floor?

It's hard for us to not be scared of their strange animals, especially those giant ones with four legs, which they call *horses*. Maybe some day, we will grow brave enough to ride them, or to train them to pull litters over these stone paths.

Yesterday when we first arrived here, and the Admiral brought the six of us to the stone hut that is as large as many villages, I was surprised to see how the foreigners' king and queen were dressed. They put so many layers of clothing upon their bodies. I was hoping that after they came and kissed the Admiral on both cheeks, that they would at least give us something to keep us warm. But instead, they only sat and talked with the Admiral, and I could tell that they were talking about us, for they looked over at us often. I perceived that they did not care, whether I was the highest king of the island of Guanahaní. Nor did they care to know that I needed to get back to my island, because my own son is too young to take my place at the throne. These people act as if we are not capable of doing anything more than to serve them. Look at me, a king, but I have chains on my hands and feet. What more shame can they bring upon me? Maybe it would have been a greater honor for me to have escaped from them on Quisqueya and have been made a *Naborian* servant. It does not matter to me, anymore, whether Anacoana sees me in my fallen state, because Quisqueya is a far better place than this land.

I am tired of marching through these stone villages. This procession is not one of respect, for these people do not revere me as my people do back home, who gather to watch me — their *cacique* — as I parade past them. But I must remember that most of them do not know any better, and they only look upon us with curiosity. They have no idea that I am a king of a special people. They are also ignorant of Yocahu. Did you notice how many of these people seem happy and excited over something, as if we are part of a celebration of an important event?

March. March. March. See how far ahead the Admiral rides in that litter, pulled by horses? It is so easy for him and his men, for they are riding on those giant animals. But we must walk, even if our body hurt, and our feet are so cold and numb that we cannot feel them. How much farther must we go?

Hui, it is raining lightly now, but the rain here is different, because it feels cold. Look at my fingers and feet. They have turned a different color. Yours are a funny color, too. All of us have changed to a strange color. I cannot bear this any more. None of us can.

Hui, hui. Admiral! Admiral! Could you give us something to place upon our shoulders and to cover our feet? He does not hear me. In fact, nobody up front hears me. They are riding too far ahead. *Hui, hui.* We need something hot to drink. Do you have cacao or *chicha* in this land? Are there *chia* seeds to chew on, to give us strength while we walk?

Hui, hui, you up ahead. You must make your litter go slower. We can't keep up with you. We all feel faint back here. Please. *Eh, eh,* look. One of us is stumbling. *Eh,* he fell. Someone, someone, call the Admiral in the litter, please. Tell him that one of us has fainted, and we can proceed no farther, for the weight of his body is too heavy for us to bear up with these chains. *Hui, hui.* There. At last, someone is coming. Thank you, thank you. He looks better already. I don't think he'll die.

Could you tell me why they force us to wear these chains on our hands and feet? Please take them off. It will make walking easier. We promise that we will not run away. And we will be your humble servants.

Just don't eat us, like the Caribs!

Book Three

16

Behind bags of grain, Mateo pushed his nose between the slats of the outside wall of Fort Navidad. During the past months, this spot had become his favorite place, because nobody would think to look for him here, and since he was small for his age, he could easily crawl through the cracks between the bags to enter this hideout. It gave him a clear view of the beach below and enabled him to search the horizon to see whether Admiral Colón's ships were returning from Castile. If he wished to spy on the natives, all he would need to do was turn his head to the left, where he could watch the activities of the Indian village below. He could also observe the Indians trading in their marketplace in their central plaza, and when dusk fell, if he lay flat on his belly and looked to the right, he could see people starting a fire in another part of the village, where the townsfolk gathered to sing and dance into the night. And he especially loved to watch canoes approaching the shore, because the villagers always ran to the beach to sit welcomes. Everyday he also saw several men entering King Guacanagarí's hut that stood propped at the top of a small hill, overlooking several hundred Indian huts and wondered why those men met there so often.

Just a couple of months before, an odd event occurred. Some kind of important woman arrived on a canoe, and many people came out to greet her. She was very beautiful. When she saw the crippled Indian boy, she embraced him, as if they were close relatives. From time to time after that, Mateo saw her among the village people, but she didn't quite fit in with them, because there was an aura about her that caused her to stand above all of them. Her hair was stylish, she walked with grace, she dressed much more elegantly than everyone else, and she even moved with dignity.

By now, Mateo calculated that it was September, or eight months, since the Niña left Española. It also meant that he was now thirteen years old. Mateo was quite concerned, because Admiral Colón should have returned from Spain months before, but thus far, there was no sign of him.

Today he spent hours in this hiding place, waiting and searching the horizon for Admiral Colón to appear on his ships. He remained faithful to the admiral's instructions, to always stay in the fort and to treat the Indians with kindness, whenever they came. He even read the Bible diligently, and because it was written in Spanish, it was easy for him to understand; and he wanted to prepare himself to teach it to the Indians, when the time was ripe.

However, the other Christians at Navidad were not as obedient, for they wandered throughout the countryside and caused a ruckus that scared the Indians out of their wits. Although the Indians offered them their riches and women to placate them, the Christians still complained that they did not have enough gold and women.

Ever since the Christians left for Spain, Admiral Colón's Bible had become Mateo's best friend. Because the men at Navidad were too engrossed in their own interests and activities to include Mateo in their affairs, he often sat in this hiding spot, reading and re-reading the stories of Joseph and his brothers, David and his battles, the wall of Jericho falling, and the teachings of Christ. Occasionally when he glanced up to see whether any ships were appearing, he felt trade winds sweep across his face through the slats, as they fluttered the pages. And each night behind these bags, without fail, Mateo removed his rosary from his pocket, and as he fingered each bead, he quietly recited the *Hail Mary's* and *Our Father's*.

Often in this hiding spot, Mateo heard the Christians bickering elsewhere in the fort. Sometimes their shouts became so loud, that he even noticed the Indians in Guarica looking over in their direction. Once in a while, the Christians got into fights that became so bad that they would start slugging at each other, but it only happened when they were drunk. Often the men quarreled over the gold they took from the Indians, but usually it was over a woman, about who belonged to whom. The worst fight occurred last week between Guitérrez and Jácome. It began with the two men arguing and calling insults so loudly, that eventually, Mateo crawled out of his hiding place to investigate.

When Mateo walked into the clearing, he discovered that both men wanted the same girl. She was beautiful and slender. As she stood within the crowd of Christians with large, frightened eyes, he saw that she must have been no more than 16 years old, or about three years older than he was. As he listened to the two men yelling, he saw that the Christians had taken sides, with one group shouting in favor of Guitérrez, and the other, siding for Jácome. Except for Guitérrez and Jácome, the men were not taking this fight seriously and were laughing, as if they were participating in a game. Since the wine that Colón left them was long gone, they now sipped from gourds of the potent Indian drink.

Jácome was extremely incensed and was shaking a fist at Guitérrez.

"I'll knock yer head right off yer shoulders!"

Suddenly he grabbed Guitérrez, and when the others tried to stop him, he pushed them aside and slammed his fist into Guitérrez's groin.

"Why, you bastard!" Guitérrez cried.

Mateo did not know what happened next, only that soon, a large squabble resulted, with all the Christians, excepting for him, pounding their fists into each other. Among bleeding noses, black eyes, and lacerations, someone drew a sword, and a mêlée ensued. As swords crashed, knives flashed in the sun, and sometimes, even a chair flew through the air and missed someone.

Suddenly someone yelled, "*Díos mío!*"

Silence fell, and the men quickly drew aside, exposing Jácome's lifeless body, lying with a large gash from a sword across his chest, while others around him bled profusely from wounds. Jácome's death brought the men abruptly to their senses. When Mateo went over and stared down at him, the very words that this man said to him only a month before came back to him.

These tropics have strange effects upon us, Mateo. They arouse our most base appetites 'n passions, 'n often, they transform us into animals. But I'm not goin' to let those forces overpower me.

But Jácome had allowed this land to seduce him, after all.

Soon after this event, the Christians gathered to discuss their situation.

"We can't live together anymore," they said. "We're drivin' each other crazy."

Some of the Christians took their gold and moved out of the fort into various Indian villages, scattering themselves thinly among the people, as they sought for the island's most desirable women. As the men filed out in twos and threes, soon, only twelve of the original thirty-five remained. Diego de Arana, the captain, was among those who stayed. Mateo was another. Although some of the wives of the *cacique* remained with them, after that fight, most of the women returned to the village.

As the days went by, Mateo was grateful to the women who remained in Navidad, for they gave him a chance to hear and learn about their Tainan language, which provided him with something else to live for, besides waiting for Admiral Colón to return and reading the Bible. These women were delighted, when he came up to them and spoke a phrase or two in their tongue. Since Admiral Colón had insisted that the Christians never leave Fort Navidad, Mateo would never have been able to pick up that Indian language, any other way.

As Mateo gazed through the slats in his hiding place and looked out into the sea, he quietly said, "Where are ye, Admiral Colón? Hurry back! There are only twelve of us left at Navidad now, 'n we need ye to come back here to take us all home." And then he paused and corrected himself. "Oh, I forgot. There are only eleven of us remainin' here now, because somebody just died yesterday. He developed a strange illness 'n had sores all over his body. He was so sick that he even went mad."

17

When Neef entered the *bohío,* he found Lida at her loom in the corner, where she usually worked. He saw that she had picked several baskets of cotton from the mountainside and had already turned much of it into thread, and now she was weaving some of it into cloth.

"I was just visiting King Guacanagarí," he said. "Another messenger arrived today at the palace to ask for Sabila's hand. But Sabila was not there to know about it."

Now that Sabila was finished with her schooling, Neef's father, King Guarionex, had sent word that she should not yet return to his kingdom and had made arrangements with King Guacanagarí of the Kingdom of Marién to take her in. He also asked Guacanagarí to find a husband for her. However, among these new developments, Guacanagarí still did not know that Sabila and Neef were siblings.

"Did our king accept that offer?" said Lida.

"Nay, he turned it down."

"Which king sent that messenger?" Lida asked.

"It was someone who ruled a small *cazicazgo* in the Kingdom of the Mines."

"Does he have any wives?"

"Three, I believe."

"Then he must be too old for Sabila, and she wouldn't be his first wife, anyway, if she marries him."

"I overheard that he was thirty and one years old."

"Sabila needs a husband, who is closer to her age."

"I still think that Sabila should have married Prince Chinya," Neef said. "In fact, I think she was wrong to turn down his proposal, for he would have made her his first wife, and his grandmother, Queen Higuanamá of the Kingdom of the Great Old Lady, would eventually give him a large portion of her kingdom to rule over. But Sabila said that she didn't want to be sent so far away."

"She has a right to her opinions, Neef."

"But it is getting too dangerous for her to remain here in Guarica any longer."

"Dangerous?"

117

"Aye, the foreigners at Fort Navidad are looking at her in funny ways."

"Oh, but they look at all of our young women that way. Besides, Sabila wouldn't let it go to her head, because she has had too high an upbringing to be like the other women, who fall for those lecherous eyes."

"But she is around the other young ladies most of the day, and they can have a powerful influence upon her thinking. I've seen how those women boldly stare back at the men at Navidad, and I've heard that some of them are even giving themselves to them, as if they have the same privileges as the wives of a king. I have every reason to believe that they are jealous of the wives of the king, because they want to also be given to those men."

"Neef, you must realize that those girls are attracted to those foreigners, because those men are a novelty to them. But Sabila would never stoop to their level."

"What makes you think she wouldn't?"

"She is a full blooded princess, and from the time she was born, she was raised to believe that she would marry a prince or king."

"Lida, I know my sister. She is a very socially oriented woman, who can be easily influenced by what is popular. With all this swooning over how beautiful those men are, how can it pass over her? Those other women are constantly saying that they would love to be married to those *zemies*."

"She's a princess, who's been raised to set an example for everyone."

"Some of those women are as young as thirteen years old, and because they aren't old enough to wear *naguas*, the men at Navidad, who come from a country where people clothe their bodies, stare at their exposed bodies, which I can tell, attracts the attention of those girls. They no longer talk about the eligible bachelors of our people anymore, but all they ever speak of, are the men at Navidad. It's disgusting, Lida."

"Neef, I know all about this problem. These young women no longer want our own men, for they consider them to be too ordinary, even if they come from the highest nobility. It doesn't help, either, that many of these women still believe that the men at Navidad are *zemies*, no matter how badly they behave. In fact, the women overlook their bad manners and are drawn to their fair skin, light eyes, and fair hair. They know every man at Navidad and are always mentioning several Pedros, Diegos, and Franciscos. They swoon over a Marco, and even a redheaded Guillermo, whom they sometimes call *William*, and giggle at his temper that bursts out of him, like a madman."

"I don't understand it, Lida, they would never tolerate a bad tempered man of our own people. Did you notice, though, that they hardly ever speak about Mateo?"

"Mateo? Oh, they consider him to be a runt. Everyone thinks he is just eight years old. But they admire his light colored hair."

In disgust, Neef began imitating the women.

"Ooooh, Pedro's eyes are as blue, as a cloudless sky. And Francisco's green eyes sparkle as nephrites! Ah, if only I could run my hand through William's lovely, flaming red hair. Ooooh, to feel Marco's beard against my cheek and to finger his tall, thin nose…"

"Neef stop that! Now, don't worry one bit about your sister, for she is too well bred to fall for those men and become like those other girls."

"Lida, why isn't our town punishing those women for their promiscuity?"

"There are too many of them."

"If Sabila behaved like any of them, would she be punished?"

"Aye, Neef, she would."

"Then what's the difference?"

"Our people expect more from those who have been taught at The School."

"That isn't fair."

"That's how it works, Neef."

"Lida, do you think that the men at Navidad are Yocahu?"

Lida looked up from her weaving.

"For a long time, that was my greatest hope. I wanted them to protect us from the foreigners, whom your grandfather said would destroy us. But I now realize that such dreams cannot materialize, unless we, ourselves, work for them. I believe that our fathers, who lived with Yocahu, had exercised efforts to earn that utopia; but the later generations forgot all about the hard work it required and only remembered the utopia. And in time, they formed philosophies that it was their right to regain those ideals, even if they were unearned, because they practiced lower standards."

"Lida, from the beginning, Basamanaco never believed the foreigners were gods, and he's firmer about it, now that they have caused so much commotion throughout the island and have raped many women."

"I know, Neef. I know my husband even better than you do. The men at Navidad also have made it hard for me to believe in them. There were many times when I saw that they had no power to help themselves. When they contracted *yaya*, they called upon me for help. But the brews I administered to them could never cure any of them, like they do our people. Instead, their sores developed into warts and became extremely painful and oozing, especially around their private parts. Recently, one of them even went mad, before *yaya* finally killed him."

Neef sighed, as he took his crutches and rose to his feet.

"Lida, I'm tired of discussing this problem. I'm going to look for Sabila, right now. I'd like to tell her about her latest marriage proposal."

He left the *bohío* and hobbled down a path toward the forest, in the direction he had always seen his sister heading. As the forest thickened, underbrush extended into the path in front of him and bumped into his legs. Occasionally, a parrot cawed, as it soared through the humid, warm air and disappeared into the verdant vegetation. As he continued along the path, he suddenly heard distant laughter coming from a man and woman. As it rose and fell, he discerned that the woman's voice was Sabila's.

A chill shot through him. *Sabila is with a man!*

Neef knew well that this was a taboo for an unmarried princess. He grew afraid of what this might mean and decided not to investigate any further, for he would rather not know whether his fears were correct. He turned abruptly to return home. As he started toward town, he could not help but glance into a clearing. There, he saw his sister leaning against a tree, as her arms encircled one of the Pedros of Navidad. This Pedro was one of the younger and better-looking men at the fort, and he had his face buried in his sister's neck, as he fondled and kissed her.

Neef stifled a gasp and looked away. With his arms trembling, he continued toward town. As his mind wracked in turmoil, he stumbled upon a root, but caught himself against a tree trunk. In his effort to keep his balance, he hit a low branch and snapped it in two, but he quickly straightened himself up, and proceeded.

"Neef!"

When Sabila called, he knew that she had heard the branch breaking, but he continued to walk, as if nothing was out of the ordinary. He heard her running, and soon, she caught up with him and grabbed at him so abruptly, that he lost his footing, dropped his crutches, and fell backwards. He reached for a bush to keep from hitting the ground, but its thin branches broke beneath his weight, and before he knew it, he was lying on his back and was looking up into Sabila's panic-stricken face. As she knelt over him, clinging to him, he felt her fingernails digging into his arm. Tears smeared the paints on her face and caused her to no longer resemble that cultured lady, who once held him in awe, when she stepped off a canoe that brought her to the Kingdom of Marién, after completing her time at the School of the Princes. Nor was she that innocent girl, who had left the Fertile Kingdom at the age of ten. Instead, he saw in her eyes that she was now a woman, with knowledge that went beyond either the traditions of the Tainos of Quisqueya or of the School of the Princes.

"I saw you looking at us!" Sabila shouted. "Promise to never, never tell on me."

Because her fingernails were hurting him, Neef was unable to reply.

When he could finally speak again, he said, "You don't need to hang on to me, Sabila. I would never tell anyone about you. Never."

Sabila then allowed him to sit up, but she still clung to him.

"You must understand that I cannot help the way I feel about Pedro. What I feel is so intense that it cannot be wrong."

"My sister, if what you are doing is right, then why must you hide?"

"Pedro is not just any man, Neef, but he is a *zemie*. Do you understand? A *ZEMIE!* And I love him."

"Is Pedro the reason why you did not want to marry Prince Chinya?"

"I can't accept anyone else, but Pedro."

"Sabila, I'm bewildered. You said that you love Pedro. But I have never been taught about that kind of love. I get a feeling that this is not the same kind of love as the *Yocahuan love* that we have known all of our lives. Ever since the foreigners arrived, I've heard many of the single girls talking about *love*, just as you are. I don't know that kind of love. I've been taught about love for my parents, love for my king, love for our *zemies*, love for my family, and even love for my fellow townsfolk. But Sabila, your kind of love puzzles me."

"You are puzzled, because on Quisqueya, we are taught that any kind of natural attraction between a man and a woman who are unmarried, is undesirable, and if it happens, it must be squelched, for the choices of our parents or matchmakers must come first. But this kind of love is acceptable on the other islands, where people are allowed to choose whom they wish to marry. This kind of love didn't use to flow freely on Quisqueya, where parents chose marriage partners, but since the foreigners came, they have opened our eyes. And now, this love has rapidly spread everywhere."

"So that means, this love that so overpowers you is irrational and independent of right or wrong."

Sabila tightened her grip on Neef's arm.

"Neef, promise, that you will never tell."

"I promise, Sabila. Trust me. I told you before that I would be quiet."

Finally, Sabila released him, and soon afterwards, Pedro came over and put his arm around her. Neef noticed how gently he spoke to her. His manners were not as harsh as those of some of the other men at Navidad. In a heavy accent and broken sentences, Pedro told Sabila to be gentle to her brother, for he was just a boy. But as kind as Pedro was, he appeared to be unaware that he was jeopardizing Sabila's safety and ignorant of why she was in such turmoil that Neef now knew about them.

As Neef picked up his crutches, he saw in Sabila's eyes that she now trusted him that he would keep her secret.

When Neef returned to the *bohio*, he found Lida still weaving at her loom. He sat and watched her for a long time. Finally he spoke.

"Lida, Basamanaco told me a while back that he didn't want to marry a giant from Guanine. He said that he wanted to marry you."

"That's right, Neef."

"Did he marry you for love?"

Lida looked at him in surprise. Then, she burst into laughter.

"Look at me. I'm not a beautiful woman. My jaw is too big, my hair is too thin, my breasts are too small, and my voice is too loud. If anybody wants to marry me for what I am, it must be for love."

"Basamanaco sees many things in you that he loves, Lida."

His words caused Lida to blush and giggle, as if she were a young girl again. Neef stared at her in amazement, for he had never seen her act this way before, and he did not think that she had it in her, to behave in this manner.

18

When Mateo grew weary of reading, he crawled out of his hiding place to stretch his legs. As he crossed the courtyard of Navidad with his Bible tucked beneath his arm, he turned his head to glance through the open gate and saw a Christian approaching the fort. This man had left Navidad weeks before, and now he was returning. An Indian woman was walking by his side, and she was extremely beautiful. In fact, she was the important looking woman Mateo once observed arriving in a canoe a few months back, who acted as if he was related to the crippled boy. The woman smiled at Mateo as she and Pedro entered the fort.

"*Hola*, Mateo," Pedro said. "Is the captain around?"

Like the rest of the Christians, Pedro was now lax with his dress, and he no longer trimmed his beard or wore a shirt.

"He's in his room *señor*."

Pedro knocked at the door of Diego de Arana's office. It opened slightly.

"Señor Capitán, I wish for ye to marry us."

"Eh? I marry none of my men to an Indian."

"But th' Indian priests will not marry us, either. Ye must understand, Sabila's not any woman. She's a princess. I want her to bear my children."

"Then let her have yer children. But not in marriage."

"But *señor...*"

"Ye know where I stand on this issue."

And then the door closed.

Mateo saw perplexity sweep across the woman's face. And then she began to weep, while Pedro comforted her.

"Sabila, Sabila, I love ye. I promise I will bring ye back to Castile with me."

And then they left Navidad.

As Mateo watched after them, wondering what would happen to Pedro and his woman, he remembered what Captain Arana said to the other Christians, who had also approached him to marry them to Indian women. *Be careful with what ye do. Ye are from a good family. To marry an Indian is steppin' down from yer social rank. It's better to just love th' women here 'n have as much fun with them as ye can, for when th' Admiral returns, ye cannot bring them back to Castile.*

And after a week passed, Mateo did not see Pedro and his woman again. Although here at Fort Navidad he lived apart from the villages, Mateo was well aware that throughout the island, a new race was emerging, for he saw from his hiding place, Indian women carrying babies with European-like features; many whom he knew would never know their fathers.

One day, as Mateo crawled into his hideout to scan the horizon and read his favorite stories in the Bible, he heard a commotion from the Indian village below. As he peered through the slats, he saw a crowd of Tainos, pushing toward their central plaza. The people were shouting and waving sticks in the air. They were tugging at something, but there were so many of them around that object, that Mateo could not see what it was. Never before did he see so much agitation among those people. As the crowd parted slightly, Mateo discerned that they were dragging a human being. A woman suddenly screamed and overpowered the shouts of the crowd. And Mateo then realized that that object was a woman. She was howling and weeping, but because she was bound so tightly, she could not break away.

One of the men who led the group began to yell above the crowd. As he waved his stick, his shouts further incensed the others and caused them to grow wild and scream louder. As Mateo watched this scene, he suddenly recognized who that woman was. She was Sabila — Pedro's princess! Something dreadful was happening to her!

Mateo dropped his book, crawled out of his hiding place, and ran.

"Captain Arana! Captain Arana! They're goin' to hurt Sabila! Come quickly."

The captain was sitting with his arm around a woman and ignored him.

Mateo did not feel that he had time to explain more to the captain, so he turned and raced out of Navidad. Soon he was clamoring down the hill toward the village. By the time he reached the plaza, the crowd had doubled in size.

"Leave her alone!" Mateo yelled in the Indian tongue.

A few in the crowd glanced over at him, surprised that he could speak their language, but then, they turned toward Sabila again. Mateo pushed past the people and grabbed hold of Sabila. He saw her terrified face and yanked at her, but could not pull her free. Angry eyes surrounded him, and now that he was close to these people, he saw that their sticks were carefully filed into extremely sharp points.

Sabila squirmed beneath the cords.

"Pedro! Pedro!"

"I'll get you free!" Mateo yelled in Tainan.

"Go away, Yocahu boy."

Sabila wept desperately. When Mateo could not untie the knots, he tried again to pull the princess away, but the people were stronger, and the crowd began to raise their pointed sticks. Then before his very eyes, Mateo saw the angry crowd plunging their sticks *en mass*, deep into Sabila's flesh. Sabila shrieked. Horrified, Mateo hung on to her, as her screams rang through the plaza. While her blood splattered across his body and face, he felt her stiffen and then relax, as she turned silent.

In shock, Mateo looked up into the enraged faces. As the people left their sticks lodged in Sabila's lifeless form, they then began spitting at her.

"Death to you, slut!"

Mateo comprehended every word they said. He was surprised that now that he understood what they were saying, their words no longer appeared to be gentle.

And then he heard shouting in the distance. Soon the man, who was much taller than the rest of the people, came running into their midst. He was the person who resembled the man to whom Mateo had given his wooden horse in Juana. And when that man saw what had happened to Sabila, he knelt over her and wept.

"Sabila, Sabila. What have they done to you? My precious little girl, my little flower, who always sat welcomes for me whenever I came to your village."

The people grew quiet, and they slunk away, as if they held a special respect for that man. With amazing strength, the large man ripped the cords off of Sabila, and then, he gently lifted her lifeless body into his arms, as he wept unashamedly.

"Slut!" someone in the crowd yelled.

"Whore!" another said.

As the crowd regained its fury and cried out further condemnations, someone said, "Basamanaco, leave her body alone. That filthy girl got what she deserved."

"Why did you kill her?" said Basamanaco. "Other women around have also been sleeping with Christians."

The crowd ignored Basamanaco's question, and someone then said, "Did she get what she deserved?"

The crowd roared.

"Aye! She was educated at The School and should have been an example to us!"

"I thought you believed those foreigners were *zemies*, who could not commit any crime, so Sabila could not have done any wrong, when she slept with one of them."

"We were wrong, Basamanaco. They were never *zemies*, but evil *mapoyas*! Who else, could have created all of those bastards, who are now being born everywhere among us?"

Basamanaco began walking away with Sabila still in his arms. With tears staining his face, he turned to the crowd again.

"Don't you know that these foreigners bring with them new times and new changes, and because of them, we must now accept those, who break practices that go contrary to our traditions?"

"Quiet, trader. Sabila received her rightful punishment."

"Aye, she knew better."

As he still held Sabila, Basamanaco continued.

"No matter what we feel is right or wrong, we now face a new era, when we must exercise a greater love of Yocahu than we ever had. We must forgive those, who no longer keep our values, even if they are part of our royalty. We must also forgive those, who are not of our royalty, who also break our laws."

The people encircled Basamanaco.

"Out of our way, Basamanaco. Let us take care of her body, ourselves. She doesn't deserve a proper burial. Let her spirit roam the earth, as a restless *mapoya*."

As the people charged at Basamanaco, Mateo could not believe the vicious behavior he witnessed, for he had believed that they were a peaceful and loving folk. But Basamanaco pushed the crowd aside, with a strength that surprised Mateo.

"Is Sabila the only woman, who illegally slept with a foreigner? Is she the first?"

"What does a trader, like you, know how a woman of high breed should behave?"

"Sabila is not alone," shouted Basamanaco. "You, Mula. Your daughter just bore a son, with skin much fairer than ours. Tuamari, who fathered the girl child, who was born in your family?"

A few people squirmed.

"I know that the foreigners raped our women, but I suspect that most of these babies are not results of rapes, but results of promiscuity. I suspect there were also taboos broken many times, when no babies were conceived, and the guilty ones believed that they were free from all consequences. But let the ancestral bones in our baskets rattle and absorb all that we do, whether good or bad, that they may lie as witnesses against both our righteous and evil, secret acts."

The people grew silent, as Basamanaco stooped to kiss the dead girl on the forehead. He then swallowed to keep from breaking into tears again, before he continued his speech.

"We all know that *yaya* now prevails among the foreigners, and we also know that it did not exist among them when they arrived, and when it attacks them, it is a sure death. But how did they catch this disease? It came from our own people."

Someone stepped forward.

"Curses to Sabila!"

"And to the others?" Basamanaco said. "If you curse her, curse them also."

The crowd repeated more emphatically, "Curses to Sabila!"

The man who led the crowd in shouts added, "Curses to Sabila's family, whoever they are!"

Then he looked across the square toward the crippled boy, who stood some distance away.

"And down with Basamanaco's Crippled Boy! He seems to know her and acts, as if he is related to her."

The crowd then started toward the crippled boy. Mateo saw fear grow in that boy's face for only a moment, but then it left him, and he arose and held himself high with his crutches.

"Go ahead. Kill me as you did Sabila."

Mateo was amazed at his bravery.

And while the people were concentrating on closing in on the crippled boy, Pedro was suddenly among them, but they were so spirited that none of them saw him approach. Pedro was breathing heavily, and his face was wild.

"Where is she? They came 'n yanked her from my arms. Where did they put..."

Pedro's voice trailed off, when he saw Basamanaco holding his lover with sticks protruding from her body. Instinctively, he withdrew his sword, and when the people saw his weapon flashing in the sun, they panicked and scattered. But Basamanaco still remained immovable among them, as Pedro started toward him. As soon as Basamanaco began to speak, Pedro stopped.

"I am her friend. I would never kill Sabila."

Mateo was impressed that Pedro appeared to understand what Basamanaco had said, even if he spoke in the Indian language. As Pedro stared at Sabila's limp body in disbelief, he suddenly stepped backward, swung around, and faced those who had not run away. In a rage, he charged madly into them. As he lashed blindly with his sword, blood flew in every direction, as people howled and fell. Finally, Pedro came to his senses and stopped, as he stared trance-like into space, while men, women and children lay dead around him.

Those who were still alive slunk away, as Pedro stood with fresh blood on his sword, as if he had not comprehended what he had just done. All this time, Basamanaco stood bravely, watching him, with Sabila in his arms. And far away, the man who had instigated the shouts against Sabila shrank from both of them.

Mateo walked over to Pedro, and when he reached him, he found that his friend needed no coaxing to follow him. But first, Mateo wiped the blood off the sword, replaced it into its sheath, and finally, began leading Pedro toward Navidad. With shock in his eyes, Pedro followed wordlessly. As they climbed the hill toward the fort, Pedro finally spoke.

"What have I done?"

He was not really talking to Mateo, but more to himself.

"I went crazy when I saw her dead. I did not mean to kill so many of them."

Mateo turned and looked at him. He couldn't help liking him.

"Pedro, I think that ye are th' most civilized Christian on this island, for ye've truly loved a woman for who she was, whether or not she was a Christian or an Indian."

And together, they continued their climb up to Navidad.

19

Canaobo the Fierce slammed his fist into his hand.

"Anacoana, I've had all I can take! King Guacanagarí refuses to admit that those men at Navidad are the foreigners, who have come to destroy our island! Does he realize how dangerous it is for him to continue to treat them as if they are Yocahu? He's jeopardizing the safety of the entire island!"

It was rare when Canaobo the Fierce came to visit Anacoana from his Kingdom of the Mines, and when he did, he often shouted about the problems of the island. As his voice rose, the baby in Anacoana's arms squirmed in its sleep. Two little girls drew close to her, with their eyes round with fear.

"Hush, my love. Thou art scaring our children."

"When will he start defending his people, I tell you? How much more abuse can he endure from those foreigners?"

Anacoana reached over to him and caressed his shoulder.

"My darling, remember that *the love* is strong with King Guacanagarí. "

"*The love?* Bah! *Cowardly* is a better word to describe him. If he is too afraid to declare war upon those strangers at Navidad, why doesn't he ask me to come to help him? I can solve his problems. I can kill every man at that fort in just a few hours, I tell you. Must my men and I march there uninvited to fight those barbarians?"

His voice awoke the baby, and when it began to wail, Nila immediately appeared in the hut to take it away, and as she carried it through the doorway, the two little girls jumped up and ran after her.

"Father's being scary again," one of them said.

When Anacoana and Canaobo the Fierce were alone, Canaobo paced back and forth, while Anacoana sat watching him, carefully thinking of what to say to calm him down. She closed her eyes, breathed deeply, and then walked over to him.

"My love, anger is not good for thee. It taketh away thy good thoughts and maketh thee become out of control."

"But I must express how I feel."

"Thou canst say the same things in gentler ways."

Anacoana placed her cheek against her husband's bare back.

"It is unwise to fight those men at Navidad, for I hear that their weapons can quickly put an end to all of us. Besides, suppose they are Yocahu?"

Canaobo waved his arms in the air.

"*Hui*! How can anyone who rape women be *Yocahu*? Do *zemies* fight and kill each other as often as those men do? Would Yocahu kill thirty-five men, women and children with a sword to protect a woman, who tramples taboos?"

Anacoana winced, when he spoke of Sabila.

"That woman whom thou speakest of was a beautiful and sensitive person. She was only ten years old, when she first came to The School."

"I tell you, she and those men at Navidad have defiled and mutilated the very goodness of what the people of this island have struggled for generations to preserve. Those men have created bastards upon this island, faster than schools of fish can multiply, and nobody has the heart to strangle any of them, when they are born."

"Canaobo, Canaobo. King Guacanagarí and his people are doing the right thing. If they endure all their trials now, they will be among the greatest people in the world someday. They are applying the correct principles with *the love*."

"Love? Bah! And let these foreigners take over the entire island? The people here have lived too long trying to keep peace. Now they do not even know how to protect themselves."

"Canaobo, we shall win with *the love*. If we fight, we will lose our status with Yocahu, and our *zemies* will cease to protect us."

Canaobo slammed his fist into his palm again.

"Stupidity! Stupidity! Stupidity! I tell you, we must declare war upon the fort! Can't you see that? Even the people on the other islands and the countries of *Guanine* have heard of those men, and fear sweeps across all of their lands. None of them want those men to come to their countries. Every day messengers bring news to me that even the Caribs are making plans to come to attack Navidad to prevent those men from reaching their islands."

"The Caribs? Can those cannibals withstand the thunder weapons and swords of Yocahu?" Anacoana's voice began to rise, because her husband's temper was finally getting to her. "The Caribs are barbarians. We must never fight as barbarians."

Anacoana closed her eyes. For eight years, she gave Canaobo the Fierce her unconditional love, but there were times when she was perplexed by his rash ways. Although his great intelligence often caused her to forget that he was never fully educated at any school for princes, she still cringed at his fascination for fighting, particularly when he mentioned wars that he lost; for at times, he even lauded his enemies for their victory over him.

"Their sabotage was brilliant, Anacoana!" Canaobo would say when he described his foes, as she listened to him in horror. Even when he was defeated, he would laugh heartily and say, "Ha, ha, they gave us a solid beating!"

"How canst thou laugh when thou hast lost a battle? There is no humor when so many of thine own men have died."

"But it was a beautiful battle, Anacoana."

When her husband was not angry, she felt that her efforts to teach him of the Yocahuan principals were winning, but just when she thought that she was finally beginning to see his temper mellowing, the foreigners arrived on the other side of the island, and his temper started exploding again.

As Anacoana stood before her husband, deep in thought, she barely heard him speaking to her.

"If you think fighting the men at Navidad is wrong, what do you suggest?"

Anacoana snapped back to the present. For the first time that day, she saw Canaobo the Fierce looking at her with a humble expression, as he waited for her to give him her opinion. This was an opportunity she must jump at.

"I think we should hold a great, solemn assembly, my love."

"A what?"

"A large conference, my dearest. The kind that we *caciques* hold in our royal *bohios* everyday, with our own panel of advisers, but this time, it should be a meeting involving all the major *caciques* of this island."

Canaobo stared at her in disbelief.

"But we *caciques* can never agree upon anything. Such a conference would mean that I must meet with Guacanagarí, but he is still angry with me for taking two of his wives last year. And Guarionex can never get along with Queen Higuanamá. He's been calling her a wrinkly, old *mapoya*, ever since she…"

"This meeting will help the rulers of this land, to learn how to work with each other. All the *caciques* of the major kingdoms — the Fertile Kingdom, the Kingdom of the Mines, the Kingdom of the Great Old Lady, the Kingdom of Marién and the Mother Kingdom — should decide what to do with the men at Navidad."

"But Anacoana, I tell you, such a meeting on this island would be futile. Do you realize how much easier it would be, for me to go over and attack Navidad?"

When Canaobo saw the determination in Anacoana's eyes, he finally said, "Very well. Let us have that meeting."

Anacoana bent over and kissed her husband behind the ear.

"Let me tell Beheccio about our plans," she said.

After she signaled a servant to fetch her brother, she turned and looked deeply into her husband's eyes.

"Hui, my love. I perceive great frustration in thee. Art thou merely agreeing with me, because thou lovest me?"

Canaobo the Fierce turned away and said nothing, for he yearned for a good fight to settle the problems of the island, because the warrior within him that was nurtured since he was born, could not be squelched.

20

From his hiding place in Fort Navidad, Mateo scanned the horizon for sails billowing in the wind, or any other signs that would tell him that the Admiral was returning. As a breeze pushed through the slats and swept across his body, he again realized that he would never tire of the salty air from the sea that now refreshed him. Today he sat here for hours behind these bags of grain, and as always, he saw no ships.

Finally Mateo plunged his hand deep between two bags of wheat, and when his fingers hit the Admiral's Bible, he pulled it out and carefully turned its wrinkly pages. It was nine months, since the Admiral had told him to teach the gospel to the heathens, but he still did not know these Indians well enough to convert them. Even if he now understood their language, they stayed in their village, and he remained in this fort. As the pages of the Bible fell to the book of Zechariah, he was grateful that it was printed in Spanish, for although the monks taught him some Latin and Greek, those languages remained extremely cumbersome to him.

Today he felt particularly isolated in Navidad, because ever since Pedro massacred the Indians, there was a growing resentment among those people. Their eyes had turned cold. More of the women had returned to Guarica and chose to have nothing to do with their lovers. Yet there were still two or three of them, who remained loyal to the Christians.

The other day, he overheard the few women who remained in Navidad whispering about a *cacique* named Canaobo the Fierce. They said that he was planning to attack this fort, but because this king was a womanizer, they did not need to worry about being killed if he came, since it was just the Christians he would be after. In fact, they said that he might even take them back to be his wives.

"Did you hear that Canaobo the Fierce has killed several Christians on this island?" one of them said.

"How many did he kill?"

"Two in his own Kingdom of the Mines last week. They were living with several women, and he was furious that they had impregnated them."

"Then he would hate me, too," said one of the women, as she patted her belly.

They snickered.

"How soon do you think Canaobo the Fierce will get here?"

"Who can tell?"

When Mateo tried to share what he heard with Captain Diego, his words met deaf ears, as the captain sat shirtless, unshaven, and unshod.

"Come, come, Mateo," Diego scoffed. "How can ye possibly understand th' Indian language? Ye never set foot out of this fort, except for th' one 'n only time when ye ran into Guarica to try to save that Indian woman. Besides, who th' hell is Canaobo th' Fierce, anyway? How could he possibly fight when th' people of this island do not even own weapons? If we were on another island, I would fear for my life, but here, on Española, th' people could never knock ye to th' ground. If anybody gave them a bow 'n arrow, those *cretinos* wouldn't even know what to do with them. Instead of shootin' th' arrow, they'd probably try to shoot th' bow, instead."

"But *señor*, I heard that this *cacique* fights better than a madman, because he 'n his men came from another island, where th' people there are taught to be good warriors."

"Look, boy. If any one of these people turned against us, we have our guns. Ye've heard what everybody's been sayin.' One of us Christians can kill two hundred of them in a minute!"

With his ears burning, Mateo turned abruptly away. It was rare, when he ever saw the captain alone, for he always had an Indian woman next to him, and now, when he finally found a chance to warn him, he laughed to his face. As Mateo stomped toward the door, he thought upon how he noticed the beginnings of a sore to the side of one of Diego's nipples. It was the same kind that Guerrero developed all over his body just before he died. But Guerrero's sores grew into enormous warts, and he went blind and was yelling things that made no sense.

"I wish somebody would listen to me," Mateo muttered.

As he reached the doorway, Diego called after him.

"Hey, *mi hijo!* Stop takin' everythin' so hard. We all like ye, but we can't be alarmed over every little thing, as ye are. Ye've been worryin' every minute since we've come to this island. Look around ye, boy. We're in a paradise ye'll never have again, once we return to Castile."

"But *señor*, I do look around," Mateo called back. "I see that we have no dignity left, 'n many of us have forgotten how to act like human bein's."

Now that Mateo was back in his hiding place, his mind was greatly disturbed. He leaned forward, stared through the slats again, and studied the waves pushing garlands of kelp to and fro below. He was surprised when he realized that he might actually miss this scene, after the Admiral brought him back home.

Just then, he saw something move on the horizon. He grew alert. There were dark spots advancing toward the island. He could see four, eight, no, ten of them approaching. As those objects drew near, Mateo soon discerned that they were canoes, and their passengers were paddling so fast that their boats whipped over the water. As the canoes came nearer, he could see that the people on them were wearing hats with large, dark feathers, and their faces were harder and more angular than the gentle features of the Tainos.

A raspy sounding conch shell soon trumpeted from one of the vessels.

Suddenly, sounds of panic burst from Guarica. Mateo turned to his left and saw that the Indians were fleeing in the direction of the mountains. They were screaming only one word: *Caribs! Caribs!* Then they grew silent, as they ran, and Mateo saw torches glowing from their towers to warn the other villages.

Caribs? Mateo thought. *Wasn't that th' word th' captured natives on th' Santa Maria kept repeatin' to Admiral Colón?* He tried to remember further and recalled how the Admiral did not believe any of the stories those natives acted out.

Wait a moment. Aren't th' Caribs th' people whom th' Indians said in their pantomimes ate humans? Mateo glanced back at the approaching canoes. *Ye mean, th' Caribs actually exist 'n are not somethin' th' natives made up?*

Mateo jumped up. He must warn the fort!

Soon Mateo was running across the courtyard, shouting until he turned crimson.

"Caribs! Caribs!"

No one in the fort stirred.

Mateo ran over to Diego. He was sitting upon a barrel and entering notes into his journal. As carefree as he had become, he still remembered his journal every day. Diego casually glanced up.

"What's stirrin' ye up now, Mateo? Didn't I tell ye to enjoy yerself?"

"Caribs are comin'! Quick, run!"

"Who?"

"Th' cannibals! They're attackin'!"

"Mateo, I told ye to stop worryin'."

Frustrated, Mateo turned and ran toward the entrance of Navidad, so he could escape to the mountains as the Tainos were. When he reached the open doorway, he glanced down at the beach. The Caribs were already close to landing, and there was no time for him to get to the mountains, without them seeing him.

"Caribs! Caribs!" he yelled again.

He turned around and ran back into the fort.

"Get yer guns, men. Fire up th' cannons!"

No one moved. A sailor lay on his back upon a blanket, sunning himself. He adjusted a pillow, which he placed over his face to protect his eyes from the sun.

"Caaaareeeeeebs!"

The conch sounded again.

"Hear that? Caribs, men, Caribs!"

Mateo attempted to run through the gate again, but several of the canoes had already landed, and he could see the Caribs pouring out of their vessels. Some of them sped across the beach and were beginning to charge uphill. Mateo pushed the gates shut and secured their locks. In panic, he ran in circles, and then, he scanned the courtyard for a safe place to conceal himself. He ran past Diego, into his office, but found that the pieces of furniture in this room were too scanty to offer him any safety. He tore through the fort, searching for closets, secret compartments, storage areas he could fit into, but found nothing.

Th' kitchen, he thought. *Maybe I can hide in th' kitchen.*

He ran there, but as he looked around, he saw that the cupboards were too small for him to squeeze into, and too poorly built, to even hold his weight. He returned to the courtyard. The ground vibrated now from the thuds of running feet outside of Navidad, which grew louder and louder.

Th' bags of grain! My hidin' place!

Mateo ran toward to his hiding spot, got down on all fours, and squeezed between the bags. With all of his strength, he pulled the burlap together behind him. Then he crouched low, burying his face into the ground, not daring to look through the slats in front of him.

Thump thumping surrounded Navidad. The Caribs pounded at the door. Their voices were loud, brash. There was a crash and sounds of wood splintering. And then the enemy entered.

Mateo heard the Christians beginning to shout. Metal swished across metal, as swords slid out of sheaths. But even then, Mateo knew that most of the Christians were neither armed nor prepared for this attack. He heard thuds and clubs slamming upon flesh. Then he heard screams, Christian screams, whose voices were in panic — Diego de Arana, Pedro, the cook, the man who was basking himself in the sun, others. They were in shock, for too long, they enjoyed only a loving, peaceful people, who pampered them with favors. But now, their swords clattered across the floor.

"*Dios mío*! These savages are damn good fighters!"

"Fight, men fight! Don't let them kill us all!"

Mateo felt braver now, and cautiously, he peered through a crack between the sacks. He saw Marco — Marco, the physician, the man who stayed up all night when the Christians developed chills and fevers. A Carib was aiming a spear at him. Mateo had seen that type of spear when he was on Juana, for the natives there showed the Admiral similar darts, spears, and arrows with that peculiar design. Mateo realized now that at that time, he understood those natives more than he gave himself credit for, but the information he perceived was so bizarre, that he quickly dismissed those ideas. When the Indians on Juana had gestured, it appeared that they said that the Caribs ate people, and those were the weapons they left behind after they attacked; they also gestured that the Caribs poisoned the tips of their weapons, so when they pierced anyone, the victims died instantly.

From the look of horror on Marco's face, Mateo wondered if he also remembered those types of weapons, as he held his arms outward in self-defense. Now, his voice quivered.

"No, no...don't use that on me! Noooo..."

The Carib flung his spear. Mateo heard a whack, as if the spear hit something solid, such as bone. Marco staggered backwards, and then fell to the ground.

The screams of women echoed everywhere. Mateo saw the warriors tying them up and flinging them across their shoulders, as if they were weightless. As they ignored the shrieks, the Caribs ran with those women down to the beach. Through the slats, Mateo could see them securing the women to trees. One of the women was bawling pretty hard.

"I don't want to be your concubine."

The cannibal smacked her unconscious with a club, and she grew limp.

Then Mateo realized that he no longer heard shouts coming from the Christians in Navidad. Instead, he heard the Caribs crashing objects about, as they wandered through the fort. Their language was not the same as the Tainos', but he picked up an occasional word, which was similar to their language. He could tell that they were yelling obscenities. He pieced together a few sentences, which they kept repeating, such as, *don't leave a single bastard alive; we can't have them coming to our island and bringing their curses*; and, *where's the boy — has anyone seen that stinker?*

Finally, the Caribs left the fort, saying, "Let's look elsewhere. We didn't get them all."

Mateo looked down at the beach. The Carib canoes were still on the sand, and the women were still tied near them. And when he saw no Caribs, he knew that they were wandering around outside of Navidad. It was a long while, before Mateo saw any Caribs again.

When they returned, they removed the women from the trees and tossed them, bound-up, into their canoes. Then they withdrew their vessels and blew their conch several times. Mateo saw neither Tainos from the village nor Christians with them. Instead, only women from Navidad were on board. As the cannibals paddled their canoes out into the sea, Mateo remained motionless, until long after their black dots disappeared over the horizon.

When Mateo finally crawled out of hiding, a silence dominated the courtyard, as a peculiar odor hovered in the air. He soon grew brave enough to allow his eyes to slowly glide across the bodies strewn throughout Navidad. Some of the Christians were plopped in grotesque positions, while others seemed only to be asleep, but most of them were mangled, with blood smeared across them.

"Señor Arana? Pedro?"

Mateo's voice croaked. No one responded. He heard not a single groan to indicate that anyone was alive or injured.

Mateo moved with caution throughout the fort. He saw the cook sprawled across the table on his back, with an awkward expression upon his face and an arrow penetrating his neck. Diego de Arana lay across the threshold of his room, as a poisonous spear protruded his side. He was no longer laughing, but at least, he looked at peace. Pedro, the only man in this fort who showed respect for Mateo, lay face down at the far end of the court in a pool of blood, with three poisonous darts in his shoulder, chest, and groin.

When Mateo went to him, Pedro appeared to have been dead for a long time, for he was stiff and cold.

Mateo turned and staggered among the scattered forms. A sailor lay in front of him; a chalkier was to his far right; the tailor sprawled across the plumber; and Marco had fallen with a spear between the ribs. There were bodies smashed from clubs and bodies with arrows, darts, or spears in them. As Mateo's vision grew blurry, he approached Pedro again. He thought of how this man had once loved an Indian princess. He knelt before his friend and sobbed.

He looked up with crazed eyes, for suddenly another scene filled his brain. It occurred years before when he was five years old, when a mob slaughtered his family. He was the only one left alive in his home, and he ran through its rooms, seized by panic. Days later, when the house stunk, Papa came and rescued him.

Mateo turned away from Pedro and rose to his feet. He could no longer endure the silence around him.

"Everybody, wake up!"

The next thing he knew, just as when he was five years old, he was running through the rooms of Navidad, as if he were insane, screaming until his lungs felt as if they were on fire. And when he stopped, exhausted and panting, he noticed that the Indians from the village had entered the fort. They kept their distance, though, as they stared at him. They said nothing, but their eyes were red, as if they were crying for him.

Mateo slunk away.

"Get away from me, ye miserable savages!"

More Indians appeared. No longer were their eyes full of hatred. Many of them were young women, who appeared to be only a few years older than he was. They wore only loincloths. When the Christians were alive, they used to cast coy looks at them. The young women wept bitterly, now. For the first time, Mateo realized that these women actually loved the Christians. He saw them walk over to certain corpses and stroke their hair, kissing them, as they allowed tears to fall upon the dead faces.

But Mateo still kept away. One of the Indians finally came to him. He was the man who was much larger than the rest of his people, whom the Indians called *Basamanaco*. He was the one who had carried Sabila the day she was killed. Mateo noticed that sometimes, this man left on a large canoe packed with goods with other men and did not return for many days.

Now Basamanaco spoke, and his voice was gentle.

"We will bury your dead for you," he said. "We will give your people a grand funeral, as all good men deserve, so their *opias* can rest in *Coaibai*."

Mateo heard Basamanaco address him as *the Yocahu boy*, and the kindness in his voice put him at ease. Yet he still backed away, filled with suspicion that these people would want to kill him also.

And all this time, the young women did not cease from weeping.

As Mateo looked upon the Indian faces, he could not bear to remain at Navidad any longer. He trusted no one and wished to be run away.

How can I survive until Admiral Colón arrives? he thought.

He remembered that biscuits and dried meat were stored upon the shelves in the kitchen. He would take as many of those supplies as he could, and then he would go out into the forest and build a shelter somewhere. He would wait for Admiral Colón there. He thought of the other Christians, who were scattered throughout Española. *Will I be able to contact them?*

Mateo spotted a cloth bag strewn upon the ground, which the Caribs must have discovered and discarded, when they rampaged the fort. He snatched it up and headed toward the food supplies. As he filled the bag, he heard the Indians shuffling about, as they lifted the bodies of the Christians to carry them out of the fort. On the other side of the wall, he could hear them beginning to dig graves. With the sack full of food, Mateo tossed it over his shoulder and turned toward the entrance of Navidad. As he passed the Indians, he felt their eyes following him. No hatred emanated from them, only pity. He felt compelled to turn back, to help them dig graves for his friends. But instead, he looked straight ahead toward the forest.

Once he reached the wilds, he stumbled across several corpses of Christians. They were the men who had left Navidad after the big fight. Judging from the clothes on one of them, Mateo was certain that he had found Guillermo. He looked as if he had been dead for some time, so the Caribs could not have killed him. As he walked on, he found other bodies scattered in the underbrush that looked as if they had been dead for a while. All of them were Christians; none were Indians.

Mateo braced himself against a tree for a second and looked back in the direction of Navidad. Should he tell the Indians about these other bodies, so they could also bury them? But he resumed his walk, reasoning that eventually, they would be found.

When dusk began to fall, Mateo already was deep in the forest. Suddenly, a thought shot through him.

That warrior king named Canaobo th' Fierce. He never attacked us! Maybe it was he, who killed those men in th' forest. Did th' Caribs beat him to Navidad?

And then a chill shot through him.

Why, I am th' only Christian left alive on Española! What would happen, if Canaobo th' Fierce found out about me? Would he come to kill me also? Or maybe, th' Caribs will return 'n will beat him to it.

21

When King Guarionex heard of the Carib attack on Fort Navidad, he immediately sent word that he wanted his son Neef out of the Kingdom of Marién and expressed a desire for him to become educated in the ways of princes in the Mother Kingdom. So Basamanaco had to take him away to the School of the Princes in Anacoana's courts. Basamanaco knew that Neef's absence would create a void in Lida's life, but when he returned from the Mother Kingdom, he was relieved to see that she had been noticing that there was much more work to do around their home, and she had been keeping herself busy.

As the summer months approached and brought the rainy season, it also became time for Lida's deep cleaning, and Basamanaco was pleased that she did not remain confined to their *bohio* or allow any pouring rain to interfere with her work. For she inspected every corner of their home for flaws, wove new hava mats, and replaced old ones, whether or not it was necessary. She also examined every gourd and wooden bowl for cracks and chips and replaced each one, even if they all looked new. And when Basamanaco was away on his trips, he often returned to discover that she had checked for weak spots in the grass walls and thatched roof of their home, and sometimes in heavy downpour, she had even performed the necessary repairs herself.

But one day, when Basamanaco was at home, Lida entered their *bohio*, dragging a huge sack behind her. He gasped in horror when he saw her with it, for he had purposely hidden it from her, since he knew that she was a practical woman and would hold no value in its contents. That bag held his treasures, which he had collected throughout the years. Although it did not matter to him, whether or not she threw out the hava mats, he could not part with any of the items in this bag.

"Someone left this sack in a hole in the ground behind our *bohio*," she said. "And they covered it over with rocks."

As she dragged the sack to the middle of the floor, Basamanaco watched her in silence, as she untied the palm fiber cords at its mouth. Then she turned it upside down to empty its contents. But when she snatched up a wooden bowl, fingered its many cracks, and then tossed it aside, he could not remain quiet any longer.

"Lida, please. Don't throw that out. That was my favorite bowl when I was a boy."

"What? These are your items? You have no use for that bowl, anymore."

She then examined an odd looking object that was carved out of wood.

"What sort of animal is this? My, it has such a long neck and long legs. And look at its tail. I've never seen anything like it before."

"It's a horse."

"A what?"

"A horse. The Yocahu boy gave it to me when I met him on Cuba, before he and his men came here to Quisqueya."

"How long do you wish to keep it?"

"I don't intend to ever dump it out. It reminds me of the llamas in the stories my grandfather used to tell me about, that live in the southern lands of Guanine."

"And this?"

Lida pulled out a cloth doll from the pile. It was sewn with tiny, neat stitches.

"A toy for a child? We have no child."

"When I was trading in the Kingdom of the Great Old Lady a long time ago, I had to bargain hard for it."

"Why?"

"I wanted it for our baby."

"What baby?"

"I got it for her when she was still alive."

"Basamanaco..."

"At that time, I thought that our baby would love to have a doll."

Basamanaco turned away, resigned, and headed toward the entrance of the hut.

"Lida, do you need me to gather herbs from the woods for you?"

"In this rain? Of course not."

"I happen to like the rain. What do you need for your brews that you make for the sick?"

"Oh, I suppose I could stand to have more *guayacan* bark."

Basamanaco stepped outside. The rain had let up, but the sky was heavily overcast. As he walked upon the soggy ground, mud squished between his toes. When he reached the forest, the merry sounds the birds were making told him that they were enjoying the wetness, as their chirps and calls resounded around him.

As he walked along, he projected various birdcalls and listened for responses. In the distance, he heard a parrot reply with a love call.

Soon he came across a large tree lying across his path, which strong winds had uprooted up. Broken branches and limbs dangling from other trees surrounded it. As Basamanaco looked upward, he was amazed that all of the guayacans continued to still stand erect and strong, unjostled by any recent storm. Lida often referred to them as *holy trees,* because they possessed unusual magical powers to heal many illnesses that other herbs could not. He carefully studied the guayacans to see which ones possessed the best bark to bring back to Lida.

Suddenly, a raspy cough came from somewhere in the forest. Basamanaco paused and looked around, but saw no one. The cough came again. It sounded as if a child was out here alone, and whoever it was, appeared to be extremely ill.

Now, what would a child be doing out here?

As Basamanaco searched the forest, his eyes fell upon a crudely built shelter hidden among some bushes. It stood beside a tall tree and hovered close to the ground. Because someone had covered it heavily with moss and leaves, it made it difficult to see. As Basamanaco approached that odd structure, lightning lit up the woods, and shortly thereafter, thunder rumbled from far away. He glanced upward and saw that the sky was blacker than moments before and noticed that the birds had turned silent.

From where he stood, he could not see anything within the shelter, but he suspected that the person who had coughed was inside of it. He could tell that inexperienced hands, ignorant of creating anything that could withstand all types of weather, were responsible for building that structure. Basamanaco tiptoed to a spot where he could peep into its entrance. He saw a boy with fair colored hair and fair skin lying inside of it. He resembled the Yocahu boy, who used to live in Fort Navidad. The boy's hair was now drenched and matted close to his head; his robes were wet and torn in places; and his scrawny body shivered as he slept. As Basamanaco came closer, he saw that the boy was breathing heavily through chapped lips, and his skin was feverish and red. Although the boy had placed leaves and moss on the floor to protect his body from the earth, the ground beneath him was so saturated that water was seeping up through the floor covering.

Rain began pelting heavily now, and soon the forest hummed, as if thousands of bees were hitting the leaves that surrounded Basamanaco. More lightning brightened the woods around him, and this time, the top of a fir tree nearby snapped and fell to the ground, leaving a faint odor of smoke. Then thunder, louder than the previous ones, vibrated the boughs above.

As the rain poured, water dripped through the moss of the shelter and sent small streams that hit steadily upon the boy's body. But the boy was unaware of what was happening, and he coughed even more, while trembling in slumber.

Basamanaco frowned. *I need to bring him back to Lida.*

Basamanaco edged closer to the door, as currents began washing over the tops of his feet and splashed against his calves. He stuck his head into the shelter and cupped his hands to his mouth.

"*Hui!*"

The Yocahu boy did not respond.

Basamanaco crouched lower and leaned further into the shelter.

"*Hui!*"

The Yocahu boy hacked a series of coughs.

Basamanaco reached in and shook the boy's feet, but he appeared to be unconscious. As Basamanaco pushed into the shelter, it was a tight squeeze, and when he was inches above the boy, he could feel his fever radiating up toward him. He shook the Yocahu boy again.

The Yocahu boy opened his eyes for a second, and then closed them. When he tried to swallow, he whimpered, and then drifted back to sleep. Basamanaco noticed that his neck was swollen. When he looked around the shelter for the boy's belongings, he saw a strange, black, square-like object in a corner. It was located in perhaps the only dry spot of this structure. Curiously, Basamanaco reached toward that object, and when he got hold of it, it fell open, revealing many thin sheets of strange material that were secured together. Each sheet felt extremely delicate and had strange marks upon them.

When the Yocahu boy whimpered again, Basamanaco replaced the black object, and turned his attention back to him. As he gathered the boy into his arms, he was surprised at how easily it was to lift him, for he was practically weightless. Basamanaco could feel the fire penetrating the boy's wet clothes. Just as he made his way toward the entrance, he stopped, returned, retrieved the strange object with thin sheets in it, and wedged it between his body and the Yocahu boy.

Once outside, Basamanaco rose to his feet with the bony and delicate bundle in his arms. He broke into a run, as the rain fell in torrents and pounded upon his shoulders and back. At that moment, he wished for *chia* seeds to chew on, because he needed something to give him greater stamina to help him run faster to his village. As he glided over the mushy ground, shallow rivers rushed beneath him, and he was glad that the boy was easy to carry.

When Basamanaco finally approached his hut, he found Lida standing at the doorway, as if she was waiting for him a long time. Her eyes widened and jaw fell, when she saw him with the boy.

"*Eh?* What do you have with you?"

"I found him in the forest."

Lida stared at the boy incredulously for a second, but then she turned and intuitively went to a hammock and untied it from its post, so Basamanaco could place the boy into it. She then reached out and examined the Yocahu boy, clucking her tongue as she checked his ears, tongue and throat, and then pulled back his eyelids to stare into his pupils. She fingered the long, infected scratches upon his arms and legs, and then tried to remove his clothes, but their wetness made it hard to loosen their ties. The buttons and his belt puzzled her. Somehow, she figured out how to unfasten the strange clothes and peeled away the soggy material that clung to the boy's skin. Finally, she shook her head.

"He needs a bath!"

Her voice came so suddenly that it startled Basamanaco.

"How sick is he, Lida?"

"Worms, I think. Worms, fever, bad infections. His lungs are filled with fluid."

"Will he live?"

"It looks like when the foreigners served their meals, they ate everything before the food ever reached him."

"Will he live?"

"I can build him up. I must first clean out his blood."

"Will he live?"

"Where is the *guayacan* bark you brought from the forest?"

"Lida, I forgot all about it."

"No matter. I still have some left. I can always gather more later."

As Lida left for the communal hut, with ingredients she needed for some brew, Basamanaco knelt beside the Yocahu boy and took one of his feverish hands into his large, callused ones. He couldn't help thinking back to when he first saw this boy on Cuba. Even at that time, he noticed that this boy was the only one of the foreigners, who did not have greed in his eyes. If the other foreigners were more like him, he, Basamanaco, would probably believe today that all of them were the promised Yocahu.

Basamanaco looked over at Lida's loom in the corner of the hut and saw many sheets of freshly woven cloth folded neatly in a stack. He went over and took one of them, returned, and wrapped it tightly around the Yocahu boy's body. Then he held the boy in his arms, as he sat upon the floor and began to sing an *areita* that his own father used to sing, when he was a boy. It was a song handed down through his family line, which told of an ancient family that came from the east upon a ship and settled in the land of Guanine. And after their sons fought among themselves, each of them went their own separate ways and became fathers of many nations.

Lida finally appeared in the doorway with rain streaming down her hair. She was holding a gourd of steaming drink and came over to the Yocahu boy and her husband. When she placed the vessel to the boy's lips, determination fired in her eyes.

"We will get him well."

She allowed only a tiny amount of brew to slip into the Yocahu boy's mouth. Even in his unconsciousness, the boy made a face when he tasted it. Lida continued to feed him in small doses. When she felt that he had enough, she placed the gourd on the floor.

"Tomorrow I will give him a bath," she said.

Then she bent over to pick up his wet clothes that lay in a heap on the ground. As she shook out each piece, two soggy biscuits fell to the ground. She picked them up and studied them, then looked at Basamanaco.

"He keeps junk, like you."

"Do you realize what this means, Lida? Now we have two sons."

Lida was silent for a while.

Finally she said, "Aye, aye," and her voice was amazingly soft.

Basamanaco gently placed the Yocahu boy back into the hammock. Then both he and Lida sat, side by side, upon the floor next to the Yocahu boy and watched him intently. Neither of them wanted to leave.

"Do you think the people of Guarica will call him *Basamanaco-el?*" Basamanaco said, for on Quisqueya, sons were often known by the names of their fathers, followed by an "el."

"Or Yocahu-el."

"Nay, Lida. The name of Yocahu will not be used in our home. I don't even like the townsfolk calling Neef *Basamanaco's Crippled Boy.*"

Tightlipped, they both continued to watch the Yocahu boy. Suddenly Lida touched the boy's arm.

"Look, look. The medicine is already working. His skin is not as red as it used to be. And he is not as hot."

They both laughed, until tears rolled down their cheeks.

But then Lida said, "Suppose he refuses to be our son? Doesn't he have a family, back in his own land?"

"We will love him so much, that he will want to stay with us."

"So he will want to be called Basamanaco-el?"

"Aye, so he will want to be called Basamanaco-el."

Basamanaco looked toward the center of the hut at the empty spot, where his sack of special belongings once stood. He noticed that Lida had saved out two items from his treasures.

"Lida, thank you!"

He arose and walked over to that spot and picked up the wooden horse and cloth doll. Then he sighed, replaced the horse, walked over to Lida, and handed her the doll.

"We do not need this toy. It is too childish for our son."

He motioned to the square-like, black object that sat near the hammock, close to the Yocahu boy.

"Our son has already come with his own toy."

But Lida firmly took the doll, walked over to the horse, and set it down where she thought it belonged.

"We never dreamed we would ever have two sons," she said. "You never know. Maybe someday, we might even have a daughter again."

22

Although the Christians were no longer alive at Fort Navidad, Queen Anacoana still felt that it was expedient that a grand meeting involving the major *caciques* of the island should be held, for she saw a need to discuss the development of any possible future problems. When messengers arrived and told the rulers of the five major kingdoms that Anacoana wished to hold a conference with all of them concerning the welfare of their island, each *cacique* agreed that it was a good idea. By now, they all realized that the outsiders, who had built Fort Navidad, could possibly have been the foreigners from the East, whom Cahoba the Great predicted would come to destroy them. Soon the rulers began sending messengers among themselves, to discuss this meeting. Because there were no more foreigners left at Fort Navidad, they chose the Kingdom of Marién to be their meeting place, for it would enable them to examine the fort and study the surrounding area, so they could fully understand the impact of the physical and psychological devastation that occurred there.

The *caciques* also agreed that the main purpose of their meeting would be to prevent further destruction from these foreigners, particularly if and when the Admiral returned for his men. And since they never before held such a meeting, they recognized that they had to also overcome their minor differences, become united, and learn how to forgive each other with a greater love than they ever practiced — particularly those who were furious at Canaobo the Fierce, who had a knack of stealing their wives.

"It is time that we change our ways to protect ourselves," Canaobo the Fierce said in his messages. "We must abandon our traditional philosophy of love and peace."

However, the other *caciques* did not respond to this advice, for they could not forget about *the love*, and they also greatly feared this ferocious king.

While the rulers discussed this meeting through messengers, Queen Higuanamá of the Kingdom of The Great Old Lady sent word that she could not be present, for she was now too old to travel, so she would be sending ambassadors to represent her. So the magistrates who planned to attend the conference were: Canaobo the Fierce of the Kingdom of the Mines, Beheccio and Anacoana of the Mother Kingdom, Guarionex of the Fertile Kingdom, and Guacanagarí of the Kingdom of Marién. It was agreed that after this conference, the attending *caciques* would report its results to the lesser *caciques* of their various kingdoms, to keep all of Quisqueya informed.

When the time for this conference arrived, processions of canoes entered Caracol Bay and approached Guarica, the hometown of King Guacanagarí, bringing with them the highest *caciques* of the island. While conchs blew, announcing arrivals, the people of Marién ran to sit welcomes, waving and shouting their usual *taynos.* Many brought gifts and flowers for these leaders. Among them were young women who carried *mestizo* babies, whose features portrayed an exquisite beauty the island had never before known.

Many people gave up their own homes to house these rulers, as well as any visiting *undercaciques* and their *Naborian* servants. And because the conference was of such importance, the people also gave up their Autumn Harvest Feast that was held at this time of the year.

Each morning of the meetings, as litters carried the rulers to the royal *bohío* of King Guacanagarí, which sat at the top of a hill overlooking the sea, people followed them, cheering and waving. Once the leaders disappeared into the royal *bohío*, the townsfolk were left wondering about what transpired in that hut. The conferences began from early morning and stretched into the night, long after the *Naborians* lit *guacanax* lamps to keep mosquitoes away.

As the people gathered in the plazas to speculate, someone said, "I hear that Canaobo the Fierce will be taking our young men, to train them to fight."

"Not only our young men, but I have heard that he will use our young women also."

But those assumptions were only guesses.

Despite the current happenings in the Kingdom of Marién, Basamanaco and Lida had withdrawn from the townsfolk and were now enjoying new experiences. Ever since they acquired their new son Mateo while Neef was away, they began to experience joy beyond their imagination. Although Mateo refused to be called *Basamanaco-el*, as Basamanaco hoped, both Basamanaco and Lida were elated that

139

the brews Lida prepared not only helped Mateo regain his health, but they also helped him put on weight and gain color in his cheeks. And soon, he became strong enough to run again, as other boys his age. But most importantly, he developed a deep love and trust for them.

Basamanaco found himself sometimes putting off trading trips, as he told people that he needed to remain at home to teach Mateo how to paddle a canoe. Since no physical handicaps plagued Mateo, he did not generate fears, as Neef did. And Basamanaco soon began teaching Mateo the art of fishing with *baygua* powders. One day, he even brought him out into the ocean and showed him how to use *ramoras* to fish with, by tying strings to these fish, which had natural suckers, and then coaxing them to attach themselves to large hosts. Both Basamanaco and Mateo laughed at Mateo's successes, especially when one day, Mateo pulled up a giant turtle with those *ramoras*! And when they caught enough for that day, Basamanaco showed him how to release their catch into fenced corrals that the villagers built on the beach, where live animals of the sea were stored for future use.

Again the *bohío* rang with Lida's singing, as she went about with her chores. She even forgot to fret over Basamanaco's accumulating treasures. Since Mateo was already speaking the Taino language when he came to live with them, in a relatively short time, he even began to loose his foreign accent. However, unlike Neef, he could never catch on to the correct rhythms of the *areitas*, nor could he understand the histories of Basamanaco's family, who lived in Guanine long ago. But both Basamanaco and Lida loved him, anyway.

And as the meetings proceeded and the common folk whispered among themselves, one day, a small canoe arrived on the beach, and a lone passenger climbed out of it. Since everyone was so occupied in their speculative discussions, they did not realize that Neef had come home, for the School of The Princes in the Mother Kingdom had dismissed its classes for the duration of the Conference of the Caciques. None of the townsfolk ever knew that he was attending The School, but instead, they assumed that Basamanaco's Crippled Boy went away somewhere, and the Yocahu Boy had taken his place in Basamanaco's home. As Neef passed the people, he overheard their conversations, and for the first time in his life, he realized the value of the daily sessions the *caciques* held in their *bohíos*. He regretted that he hated the solemn assemblies in his younger days, when he lived in the Fertile Kingdom.

When Neef came home from The School, Basamanaco and Lida were elated to experience the joy of having *two sons* in their home, and their happiness greatly multiplied. Although Neef noticed that Basamanaco had taught Mateo many skills that he never taught him, which he had to acquire himself, he said nothing, but instead, he was happy for his brother's accomplishments. For by now, he had gained many *ayiti* experiences at The School, which elevated him to greater spiritual heights, and there was no room in his heart and spirit for jealousy and other base, human emotions. Instead, he instantly loved his brother, Mateo.

One day, Neef appeared before Mateo, with an object under his arm.

"I was just exploring Fort Navidad," he said. "Look, what I found. What is this? And what are these funny marks in it?"

Mateo looked over at the object that Neef held.

"You have a book," he said. "And those marks are words."

And then Mateo went to a corner, where he kept his black, square-like object, and returned with it.

"This is also a book. It is something that Admiral Colón gave me before he left."

"What do you do with books, anyway, Mateo?"

The two boys then sat together upon the floor, as Mateo spread out the two books in front of them and explained about their uses to Neef. Then he read a portion of the first chapter of Genesis and translated it into the Taino language. He thumbed to one of his favorite stories in the Bible and also read and translated it.

"Why, your people also have *areitas*, but they have no tunes to sing them to," said Neef, as he listened to Mateo.

"I actually think some of these passages were sung at one time," said Mateo.

As with many of his people, Neef had already picked up a few Spanish words by listening to the men from Navidad, so he understood many words Mateo read, before they were translated.

As Neef sat entranced, he finally said, "Please teach me to read, Mateo."

Unbeknownst to those boys, as Basamanaco watched them discussing the books, as far as he was concerned, the conference with the *caciques* could last forever, for the longer it stretched out, the longer Neef would remain with them, and he could never be happier.

While the conference continued, day after day, it did not progress as well as the *caciques* had hoped. Because they had never worked closely with each other before, each of the caciques was certain that his viewpoint was correct. King Guacanagarí declared that he understood the foreigners better than any of them, because he was the only *cacique* on Quisqueya, who knew the Admiral and his men. He said that the best way to keep the island safe from those foreigners, if they returned, was to give them constant favors, never anger them, and to always make them feel welcome.

"But look how they treated your people," Canaobo the Fierce protested. "I tell you, it is because you were too soft with them. You should have killed them from the start."

"You know I could never kill anyone. Besides, I got my revenge. I made sure that some of the women I gave them were infected with *yaya*. And those men could not withstand that disease. Maybe it would have taken more of their lives, if the Caribs didn't finish them off."

With the exception of Queen Anacoana, the other rulers were afraid of Canaobo the Fierce's temper, so they did not oppose him too strongly.

"Canaobo the Fierce is right," King Guarionex said. "You should not have allowed any of the foreigners to take advantage of you. When I return to my home, I am going to form armies and teach my own people how to fight, just as Canaobo the Fierce is doing in his kingdom. I think more of us should be doing this."

"Us? Have armies?" an ambassador from the Kingdom of the Great Old Lady said.

A long silence followed. Finally, King Guacanagarí spoke.

"For each of us to form armies, would mean our own destruction. Little do any of you know the power and strength those foreigners bring with them. You have never seen their thunder weapons release objects that rip through trees, as I have, and if they should ever use them on us, they could crush us all, as frail, dried leaves."

"Don't let their weapons scare you," Canaobo the Fierce said. "I tell you, we must let those foreigners know that we can be even more powerful than they are. We can't just smile and give them the best of all we own, as you did, Guacanagarí. And worst of all, you gave them your best wives."

After many weeks of meetings, Canaobo the Fierce no longer intimidated King Guacanagarí, and Guacanagarí suddenly allowed his irritation towards him to flare up.

"Who are you, to talk about not parting with wives? After all, you've stolen three of my favorite ones and will not give them back."

"Why should they want to come back to you, when I'm a better lo —"

King Beheccio jumped up.

"Gentlemen, gentleman. Ye must remember the intent of these meetings. Ye must understand that we are weary from many days of talks, and we all wish to return unto our own countries. But we cannot do so, until we come to a consensus on how we can save our island."

At that moment, both a *Naborian* and a messenger entered the royal *bohío*. As soon as they dropped to the ground to kowtow before the rulers, the *caciques* turned their attention toward them.

"Your majesties," the *Naborian* said. "This messenger just arrived. He says that he must speak to all of you."

"Well, state your reason for interrupting this meeting," said King Guacanagarí, who was short tempered, because he was still irritated at Canaobo the Fierce.

The messenger looked up from his position on the ground and remained kneeling.

"Oh, great kings. I apologize for disturbing your conference, but my king said that I should deliver this news to you right away."

He bowed again.

"Well, get on with it, then."

"I am from the island of Huino, which is south of Quisqueya. My people, as well as those on many other islands, have heard of the great troubles the foreigners have inflicted upon you, particularly here in the Kingdom of Marién. We send you our sympathies and grieve with you."

The messenger looked into each of the faces of the *caciques* and continued.

"Your majesties, I bring tidings of the arrival of new foreigners. They have come to my island and were looking for Quisqueya."

Gasps echoed throughout the *bohío*.

"Seventeen giant birds carrying many men, women and children with fair skins, fair hair, and much clothes upon their bodies, came to Huino. These people were lost, and when they asked how to reach Quisqueya, we gave them false and confusing directions, so they would not find you right away. We believe that the Admiral is with them."

The royal *bohío* turned deathly silent.

King Beheccio finally spoke.

"What do we do, now?" He turned to King Guacanagarí. "If the Admiral is as powerful as thou sayest he is, what thinkst thou that he will do unto thy people when he arriveth here and discovereth that all at Navidad have been killed?"

"That is why I kept saying, that if we show the foreigners that we are their friends, they will not hurt us," Guacanagarí said.

Canaobo the Fierce began pacing the floor.

"I tell you, before the Caribs attacked Fort Navidad, I've killed as many of the foreigners I could, who strayed away from that fort. I don't think there are any more of them wandering around on Quisqueya."

"Are you sure all the foreigners on this island are dead?" King Guarionex said.

Everyone turned to Guacanagarí, as if he was the only one, who could account for the whereabouts of all of the foreigners.

Guacanagarí appeared reluctant to say anything more about this matter, but finally he said, "There is still one of them left."

"Then the best thing to do is to kill him, I tell you," said Canaobo the Fierce.

All of the other caciques agreed, and they quickly appointed Canaobo the Fierce to do the job, but Guacanagarí arose and held up his hand for silence.

"This person is the only foreigner, whom I think that we should keep alive. If you want him killed, I can never tell you who and where he is."

The *caciques* murmured among themselves, and Canaobo the Fierce slammed his fist into his hand.

"And why is he so privileged?"

"He was the only one at Navidad, who never hurt any of us. He didn't take our gold, he didn't take our women, he didn't take advantage of us, and he even learned our language."

The voices murmured again, as they discussed Guacanagarí's stand.

Finally Guarionex arose and said, "All right. We've all agreed that we won't have him killed. Tell us who he is."

"It is the Yocahu boy."

"So when the Admiral returns, what will this boy tell him about what happened at Navidad?" Guarionex said.

"He will tell him the truth, most likely."

"But can he discern our people from the Caribs? I've heard that the foreigners could never see the differences among the people from one village to another on Quisqueya. And they were even worse with knowing who belongs to which island. Will that boy be able to say that it were the Caribs, who had killed those at Navidad, and not any of us? If he can't, the Admiral might take revenge upon us."

"Wouldn't you think that if he is smart enough to learn our language, that he must also be smart enough to know the difference between us and the Caribs?

Canaobo the Fierce then said, "Maybe when the Admiral returns, he might think that you slaughtered them, Guacanagarí. Then what?"

"How could I kill anybody? The Admiral knows I have done mostly good to his people. Besides, that boy will never say anything that will bring harm to us. I have observed him closely."

"You can never be sure of that, I tell you. I still think the best solution is to kill him, to keep him quiet."

Anacoana stood up suddenly and put her hand on her husband's shoulder.

"Wait, my love."

Then she turned to King Guacanagarí.

"Where is this boy?"

"I'm not telling any of you anything more about him, until your husband promises me again, that he won't kill him."

Canaobo the Fierce promised.

"He is living here in Guarica with Basamanaco the Trader."

Anacoana caressed the back of Canaobo's neck, and her voice turned extremely gentle, as she spoke. She surprised the others, when her husband immediately softened and sat up to listen to her.

"I have an idea," she said. "Let us have that boy work for our good."

When the men turned questioning eyes toward her, she continued.

"We must train him to have a position of honor, such as a prince or a ruler among our people, so that when the foreigners return, they will see that we have treated him well."

"What good will it do?"

"As a prince, that boy will be able to act as a mediator between us and the foreigners, to protect us and keep peace. I will personally take charge of him at the School of the Princes."

"But the foreigners are nearly here. Suppose they reach the Mother Kingdom and find him, before you have properly trained him?"

"They will find him not, because he will be well hidden."

"Impossible!"

"I will give unto him the *bohutio* test, before any other training. As you all know, this test usually cometh at the end of the schooling for students who are studying to become priests, but with the Yocahu boy, it will be his first test, and maybe, the only test he will need in preparation for becoming a prince."

"But my queen, what you are suggesting is unreasonable," a king said.

"There are many reasons why I suggest giving him only a *bohutio* test. First of all, it giveth him a quick and short education; second, this test teacheth one how to become close to the unseen world, and it is this kind of sensitivity that will help the Yocahu boy to defend us; third, this test requireth one to be concealed in the wilderness, in places no one will know about; and fourth, it is a test that taketh many *uinals* to complete, which will allow us more time to decide how we can deal with the foreigners, after they arrive."

"But, my dear queen," another king said. "He will then only be partially educated."

"He needeth not six years of refinement, as the other princes. For as our mediator and protector, he needeth not to know about the stars, the histories of the *caciques*, or how to behave in kingly manners. The *bohutio* test, alone, teacheth one much about *the love* and the world of *zemies*."

When the *caciques* finally agreed unanimously to Queen Anacoana's proposal, Guacanagarí turned to the *Naborian*, who had introduced the messenger.

"Bring Basamanaco the Trader here at once."

When Basamanaco was summoned to the royal *bohio* and heard what the *caciques* wanted, he was filled with grief, for it meant that if Mateo left for the Mother Kingdom, he would lose two sons; but he also knew that if Mateo remained here, when the foreigners arrived, they would take him back to his homeland.

"Thou must deliver the Yocahu boy to the Mother Kingdom, as soon as possible," Queen Anacoana said.

Basamanaco had heard all about that *bohutio* test, and it was an idea that did not appeal to him.

"The *bohutio* test involves going into the wilderness alone," he protested. "That boy possesses no skills to survive."

"Then we will send him into the wilderness with another prince, who can teach him how to live in the wilds," Anacoana said.

When Basamanaco heard this comment, a thought flashed through him.

"Oh, kings, may I suggest an idea?"

"Tell us."

"How about Neef? How about sending him with Mateo into the wilderness?"

"The crippled boy, whom thou hast recently brought to my school?" said Queen Anacoana.

"Aye, your majesty."

King Guarionex nearly fell over and weakly said, "My son?"

"Aye, oh, great King Guarionex. Your son. When Neef took his solo, he prepared for it, without the help of anyone. He is extremely determined and clever, and when he took that trip, he was gone for two weeks. He even taught himself how to climb trees."

After the *caciques* discussed Basamanaco's proposal, they finally agreed to have Neef accompany Mateo. And before he left, Guarionex came up to Basamanaco.

"Could you send my son to me? I have not seen him in years."

"I'd be happy to."

Then Basamanaco added, "Do you think the boys will be safe from your older brother in the wilderness?"

"How could Eldest-Son-of-My-First-Wife harm them out there?"

"When Neef took his solo, he said that he ran into one of your brother's followers, who nearly killed him. And on the night the Santa Maria sank, we also saw your brother here on the beach."

"I can't answer for when Neef saw one of his followers in the wilderness, but I happen to know that when the foreigners arrived, my brother traveled to this kingdom to check them out, and when he decided that they were harmless, he returned home soon afterwards. I didn't send anyone to warn you that he was coming, because I assumed that you were watching Neef closely. Anyway, after the Admiral returns with more of his people, my brother will have greater issues to deal with."

Somewhat dissatisfied, Basamanaco left to tell Neef that his father wished to see him.

After the conference ended, only a few problems were resolved, and each *cacique* left for home, with a different agenda. However, they all agreed to have both Mateo and Neef perform their *bohutio* tests together in the wilderness of the Mother Kingdom. They also agreed that Mateo should never be told that his people had returned, until he was sufficiently qualified to be a prince and able to serve as their mediator; for by then, he would have gained greater political influence in the land and could help to protect the people of Quisqueya from further manipulation. And although they were taught the philosophies of *the love* all their lives, Beheccio and Guarionex decided to accept Canaobo's suggestion, that they should organize armies and be prepared for war against the foreigners, if necessary. Yet both kings were reluctant to create armies as massive and extensive as Canaobo the Fierce's. And only Guacanagarí stuck to his idea of remaining friends with the foreigners. To some extent, Queen Anacoana understood Guacanagarí's views, for as Canaobo's wife, she knew that through the art of love, a woman could soften many men's hearts, just as Guacanagarí felt that he could soften the Admiral's heart.

Among these great *caciques,* perhaps the one who was the most frustrated was Canaobo the Fierce. Angered that the only consensus resulting from the conference was the issue concerning Mateo, before he left for his home in the Kingdom of the Mines, he called his armies together and set fire to Fort Navidad.

When he turned to the onlookers, who watched him in amazement, he yelled, "Spread this news around! When the foreigners return, tell them that Canaobo the Fierce burned this fort! Those foreigners must know that *someone* on this island, has power, just as great as theirs."

In fear of what the Admiral and his men would do when they discovered the fort burned and the men of Navidad dead, Guacanagarí planned further instructions of his own, for his people to carry out.

"Aye, you should tell the foreigners that Canaobo the Fierce killed their men and burned the fort, but you must also tell them that I, your King Guacanagarí, was trying to save the men at Navidad from Canaobo the Fierce. And while I battled against him, I became badly injured."

But the person who was even more troubled than any of the *caciques* was Basamanaco, for he did not know how he could break the news to Lida that both of their sons, Mateo and Neef, would soon have to leave them.

23

Mateo grew weary of synchronizing his paddling with the traders, and he yearned for the party to stop to rest, but the men rarely interrupted their journey, except for at night. The trip to the Mother Kingdom was harder and longer than he had imagined, and it did not seem that they left Guarica only yesterday. Two days before, when Basamanaco told him that the kings of the island wished for him to travel to a strange place to take a *bohutio* test so he could become a prince, he refused to leave. He wanted to remain in Guarica, so that Admiral Colón could find him there when he returned. But as Mateo deliberated over Basamanaco's proposal, he realized that he had waited long enough for Admiral Colón, for he had calculated that it was already in the middle of November and over a year, since Admiral Colón and his crew made their first landfall; and it was over eleven months, since Colón left for Spain.

Mateo reasoned that perhaps a tragedy occurred at sea, the Niña had sunk, and Admiral Colón never reached Castile to tell its sovereigns about his discovery. As he thus pondered, Mateo finally admitted that it was best to accompany Basamanaco and Neef to the School of the Princes, although he saw no value in becoming a prince. But he needed to forget that he would never see Castile again, nor would he return to the monastery La Rábida in Palos, which he called home.

So yesterday at dawn, as the canoe pulled away, he watched after a touching scene of townsfolk crowding at the shore to bid farewell, particularly to him. Some of them wept, especially Lida. And even while they no longer believed that the Christians were gods, they still addressed him as the *Yocahu Boy*, or sometimes even, *Son of Yocahu*. By now, Mateo perceived that Yocahu was one of their greater gods. And he still agreed with Admiral Colón that these people were gentle folk, excepting for a few times, such as on Christmas Eve last year during a feast, when a tall man wearing a feathered hat stepped out of the shadows and shot at him and Admiral Colón, as they rowed back to the Santa Maria; and another time, when these people killed Sabila.

Basamanaco tapped Mateo on the shoulder.
"In two days we shall reach the waterways of the Mother Kingdom," he said.
"Waterways? What are they?"
"They are canals that the fathers of the Mother Kingdom built long ago to channel river water to their fields. The people made their longest canal cut through the west end of Guayacarima, which saved travelers from going around that peninsula."
"How could they have done that? Your people could never change the course of rivers. They don't have tools that are advanced or good enough."
Mateo perceived hurt grow in Basamanaco's eyes.
"What do you mean? We have good tools. And our fathers also had very good tools. Our people could always build excellent canals, plazas and homes. Nowhere else in the world are there cultures as refined and as advanced as the ones here on this island. And kings and nations that surround us, revere us as being the richest land around."
Mateo could not believe what Basamanaco just said.
"Basamanaco, you have no idea about the wealth of Europe. People there live in furnished homes with tables, chairs, beds, mirrors, rugs, and scissors. The wealthy Europeans own items of fine, carved wood, which are smooth and polished. And tapestries hang on their walls, with intricate designs woven into them. They also wear fancy clothes for different occasions. Their homes also contain many spacious rooms, with stairways, which they climb to different levels."
But when Mateo ended this description of Europe, he could tell that Basamanaco did not understand a word he said. And although Basamanaco claimed to know the sea, Mateo wondered whether he had any idea of the expanse of the Western Ocean, which took several weeks to cross. And he wondered whether Basamanaco also had any notion that the Western Ocean, alone, was a third of the width of the globe, as Admiral Colón often said it was.
Mateo thought of how Admiral Colón often expressed the ignorance of these Indians to him. He had said that maybe it was possible to teach them that God created the heaven and the earth. Little did Basamanaco know that the Christians at Navidad often called his people dirty, bestial, and heathen. Yet the longer Mateo lived with these people, the more he wondered whether the perceptions the Christians held were true. He found that in many ways, these Indians were cleaner than the Europeans, for Lida kept their *bohio* immaculate. And the Indians here took baths every nine days in the river and soaped their bodies well with sudsy plants, and sometimes, they used sweet scents. When Lida first insisted that Mateo should bathe often, he feared that it would make him ill, for it had been two years since he had washed his body. But he discovered that baths made him stronger, and now, he loved the feel of a clean skin and even enjoyed the sweet scents. And when he was ill and drank Lida's herbs, he felt their miraculous, healing powers that saved his life. Her concoctions caused him to realize that the Indians had much more knowledge than the Admiral perceived they had, and they could not be as ignorant and bestial, as the Christians thought they were. Even if these people owned no metal hooks for fishing,

he now knew that they used other methods to catch fish, which he believed were often ingenious and superior to anything the Europeans ever practiced.

As Mateo sank his oar into the water, his arms burned from the constant movement of paddling all day. His mind was now cluttered and confused, as his thoughts tottered between two cultures. The more he learned about Basamanaco, the more fascinated he became by his strange knowledge, skills, life, and people. But still, the Admiral said that they couldn't count to ten and add or subtract.

Mateo then called over his shoulder.

"Basamanaco, can you count?"

"Count?"

"Can you figure with numbers?"

"Numbers?"

"How many fish would you have if you had seven, and then you caught three more?"

"I would have half a man."

"Half a man?"

"See? Two hands make half a man. And together, your hands and feet make a whole man."

Mateo paused to comprehend what Basamanaco meant. And then he understood.

"And if you had half a man of fish, and someone gave you half a man and two more?"

"I would have two fish more than a whole man."

"Tell me how many whole men of people live on this island."

"There are too many of them to describe. They are as many as ants."

Mateo grew quiet.

"Basamanaco, I think for a long time I misunderstood your people."

"I know, my son. Everywhere I travel, I find that people are basically alike. They feel that their own people, their own beliefs, and their own values are the best in the world, and sometimes, they do much to hurt their brothers, who are not of their lands. Often it is only out of ignorance, for they do not know what they are doing. Yet even after all of my journeys, I cannot help but believe that there is no better place than Quisqueya, for nowhere else does peace prevail as strongly."

Mateo did not comprehend what Basamanaco was saying, and his mind grew confused and filled with questions, concerning matters he could not understand.

"Basamanaco, how can they teach anything at the School of the Princes, when your people have no books, and they cannot even read and write?"

"What do you mean?"

"Without writing, there is nothing to teach."

Basamanaco called to the traders to paddle faster. Then he turned to Mateo again.

"Oh, my son. You must develop eyes to see the beauty of our people. Look at the tattoos on our bodies. Every curve and cross means something and tells a story. And in our plazas and stadiums, there are pictures and symbols carved on the stones that record our histories. We even write on our baskets and carve messages into our dishes. One little design can be a poem or an emblem for entire stories. Our writing is not like anything your people have created, but they hold the same magic."

"Then what is taught at The School?"

148

When Basamanaco looked at Mateo, his eyes were humble.

"I've never attended there, for I am only a trader. On Quisqueya, common people do not go to school. But I have taken many children of the *caciques* back to their homes, after they completed their education, and they told me much about their schooling. I cannot begin to tell you all the subjects they learned. Not only did they mention the position of the stars, but they also talked about the phases of the moon and the planets. They talked of legends, *areitas*, and history that went back before the world was created. What else do they learn there, Neef?"

All this time, Neef was quietly listening to this conversation, but had not contributed anything.

"There is wood carving, canoe building, etiquette, poetry writing...I could go on and on," he said.

"It takes many years to create a true prince, Mateo," said Basamanaco. "Can you repeat the genealogy of your fathers, back to the beginning of humans? Every *cacique* can."

"I've never heard of such a thing. In fact, I can hardly remember my own family, for they were killed when I was little. But I vaguely recall my father telling me about my great grandfather."

"My father taught me all that he knew."

"Basamanaco, Neef told me that your forefathers were kings. So, why are you only a trader?"

"Hui, that was long ago, when my fathers lived in the land of *Guanine*."

"They were the giants," said Neef. "I think Basamanaco is the only one of them still alive today."

"But unlike on Quisqueya, in my ancient people's kingdom, not only was the royalty educated, but so were the common people," said Basamanaco. "Our education encompassed many subjects, but reading and writing was only reserved for the royalty. My father said that, like your people, we also had books called *codices* that were made of thin pieces of bark. However, in other places, I heard that some of their records were written on stone. Some people even had books made of thin sheets of metal. I never learned to read as my ancestors did, but my father gave me lessons on history and genealogy. He even taught me about the travels of my forefathers and sang *areitas* to me, which he insisted that I recite without a flaw."

Mateo joined into the conversation again.

"My father and grandfather also taught me when I lived with them. My father even brought me to the solemn assemblies that he held everyday. How are you taught in your country, Mateo?"

"In Castile, the monks teach me in the place where I live. They are holy men, like your *bohutios*. But some of the other children in my country go to school. And I hear that the very rich are often taught by private tutors."

Pride shone in Basamanaco's eyes.

"My father was my only private tutor, and his learning went further than most men, because he also possessed the knowledge of my trader ancestors, and their school was the world. In many ways, Father knew more than the *caciques*."

"Where did your ancestors travel, Basamanaco?"

"Before the Caribs came from the mainland, everywhere. Often they traded in the nations of Guanine."

"There you go again, talking about Guanine. Doesn't that word mean *gold* in my people's language? Where is this place, anyway?"

"Guanine is many days' travel west of here. It is across the water. Some people call it our mainland, because it is so massive. It has giant cities, where many of them have amazing buildings, which stretch to the sky. In some places, people there have developed the finest pieces of art, with many intricate sculptures made of *guanine*. Some places there even have streets made of *guanine*. Their cures for illnesses go far beyond our herbs."

"Wait a moment. You must be talking about Cathay! It's on your mainland, where there are marble palaces and bridges. That means that when I first met you on Juana, we were on Guanine, weren't we? But somehow, Admiral Colón could not find those wonderful places on Juana."

"The name of the place where we first met is Cuba, Mateo. It's not Juana. And Cuba is not the mainland, either. It is only another island — a very large island."

"Cuba? An island? Is that why the Admiral could not find the Khan there?"

"Who is the Khan?"

"Don't you know? About five hundred years ago, an Italian named Marco Polo came to your mainland, where he lived in Cathay, with an emperor by the name of Kubla Khan."

"His name was Marco — who?"

"Marco Polo. The Great Khan gave him an important position, and he traveled to many places in these Indies. He even came to these islands of Cipango. I studied all about this in the lessons the monks gave me."

"Cipango?"

"That's what you call these islands, don't you?"

"I've never heard of that name. And who is this Marco Polo? I never heard of him, either."

"Maybe your ancestors wrote about him in their *codices*."

"My father told me of no such person."

Mateo was perplexed.

"Surely, your ancestors must have known about him. The Admiral said that your people remembered him, for hundreds of years. He said that your people have also been waiting for my people to bring them the true religion. He told me that about two hundred years ago, the ancestor of the Khan assigned some of his ambassadors to find the Pope in Europe, because he wanted monks sent to his land to teach his people about Christianity."

"No, I have never heard of such a story."

Mateo was extremely disturbed, for he was certain that the people of Guanine must have remembered Marco Polo, and Basamanaco's ancestors were from Guanine. But maybe it was because Basamanaco was only a simple trader, who did not know as much as the Admiral.

Because Mateo had become so troubled, he turned his thoughts elsewhere.

"If your ancestors were royalty, that means that they could read from their *codices*."

"Of course."

"What kinds of things did those books say?"

"They recorded more subjects than you can imagine. Medicine, philosophy, astronomy, history, and *areitas* — you know — those stories that I sing to you, with those rhythms, which you have trouble doing. Of course, my father could only remember a small portion of the *areitas* of his people. He liked to sing *areitas* that told of the first family that came on a ship from the East from Tulan. That family consisted of seven tribes."

"Will you take me to Guanine some day, Basamanaco? I want to see those streets of gold."

"It is too dangerous these days. The Caribs might capture us. It was safer for our fathers long ago, before the Caribs came to these islands from Guanine."

For a moment, Basamanaco appeared tired of talking, and he closed his eyes, as if he was withdrawing into a trance. Then he began to chant one of the *areitas*, which Mateo had trouble learning, in a singsong voice.

> Our fathers, strong, rich men of Tulan,
> Thirteen clans of seven tribes,
> Were told to flee,
> To find the mountains and the other shore
> Of the sea
> But when they gathered on the strands
> The warriors wept
> For they could not conquer the waves
> Could not conquer, could not conquer
> Until their brother gave them hope
> Gave them hope, gave them hope.

When Basamanaco finished his song, he turned to Neef and Mateo.

"My sons, my sons. My ancestors believed that all men are brothers. They believed that long before our fathers crossed the waters, they all came from a common set of parents."

Mateo found these comments disturbing, and he covered his face with his hands, so Neef and Basamanaco could not see how troubled he was. He could not believe that he could possibly be related to the Indians. He madly thought of something else to say, to again change the subject.

"Basamanaco, about the *bohutio* test Neef and I are supposed to take, what happens...if...if Neef and I do not pass it? Will we fail to become princes?"

Basamanaco appeared to be reluctant to reply, as he silently struck the water with even strokes.

At last he said, "I know very well of that test. I have taken many people home from The School, who earned the position of *bohutios*. They told me much about it. It is not a test for princes."

"Then why must we take it?" Neef said.

"It is a test for priests at the end of their training to teach them how to communicate with the world of spirits."

"I do not understand..." Mateo said. "You mean, we must communicate with ghosts?"

"The purpose of your test is to receive a vision, to learn of your special mission here in this life. You will need to survive in the wilderness totally on your own, and take nothing with you. As you wander in the wilds, you must find the Canta Mountains, where you will climb up a trail, which leads to the two caves where humans originated. Soon after you find those caves, you must begin a fast, where you are to consume nothing but sacred herbs to purify your bodies. And as you fast, you must climb to the top of the mountain.

"The mountains belong to the *zemies*. They are sacred places. And there, while you fast and only drink sacred herbs, you shall learn from the *zemies* what they would like you to do for them. I heard that it is not the vision that is the hardest to achieve, but it is fulfilling its challenges, once a priest goes home."

"Then when one works to become a *bohutio,* he must become like Admiral Colón," Mateo said. "Admiral Colón feels he has a special mission, so he says that he must live a saintly life to keep sight of his goals."

For a brief moment, Mateo wondered whether his participating in the heathen *bohutio* test would interfere with his ability to bring the gospel to these people.

He pushed those thoughts aside and said, "And if we fail to fill our missions?"

Basamanaco's voice trembled, when he spoke.

"I never knew anyone who successfully filled their mission."

"No one? Did it make them cease to become priests?"

"They did not lose their positions."

"Then what is the purpose of their vision?"

"I do not know their purposes. I only know that their visions were powerful experiences, which made them feel that they were the only ones who could save humankind. Maybe the *zemies* asked too much of them."

"What you're saying, is that it is not possible to reach those goals," Neef said.

Basamanaco sighed.

"Maybe. But on the other hand, I do not think anything is impossible. I think that the standards of human beings are not as high as those of the gods.' I think each person actually has the ability to achieve the standards of the gods, but people tend to give up too soon, when the task becomes difficult and when they do not understand themselves."

"Admiral Colón believed God gave him a challenge," said Mateo. "He persisted, long after others gave up."

"But I can see that the Admiral is still a man in many ways," Basamanaco said. "Yet if he allowed himself, I think he would greatly understand the *zemies*. He is the kind of man who appears to be able to comprehend that the gods would never ask anyone to do anything they could not do. And he would understand that each *bohutio* has the strength to achieve the challenges which they were given."

"Why does Queen Anacoana want us to take a test for the priests?" Neef asked. "We are not going to be priests, but princes. And besides, does this mean that my education at The School must be cut short, because I must take that test with Mateo?"

Again, Basamanaco appeared reluctant to answer.

But finally he said, "Queen Anacoana wants both of you to remain away from the rest of the people. She wants..." He floundered for words, so he would not reveal Anacoana's true purpose for keeping Mateo concealed from the foreigners, who were now close to returning to Quisqueya. "She wants you both to understand that...that…you both are very special and have unique missions. And she feels that the *zemies* can help you in this way."

Basamanaco did not speak much afterwards, and when he did, it was only to give instructions to his men. But his silence made Mateo uneasy. As Mateo withdrew within himself, he began to hear Admiral Colón's words echoing in his mind, *God is with me, Mateo.*

And Mateo wondered, *If God is always with him, maybe God actually brought him back safely to Castile, after all. But if that happened, why didn't he ever return?*

24

"All dead! Canaobo th' Fierce. Him come. Him kill all."

"*Hui*, Canaobo th' Fierce 'n his men. They burn Navidad."

As the Admiral stood with a few of his men among the charred ruins of Fort Navidad, he was amazed at how well the Indians could now speak in broken Spanish. Yet he was not convinced that every Christian he left at the fort was dead, as the Indians here said, for the fear in their eyes and their cowering from him told that these people were afraid to disclose what actually had happened. Last year, the Indians in this village pressed around him in crowds, but now, only a few of them came to greet him. And instead of their happy *taynos* and showers of gifts, they now hardly spoke.

The Admiral turned to the two Christians nearest him, Señor Mendoza and Señor Hojeda.

"How could this have happened? I left my men well armed."

Señor Mendoza did not hear a word the Admiral said, as he shook his head at the scattered remains of Fort Navidad. He turned to his eighteen-year-old son, Tomas.

"When ye live in these Indies, it will never be safe, until th' people around are pacified."

His son Tomas was one of several people, whom Queen Isabella of Spain promised parcels of land to manage on Española. Since Tomas' eldest brother would be inheriting his father's property back home, there would be nothing left for him once his father died. So Tomas accepted this offer from the queen and came to this island to enjoy whatever excitement and adventure it offered.

But unlike Señor Mendoza, Señor Hojeda was paying attention to what Colón said, and he walked over to him.

"Admiral, it's obvious that these people killed our Christians."

Colón waved his arms in the air.

"I don't understand it. Before I left, these Indians were th' gentlest people on earth. They seemed so kind 'n generous, 'n I felt that they would never hurt a soul. I was convinced that this was th' best place I could possibly leave my men."

As Colón ambled through the blackened heaps that lay damp from recent rains, the Indians standing nearby inched farther away. From their distances, they watched the Christians' every move and appeared to be listening closely to what they said. Colón then discovered his Lombard among the debris. Although it was coated with carbon, and pieces of timber had fallen over it when Navidad burned, it was still standing in the exact spot where he left it.

The Admiral began calling the names of his men.

"Diego de Arana?"

"Him burned in Navidad," an Indian called.

"Guillermo!"

"Him dead. Lyin' in woods. Canaobo th' Fierce find him livin' with many Indian womun. Drag him into woods. Kill him there."

"Alonso!"

"Him also burned in fort."

"Guitiérrez!"

"After big fight in Navidad when Jácome killed, him go 'way with nine men. Live far 'way in another town. Him take all his gold 'n all his womun with him. Him look for more gold 'n womun where he go."

"*Hui*, then Canaobo th' Fierce come 'n kill him."

"Aye, Canaobo th' Fierce. Him kill everybody. Him burn everything."

Señor Mendoza turned a deep crimson, and his eyes grew wild with rage.

"These Indians keep mentionin' Canaobo th' Fierce. Who in hell's name is that devil, anyway?"

"Him strong *cacique* in Kingdom of th' Mines. Him own most gold mines of Quisqueya. Him good warrior. Fight strong."

Colón continued to call the names of the men he left behind, but there were no responses, and his voice only echoed off the blackened walls. He and his men turned over planks and kicked portions of chairs across the dirt. They stumbled across carbon stained shards of glass, a mutilated chest, splintered kegs that once contained the wine of Spain, pieces that looked as if they were once part of European weaponry, and other fragmented remains.

The Admiral turned to the forest behind Navidad. He well remembered those woods. But now, a stench lingered in the air. As he ventured deep among the trees, calling for his men, he pushed through brush that came up past his waistline. He soon stumbled across several corpses, clothed in European attire, with worms infesting their rotting flesh. They looked as if they had been dead for about a month. The bodies were too deteriorated for him to recognize, but the hair and clothes on one of them could possibly pass for Guillermo — Guillermo, the Englishman. When he was alive, his men sometimes called him William, because he was the only Englishman in the crew. But now the sight of him caused the Admiral's stomach to churn, and he ran toward Navidad, gagging.

At Navidad, the Admiral found Señor Mendoza still searching the charred remains with his son Tomas. At another part of Navidad, Señor Hojeda was rummaging through the debris with a *padre*, whom Queen Isabella assigned to teach the gospel to the heathens on Quisqueya. Other men held their weapons with one hand, as they cast occasional glances at the Indians with caution. And the Indians remained far away, with beads of sweat rolling down their foreheads, as they curiously studied the *padre*, whose brown robe reached to his ankles and large cross dangled from his neck. And when the Indians noticed the interpreter Don Diego Columbus walking up to the Admiral, their faces suddenly filled with repulsion. Don Diego was once an Indian king from the island of San Salvador, where the Admiral made his first landfall, which he did not know the Indians called Guanahaní. Don Diego was one of two Indians, who had survived the harshness of Spain, and now he was dressed properly as a Christian, in a shirt with sleeves that reached to his wrists. He wore brown trousers that came to his ankles, and a pair of polished, leather shoes. When he crossed the ocean to Castile, the natives upon the ship used to call him Semola. Because Semola had readily accepted Christianity in Castile and even had asked to be baptized, Colón renamed him Don Diego Columbus. He rewarded him with a promise that he would be returned to the Indies. But despite Don Diego's pleading to be returned to his island of San Salvador, Colón insisted that he come to Española with him, instead. He assured him that all would be well there; that upon

154

this island, he would never be made a slave, as he feared. In fact, the Admiral said that he would personally make him a king on this island, and he would give him his own piece of land for his kingdom. And while the natives stared at Don Diego with hardened eyes, Colón perceived that they viewed him as a traitor.

As Don Diego stood near Colón, Colón walked through the rubble, muttering.

"What could've happened? All th' artillery I left my men were superior to anythin' these Indians owned."

Señor Hojeda bent over the debris, isolated a small object from a pile, and blew the soot off of it. It was a piece of jewelry, European in make, and it appeared to be unharmed by the flames. After he polished this piece off with his sleeve, he held it up to the sun for a better view.

"Why haven't these savages taken our men's valuables?" he said.

The Admiral walked over to him and also studied the jewelry Hojeda held.

"Ye must know that these people do not steal."

"So, ye are sayin' now that they are not robbers, eh? But ye also said that they are not murderers. Somethin' is not right, Admiral."

Then Colón remembered something, and he swung around and faced the Indians.

"Th' boy. Where is he?"

None of the Indians answered, but slunk farther away.

"Where is Mateo?"

"E-e-every man who live in this fort...all killed."

Señor Hojeda slipped the piece of jewelry into his pocket.

"These men are guilty, I tell ye," he said. "Can't ye see th' lies written in their faces? Look how wickedness gleams from each of them. I just know they've murdered every one of our men."

The Indians winced, when they heard Hojeda, as if they understood everything he said. Then all, but one of them, began to run away. The Indian who remained, stood shivering.

Some of the Christians raised their weapons and began to start after them, but the Admiral shouted, "Leave these people be!"

A sailor yelled, "Hojeda is right, *señor*. It's no use for Christians to be trustin' these savages. As soon as a man looks th' other way, they'll shoot an arrow right in his back."

"Listen to me, all of ye. None of ye here have ever experienced th' kind receptions these people gave me 'n my men. They threw grand feasts, 'n gave us many gifts of precious metals 'n stones. They even gave us their women. I still think that they are th' kindest, most generous people in all th' world. Believe me, they will make th' best Christians."

Then the Admiral turned to the only Indian, who had not run away.

"Where's yer King Guacanagarí?"

When the Indian spoke, Colón realized why he did not leave as the others had. He was too terrified to move.

"H-h-him in his *b-b-bohío*. H-h-him hurt bad. W-w-when Canaobo th' F-F-Fierce c-c-come, our king fight him. Try to protect N-N-Navidad 'n yer men."

Señor Hojeda was furious.

"He's lyin', Colón!"

The Indian stood rigidly, while sweat poured down his cheeks and neck. He began to weep.

"Canaobo th' Fierce h-h-hurt many of our m-m-men also. We never, never attack yer people. We l-l-love them. We always yer fr-fr-friends. 'N always King Gu-Gu-Guacanagarí y-y-yer friend."

Hojeda pointed at the Indian.

"This man 'n his people should be punished."

"Admiral, maybe we should give these people 'n their king a trial," Tomas said.

"W-w-we yer fr-fr-friends."

Señor Hojeda's face was hard.

"No trial! These people deserve no trial. They've committed a most grievous crime against us, where justice is due."

The Indian was bawling now.

"N-n-no, no. My people no kill. We y-y-yer friends."

Señor Hojeda persisted.

"Colón, ye are too much a man of dreams with too big a heart. It has made ye open to deceptions. These savages are really devils from th' inside out. They've deceived ye with their generous gestures. Ye can't let them fool ye, any longer."

Don Diego, the interpreter, had been quietly observing this scene for a long time. Finally he intervened.

"Señor Colón, these people would never kill. I know them."

"I believe ye, Don Diego."

The Admiral turned to the Indian, who was frozen in his spot.

"Ye must take me to yer king. I wish to see him now."

When the Indian remained shivering and did not move, the Admiral went over and pulled him by the wrist to lead him. The Indian was stiff beneath Colón's grip, but then he relaxed slightly and seemed to regain his ability to walk. Obediently, the Indian headed in the direction of King Guacanagarí's royal hut.

"Where are ye goin'?" Señor Hojeda called after them. "Are ye lettin' these savages go unpunished?"

The Admiral called over his shoulder.

"I wish to see an old friend."

Colón followed the Indian as they both walked down the hill, away from the ruins of Fort Navidad, into a ravine. Then they climbed up another, smaller hill, toward the royal hut of King Guacanagarí. When they reached the doorway of Guacanagarí's *bohío*, Colón could see the king lying against a pile of pillows inside. From where he stood, he could hear the king's labored breathing, and the king was also groaning, as if he were in pain. When Guacanagarí saw the Admiral, he called out to him and invited him in, as though he had been expecting him for a long time. As Colón entered the hut, he saw the familiar baskets hanging from the ceiling, which held the bones of the *caciques* of the past. His eyes took in the hava mats spread across the floor that were always kept scrupulously clean, because *Naborians* scrubbed them every day. He approached the king and knelt by him and saw open wounds and lacerations upon the king's body. The sheet that the king used as a blanket was soaked with blood. Somehow, though, those wounds appeared to be too new to have been inflicted a month before, when the battle with Canaobo the Fierce must have happened at the time the Christians were killed. The Admiral dismissed these thoughts, when he saw Guacanagarí's face contorted in pain. Guacanagarí extended a limp hand toward him, and Colón took it between both of his.

"*Mi amigo*, ye come at last," Guacanagarí said.

The Admiral was taken aback that the *cacique* also now spoke in broken Spanish, like the rest of the Indians.

"I am honored to be back."

"Sorry yer people killed."

Guacanagarí shed tears, and he wept as if the Christians were his own people.

The Admiral was touched by it and said, "Ye are badly wounded."

"*Si, si*. Canaobo th' Fierce, he..."

"I know. I've heard enough about that rascal."

"I always yer *amigo*. Even if other *caciques* turn against ye, I always yer *amigo*. Whatever ye need, ask me. I give to ye."

The *cacique* looked at the Admiral, his eyes brimming with tears.

"I've brought many more of my people this time, 'n many more ships. "

For a split second, the Admiral thought he saw horror flash across the *cacique*'s face, but it was so brief that he was not sure he saw correctly, and when the king smiled again, his smile seemed forced.

"There are men, women 'n children," the Admiral continued. "When my people heard about yer land, they wished to live here among yer good people. So many of them wanted to come with me, that I did not have enough room in my ships to hold them all, 'n I had to turn many of them away."

"Yer people welcome any time."

And then Guacanagarí called to his *Naborians* to bring gifts to Colón. They came with three small gourds filled with gold pieces, a crown of gold, and numerous stone beads that were green, red and white in color. After the Admiral received them thankfully, he removed a silver image of the Virgin from his neck and placed it upon the king.

"This yer queen?" Guacanagarí said, as he fingered the image of the Virgin, with his eyes flowing with tears.

The Admiral did not understand what Guacanagarí just asked, nor was he sure why the king wept, but his heart went out to him, for he knew that such friendly exchanges between him and this *cacique* must soon come to an end, for he must remain true to the instructions that the sovereigns of Spain gave to him. During this voyage, he was told that once he returned to these Indies, he must show the people here his superiority. He must exercise dominion over this king and his people, as well as over the other kings and Indians in all of these lands. Every heathen must now understand that they must be pacified, that they must be converted to the true religion, for the Christians have come with great power.

25

As soon as the boys arrived in the Mother Kingdom, Queen Anacoana was eagerly waiting for them, but instead of allowing them to attend classes with the other princes that Neef would have done if it were not for Mateo, she quickly began to whisk them into the forest to take their test.

When they cast questioning eyes at her, she said, "You must realize that you are both special boys, who were chosen to do some extremely important tasks. I am sending you far away for your test, because I know that you both have unique spiritual abilities. Few of my students can discern the world of spirits, as well as the *bohutios* can, but because I can tell that both of you have these abilities, I am trying out a new program with you. Through your *bohutio* test in the wilderness, I feel that it is important that you gain a deeper understanding of the goodly *opias* and the mischievous *mapoyas*. This experience will enable you to know who you are. You will then become much stronger students, when you return to the school."

"But your majesty, suppose we get lost in the forest?" Neef said. "We just arrived yesterday, and we do not know your kingdom, at all."

"My son, my mind is at rest with both of you. Neef, I've heard of how well thou hast survived in the wilderness during thy solo."

"But your majesty..."

"I will give both of you three *uinals* to find those caves. If ye do not return after three *uinals*, I will send messengers to search for you. My men know these forests so well, that they can find anyone in it. Then they will help you get to those caves to receive your vision."

But Anacoana's instructions to the caves were unclear to the boys. Within a week from the time they left The School, they became lost. After three *uinals* passed, as they still wandered about, no messengers appeared to rescue them. And now, after eight *uinals*, Neef and Mateo had wandered so far that they were not even sure, whether they were still in the Mother Kingdom. Even if Neef had taken a solo and developed a good sense of direction from this experience, he still could not find his way back to The School, but fortunately, his skills of survival kept them both alive. In the wilds, Neef taught Mateo everything he knew about survival. He even taught him how to climb trees, but without the help of a rope. And since Basamanaco had already shown Mateo how to make *baygua* powder that could stun fish, Mateo's skills continued to develop beyond that point, so that now he could not only quickly spot *liana* plants, from which the powder was made, but he could even smell them long before he saw them. And he said that he could produce enough powder to stun every fish in the hundreds of streams of Quisqueya, if he had to.

But all this time, Mateo worried that the Admiral would have returned and would be looking for him. To comfort him, Neef assured him that someday someone would find them, or maybe, they would eventually find their way back to The School.

But eight *uinals* was a long time to be lost, and as Mateo and Neef searched for the caves *Cacibagiuagua* and *Amaiuaba*, they found many caves, which often had guardians that someone painted at their entrances, but none of them matched the description of the famous two they were looking for, where the first humans were believed to have been originated. In their search, the mountains of Quisqueya amazed them. Neef kept reminding Mateo that these were the sacred grounds of the *zemies*. He also reminded him of the sacredness of the other mountains they saw along the coast, whose cliffs appeared to plunge straight into the ocean, which they recently passed on canoe, while they traveled from Guarica to the Mother Kingdom with Basamanaco and his traders.

Queen Anacoana had made one concession with the boys. Although they were supposed to take nothing with them, while they were in the wilds, she allowed Mateo to bring the Admiral's Bible along. So when the boys were not traveling, they sat together and took turns reading aloud from it.

As they read its psalms, Neef said, *These passages remind me of our areitas.* The genealogies also impressed him. When they read about Noah and the flood, he also said, *This is the kind of story Basamanaco would tell.* Neef also commented that the teachings of Christ made him think of the philosophy of Yocahu.

And finally one day, Mateo said, "You are reading better than most of the people in Spain. And since people do not have Bibles written in their language, I think that you also know the Bible even better than most Christians. The monks at La Rábida tell me often that Spain is very unique, because many people there can read and write, but in other parts of Europe, the people are illiterate. So that means, you are reading better than most people in all of Europe."

But Neef did believe Mateo and thought that he was only complimenting him to make him feel good about himself. So he only frowned and said, "I don't understand why the Christians do not memorize long passages from the Bible, as my people do with our *areitas.*"

"Do you want to become a Christian, Neef?"

"*Hui,* of course, of course, " Neef said.

"Then as soon as the Admiral returns, I will see that you are baptized."

"What does *baptize* mean?"

After Mateo explained about baptism, he took out his rosary from his pocket and taught Neef the proper words to recite as he fingered it. While Neef said the *Hail Marys* he included passages about Atabey, the mother of Yocahu. When he said the *Our Fathers* he also added chants about Makanaima, his creator. As he repeated this Christian ritual, he added his sacred *areitas* in a singsong voice, which included the *zemie* of the mountain, the *zemie* of the sun, and the *zemie* of the moon. And he also gave reverence to his everyday *zemie* that hung around his neck, which he wore for protection.

As Mateo listened to Neef, he said, "You're not ready to become a Christian."

"Aye, I am, Mateo. Learning about Christianity has greatly expanded my spiritual powers. It also deepened my *ayiti.* After I'm baptized, I will become an even greater Christian than all the other Christians put together."

As the boys talked throughout the day, Neef learned much about the ways and customs of Mateo's land. Spain impressed him, as much as Quisqueya did Mateo.

The boys had much in common, for they both had lost their families at a young age. Although Neef knew that his parents were still alive, excepting for a brief meeting with his father recently, he had not seen them in years. And Mateo was greatly attached to the Admiral's Bible, while Neef often took out a black object from his pouch and fingered it affectionately with a far away look.

"Why do you carry that black rock around with you?" Mateo asked.

"It's a piece of coral that my Grandfather found on the beach long ago. I have kept it with me, since I was five years old, because it reminds me of him. I think he loved me more than my father ever did."

"Why do you say that?"

"Grandfather saw me as the person I actually am, but sometimes I think my father never knew me, and when I lived with him, he acted as if he was ashamed of me, because I'm crippled."

And throughout the day, Neef often scratched images into the dirt with his piece of coral, just as he did when he was younger, when he used to accompany his father to the daily solemn assemblies. But now, instead of making up stories, he was creating an alphabet for his own people. At times he daydreamed of how he would some day produce books for the Tainos. He planned to record the *areitas*, history, astronomy and even the poetry that he learned at the School of the Princes. Then he would put them into volumes that would be similar to the book he found in Fort Navidad, the Admiral's Bible and the codices that Basamanaco mentioned. Since he was a student of the School of the Princes, it meant that someday he would became a ruler, and when that day arrived, he would teach his people his alphabet and how to read and write in their language, so that Quisqueya would have literary works that could be preserved for generations, as the codices of Guanine.

While the boys passed their days away, they grew to love the enchantments of the jungle, as they adjusted to a diet of wild cassavas, roots, fish, hutias, birds and, if they were lucky, an iguana. If they hurt themselves and developed fevers or infections, both of them knew which herbs to look for, for Lida had taught them well.

The *zemies* were with them during this trip, for the weather was never harsh. The shelters, which Neef taught Mateo how to build, kept them warm and dry. And as more *uinals* passed, Mateo finally said that if he had counted the days correctly, it was around October 1494, according to his people's calendar. Then Mateo prayed to his God to send a messenger from Anacoana, while Neef appealed to the *zemie* around his neck, for that same messenger.

One day as Neef and Mateo walked up a mountain path, just as they had with many other mountain paths before, they discovered that this time, they could see the ocean in the horizon. As Neef panted and struggled with his crutches, keeping good balance whenever he stumbled over rocks, he looked up and saw an opening on the side of the mountain ahead of him that looked as if it led into a cavern. As he and Mateo neared that entrance, he saw that it was somewhat different from the other caves they saw, for in front of it, stood a tall rock with human-like features, with ear-like objects on either side of it that resembled large ear clips that people of importance always wore.

Both boys could not help but stare at that rock.

"Who could have come up here to carve out that image out of stone?" Mateo said.

Neef said nothing, but instead, scanned the mountainside. Although he was exhausted from his climb, he walked ahead on the path that curved around a bend and disappeared. Mateo followed him, and when he caught up with him, Neef was studying the mountain above him. As soon as Mateo approached, Neef pointed upward.

"There it is, Mateo."

"Where's what?"

"The other cave. You know, *Amaiuaba*. That's the cave where the first human beings, who were commoners, came from. The cave we just saw back there must have been *Cacibagiuagua*."

"Then that strange rock in front of it, is Marocael?"

"*Hui*, that's right, my brother."

It was the first time that Neef had ever addressed Mateo as *my brother*.

The boys then returned to the image of Marocael. As soon as Neef reached that figure, he surprised Mateo when he suddenly fell to his knees. As Mateo watched him in silence, he saw Neef kowtow upon the ground and tap his forehead against the earth several times. Then he reached into his pack that he had created in the wilderness and pulled out a piece of fruit, which he had picked earlier from a tree they passed, and placed it in front of Marocael. And finally, he took some odd objects out from his pack that Mateo never before saw and proceeded to rub sticks together to begin a fire to light them.

As Mateo stared after Neef, he became enveloped with disgust, for the weeks he had spent with Neef, patiently teaching him from the Bible about what he felt was the true religion descended upon him, and now, despite those efforts, Neef was participating in a heathen practice. With resentment still swelling inside of him, Mateo turned away abruptly and looked out toward the sea. The distant ocean diverted his mind away from this scene, and he began wondering if both he and Neef should travel to the shore and follow it, until they came to a town where people could direct them to the city where Queen Anacoana lived.

As Neef's strange objects smoldered and filled the air with their aroma, Mateo turned back and saw that Neef was now raising his hands toward the sky and chanting. Even if he could now understand the Tainan language, Neef's muttered prayer was incomprehensible to him. Mateo then realized that Neef was weeping, as he repeatedly bowed in front of Marocael. Mateo walked further away, greatly repulsed.

Mateo again looked out toward the sea, and once more, he began to plot how he and Neef could get back to Anacoana. And then, he noticed some tiny objects in the water far away. Parts of them were white. He stared, trying to decipher what they were. Then he realized that those white parts were sails, filled with wind. *Why, I see ships from Europe!* When he turned back to Neef, he saw that he was still involved in his worship.

"Neef! I see some boats down there!"

Neef remained deep in his trance.

"Neef, the Admiral is back!"

Neef finally stopped what he was doing and looked up. He pulled himself up with his crutches, walked over to Mateo, and looked out at the sea.

"The Admiral is looking for me," said Mateo. "We must go to those ships, at once."

Neef stared at Mateo, with disbelief in his eyes.

"And forget all about our visions, my brother? Is going to those giant birds more important than our visions?"

It was Mateo's turn to stare at Neef in disbelief.

"Neef, I need to get back home."

"It will take us a long time to reach that shore, and by the time we get there, those boats may be gone."

When Mateo heard those words, he knew that Neef was right.

"We have gotten this far, and now that we are here, we must remain to receive our visions, my brother. When my people see the Admiral, they will tell him that you are alive, and he will wait for you to return — if not in the Kingdom of Marién, in the Mother Kingdom."

Mateo looked out at the sea again.

"Are you sure, everything will turn out well?"

"Why shouldn't it? The Admiral is our friend, and our people are his friends."

Mateo looked back into the sea.

"Oh, Neef, I've been waiting for those ships for a long time." As he wept for several minutes, he finally added, "When I return to Castile, will you forget me?"

"How can I? You are my brother. If I forget you, it means forgetting your books with their *areitas* and stories. I could never do that."

"I hope after I go, you will not forget how to read."

Neef gave a strange laugh.

"Do you think that I can forget those words that I have written into the dirt so many times? Because of what you've taught me, I have finally completed an alphabet for my own people."

"You have been so willing to learn from me, Neef. Yet, I am not always ready to learn from you. There are many things I cannot understand. I can't see how you must worship Marocael and depend so much on your *zemies*. And can't understand why Queen Anacoana wants me to be a prince. I see no purpose in acquiring that position, or even receiving a vision."

"I don't understand the queen, either. But sometimes when I don't know why my king or any other ruler tells me to do something, I must remember that they are guided by the *zemies*, and I don't have as great spiritual sensitivities, as they do. Their priests, who work with them, are also constantly talking to the gods. It is easy for me to question my rulers, because I am not receiving communication from the spirits, as they are, and often I should remain silent and obey them, for the wisdom they receive come from greater powers than I can ever understand."

Mateo stared after the ships again, and with tears trickling down his cheeks because he yearned to go to them, he said, "You are right. As long as you and I have finally found those caves, we might as well get our visions over with, whatever they are. That means that in the morning, we should begin a fast and should start to climb to the summit. And if it makes you happy, I'll even take those herbs that we're supposed to drink for it."

"Shall we look in the cave nearest us?" Neef suggested.

Mateo nodded, as he remembered how sacred these mountains were to Neef.

As Neef led his brother through the entrance of the cave closest to the image of Marocael, they soon found themselves in a chamber that was cool and dim.

"How can your people believe that the first humans crowded into such a small space?" Mateo said.

Neef did not answer, for he was busy studying the chamber in silence, as he searched the walls and scrutinized every rock and crevice. He hobbled over to a dark corner.

"There is an entrance here," he said.

Neef knelt down and placed his crutches on the ground, then crawled to the opening and peered in.

"I see only blackness."

He stuck his arms into the darkness, waving them around in the air, and then he felt an object that was long, thin, and stick-like. He pulled it out and saw that it was a torch, which had never been lit. He plunged his arms into the blackness again and pulled out several other torches.

"Someone left these here for anyone, who may come here."

"Does that opening lead into a tunnel?" asked Mateo.

"I believe so, my brother."

After they lit one of the torches, the two boys crawled into the tunnel, with Mateo leading and holding the light, and Neef dragging his crutches behind him. And then they reached an inner room. As they pulled themselves to standing position, their torchlight reflected off a row of huge clay urns, which lined against the walls. Some of them came up to almost as high as their shoulders. As the boys examined the pottery containers, they found that every one of them was sealed at the top. When Mateo tried to move one of them, it was too heavy for him to budge. The boys beheld figurines of gold, of a quality that was finer than anything else they saw on Quisqueya. They also saw cold, hard pans, which appeared to be of similar material to the armors some of the Spaniards wore. Wooden boxes, with tightly fitted lids, balanced high in stacks, and when Neef lifted the top of one of them, he discovered trinkets and more golden objects in them. *Dohus*, the chairs for *caciques*, with smiling faces of *zemies* carved into them, were piled next to these boxes. Some of them were so old and brittle that bits of wood broke away, when the boys pressed their fingers against them. And then Neef uncovered a container with many sides. When he lifted its lid, an odor of dried herbs shot up his nose and caused him to sneeze. Quickly he closed the box and replaced it, almost dropping it as he sneezed again.

"What sort of place is this cave?" Mateo asked. "Everything looks so old."

Neef took one of the gold figurines and examined it. He studied some metal objects near them.

"Could these objects have been imported from Guanine extremely long ago? Grandfather Cahoba said that many generations back, our fathers used to trade with Guanine, and they received many riches of fine workmanship that they could never obtain anywhere else."

"Then what are these objects doing here in this cave?"

Neef grew silent and suddenly replaced the items.

"Mateo, I do not think we should be here."

"What do you mean?"

"We are on hallowed ground."

"What?"

"I think this cave is a tomb that was used for the ancient *caciques*. I am absolutely certain now that we must be in *Cacibagiuagua*."

"But why shouldn't we be here?"

"This tomb is sacred, Mateo. There are a few such caves, like this one, in the Kingdom of Marién and the Fertile Kingdom, but the objects in them are not as ancient. Grandfather used to tell me about those large urns along the wall. He said that they contain the bodies of *caciques* from many generations back. The kings are placed in them in fetal position, because it is the way they entered this world, and when they die, they must also enter the next world in that same position."

"What are those boxes for?"

"They hold the possessions the *caciques* wanted to bring with them to *Coaibai*."

"*Coaibai*?"

"It is the world where all the spirits of the good enter, when they die. It is supposed to be very beautiful, with lovely fruit you can pick off trees, and a land with much water. Come, Mateo, we have no business being here."

As the boys crawled through the tunnel to get back to the outside world, Mateo said, "I'm glad that I did not try to reach the Admiral today, Neef. I am so glad that we saw that tomb instead, even if we should not be there. For a moment, I thought that I was on Mount Olympus."

"Is that a place like *Coaibai*?"

"Ah, nay. It is a home for the gods. Olympus is a mountain, where some people, called the Greeks, believed their gods gathered in a great hall. In that inner chamber, I almost could feel the ancient *caciques* talking among themselves, as if they were in a large meeting place."

The torch grew dim, and then flickered out. As the boys groped in the dark and crawled toward the outside world, Neef finally said, "I think you are ready for your vision, my brother."

And Mateo knew that he was right.

In the morning when Neef awoke, he saw his brother sitting in silence by a fire he had built, with his eyes turned inward and his countenance sage-like. Mateo blew into his hands, rubbed them together, and extended his bony fingers toward the flames.

"I received my vision, my brother," he said.

"But we haven't even begun to climb to the summit."

"It was a vision."

Mateo withdrew into silence again and moved closer to the fire, while Neef waited for him to speak again, but he didn't, so he said, "Tell me about it."

"I saw a man. He was tall and handsome, with scars upon his chest, like the scars of your people, who escaped from the hands of the Caribs. He wore a gold crown with green jewels in them. He was a king, with a funny name that sounded something like *Cah-how-bah*.

"You saw my Grandfather Cahoba?"

"He said that his bones hung in a basket from the ceiling of his family's hut. And then he told me that the people of this island are in great danger. He said that because I am a foreigner, I would be able to help you and your people in a special way. And I must do all I can for them."

"What else did he say?"

"That was all."

"Why would my people be in danger?"

"I was not told why."

"Did you ask him, if I should finish my alphabet?"

The fire crackled, snapped, and sparked.

"I did not even think of your alphabet." Then Neef added, "I will not eat, until you receive your vision, my brother."

Then Mateo stood up, helped Neef to his feet, handed him his crutches, and said, "I have already prepared your herbs for you, my brother." He had a sheepish expression. "Last night after you went to sleep, I created a brew of herbs for myself and drank it, because I felt that I was ready for my vision."

Neef looked into the gourd Mateo handed him, and as he brought it to his mouth, he breathed the warm fumes of the sacred herbs. He had never tasted them before. He took a sip.

When the boys began to ascend the path toward the summit, Neef took a drink of the brew again. He felt his head turn light, and the world began to spin around him.

"Are you all right, my brother?" he heard Mateo say.

"Of course. Let us keep walking."

When they reached the top of the mountain, Neef's head had cleared. As Mateo started a fire, Neef hobbled with his crutches to the edge of the cliff and stared down at the valley below. As he saw the ocean stretched out in the distance, he also saw that the ships were no longer present, and he thought of the land of Guanine, which lay somewhere on the other side of that sea.

He brought the gourd up to his mouth and swallowed again. His head began to reel wildly this time, and his heart throbbed madly. He turned to look out at the sea once more, but instead, he saw only bright colors spinning around him. His body had turned weightless, as though it was floating in air. And in the distance, he heard two thumps, as his crutches hit the earth.

26

Neef found himself spiraling through a deep abyss, thrashing for something solid to latch on to, and crying for the endless falling to cease; but as soon as he realized that he was heading toward a tiny dot of light in the distance, he forced himself to relax and watched as he neared that spot. Soon he saw that he was approaching a world, surrounded by a cloudless sky. It was filled with trees of yellow, green, red, and turquoise, among waterfalls, rivers, and streams. And then, he saw a man standing at the edge of that scene, waving both arms.

"Welcome to *Coaibai!*"

When Neef finally reached that man, the gentleman clasped him by the hand and pulled him out of the blackness. He felt his feet hit solid ground, but even if he was still encompassed by shadows, he could tell that the man before him was tall and dressed in a light robe. As the stranger guided him into his world, Neef soon found himself within colorful and brilliant surroundings. And then, he suddenly discerned who that man was.

"Grandfather!"

Grandfather Cahoba and Neef embraced. Neef then stared at his grandfather and noticed that he now had a youthful face and was not the old man that he remembered, when he was a little boy.

"Grandfather, did you say that we are in *Coaibai*? Does that mean that I am now dead?"

"Be not concerned, whether thou art dead or alive, Neef, for thy visit here will be for but a moment. I have been waiting a long time for thee."

Grandfather stepped back to look at him.

"Thou hast, indeed, grown into a comely young man."

"Why do you speak in the mother tongue, Grandfather?"

"It is the language of this land, my son. In *Coaibai*, everybody speaks it. Come, let me show thee around."

As Grandfather led the way, Neef realized that he did not have his crutches with him, so he reached for a nearby tree to keep his balance. As he rested against the tree trunk, he cast his eyes about and saw that all of the trees bore so much fruit, that their branches bent close to the ground. At the same time, each of them produced several varieties of flowers, whose combination of perfumes filled the air. Not too far away, large and small waterfalls cascaded into lakes, rivers, streams, and fountains.

Grandfather Cahoba looked back and saw Neef still leaning against the tree.

"Come along, now. In this land, thou art whole, and thou needest no crutches to help thee walk."

Neef was not certain of what he heard, but Grandfather acted as if he was expecting him to keep right up with him. Cautiously, Neef attempted to step forward, while still hanging on to the tree trunk. His legs felt strong, his balance, steady. He took a step away from the tree, and when he found that he could stand steadily alone, he took another step, and then another. Then he broke into a run, and laughing, he caught up with his grandfather.

"Look, Grandfather! I can run!"

"We must hurry, for time is short."

Surprised that his grandfather was not impressed that he could now walk and run without crutches as normal people, Neef continued alongside Cahoba the Great in silence. For the first time, he noticed that Cahoba was wearing his crown of gold with greenish stones, as he did during special occasions when he was alive. Although his face was now young, his hair was still streaked with gray, just as it was when he died. Neef saw a deep wisdom in his eyes that he never noticed when he was a little boy. And when Grandfather spoke, his voice was kinder and gentler than even the voices of the people in the Mother Kingdom.

"I am allowed only a little while to spend with thee, Neef. Right now, I must take thee on a journey. Thou wilt experience many strange events, which may be troubling to thee, but do not be frightened by them, for nothing will hurt thee. And bear in mind, that some of them will only be symbolic of what will happen, while others, will represent actual events. The first incident will be a true one, which will soon occur on Quisqueya. It will happen in an inland village called Trajeeda that is set high in the mountains of the Kingdom of Marién."

And then, Grandfather took one of Neef's hands.

"Come."

Before Neef could ask any questions, he found himself standing next to Grandfather Cahoba in the center of a town plaza.

"The people here are the spirits of the future," Grandfather said. "Although thou wilt be able to see them, they will not be able to see thee."

Neef saw that a palisade wall was built around the town they were in. Its front gates were left wide open, and through them, he could see that Trajeeda was located on high elevation. Curved paths, which wound through lush forests, led up to this town. Outside, close to the edge of a forest, he saw men hoeing at small hills of manioc plants, called monotones, while tiny boys ran to and fro, chasing birds away from manioc seedlings.

This town was considerably smaller than Guarica, yet it was similar to it in many ways, for in the shade of trees, women also gathered to scrape manioc, as they chatted about their husbands and children. While toddlers romped close to these women, older girls, who propped babies over their hips, played games among themselves.

Then Neef discerned an excited voice calling from far away. Through the front gate, he saw a young man, who was about fourteen years old — about the same age, as he was — who was running up the mountain path and cupping his hands to his mouth, so his shouts would carry.

"Foreigners are coming!"

The townsfolk grew alert, and every one of them dropped what they were doing. The young man entered through the gates, with some of the workers from the manioc fields trailing behind him. As he ran past the *bohíos*, he continued his shouts.

"Get ready for guests of honor! Everybody, sit a welcome!"

By the time he reached the center of town, many of the townsfolk had already gathered together to meet him.

"What's happening, Marrut?"

"Foreigners. I saw them coming up the trail. They were friendly and smiled at me. They're heading this way."

"Do you mean the strangers from heaven?"

As the villagers chatted, someone said, "I wonder what they look like."

"If they're coming here, we shall find out, soon enough."

"Did you hear of the clothes many of them wear, called armor? People say that they are hard and stiff and shine in the sun, as ripples in streams."

"And they ride upon huge four legged animals that they call horses, which are beautiful, but frightening."

"Does our king know they are coming?"

"I'm going to tell him, now," said Marrut.

Marrut ran toward the royal *bohío*, leaving the people behind.

"What gifts shall we give them?"

"I heard they like *guanine*."

While townsfolk ran off to their huts to find items of value for their guests, a woman stepped forward.

"Quick, everybody. Quick, children. Gather in the plaza. Everyone sit on the ground. Let us show these strangers how much we honor them!"

People scampered about. Some ran to get their children, cousins, aunts, and parents. Others went to call in the rest of the men and boys from the manioc fields. As they left, still others were returning from their homes, holding their best treasures as gifts. Neef knew that because many of them had little means, they were giving away the only objects of gold they owned.

"Everybody, gather! My-Father's-Oldest-Brother! My-Mother's-Mother! My mother! All of my children. Come sit a welcome! Come sit a welcome!"

The children giggled.

"Listen! I can hear their animals walking."

"Children, children, stop your chatter. We must be respectful of our guests. Remember that they came from heaven. Smile, now. Sit quietly."

"There they are. You can see them through the gates now. They're coming around the bend. *Hui*, look at those animals! They are so majestic!"

While the people sat their welcomes, whispering among themselves, Neef saw that others were still arriving with gifts. As he sat with Grandfather Cahoba among the townsfolk, he was aware that they could not see him. Soon he heard boisterous laughter coming from the Spaniards. It was a sharp contrast to the voices of the people around him. As the Spaniards approached, he stared at awe at their horses, for it was the first time he had ever seen such animals.

"Hui, look at their horses!" a woman said.

"Those men! I can't believe how beautiful they are. Oh, the color of their hair."

Neef turned toward the person, who had just spoken. She was a girl, with hair arranged in tufts, and she looked about two or three years older than he was. Then, a child two rows in front of him began to cry.

"I am afraid, Mama."

"Quiet, now. Smile. Show respect."

"But they scare me."

"Children, children, show respect, I say."

The Spaniards entered the town, and Neef heard the girl near him gasp.

"Gorgeous. Such gorgeous men."

The foreigners studied their surroundings, not realizing that the first place they should look for townsfolk was in the center of the main plaza, because that was the customary place where they would be sitting welcomes. Instead, the men peered into the *bohios,* looked around them, and stopped their horses to examine insignificant items, such as a jug of water, or a wooden bowl. Their armor sparkled in the sun, and the *clop-clop-clopping* of their horses echoed through the town.

While the Spaniards searched the premises, one of them said, "Where th' devil is everybody?"

The townsfolk did not appear to understand what he said, but Neef did. The Spaniard's horse stopped to nibble the leaves off a *bohio* wall, but the man dug his spikes into its side, and his horse continued on.

"They'll be coming here soon," a townsperson whispered. "Smile, everybody."

"Look at their beautiful eyes!" the girl next to Neef said.

The *cacique* of the town, who had since had come out of his hut, was also waiting for the Spaniards in an open sided structure. When the Spaniards came near, he arose to greet them, with the usual gift that he and many other *caciques* on this island treasured the most, which was a girdle with a mask covered with small gold tiles. His queen who had been sitting beside him also arose and followed him, while the rest of the king's wives remained sitting in a row behind the king's *dohu.* As the townsfolk watched their king walk up to welcome the foreigners, they eagerly waited for their turn to offer their gifts.

Some of the people around Neef became teary eyed.

One of the mothers whispered, "Let us hope that they are actually from heaven."

The clatter of hooves grew louder, as more Spaniards filed through the palisade gates. Since the men at the end of the procession were on foot and had no horses, the climb uphill had caused them to become out of breath. When the procession finally stopped in front of the *cacique,* he extended his gift toward the leader of the brigade. As he stepped forward, his queen removed her necklace, which held a trinket of *guanine,* and followed him.

"Welcome, oh great Yocahu," the king said. "Here is my greatest treasure, as a token of my friendship."

"And here is mine," said the queen.

As the people sat their welcomes, they expected Yocahu to praise their king for his generosity. But the Spaniard at the lead said nothing. Instead, he withdrew his sword from its sheath. The people had never seen a sword before, and they continued to smile through their tears.

But a child broke the silence.

"Mama, I don't like that shiny thing in that man's hand."

"Hush, hush."

"But Mama..."

"I think Yocahu is making a sign that he is accepting our king's gift."

"Mama, I am scared."

The Spaniard wordlessly took the girdle, briefly examined it, and then tucked it in his pack that hung from his saddle. Then he glanced down at the king and lifted his sword. The sword sung through the air. When its blade struck the king in the neck, the *cacique* staggered backwards, gasping, while blood spurted across the horse.

The people sat horrified, afraid to move, and unsure of what they saw.

The sword sung again. Paralyzed, the people saw one of their king's arms fall to the ground. Their king looked up at the man who had struck him, with surprise on his face.

"Yocahu, why...?"

He fell to the ground, groaning.

"Look, Mama. Another man is lifting his shiny thing."

This time, a Spaniard lashed at the queen. Someone in the crowd screamed. As the people watched helplessly, their queen's head fell from her shoulders and rolled toward the center of the plaza. This scene was more than they could take, and panic swept through them. Suddenly everyone jumped up and began running in all directions, yelling uncontrollably. Immediately the Spaniards looked over at them and the rest of those men whipped out their swords and turned their horses toward the people. The Spaniards on foot ran over to them and began slashing left and right with their blades. The horses reared and neighed, refusing to trample anyone. And all around Neef, people fell in heaps as if they were fish unloading from a net after a heavy catch.

"Aiiiiieeee!"

"Stop! Stop! We are your friends. You must not kill us."

"Yocahu, why are you angry at us? What have we done that is out of favor with you?"

"Please, don't kill us!"

Mothers gathered their children, yelling, "Quick, children, run! Follow me!"

But the Spaniards on the horses were faster than those mothers and prevented them from escaping. They made their slaughter complete, by killing both mothers and children.

"Mama! Mama! Mama!"

"Children, children, I am hit. Save yourselves. Run!"

As shouts rang everywhere, a Spaniard ran in Neef's direction, but he ran right through him, and when he swung his sword, his weapon also whipped through Neef, painlessly. When it hit the person behind him, Neef heard a chilling shriek. Although he remembered that Grandfather Cahoba had told him that these people only represented the spirits of the future, he never knew that spirits had odors, for he could smell the sweat of the Spaniards, as they rode through him, while they caused bodies and body parts to fly with their swords. He also could smell the horses, as those giant animals treaded around bodies. Yet he could only watch helplessly, as men, women, and children fell everywhere.

When all were dead, and only small barkless dogs remained as survivors, an eerie silence prevailed. After the Spaniards, with haggard and expressionless faces, paused to wipe the blood off their swords and returned them to their sheaths, they walked among the dead and occasionally picked up an item or two of value.

"Tomorrow the whole countryside will learn of this slaughter," the Spanish leader said. "And everyone will know of our power."

As the riders turned to leave the town, the horses whinnied and balked, afraid to step on the bodies. Stoically, the Spaniards on foot followed the cavalry, leaving not a single person alive in the village of Trajeeda.

When the Spaniards were without the city gates, Neef watched after their sleek animals, as they descended the path down the mountain, with foreigners on their backs. The puny dogs near him sniffed at the death in the air and whistled whines, as if they were trying to howl, but could not, because they were mute. Neef glanced at the people that lay around him, and in horror, he noticed that the trinkets of gold and other gifts, which they had prepared to give the Spaniards, were no longer around.

Suddenly thoughts of all the troubles that the foreigners had caused returned to him — of the ruckus at Navidad, the rapes in Guarica and the countryside, and women, such as his sister Sabila, who broke taboos to either please the foreigners or because they had fallen in love with them. With anger, Neef faced Grandfather Cahoba.

"What was the purpose of that massacre? Why did those foreigners kill those people, when they were giving them all that they had? Did it not mean anything to them, that they were being treated with the greatest honor? Didn't they know that the *cacique* was giving them a rare gift, few on earth ever receive?"

"Thou must understand that what is honorable to us, is no honor to the foreigners. What our people prize most, sometimes holds no value to those men or others. Come. Our journey is not over."

Cahoba the Great then led Neef down the mountain path. Neef recognized many of the mountains he saw in the distance, for he remembered them from when he took his solo trip four years before.

"With the next scenes that I will show thee, thou must realize that a few years have passed, since that massacre we just witnessed," Grandfather Cahoba said.

As they descended, Neef could see that the land he approached was spotted with strange buildings; some were made of wood; and some were constructed of stone-like material. He saw foreigners walking about in this town in clothes of different colors. The clothes the women wore came down to their ankles. Some of these people rode upon horses, while others sat in wheeled litters, pulled by those animals. Grandfather then pointed to a building, which was larger and taller than many of the others.

"That is where the foreigners worship their invisible god. They call it a *church.*"

As they walked on, they soon passed towns, peppered with *bohíos*, where their own people lived. Outside of those towns stretched fields, where townsfolk bent low, with large bags on their backs, picking cotton balls under the direction of the foreigners. Neef saw *Nytainos*, commoners, *Naborians*, *undercaciques*, and even *caciques* working side by side. The people of the upper class no longer wore their hair in tufts, nor did the *undercaciques* wear their feathered hats. Instead, everyone had their hair styled as commoners that they pulled back and tied behind their necks;

they also were clothed in simple styles of the foreigners' attire. Neef saw naked children playing beside women, and many of them appeared to be of mixed blood, similar to the new breed of children, whom he saw emerging in Guarica. He then turned to Grandfather Cahoba.

"Are our people prisoners?"

Grandfather's expression did not change, as he led Neef into another town. As they passed people in plazas, Neef gasped at their protruding ribs and the gauntness in their sunken eyes, which gave them the appearance of walking skeletons.

"The town we are now in lies the Cibao Valley of the Kingdom of the Mines," Grandfather Cahoba said. "Here, each person must produce a hawk's bell full of gold dust, every two months, which is a difficult task to do. In addition, our people must also produce food for the foreigners. They are not given enough time to even raise food for themselves, because they are spending most of the day laboring to meet their quotas and working for the foreigners."

Neef saw that the Quisqueyans no longer had *zemies* around their necks, but some of them wore necklaces with crosses hanging from them. As he wondered about those crosses, Grandfather appeared to read his mind.

"Those charms hanging from their necks are symbols of Christianity. They signify the cross, upon which the Christian Son of God died. Those who wear them are showing that they are converted to the Christian religion."

Cahoba the Great pointed to a Christian church that stood among *bohios* in this town. It was not as grand, as the other church he saw in the foreigners' community.

"That is a Christian church built for the Quisqueyans. Come, let us go inside."

As they entered that building, it was dark, quiet, and filled with the foreigners' furniture. Figures that resembled foreigners stood in that hall.

"Are those the foreigners' gods?" Neef asked, pointing to the figures.

"They are symbols of their saints."

"So our *zemies* are no longer around."

"No, Neef. Our *zemies* still exist, but our people keep them hidden. And many of those, who are wearing those crosses, still worship them. They have not forgotten Yocahu, but if the Christians catch them with any of our *zemies*, they flog them."

"Why are they treating our people, as if they have no worth?"

"Canst thou not see the similarities between us and those foreigners? We on Quisqueya have for many generations believed that we were better than everyone else, that all other nations were inferior to our island. Within our minds, we, too, have destroyed the worth of others, just as these foreigners will also destroy our worth, with their swords and dominion. Understandest thou this great flaw of humans? We on Quisqueya are equally guilty of it. For hundreds of years we have held our heads high, confidant that we led the world, confidant that we were the chosen people of Yocahu. We believed that the Caribs, the people of Guanine, and others in this world were inferior to us; and we felt that they were bloodthirsty people, who had no understanding of Yocahu. But do our people have any better understanding of this great *zemie*?

"For generations we packed our heads so tightly with unrealistic ideals, that we blinded ourselves from seeing that the fragments of our own system had broken down a long time ago. We were too proud to change, and we often chose our own destruction in ignorance, for others in this world, who have made themselves far more powerful than we are, have long emerged. And these people are now ripening to come to change us.

"Neef, Neef, our Quisqueya is only a tiny spot on this earth."

"How can that be, Grandfather? Remember how, when I was a little boy, you used to tell me that no other place could be as great as our island?"

"Neef, I was wrong. Since I've come to *Coaibai*, I've learned otherwise."

Cahoba the Great extended his hand, and flashing before them, Neef saw the expanse of the ocean, of not just one ocean, but several oceans and many lands. And he saw foreigners living in lands across the seas. Many of those lands were much larger than Quisqueya, and their inhabitants, who had various shades of skin, peopled those countries. And when Neef next beheld the entire island of Quisqueya flashing in front of him, he realized that it was, indeed, only a spot, a mere smudge, compared to most of the other lands.

"The next scenes will be the most painful of all to view, Neef, but I must show thee what can happen to us," Cahoba said.

Suddenly Neef heard a great weeping spreading across Quisqueya, from the Kingdom of Marién, down to the Mother Kingdom. It also swept across the Kingdom of the Great Old Lady, up the Kingdom of the Mines, and even farther up, to the Fertile Kingdom. He saw everywhere — tortures, forced labors, mass robberies, genocide, and great destruction of the treasures of his culture that were preserved for generations. Slavery, vast and foreign diseases, rapes, murder, and starvation prevailed. There were foreigners with whips and foreigners with swords, slashing at his people, as they performed massacres, similar to what he recently witnessed in the town of Trajeeda.

Yet he noticed among the Spaniards, a few who allowed their hearts to be kind and compassionate, and his people recognized them immediately to be their friends. There was a man among these particular individuals, who wore a brown robe with a cross hanging from his shoulders. Neef heard his people addressing him as *Father de Las Casas*. Las Casas was troubled, not only because of the destruction in Quisqueya, but because it had spread to all the surrounding islands, and even throughout the land of Guanine. This goodly man traveled back and forth many times over the waters on the foreigner's giant birds to appeal to the sovereign of his land. He tried to bring a halt to the terror and bloodshed, but within his own country, he was scorned, because few there believed that such rashness could ever happen, and he was labeled as being mentally ill.

Neef saw time pass, and he noticed that his people no longer looked like his people, for they were interbreeding with foreigners. Even the women of the Mother Kingdom, who were once known far and wide to be the most beautiful in the world, no longer existed. Time elapsed even further, and Neef saw many of his people dying from the stresses of slavery. Their numbers were disappearing rapidly.

He saw the foreigners' giant birds arriving in the harbors of his land, and unloading from them, were people with black skins, with chains around their ankles and wrists. They were being imported from far away lands from across the great waters, because his people no longer possessed the physical stamina to perform the work as slaves, and their numbers were drastically reduced. And again, a new combination of people began to breed, for now, there were a mixture of whites, blacks, Tainos, and other people of the other islands, who were brought into the land as slaves, whom the foreigners referred to as *Indians*. And the Tainos of Quisqueya, whom Neef knew well, were no more.

Neef realized that he was weeping, for he could not take any more. This burden was far too much for a fourteen-year-old boy to bear.

"Take me away from here, Grandfather."

Grandfather Cahoba came over to him and caressed his shoulder to comfort him, but Neef still could not stop weeping.

"Neef, Neef. Thou hast been granted a purpose in life that parallels our people's. Although it was through no fault of thine that thou wast born a cripple, our people shall also someday become a crippled people, through no fault of theirs. Nevertheless, thou art blessed with a brilliant mind that far surpasses others, but thy talents remain unnoticed, because others only see thy physical condition, just as someday, the brilliance of our own crippled people shall be trampled upon, ignored, and forgotten. But thou canst be a great help to them someday."

Neef backed away from his grandfather.

"How can an insignificant person, such as I, help all of those masses?"

"Remember, my son, it was I who foresaw the destruction of our people long ago, before thou wast ever born. But that is not all. Once I reached *Coaibai,* I learned that thy mission in life should be to preserve our people."

"Me? How can I do that?"

"With thine alphabet, Neef. Our people have no reading and writing system. It is reading and writing that can raise our people up and make them strong. Knowest thou not, that when great knowledge leaveth a people — either by it being taken away by force, or by their developing a hatred for it — that they become weaker? They can even fall."

Neef paused, as he tried to comprehend what Cahoba the Great meant, and he finally asked, "Did our people have books at one time, Grandfather? Did we have books, as the people of Guanine, and somehow, we lost that knowledge?"

Grandfather nodded.

"Aye, long ago, our ancients had them, Neef."

"The Quisqueyans did?"

"I am referring to the ancestors of the Quisqueyans, as well as the ancestors of many of the other people scattered throughout Guanine. I'm talking about an ancient, first family, who came across the ocean, and other people like them, who came to Guanine hundreds of years before. They came with records, reading, writing, and other knowledge that the Quisqueyans and many others have long lost and wasted."

"You mean, that story of the first family, who crossed the ocean, which Basamanaco told me about, was true?"

"I never knew this for a fact until after my death, when I came here and dwelled with my ancestors, my son."

"But Grandfather, how do some of our Quisqueyan beliefs fit into the entire scheme of history? How do we account for our legends, such as the one about the two caves, where humans originated? Do you realize that the story of the first family rejects our belief of those caves? Grandfather, I don't understand."

"I have not much time to explain more to thee, my son. Just remember, thou canst save our people with thine alphabet."

"Wait. How can a crippled boy, such as I, save Quisqueya?"

"Thou art better able to help our people than thy father, Guarionex, for the foreigners will leave thee alone, because of thy physical condition, but they shall never forget my son Guarionex, because he is a king with power. And with thine alphabet and thy desire for intellectual pursuits, thou canst bring back the abilities that our people have lost for generations. Thine alphabet can be a start of a long trail upward to prepare us for the higher degree of learning that Yocahu will bring to us some day."

"What are you talking about? I still don't understand how I can save our people with an alphabet. Is there a safer place for us to be? Can we escape to another island, or perhaps to Guanine?"

"Neef, listen. My time is running out. I must still show thee some other important scenes, and then I must depart. Do not be afraid of what thou shalt see. Please remember that the crippling of our people shall only be temporary, just as thy crippled body shall be temporary. Always remember that, with thy help and with the help of many others like thee, we shall someday become a mighty people and shall rise to be among the greatest on the earth."

King Cahoba extended his hand, and when Neef turned in the direction to where he pointed, he saw before him, an immense devastation throughout the islands, which surrounded Quisqueya. Then Cahoba pointed in the direction of Guanine, and across the waters, Neef saw civilizations — great civilizations — with buildings Basamanaco often mentioned that stood much greater and taller than he ever imagined. Many of them appeared to reach the sky. And surrounding them, were streets lined with *guanine*. Then he saw their libraries. He found that his eyes could penetrate their walls, and he observed the *codices* within them, packed within shelves. There were histories and genealogies, stemming back to the beginning of humankind. He saw records of kingdoms, wars, murders, glories, and subjects of all sorts of learning. They told of no caves at the beginning, but they mentioned a story of a single man and woman, alone in a garden. They spoke of a huge flood. They spoke of a ship that traveled across the great waters, carrying a family with quarreling sons. They spoke of other ships that crossed the waters.

And then Neef saw Spaniards, called *conquistadors*, approaching the great cities of Guanine upon their horses, with not only swords, but with weapons that roared like thunder, much like the Lombard that the Admiral periodically set off from his ship that scared his people. And these men came eradicating the civilizations through trickery and powerful weapons. Neef then saw fires, monstrous fires. He saw the Spaniards taking the *codices* and placing them in huge piles to burn them, so there would be no more histories, no more genealogies, and no more records of Guanine that told that all men were brothers.

When Neef saw the fires, he lost control of himself.

"The *codices*! They must not burn those *codices*! Nay...nay...nay..."

He turned toward Cahoba the Great, but the king was gone. Desperately he spun around, searching for his grandfather, but instead, he found himself enveloped in darkness, just as he was before he reached *Coaibai*. A droning suddenly came to his ears, as if millions of bees were buzzing around him. It began as a whisper, but then gradually increased in volume. As it grew louder, he discerned that it consisted of human voices, of *human screams*, thousands and thousands of screams, from over a period of hundreds of years. The voices burned into his soul. They came from *his people* of Quisqueya, from the people of the surrounding islands, from the people from every corner of Guanine, from people who originated from a family who came on a boat, from people who crossed over to Guanine to the north from another huge mass of land, and from several other people who came to Guanine by other means. The darkness lifted, and Neef saw that the blood of these people was buried deep within the ground of their lands, and there was so much of it, that it formed massive rivers. The screams grew deafening, and they were crying up to the heavens for justice.

The entire image of Guanine swept before Neef, and he gasped at its greatness. Throughout this land, the screams continued to increase, beyond deafening levels. Neef covered his ears, but their intensity was so great and refused to be silenced, that he could not shut them out.

In desperation, Neef looked for his grandfather again. He called out to him in the direction, where he once stood.

"Grandfather Cahoba! I cannot! I, alone, cannot save all of these people! I am only a boy — a crippled boy, who no one knows."

A small voice close to him whispered, "Thou art no longer a boy, Neef, but thou art now a man."

Then Neef found himself beginning to spin into the deep darkness again, but this time, the screams roared all about him. He groped for solid ground, and when he found none, he yelled with all his might, trying to be heard above all the noise.

"I cannot, can you hear me? I cannot! Grandfather Cahoba, do you hear meeeeeee?"

When Neef opened his eyes he saw Mateo kneeling over him.

"You had your vision, my brother. You were shouting, as if the *mapoyas* were after you."

"Th-th-they were."

Mateo held a pouch filled with water to his lips, but Neef pushed it away. Then he remembered that now that his vision was over, he could take a drink, for his fast was also over. He reached for the water.

"Only a sip, my brother," said Mateo. "Remember that your body must get used to nourishment again."

The water refreshed Neef, and its warmth felt strange as it slid down his throat to his stomach. He sniffed. Something was cooking. He saw that Mateo was roasting a bird on a spit. His brother had learned his skills of survival well.

Mateo handed him his crutches.

"Come sit by the fire."

For a moment, Neef did not know what to do with his crutches, for still fresh in his mind was his vision, in which he enjoyed the freedom of walking unassisted. But when he found that he no longer could get up and walk alone, he took the crutches and hobbled to the fire.

"I think something bad will happen, my brother," Neef said. "You had a bad vision, and I had a bad vision."

"But something wonderful will also happen soon, Neef. While you were having your vision, I saw the European ships appear close to the shore again. I am sure if we travel to the shore, we are bound to find someone there, who can help us get back to the Mother Kingdom. And you know what those ships mean? It means that I will soon find the Admiral, so I can go back home."

"But your vision, Mateo. What are you going to do about what you've learned in your vision?"

"I've been thinking much about it. I think if you and I work together, we both can do something to help your people. After I go back to Castile, I will return to help you, as soon as I can. I promise."

"Go back to Castile? Mateo. You can't go back now. You must remain here. We don't have much time. You have no reason to return to your homeland, because you have no family there."

"But I still have my Papa. He comes to see me at the monastery, from time to time."

When Mateo said what he did, Neef knew that he had his mind made up to return to Spain, and nothing could change him.

27

Tomas Santiago Mendoza staggered across the Indian hut, and as he approached its doorway, he threw his weight against a post at its entrance and shook his head to rid it of its dizziness. As the world spun around him, he was reminded of the huge quantities of Indian drink that he consumed the night before. That *chicha* always had so much power over him — more than all the wine of Spain ever did. Yet he heard that this drink was only extracted from maize, and its potency was only that of beer. But it still acted strangely with him, and yesterday on 24 March 1495, when he and his men defeated 100,000 Indians here in Santo Domingo, he absolutely had to celebrate with *chicha*. In fact, ever since his father left this island and returned to Spain, he was always celebrating with *chicha*.

That battle was an easy victory for him and 200 other Christians. Those natives were angry, because they did not want to make payments to Spain, and they wanted to continue in their lazy lives. They came charging at the Christians with their crude weapons. He never saw those dirty dogs fight before, nor did he ever see those cowards with weapons. But they came with stone axes, bows and arrows, yelling like crazy. Señor Hojeda said that it was that troublesome Indian king, Canaobo the Fierce, who must have talked those people into fighting. Tomas could tell that those dirty dogs were extremely frightened of them, because they were shaking like mad in their flimsy loincloths, and they dared not come too close. When they shot with their bows, they kept so far away, that their arrows never reached the Christians. And all he and his men had to do, was to charge into that crowd of wimps with their horses and war hounds, and apply their swords. Occasionally they even set off a few Lombards. And all 100,000 of those devils ran off, as scared as *una manada* of pampered dogs, which only rich ladies keep as pets.

When the Admiral heard of this victory, he was ecstatic, for he always said that those Indians needed to be constantly reminded of who was with power.

As Tomas stared out of the *bohió* into the distance, he cried, "*Viva España!*"

His glazed eyes noted that the position of the sun was directly overhead.

Dios mío, he thought. *It is nearly noon. I've been asleep for almost an entire day.*

Slowly, Tomas saw the lush landscape of Santo Domingo come into focus before him, and even with this hangover, he could still comprehend its beauty. Everywhere in these Indies, the view was stunning, but they were especially so in this southeast corner of the island.

Before his father returned to Spain, he said, "Son, after they assign ye to a parcel of land, as its *repartimiendero*, ye have a responsibility to spread 'n increase th' power of Spain. Ye must see that th' Indians below ye are pacified to a state of complete obedience at all times 'n that they always pay their tributes. 'N make sure that ye teach them good Christian habits."

But after his father left and Tomas was assigned to manage this property, he didn't even need to teach his Indians Christian habits, for the *padres* began to labor with such zeal, that he could forget about teaching religion altogether, since this job was already done for him. If the Indians were caught with their idols, he didn't even need to do any punishing, because the friars gave them thorough floggings, themselves.

And when the Indians failed to pay their tributes, all he needed to do was slash off a few hands, or give a few whippings. The quotas were not always filled, but a few lashings kept them obedient. Whenever the Indians paid him, he rewarded them with a brass token to wear around their necks, which bore his last name of *Mendoza* upon it. Of course, he provided them with clothing and some food. And he always made sure that all able-bodied Indians on his land, aged fourteen and up, wore a brass token to show that they were doing their duties; and if he found them to have no such token, he punished them severely. Tomas felt confidant that in time, these natives would adjust to this *repartimiento* system. Yet he could see that there still remained something in their eyes, which told him that they would never totally submit to the Spanish will.

Tomas' head felt a bit clearer now. As he turned to look back into the hut, he stared at the empty space, where he slept the day before. The Indian woman, whom he brought here yesterday, was gone. She was beautiful, with exotic eyes and a perfect form. He had watched her for days, and he heard from the natives that she was a woman of honor, who was educated at the School of the Princes, whatever that meant. All he knew was that she was his to do with as he pleased, because she lived on his *repartimiento*. And yesterday after the victory, he saw her, as he was riding toward his home. Since he felt that he must celebrate, he forced her upon his horse. As she screamed, scratched, and stretched out toward her husband, who stood with a cowardly look on his face, they rode away. He could feel her husband's eyes helplessly looking after them. If that man tried to fight, he, Mendoza, would have killed him. Anyway, he knew that fresh on that man's mind, was the recent battle — the horses, the swords, the dogs, and all of the Spanish weapons that showed power and strength. Just as with all the other Indian men, that man was too afraid to defend his own wife.

As Tomas and the woman galloped away upon his horse, he eventually turned toward a hut at the edge of the village. When they approached it, the people who lived within it, fled — leaving it empty for them to enter. The woman was not afraid of him, as her husband was, and she fought him tooth and nail.

"Settle down, *señora*, or I'll kill ye!"

"What good am I to ye, if I'm dead?"

Her Spanish was perfect, but not as perfect as her face and body. Yet there was something brave about her, as her eyes pled for him to leave her alone, which gave his heart a twinge of pity. But that was before he discovered the gourd of *chicha* in a corner of the hut. He knew that if he drank its contents, it would squelch out all pity he had for her, and would thus make his victory celebration more complete. After he tied her up, so that he could have both hands free to drink the *chicha*, that drink certainly felt wonderful as it slid down his throat; and when he had enough of it, he drank even more, until long after his head turned light, and all tender feelings left him. Then he proceeded to do with that woman what he intended to do with her, in the first place.

Here in Española, there was no law. Of course, the Admiral tried to enforce order and stressed the three monastic vows. But who in these tropics cared about the virtues of poverty, chastity and obedience? They stifled a man's natural ways, and this island aroused too many desires.

Just then, Tomas thought he heard someone calling his name. Then he heard the hollow clopping of hooves. As he leaned against the support post of the hut, he ignored those sounds and began to sing as loud as he could.

"Viiiivaaa Espaaañaaaa! Viiiivaaa....viva....viva...."

He saw his friend, Ricardo, approaching upon his scraggly horse. He turned his back toward him and pressed his forehead against the post.

"Mendoza!"

Ricardo's voice irritated him. He heard him come near and dismount a few feet from him.

"*Hola*! I see ye had too much again."

"What th' devil do ye want? Leave me be."

"Hojeda is lookin' for ye."

Tomas shuddered, when he heard that name. He knew how the Indians feared Hojeda, for he was their greatest enemy. But to him, *Hojeda* meant another job that he did not want to do, and taking orders from someone who didn't care, if he already had too much work to do.

"Hojeda, Hojeda, Hojeda. What does that bastard want from me, now? Tell him to burn in hell. Besides, I just helped him 'n th' Admiral win a battle yesterday."

"He wants ye to accompany him in a posse to tame Canaobo th' Fierce."

"Again? How many times do we have to fight him? What th' hell did Canaobo th' Fierce do, this time?"

"Burned a lot of Christian homes last night. Hojeda is askin' for th' toughest men around, 'n yer're one of them. We'll break that *cacique*, yet."

"There are plenty of tough men on this island. Ask them. Go away 'n don't bother me, ever again."

"Hojeda particularly asked for ye, *amigo*. Come on, let's sober ye up."

Ricardo looked around the hut and found a gourd of water. He retrieved it, walked over to Tomas, and dumped its contents over his head. As Tomas sputtered, he took a slug at Ricardo, but missed.

"*Qué diantre!*"

"Relax, *mi amigo*, I'm only tryin' to help ye. Ye're as drunk as death, itself."

"Some friend, ye are."

"Be happy that ye have no wife to yell at ye, when ye're in yer condition. Ye cannot even imagine what my Estrellita would do to me, if came home as drunk as ye are. Th' other day, she yelled at me like a drunk, herself. When she started throwin' things at me, all hell broke loose. 'N *amigo*, I can never keep secrets from her. Somehow she knows every single Indian woman, whom I've brought to bed."

"*Si?*"

"She hates every single one of them, I tell ye."

Ricardo then grabbed hold of Tomas' arm and jerked him away from the post. The horse, which carried Tomas and the woman the day before, was quietly munching upon a bush.

"Hurry up now, *mí amigo*! Get yerself up on yer horse, 'n let's be off!"

28

Shortly after Neef and Mateo left for the wilderness, messengers brought news to Queen Anacoana that the Admiral had returned to Quisqueya. They told her that he was now in the town of Guarica, where she and the other *caciques* had met in the Kingdom of Marién, and he was establishing a new system in the land. The Admiral had informed the people there that the island no longer was theirs, for now it belonged to Spain; and every able-bodied man, woman, and child over the age of fourteen, was required to work and pay tributes to the king and queen of Spain. If anyone failed to fill their quotas, they were told that they would be punished. When Anacoana heard how the Admiral was parceling her island into *repartimientos,* where the people were forced to act as serfs to the foreigners, she immediately sent away for her husband, Canaobo the Fierce.

But Canaobo the Fierce could not come to her in the Mother Kingdom, for he, himself, faced innumerable problems in defending his own Kingdom of the Mines. It was enough that these foreigners were rapidly infiltrating his land, but some of his people further complicated issues, because in ignorance, they showed these foreigners the gold, silver and copper mines in the Cibao Valley of his kingdom. His people had never revealed these mines to strangers before, but because some of them still believed that the foreigners were Yocahu, they wanted to share their deepest secrets with them, whom they believed were *zemies*. To the Quisqueyans, only special men could gather gold pieces from the riverbeds. And these men were required to fast for three days, while they drank sacred herbs to purify their bodies, before they could even collect any gold. But they always left the mountains alone, for they considered them to be holy grounds, and they only collected the gold from the riverbeds. Because the foreigners saw no sacredness in the gathering of gold or silver, when they moved into the land, they coerced ordinary people, with unpurified bodies, to not only gather the precious metals from the riverbeds, but also to dig, deep into the hallowed mountains.

"I am constantly at war," Canaobo the Fierce told his messenger to tell Anacoana. "Never before, have I been required to organize my armies so intensely. But I will come to you, as soon as I can, my dearest."

Every day messengers brought the queen news of how her husband attacked the foreigners, as he burned their homes, killed their men, women, and children, and subdued their soldiers through ambush. And finally when these foreigners grew weary and longed for their homeland, most of them left upon their ships for their country that lay somewhere across the great waters. And as Anacoana repeatedly sent for her husband, he always returned messages to her that he was still occupied with war. Canaobo the Fierce pointed out that although many of the foreigners were now gone, those who remained on Quisqueya were the rough and hardened men, who feared nothing; and they fought with great ferocity.

Then one day, foreign ships appeared at the Mother Kingdom. Anacoana was at awe at the beauty of the men, who disembarked from those ships. Their leader, Veláquez, informed her and her brother Beheccio of the tributes that their kingdom must pay to Spain. At that time, the people kept Anacoana's storehouses well filled.

"Whatever yer queen wants, I will give her," said Anacoana, speaking Spanish the best she could.

Although Beheccio had begun to form and train armies to defend their kingdom, once he faced the Spaniards and saw how fierce and powerful they were, he changed his mind. And soon, he and Anacoana decided that they would, instead, work together to win these men over by establishing peace, especially by treating them with *the love*. Even after the people of the Mother Kingdom labored under these foreigners and Anacoana's storehouses grew empty, Queen Anacoana and King Beheccio still told the Spaniards, *We will give ye whatever ye would like.* Beheccio provided the foreigners with wives, and even Anacoana gave herself to Veláquez and his soldiers. She taught them arts of love the men never knew. Yet she loathed the way they looked upon the princesses of The School, for she felt responsible to protect the purity of each of her students, especially her princesses. And everyone knew — even the Spaniards — that they were the most attractive women in the world.

As these burdens weighed heavily upon Anacoana's shoulders, she still remembered the two boys, Mateo and Neef, in the mountains. Since five, six, ten, and twelve *uinals* passed and they did not return, she assumed that they were either

180

lost, or captured by Caribs. But she could not send her messengers to search for them, because none of her men were free any longer.

As the Mother Kingdom was carved up into *repartimientos*, Canaobo the Fierce sent word one day that he was coming with his forces to save this kingdom. But Anacoana sent her messengers back to him, with word that she wanted *no wars* in her kingdom. So when Canaobo the Fierce finally appeared, he came alone in the middle of the night, disguised as a commoner, so he would not be captured, for the foreigners were now looking for him and had a price upon his head.

When Canaobo the Fierce finally appeared in the dark in Anacoana's *bohio* one night, she accepted his kisses. To the world, he was a fierce and heartless warrior, but to her, he was a passionate lover, who was both intelligent and gentle, except for his explosive temper. It paid off to win his love. And that night, as they lay in each other's arms in Anacoana's hammock, speaking in whispers, Canaobo the Fierce was deeply troubled.

"I cannot keep those foreigners out of my kingdom much longer, I tell you," he said. "They are much better fighters than the Caribs. I have lost too many of my men. Most of my brothers, whom I brought with me from my homeland, are killed. I believe the Caribs will last much longer than I will, because, as soon as the foreigners arrived in their lands, they fought to preserve themselves, but my men and I were the only people on Quisqueya, who fought for the welfare of its people. And now, there is only one of me and a few of my men left, but plenty of Caribs left on their islands.

"And, oh, the weapons the foreigners own! Ah, those marvelous weapons! If only I could have their swords and thunder things, I would defeat them all."

"Perhaps for thy safety, thou shouldst make peace with the foreigners, my love."

"Never. If I die, I must die with honor."

"Is there no honor in showing *the love*?"

"Anacoana, you must understand. I am a Lucanyan. As long as I am alive, my highest honor is to be a great warrior. To die the greatest death, is to earn the integrity of being killed in battle or to die in captivity, under the hands of my most powerful enemy. Do you see? If I die with such glory, I will inherit the highest position in the next life. Your brother Beheccio is no warrior, whatsoever, so to him, there is no honor to be captured. But for me, to die from the sword of Hojeda, would be the greatest compliment I could ever receive."

Anacoana shook her head.

"My love, my love. I understand thee not. Oh, Canaobo, Canaobo, speak not of thy death to me. Why canst thou not be at peace with these men? Why must thou constantly threaten thine own life and shed so much blood?"

"You say you must love your enemies, Anacoana. But do you love me, your husband?"

"Canaobo, of course, I love thee more than anyone, or anything else in the world."

"Then understand *me*, Anacoana. That is all I ask. When you understand me, you show me that you love me."

Anacoana thought for a long time, and finally she said, "No one else is as strong or as brave as thee, my love. It is a deep honor for me to have thee as my husband."

And then Canaobo the Fierce took her into his arms again.

The next morning, Canaobo the Fierce was gone. And Anacoana again felt the burdens of the Mother Kingdom. When Nila came to dress her and arrange her hair into tufts, Anacoana said, "Nila, when thou first came to this island and wast sold as a slave, was it hard to change to our Quisqueyan ways?"

"Yes, Princess. But I grew to cherish the Quisqueyan love. It cannot be found anywhere else."

"Then why is this love so hard for my husband Canaobo to accept?"

"He is a proud man, Princess. But sometimes, the best men are the proudest."

But Anacoana hardly heard her, for she was wondering what battle her husband was fighting that day.

29

As the posse progressed inland into the Kingdom of the Mines with Señor Hojeda at its lead, Ricardo and Tomas Mendoza followed behind him. As an occasional cry of a parrot pierced the jungle, by now, Tomas knew that many of those birdcalls were often not really from parrots, at all, but they were warnings and signals emitted from Indians, as they hid within the thick foliage. He knew how clever and sharp Canaobo the Fierce and his men were, for they had beaten the Christians so often in battle that they had become the major cause for three-fourths of the Europeans in Española, to return to Spain. Tomas could not recall how many times he came with Hojeda and his men to Canaobo the Fierce country to overtake that wild *cacique*, but had failed. And now, as the posse rode past trees and brush, just as Tomas always did whenever he was here, he felt unseen eyes peering at him, as if they lurked in hiding. Once in awhile, he thought he heard an arrow whiz past him and his men, but when he turned, he saw no evidence of it and wondered if it was only his imagination, or maybe, he was going insane; and as he glanced at the other men in the posse, their faces appeared to be unaware that they were being watched or shot at, as they continued their trek.

The Christians said that this land was the only *cacicazgo* on the island, where boys were taught to be warriors from the time they were babies, because their king had come from an island from far away, where the people believed in fighting. Tomas fought many battles in this kingdom, and he saw many Christians killed in them, for the natives here sometimes fought even more skillfully than the best

182

trained Christians, with their sophisticated weapons. Now that he was sober, Tomas tried not to let the others know that he was afraid, but whenever he came to Canaobo the Fierce country, he was always afraid. And as the posse continued, he glanced down and noticed that the crotches of the men in front of him were soaked, and then and he knew that he was not the only person who feared for his life. As the men rode on and passed villages, women screamed when they saw them coming, and children ran away in panic. But Hojeda proceeded to lead his procession, undaunted by those people, as he insisted out loud that they must capture that rascal Canaobo the Fierce, once and for all.

At last, they arrived at the village, where Canaobo the Fierce lived. One glance at its palisade gates told the men that something was different today, for the entire town appeared to be deserted. This time, it was an easy entry through its gates, and an immense eeriness hovered everywhere. Its huts, paths, plazas, and shrines of stone stood deathly silent. Although he and his men had ridden through vacant villages many times before, Tomas was surprised that today, no one was present in this village, for Canaobo the Fierce and his warriors always stood and fought.

Within this ghost-like town, Hojeda called over his shoulder.

"See? Even Canaobo th' Fierce 'n his people can turn coward."

As they wandered through this village for the first time, the horses' hooves echoed off the stone walkways and became annoyingly loud to Tomas' ears. When the posse came to the main paths, the men determined which one would lead up to Canaobo's royal hut, and followed it. Although no one seemed to occupy the homes, Tomas thought that he heard people whispering, *Hojeda, Hojeda, Hojeda*, but he knew it was impossible, for he saw no humans around.

Finally the Christians approached at what appeared to be the royal hut, and Tomas saw two guards standing in front of it. They stood alone, holding spears against their shoulders, with obsidian tips secured to them. They were unlike the spears with fishbone tips that Tomas was used to seeing, for these looked as if they were assembled in three parts, and their curious construction caused him to wonder how they worked. And he wondered whether their tips had been soaked with poison, such as the ones the Caribs used, which killed instantly.

The guards did not turn their heads, as the Christians approached. When Hojeda stopped before them, he reached for his sword, but changed his mind, and drew his whip, instead.

"Where's Canaobo th' Fierce?"

The guards barely glanced at him and did not answer, but only looked straight ahead.

Hojeda raised the whip above his head and swung it in mid air. Its crack startled the men, but unlike the usual Indians Tomas saw on Quisqueya, they did not run.

"Where's Canaobo th' Fierce, I said? Have ye no ears?"

"Him not here."

Hojeda turned around and faced the posse. Tomas felt his eyes boring into him.

"Mendoza 'n Ricardo, check th' hut."

When he heard his last name mentioned, Tomas dismounted and withdrew his sword, and as he walked toward the royal hut with Ricardo by his side, they entered into the home of Canaobo the Fierce. Baskets hung from its ceiling, which Tomas knew held the bones of kings of the past. He glanced at the simple furnishings and saw a mere *dohu* at one side of the room. Scattered here and there, were a few pieces of pottery, with detailed geometric designs. And a vase in the shape of a turtle stood at the opposite side of the hut from the *dohu*. He saw Ricardo raise his sword and swing, severing the cords, which connected the baskets of *cacique* bones to the beams of the hut. The ancient bones tumbled to the floor. Tomas immediately responded to Ricardo's behavior, by kicking at the clay pots. Their intricate designs shattered beneath his heels. Ricardo then hacked at the *dohu* with his sword.

"Take that, ye slimy *cacique!*" he yelled.

He did not stop striking at that throne, until it lay as a heap of splinters upon the floor. Out of the corner of his eyes, Tomas could see the guards outside, as they still remained immovable and stiff in their places, with their spears upon their shoulders.

"Why do ye think those guards are th' only ones left in this village?" he asked Ricardo.

But Ricardo was already on his way out, to report to Hojeda.

"No one in there," he heard Ricardo shouting.

After Tomas and Ricardo leaped upon their horses, the posse galloped out of the village to continue its search along the countryside for their wanted *cacique*. When they reached some hills, Hojeda turned around again.

"Men, my guts tell me that he's in hidin' somewhere around here. Start searchin' every weed 'n hole. When th' sun reaches above that tree over there, then return 'n report to this spot."

Tomas glanced at the sun, studied the tree at which Hojeda had pointed, and calculated that they were to meet back in an hour. He dismounted his horse, headed toward the hills, and began to climb, sometimes clutching at clumps of greenery. Tiny bits of limestone crumbled beneath his weight. As he pulled himself upon a large rock, he let nothing escape his eyes; he paused and scrutinized every crevice, each tree and bush; he scanned the area below him, and even sniffed the air. Then he started up again. A small stone rolled downhill and bounced off his arm. He continued his ascent, slowly, cautiously. As he pulled himself up upon a higher ledge, he stopped to rest, but then, he thought he heard movement coming from above him. He waited. He heard it again. And when he advanced uphill, his ears remained alert. He came to an upper ledge and found himself in front of an entrance to a cave. As he peeked in, he thought he heard a gasp, but he saw nothing. To Tomas, it seemed like all day long, he was hearing strange, soft sounds coming from vacant places. Today his imagination was really going wild. Nevertheless, he turned, cupped his hands to his mouth, and yelled to the bottom of the hill.

"Hojeda! I think there's somethin' funny goin' on up here. Come 'n see for yerself."

Within minutes, Hojeda was by his side, panting from the climb. He surveyed the cave at its entrance and held his hand behind his ear to see if he could pick up any sounds from within.

"Do ye hear anythin'?"

"I don't think so."

As Hojeda leaned into the cave entrance, he cleared his throat and made his voice sound as ferocious as he could.

"Canaobo th' Fierce, I know ye're in there."

His shout resounded off the cave walls, but there was no answer. When he repeatedly called into the cave, a chorus of voices echoed back. When the echoing ceased, he paused and turned to Tomas.

"Listen."

Tomas heard someone breathing, ever so faintly.

He whispered, "Hojeda? Shall we go in after him?"

Hojeda shook his head.

"Are ye *loco*? 'N lose him in that cave? It might lead on forever."

"Then we should find a way to get him to come out to us, *señor*."

"Hmmmmm, what can we do?"

As Hojeda gazed across the countryside below, deep in thought, the hilt of his sword flashed in the sun, and a pair of handcuffs also sparkled, as it hung from his belt.

"It would take many days to starve him out of there," Hojeda said.

"Señor, what if we offered him somethin' that would be really special to him? Ye know, somethin' he would think is from heaven, that th' Indians call *turey*."

Hojeda looked around him, pondering, then stared at his sword, but shrugged.

"I'd be a fool to give him my sword. Maybe one of us should climb down that hill to see what any of th' other men may have with them."

Tomas snapped his fingers.

"I know what we can do, *señor*."

He quickly reached toward the pair of handcuffs that dangled from Hojeda's belt.

"Señor...this is th' best *turey* we could offer him. See how it shines? I bet that *cacique* doesn't even know what it is."

Hojeda gave a laugh.

"Ah, *sí, sí...* "

Hojeda unlocked the handcuffs and caused them to jingle conspicuously, as he turned towards the mouth of the cave. This time when he spoke, his voice had greatly softened.

"Canaobo th' Fierce, do ye know why we're here? We want to be yer friends."

He forced a smile and then laughed.

"Ye are too great a warrior for all of us, 'n because ye are so strong, we want to make peace with ye. See? We even brought ye a gift."

Hojeda stood back from the entrance, holding his handcuffs in front of him, allowing them to flash in the sun.

"This is *turey*, Canaobo th' Fierce. We brought it just for ye from heaven."

Tomas watched Hojeda force a smile again, as a spot in his neck throbbed, while he stood in the direct sunlight. Then something in the cave stirred, and Tomas could hear slight sounds of someone breathing again. Hojeda continued to hold the handcuffs outward, as he carefully made sure that they were always directly under the sun's rays, so that they would gleam and glitter. He shook them hard, so the *cacique* could hear them jingling. As sweat streamed down Hojeda's forehead under the heat of the sun, he pulled a handkerchief from his pocket and blotted his face. And then, a shuffling sound came from the cave, as if someone was approaching. And soon, Canaobo the Fierce appeared at the entrance and stood before them, with his eyes squinting to adjust to the light, as he steadily stared at the handcuffs dangling in midair.

"See? Ye wear this turey around here," Hojeda said, encircling his wrists. The *cacique* smiled slightly at first, but then he broke into a broad grin. "Come here, so I can put them on ye."

Canaobo the Fierce cautiously came forward, as a breeze brushed against the feathers that extended from his crown. Tomas noticed that this king was not tattooed, as the other *caciques*. Nor did he wear a golden crown. As Canaobo the Fierce came nearer, he held out his hands toward Hojeda to receive the gift. Tomas could hardly breathe, nor could he believe what he saw, for he thought he perceived in this *cacique's* eyes, an admiration for Hojeda.

"Me honored to accept gift from ye."

Tomas dared not take his eyes off this *cacique*, lest he disappeared. No other Spaniard had ever been this close to him before and survived. He watched as the Indian warrior lifted his hands toward Hojeda, like an innocent-eyed lamb walking up to its owner, just before its slaughter. He saw Hojeda hesitating for a moment, as awe swept across his face at the handsome and perfectly built *cacique*, standing before him; and then, he quickly clamped the handcuffs over Canaobo the Fierce's wrists.

As the posse headed towards Santo Domingo, with Canaobo the Fierce riding at its lead next to Hojeda, Tomas was impressed at how fast the news of the *cacique's* capture had swept across the island, for the people now gathered outside of their huts and were no longer afraid of the posse, as it passed by. Strangely, no opposition erupted, and the behavior of the mothers and children had suddenly turned passive, unlike the previous times, when they ran away from the Christians. Instead, the people lined up, with their faces silvery with tears, as an ambience of gloom and mourning hovered throughout the countryside. Some of them even tossed flowers to their *cacique*, as he went by. Although Canaobo the Fierce had influenced his subjects to be in constant battle, now that he was no longer in power, his people appeared to have resorted back to their peaceful, Tainan ways, for no one put up any fight to save him, but all they did was stand weeping, with resignation that the Christians had finally won.

As Tomas stared after the *cacique* riding up front, with handcuffs encircling his wrists, he knew that Hojeda had given this king a place of honor, for Canaobo the Fierce was being treated differently. Whenever *caciques* were captured, they were usually burned immediately at the stake in the town plaza, for all their subjects to observe; or sometimes, they were hung.

But instead, Hojeda said, "I just can't kill this king. I guess I'll send him back to our queen in Castile. She'll know what to do with him."

Now as Canaobo the Fierce rode next to Hojeda, Tomas perceived that to his leader, this king was a grand prize that he could never bring himself to destroy. And Tomas also noticed an unmistakable pride in the eyes of that Indian king, for instead of having defeat on his countenance, he held his head high. Even as he passed his weeping people, he cast occasional glances of admiration at Hojeda.

All this time, Tomas swore he was hearing things again, for he thought he overheard Canaobo the Fierce muttering and chuckling beneath his breath in broken Spanish, "Heh, heh, heh, ye great warrior. Hui, ye capture me. Nobody else good enough to catch me, but ye good enough. Heh, heh."

If Tomas was not imagining things, he did not know how to interpret this *cacique's* words. A Spaniard would have detested his captor, but this man showed no
186

such hatred. In fact, he actually appeared to be pleased that Hojeda had gained power over him, and he appeared to have a strange humility about it. Tomas couldn't see why, when after all these months of battling against this king, his capture was so simple. As Tomas rode in silence, the teary-eyed Indians he passed reminded him of the pleading eyes of the woman he raped a while back, but this time, he had no *chicha* to squelch his pity for these people. In fact, now that he was sober, he found that he was experiencing a tremendous compassion for them. As his high-spirited companions spoke with exhilaration, because of the defeat of Canaobo the Fierce, their excitement held no effect upon him, because the surrounding Indian faces haunted him, and the sight of the *cacique* ahead of him, penetrated him to the core.

When they finally reached the Kingdom of the Great Old Lady several days later, it was dark. And the men filed into a town bar with their loud laughter. As glasses clicked, there were toasts to Hojeda and his accomplishment; toasts to Canaobo the Fierce and his downfall; toasts to the Catholic Sovereigns of Spain for their victory in the Indies; toasts to the Admiral and his success in the pacification of the island; and toasts to anyone else, who came to their minds. And as Tomas toasted with them, he did not take a single sip, for the eyes of those Indians left their mark in his brain and spoke deeply inside of him. He knew that if he drank, all communication with his inner feelings would be cut off from those images.

Tomas placed his glass down in front of him, as the men gruffly spoke around him.

"When will Canaobo th' Fierce leave for Castile?"

"They'll bring him to th' docks in th' mornin', where he'll be put on a ship that will be leavin' Santo Domingo for Spain th' followin' day."

Tomas stared into space like a dead man, whose eyes were left open, and he did not even bother to look in the direction of anyone who spoke. Ever since this settlement of Santo Domingo opened up, and he was assigned to manage a *repartimiento* nearby, restlessness raged through him. It started when the Christians hung that old Queen Higuanamá from a tree to get rid of her kingdom and power, and also, because they said that she was a heathen. And now as Tomas sat thinking of the murder of that elderly queen, as well as the capture of Canaobo the Fierce, he muttered softly, so no one could hear him.

"Only *Dios* knows what we are doin'."

"Did ye know that on th' ship where they're puttin' Canaobo th' Fierce, they are also bringin' to Spain th' largest piece of gold ever found in these Indies," someone said. This comment drew the immediate attention of everyone around, except for Tomas. "An Indian girl, who lives in this area, just dug up that gold piece th' other day."

"How big is it?"

The person spread his hands apart to show the size of the gold piece.

"About this big."

Some of the men whistled.

"Ah, so th' ship that th' king will be on, will be th' luckiest vessel that ever crossed th' ocean, eh?"

Someone nudged Tomas.

"Ye haven't touched yer wine. Would ye want to drink somethin' else?"

Tomas looked up and saw Ricardo leaning toward him. The sight of him repulsed him, and he slunk away. Surprised at his unexpected reaction, Tomas wondered what was happening to him. And then he realized that it was Ricardo's doing that had forced him each time into Hojeda's wild escapades.

"Naw, I don't feel like havin' anythin', right now. Too much excitement, I guess."

Tomas arose and left the building, glad to be away from the coarse laughter. When he reached his home, he lay awake throughout the night. In the distance, he could hear Indians singing, accompanied by their rhythmic and sonorous instruments. These people were not usually up at this time of the night, and they sounded as if they were also dancing. It was strange to hear them singing at this hour these days, especially when they knew that they were breaking the law, for the Admiral had put a stop to those heathen rituals. But tonight, no one bothered to break up their ceremony, for the Christians were too engrossed in their celebration of the conquest of Canaobo the Fierce.

As Tomas lay, staring into the darkness, his mind drifted to his family back in Castile. It was three years, since he announced to them that the queen had given him an assignment to be a grantee over a *repartimiento* in the Indies. His father was particularly proud of him, for back then, Tomas was only eighteen years old. His father was so excited over this prospect that he decided to accompany Tomas to Española to study this island for himself.

Once they reached Española, although Tomas was not yet been granted a specific piece of property, his father wandered through the island in amazement, exclaiming, "*Es fabuloso!* If ye do well here, ye'll be rich in no time!"

Now that Tomas was twenty-one years old and was managing land in the Santo Domingo area for some time, no matter how much wealth he accumulated, he still did not feel any richer than before. How could he, if the Christians who surrounded him, lived by their base desires? Within a year since his arrival in these Indies, he ceased to be that well-mannered gentleman he once was. The longer he remained on this island, the coarser he became, and he well knew that he was now dealing with people, whom he would never associate with back in Castile. And he also realized that because of it, he had grown beyond human feelings, and he wanted those feelings to return.

And as he lay alone in the dark, the scenes of Canaobo the Fierce riding in front of the posse — with his muscular arms, imprisoned by handcuffs, and his crown of feathers, drooping over his shoulders — would not leave his mind. Somehow, he, Tomas, could not see that Canaobo the Fierce deserved that fate.

When morning came and Tomas arose, still sleepless and with images of Canaobo the Fierce haunting him, he began pacing the floor. Finally he knew that he must see that Indian warrior king again. He walked to a shelf, filled a pack with some of his belongings, and headed across town to a building where they kept the captured slaves, who were about to be sent to Spain. He paid the guard at the door a gold coin to allow him to enter, and he found Canaobo the Fierce in chains, among other Indians.

As soon as he approached, Canaobo the Fierce recognized him, and his countenance brightened.

"Where Hojeda? Him come, too?"

"No. I came alone. I brought some gifts for ye." Tomas paused, and then added, "But this time, none of them are *turey*."

188

Tomas pulled out a blanket from his pack.

"It's cold in my homeland at this time of th' year, 'n ye'll need this."

Next he handed the *cacique* a large slab of dried meat.

"Sometimes on these ships, they will not give ye 'n yer people enough to eat. Ye'll need this to share with th' others."

And last, he pulled out a rosary. He had never used it, but his mother had placed it into his hands, just before he boarded the ship to come to this island.

"And here's somethin' that can help ye with th' white man's *zemie*. It will give ye protection."

But after he said this about the rosary, Tomas was not certain whether he was telling the king the truth. While he watched Canaobo the Fierce examining his presents and nodding gratefully at him, Tomas saw no malice or resentment in his eyes.

"Ye great warrior, just like Hojeda."

"Canaobo th' Fierce, did ye hear yer people dancin' 'n singin' last night?"

"I hear them. They dance for me. They make up new *areita*, just for me."

"It was a strange kind of song. It didn't sound like their usual music. What were they singin' about?"

The king was silent for a while. Then he began to snicker. His laughter grew louder, until he nearly turned hysterical, and tears streamed down his cheeks. The slaves next to him reached out, and with their chains clattering, they tried to calm him down. Finally Canaobo the Fierce gained control of himself, and he grew silent again. At last, he looked up at Tomas.

"They say, *Canaobo th' Fierce, king of th' Kingdom of th' Mines. Him captured. Will go on foreigner's ship as slave. We not see him again. Big military genius. Beaten by stupidity.*"

The king looked at Tomas, his face still wet from laughing so hard.

"Those people not understand. I not stupid. I die with honor. I know gift Hojeda give me not *turey*. My people not understand. *I save them.* My battles kill too many of them. Better for them that I die with honor 'n go away from them."

The broken Spanish that the *cacique* spoke confused Tomas, for he could not understand what the king was trying to tell him. He turned to go, but Canaobo the Fierce called after him.

"My two guards…Hojeda kill them?"

Tomas understood Canaobo the Fierce, this time.

"Ye mean, those two men who were standin' in front of yer hut?"

"Them dead, now?"

"Why, no. We left them alone."

Tomas saw disappointment fill the *cacique's* eyes.

"Them two bravest men in my army. They stay to watch for Hojeda. They want to die for me 'n receive highest honor in next world. They want Hojeda to kill them. They not want to be around, when yer people take over th' Kingdom of th' Mines."

Again, Tomas did not comprehend what the king was saying.

The following day when a fleet of ships finally withdrew from Santo Domingo, with Canaobo the Fierce on one its vessels, Tomas realized that he was watching the most valuable ship to ever leave this island. For not only did it sail with the largest piece of gold ever to be found in the Indies, but most important of all, it held the bravest *cacique* in history.

189

A few days later, a hurricane hit the island, and with its winds and battering rains, it tore up many European homes, but not one of the Indian *bohíos* was damaged, for these *bohíos* had always withstood such storms for generations. A week after that storm passed, as Tomas stood on the docks again, he saw a bedraggled ship arrive. It was from the fleet that had left with the ship that took Canaobo the Fierce away. After it docked, its crew told Tomas and others, who gathered around, what had happened out at sea. As the men described monstrous waves that tossed the vessels about as toys, they told how, one by one, the sea swallowed all of the other ships, including the one with Canaobo the Fierce and the giant piece of gold.

As Tomas listened to these men, saddened that Canaobo the Fierce was no longer alive, a *padre* who stood next to him muttered beneath his breath, "It is an act of God. I know it is. Ye can't tell me that God is not angry that we have stolen one of th' greatest kings of this island."

But no one, but Tomas, heard this *padre's* comments, for the toughened men around him were only concerned over the monetary losses involved with this destruction, as they also complimented themselves.

"God is with us. He helped us conquer Canaobo th' Fierce. And now it is His will that we pacify th' rest of th' heathens on this island."

As time passed, now that the most powerful *cacique* was no more, Tomas saw peace begin to spread across the island. Soon the Christians were enjoying being carried pick-a-back upon the shoulders of Indians, who took them everywhere they pleased. Yet Tomas still could not agree with the comments that his hardened colleagues were repeating, about the grace of God that now prevailed, for he could never see that it was His will, that the population of the Indians of Española was now reduced to just two-thirds its original size, in just a year's time.

And among these hardened men, Tomas again turned to *chicha*, so he could erase his human feelings.

30

When a runner came and gave his message to Anacoana and Beheccio, while he was still on his knees after delivering this news, Anacoana got up and walked to the open doorway of her *bohío* and stared out of it. Then she turned back and faced the messenger.

"So, tell me again why do the Christians wish for Beheccio and me to meet with them."

"The foreigners said that they wish to discuss the tributes we owe Spain and the quotas we are not meeting, your majesty."

"But we *are* meeting our quotas," said King Beheccio, with exasperation in his voice. "Canst thou not see that those men are changing the figures in their records to make our people appear unproductive, because they wish to take in more than their share?"

"I'm only following orders and am telling you what I am told, your majesty."

Anacoana quickly intervened.

"Fine. We will meet with them. Just tell us when."

"They said to tell both of you that they will be arriving at your royal *bohío* shortly."

After the messenger left, Anacoana faced her brother.

"The foreigners give us not enough time to think about this situation, don't they?

"Aye. It maketh me uncomfortable," Beheccio said.

"Thinkst thou that Ricardo is among those who have requested for us?"

"I have seen him in our kingdom lately, so he probably will be at that meeting."

"I wish Ricardo would remain in the Kingdom of the Mines, or the Kingdom of Marién, or wherever his *repartimiento* is. Whenever he cometh to meet with the *repartimienderos* in our kingdom, he causeth much damage among us."

"But his Christian friends look up to him with great respect, Anacoana. His gentlemanly manners and smooth tongue cause them to believe that he is a goodly person."

"I have heard that he hath been most active in rounding up the foreigners for Hojeda and hath served as the main cause for the havoc on this island. Hast thou heard that he and the Spaniards refer to their massive destructions in our villages as *pacifying the Indians*? I have every reason to believe that Ricardo is responsible for the death of my husband. I can apply *the love* no longer with him, and he and his men cause me to tremble with fear. When the Christians first came and told me that they were breaking our kingdom up into *repartimientos*, I explained to them that this process should interfere not with the operation of my school, and under no conditions, should I be forced to close it down. I explained how important it was, to not only the people of Quisqueya to have this school continue, but also to the other people on the surrounding islands, for this school hath been in operation for generations and is part of a proud legacy and heritage. I also emphasized that they must bother not my princesses. At first they respected my desires, until Ricardo arrived on his first visit. From then on, my princesses began to be harassed. When I appealed to the foreigners again, it took all of my strength to tell them that my princesses are not just for any man on this island, or even for most of the men anywhere else, for they are special and elite women, who were raised for certain purposes.

"Instead of respecting my wishes, they look at me, as if I were being a hypocrite, because I, the queen, sometimes share my body with some of them to improve political relations. And as long as Ricardo is with them, he stirreth up the Christians, so they wish not to respect our taboos any longer."

"Anacoana, from now on, we should be cautious with what we say around the foreigners, lest our words bring them to anger. Hast thou noticed that they've become more violent lately? This situation could turn extremely dangerous.

"And also, Anacoana, hast thou also heard about the happenings in Santo Domingo? Ricardo is also responsible for a war there that hath created a great division among the Christians. As he and his men were rounding up Quisqueyans to send back to Spain as slaves upon ships, a great protest burst out. Both Christians and *caciques* united in a revolt against this deportation. The Christians were protesting, because they were angry that many of the women, who were being taken, were pregnant with their children, and they wished not for their children to be sold into slavery; and the *caciques*, of course, were protesting, because they wished not that their own people be taken away."

191

"Doth that mean that our *caciques* are finally uniting on an issue?"

"Not completely, Anacoana. King Guacanagarí traveled to Santo Domingo from his Kingdom of Marién, because he wished to be involved in that fight. But he fought on the side of the foreigners, because he wished not to oppose the Admiral. As the Christians fought each other with swords and ammunition, the Admiral finally ended that dissension by punishing those who revolted for insubordination."

"What? He penalized the men, who were standing up for their own unborn children? I believe that not."

"I know not what is right or wrong, anymore, Anacoana. I have given the foreigners my best wives, but Ricardo still demandeth that he and his men are entitled to more women. In fact, he saith that they can have any princess, virgin, wife of *cacique*, or commoner they please, especially in our kingdom, where the women are the most attractive of all."

"I am finally understanding my past husband's views," Anacoana said. "He always used to tell me that if it were not for *the love*, we could have done much more from the beginning to protect ourselves."

"Aye, Anacoana. And maybe if I had not been so afraid of them, the armies that I hath disbanded, would have killed Ricardo long before, and fewer of the tragedies in our kingdom would have happened. Every time the Admiral is away from Quisqueya in search for Guanine, Ricardo taketh advantage of his absence by turning our island into frenzy. Now throughout our island, Christians war against Christians, Christians attack Quisqueyans, and once in a while, even the Quisqueyans fight back."

Anacoana covered her face.

"Terrible."

"Anacoana, didst thou know that those foreigners must also pay tributes to Spain?"

"No, I knew that not."

"Aye, in Santo Domingo, the Christians are protesting against those payments, because they say their queen in Spain demandeth too much. And some of them have stopped their tributes and have told the Quisqueyans, who work beneath them, that they need not pay tributes to them. And more wars have resulted from it."

"And on which side is Ricardo? Is he for, or against, paying tributes to his queen?"

"He is loyal to his queen, Anacoana, and he wisheth to continue the payments."

Anacoana sighed.

"So there is no need for my husband to perpetuate battles upon this island anymore, for others are doing it for him," she said. "Hui, at least, he had a noble cause, when he was alive, for he was only trying to preserve us all."

Just then, Nila put her head into the *bohio*.

"Two litters are waiting outside to take both of you to the royal *bohio*. The foreigners are waiting there."

Anacoana turned to her brother and whispered.

"They are here, already? I still see not any reason for this meeting, Beheccio."

She then turned toward Nila and smiled.

As Anacoana entered the royal *bohío* with her brother Beheccio, the people in the room arose. She saw her advisors, priests, and princes of the court standing at one side of the hut, while Ricardo, various Christians, and the *repartimienderos* of the Mother Kingdom stood in a small group, at the opposite side. She searched among the foreigners for her lover, Velasquez, but she did not see him. And then, her heart gave a jolt, for her eyes fell upon Semola, standing among the foreigners. She wondered why he was dressed in European clothes. She smiled in the direction of the foreigners, and then walked to her *dohu*. As she sat upon her throne, she felt self-conscious that she was no longer dressed as elegantly as she used to be. This morning was like many other mornings lately, when she was so rushed over the concerns of what the foreigners brought to her land, that she no longer had time left to call Nila to come to arrange her hair in tufts and dress her in a fine *nagua*. And now, her hair was only simply tied back behind her neck, as a commoner's.

When everyone was seated, Ricardo came forward. As always, he put on his gentlemanly smile and airs that hid his cold, coarse interior that often, only Anacoana saw. His smile briefly reminded her of the many times he deceived the Christians and convinced them that his ideas were only for the good of the island. But somehow, Anacoana knew from experience, that by the end of this meeting, he would have manipulated the other *repartimienderos* to become agitated and angry with her and her people.

Ricardo motioned for Semola to come forward and stand next to him, so he could translate for him. He then cleared his throat and began to speak.

"Yer majesties, King Beheccio 'n Queen Anacoana, as a representative of th' *repartimienderos* of th' Mother Kingdom, I am here to tell ye that our Queen Isabella of Castile has expressed th' need for an increased quota of cotton production to fill th' growin' demands of Castile. We, th' *repartimienderos* of yer Mother Kingdom, are disturbed that th' cotton gathered by yer people have decreased steadily during th' last nine months, which will make meetin' th' new demands impossible.

"Let me remind yer majesties that th' Admiral Don Christoforo Colón has set th' realistic 'n reasonable mark, that within th' Mother Kingdom, all able-bodied individuals, both men 'n women, who are fourteen years of age 'n older, are required to produce twenty-five pounds of cotton every three months. While reviewin' th' average rate of cotton since last May in th' Mother Kingdom, we have obtained th' followin' figures: Friday, 1 May 1495, th' average person brought in twenty-two pounds of cotton for that three month period. Monday, 3 August 1495, th' average was seventeen pounds. Monday, 2 November 1495, fifteen pounds. 'N last week, Tuesday, 2 February 1496, th' average dropped to twelve pounds.

"These totals are insufficient 'n deplorable, 'n fall far short of th' original 'n reasonable goals th' Admiral has set. Yer majesties should keep in mind that at all times, this island must be reduced to complete obedience to th' sovereigns of Spain, where all idle habits 'n heathen practices shall be abolished. Th' thrift 'n hard work, conducive to Christianity, should always be observed."

Anacoana glanced at Beheccio, then at her priests and advisors. None of them had anything to say to Ricardo, so she arose in their behalf and spoke in the mother tongue.

"*Señor*, I believe those figures are inaccurate. My people are constantly working hard for your queen, from early morning until the sun goes down."

"What did she say, Don Diego?" Ricardo said to Semola.

Semola immediately translated her words into Spanish.

Anacoana continued.

"I, myself, observed their production. Everything thy queen asked for, we gave unto her. If this were the Kingdom of the Mines and we had access to the gold of the Cibao Valley, we would also give unto her as much gold dust her heart desired, for it is the nature of our people to give all that we have to those we honor. We are a generous people, and we are never an idle people."

Ricardo waved his papers in his hand.

"Th' figures are here, yer majesty. My men have tediously recorded them, as soon as yer people brought their cotton to them. It shows here that th' people of th' Mother Kingdom have been frivolously idlin' away their time."

"I can believe not those numbers, *señor*. There either was a mistake, or someone hath altered them."

Her words caused Beheccio to jump up.

"*Señor, señor*. Please forgive us. We apologize for falling back on the production of cotton. Perhaps the rain hath caused the yield to become poor."

"Rain? Bah! It was not rainin' terribly three months back, 'n yer people still fell short on their quota. 'N three months before that, when it was sunny, they still did not reach their goals, either."

"We will work hard to give your queen whatever she needeth," Beheccio said.

Anacoana stood taller now, suspicious of everything Ricardo said.

"I still can believe not those figures, Señor Ricardo. I also wonder whether the Admiral and your queen in Spain are aware of this meeting."

She saw Ricardo turn crimson. He walked over to her and suddenly threw the papers down at her feet. When he leaned toward her and bore his teeth, she could tell that he was recently drinking heavily.

"Yer majesty," he said. "Do ye remember what we said last May, if yer people failed to meet their quotas?"

"Your men have punished my people enough," said Anacoana. "They need not more punishment."

"No, yer majesty. I don't believe ye remember anythin' we said. Besides our tellin' ye that yer people would be punished, we also said that if yer quotas were not met, ye, *their queen*, will be also punished."

Anacoana froze. This was another fabrication that she knew that Ricardo created, for she recalled him saying nothing of the sort.

Through the corner of her eyes, she saw Semola. He was standing silently with horror on his face. He did not translate what Ricardo just said, but Anacoana could understand every word Ricardo spoke in Spanish, and she needed no translator, even if Ricardo did. She continued to hold herself high, as Ricardo picked up his papers from the ground, and then, he pointed to some writing upon one of the sheets, which she could not read. She saw her symbol drawn on that particular sheet of paper.

"See, yer majesty? It is written right here. Ye agreed to it yerself, that ye would be punished if yer people failed. Here is yer symbol, which ye signed with yer own hand."

Anacoana stared at the paper. The symbol, indeed, looked like the one she used, but it was not quite like her drawing, for the curve on the beak of the bird that she always drew, was not right. Although she could not read or write in the foreigner's language, often these men made her sign their papers. Because she could not write her name, she drew her special symbol on them, instead. Often these papers contained agreements and proposals, which she could not even begin to understand.

But she happened to know that she did not put her symbol on that particular sheet of paper. She knew that what Ricardo was saying was a lie, for she would never agree to her own punishment, for why should she, who was always striving to be an upright leader, deserve any punishment? And then she realized that Ricardo must have planned this meeting with his men, so that they could carry on something dreadful that they must have agreed upon beforehand.

Anacoana looked over at Semola. His eyes were now round with fear. He must not have known why Ricardo had brought him along to this meeting, save only to do translating, but now, she could tell that he was probably experiencing similar suspicions that she was. But whatever these foreigners were planning, she, the queen of her people, still had the responsibility to represent her subjects.

"Señor Ricardo, my people are having a difficult time. In one year, our food supplies have diminished drastically. My people no longer have enough to eat, and they are exhausted from working under the Christians. Before thy people came, my storehouses were always full, but now they are bare, for we have not time left to fill them, after a long day of work. Whether or not those figures are true, if thou wilt *decrease* our work time but only a little, we can sufficiently work in our gardens to prepare enough food for ourselves. When we are allowed to become a stronger people, we will be able to produce much more for thee, thy people, and thy queen."

She heard Semola translating her words perfectly, but his voice trembled.

Ricardo slammed the papers down again and walked up to her, and as he spoke, not only could Anacoana smell the stench of alcohol upon his breath, but she also felt his spit flying into her face, as he carefully enunciated his words.

"Why should I give yer people less work time, when they cannot even produce *half* of what we need by working a full day? Ye have made promises, month after month, 'n have never kept them."

Anacoana turned away, close to tears, but when she looked back at Ricardo, she forced a smile.

"I will talk to my people."

Ricardo moved closer to her.

"Yer majesty, prepare for yer punishment."

Anacoana backed away from him.

Ricardo waved his arm as a signal to his men behind him, and they began to close in around her. Desperately she looked toward Beheccio for help, but when he did not move, she turned to her advisors and priests. They, too, did nothing and said nothing, but only sat tensely in their places. She then looked at Semola, but he also did not move.

"I told you, Señor Ricardo, I will talk to my people." Anacoana was trying to keep her voice steady. "We need but only more time to produce food for ourselves. Because the spirits of my people have now become so low, they must be given a little more time to help them rebuild hope in themselves."

The Spaniards continued to edge forward. Anacoana saw their grins coming close to her face. Unlike the Quisqueyans, their teeth were badly decayed. She turned to her brother again.

"Beheccio, Beheccio. Do something! Allow them not to hurt me."

She turned to run, but she felt their hands gripping her arms. As she screamed, the Christians responded, by shouting all around her. She heard Ricardo's voice above the others.

"We warned ye! We warned ye!"

She looked in the direction of the men of her court again. Her advisors sat staring at her, immovable, with horror in their eyes. And then the words of her husband, Canaobo the Fierce, returned to her. *Love? Bah! And let these foreigners take over the entire island? The people here have lived too long trying to keep peace. Now they do not even know how to fight to protect themselves.*

"Beheccio, thou must help me!"

She saw her brother jump up from his *dohu*. He was weeping. He took a step forward, but when one of the Christians saw him and drew his sword, he backed away. The Christians began to pin her arms behind her back, and Anacoana could not free herself, no matter how hard she struggled. The more she tried, the tighter they held her. They yelled curses at her, and she heard the familiar term *dirty dog*, as they pounded their fists into her face, chest, and abdomen. Then she felt their brutal hands, fondling her body through her *nagua*, and one of them grabbed hold of her necklace and yanked it from her shoulders. Beads scattered around her. She heard a rip. And then another. The next thing she knew, she was standing completely naked in front of the princes, her advisors, her priests, the whole court, and even Semola. The Christians scorned and laughed at her. She could smell Ricardo's breath upon her throat, and then, he had his arms around her. She fell backwards beneath his weight, and when she landed, he was still upon her.

He was yelling into her ear, "We told ye this would happen!"

"Behecciooooo!"

She looked over at her brother. He was now running out of the *bohío*. And he was weeping hard. Once he reached outside, she saw him turn in the direction of the forest.

It was no use calling out to him, or to any of the men of her court. She turned to Semola.

"Semola, please. Help me!"

But Semola stood, as if he were the stone figure of Marocael. Like Beheccio, he was also weeping.

Helplessly, Anacoana screamed with all her might. "Canaoboooo!"

She knew that if her husband were present, he would have killed all of her attackers, and maybe even all the people of this court, who were too afraid to defend her.

"Canaobo, my love, please. Thou must come now to help me. Oh, how I can believe not that thou art dead!"

31

Nila's wax lamp bobbed up and down, as she carefully led Mateo and Neef into Anacoana's dark *bohío* in the wee hours of the night.

"Shhhh! The princess is in no condition to see anyone, but she insisted that I bring ye both to her, as soon as ye returned, no matter how late it was."

Nila walked up to the queen's hammock and whispered, "Princess, Princess. The boys are here."

Neef heard a groan, and then he saw a dark form lying in a hammock in front of him. It tried to rise, but Nila leaned over and gently held it back.

"Nay, Princess. Thou must stay down."

Neef then saw the silhouette extend a hand in his direction.

"Neef? Mateo?"

As Neef came forward with Mateo, he could barely see the queen, but gradually, his eyes adjusted to the flickering light, and he saw a figure with a swollen face and puffy eyes, looking in his direction. Even in the dimness, he could see that its lips were extremely swollen.

"Your majesty, whatever happened?"

"It was terrible," Nila said. "The foreigners beat and raped her in front of the entire court. Everyone in the Mother Kingdom is disgraced that anything like this should happen to our queen."

"I am sorry that I was unable to send anyone out to find you in the wilderness," Anacoana said. "The foreigners came soon after you left and prevented anyone from leaving."

Neef took Anacoana's hand that was still held out to him. It felt cold and limp. He stared at her battered face. Before he could speak again, Mateo spoke.

"Is Admiral Colón on this island, your majesty?"

"Aye, aye." The queen's voice was unusually soft. "I heard that he hath returned from exploring five days ago, and he is now back in the Kingdom of Marién, in Guarica. We were lucky to receive this news, because it is rare when messengers come to us anymore, excepting for when the foreigners want to use them. There are now some ships that belong to the foreigners docked in our harbor, and when it is time for one of them to sail for the Kingdom of Marién, ye both can leave on it to return to the Admiral."

The thought of boarding a foreigner's giant bird turned Neef cold, especially after what they did to Queen Anacoana. He was glad that when he and Mateo started back to find the queen after their visions, they came across people who could direct them here and did not need to attract the giant ships, as Mateo suggested.

"Your majesty," Neef said. "Could you send word to Basamanaco that we want him to come and get us, instead?"

"It may not be possible, Neef, but I shall do my best."

The queen coughed.

"Ye both must understand, that ye cannot stay in the Mother Kingdom, anymore," she said. "It is no longer safe for anyone here. I just closed down the School of the Princes, for even my students were in grave danger. Some of them have already been forced to work under *repartimienderos* here, but I intend to eventually send all of them back home to their various lands."

The queen's voice broke, as if she was fighting back tears, and then she gained control over herself.

"Oh, my sons, I apologize that I cannot make both of ye princes, as I planned."

"Why not?" Mateo said.

"No one is left at The School. My teachers and officials must now work in cotton fields for the foreigners, and I have not any political power left."

"Then our visions were all for naught, your majesty?" Mateo said.

"Why should they be? Does their significance end when The School closeth? Is a school the only place, where one can apply anything of value?"

As the wax lamp flickered, Neef studied the queen's face, neck, and shoulders and saw that they were badly bruised, and many parts of her body had swelled to twice their original size. Her left arm appeared to be broken, for it was bandaged to a stick.

"Both of you must tell me about your visions, now," the queen said. "I can wait not until morning. "

When the boys finished relating their experiences to Anacoana, she sighed, as she lay back upon her pillows.

"Basamanaco said that nobody accomplished their visions," Neef said. "He said that the challenges that the *zemies* give are always too difficult."

The queen said nothing, as if she was thinking of an answer to give them.

"But we will fulfill our visions, your majesty," Mateo said. "When I return from Castile, both Neef and I will work together to save the people on this island."

"And how will ye both save our people?" she said. "The Christians have returned with a much greater power than ever."

"We will find solutions, your majesty."

"Ah, so I see…ye both have the right attitude toward your visions. My sons, my sons, I do not believe Basamanaco is correct. There are many who fulfill their visions, but it was not while they were alive. Sometimes they fulfilled them after they died and went to *Coaibai*. Before ye left for the wilderness, ye understood not what I meant when I said that ye would be learning about the *mapoyas* and *opias*. Now that ye have had your visions, ye are ready to hear more about them."

When the queen coughed again, Neef wondered whether the foreigners caused her to have injuries to her internal organs. Lida told him about people who received such injuries in accidents, and she had to brew special herbs to help their organs heal. He waited for the queen to stop coughing, so she could speak again.

"Sometimes *opias* are spirits of people who lived good lives, while they were alive. *Opias* can look just like you and me, but if ye look at their bellies, they have no navels. It is because their bodies were not developed from women, like yours and mine that required placentas while in the womb. The visions ye both saw, consisted of *opias* that acted out lessons for you. When these *opias* are not performing visions, they are working to achieve the missions they have learned from their *own* earthly visions, long after their bodies of flesh have been dead."

"You mean, I did not actually see my Grandfather Cahoba in my vision, but it was an *opia* who was pretending to be him?" said Neef.

"Neef, the *bohutios* informed me that your grandfather's *opia* hath actually asked to participate in both thy and Mateo's visions."

"And the *mapoyas*?" Mateo said. "Can you tell us about them?"

After his vision, Mateo was intrigued with the concept of spirits. As a Christian, he heard of ghosts, which wandered the earth, haunting and frightening people. Until recently, to him, visions did not involve friendly spirits, but rather, angels, the saints, Christ, and God. So now that both he and Neef received their individual visions, such experiences took on deeper meaning to him.

"Many of the *mapoyas* are spirits of wicked people, who had died, but because they are not given rest in *Coaibai*, they must constantly roam the earth. They are also the wicked spirits, who tempt people to do harm. They can blind us from knowing the difference between right from wrong, as well as from understanding the value and potential of each human soul. They keep us from improving our cultures, traditions, and minds. *Mapoyas* can also possess and torment the bodies of people, who have turned wicked. Bear in mind that they have participated not in your

198

visions, but instead, the *opias* have acted out the roles of the wicked spirits, to teach both of you lessons.

"Although I have said that people continue to fulfill their vision after they die, I know of only one person who hath accomplished his mission, while he was still alive. He was like both of ye, for he received not a full education from The School. And he was only given a *bohutio* test. No one knew about it, but my family."

Neef's eyes grew wide.

"What? Mateo and I were not the only people who were given only the *buhutio* test at The School? It was not your original idea?"

"It happened once before, my sons. It happened with Canaobo the Fierce, my late husband. He died at sea, while ye were both in the wilderness. When he first came to Quisqueya from the Lucanyan Islands with his men, he was only about your age. Back in those days, I saw him not, but my father hath met him, when he was visiting the Kingdom of the Great Old Lady. Father was so impressed with him, that he wished to give him an education at The School, but because Canaobo The Fierce hath not the breeding of a prince, and he was only born a commoner, Father thought that perhaps a *bohutio* test experience would be the best kind of schooling he could have.

"While I was a little girl, I heard much about Canaobo the Fierce. But I never saw him until my wedding day, after he was made ruler of the Kingdom of the Mines. Up until that time, the stories I heard about him frightened me. But after I married him, I realized that my fears were unfounded."

"What challenge did the *zemies* give him, your majesty?" Neef said.

"He was told to clear this island of the Caribs. At that time, every person on Quisqueya ran away from those cannibals. Nobody was brave enough to face them, except for Canaobo and his men. After my parents died, no one alive knew of Canaobo's vision, except for my brother and I."

As the queen leaned back in her hammock, exhausted from her long conversation, the boys stood up to leave, but she waved her good arm at them to remain.

"Not yet, my sons. Abide here just a little longer, for we have one more matter of business."

The queen turned to Nila.

"Get the royal tattooer," she said.

When Nila returned, a *bohutio* and a group of servants followed her, as she led them by the light of her wax lamp. One of the servants was carrying a basket that held some sharpened sticks and dyes in tightly closed containers.

"My sons, the world must know of your accomplishments," Anacoana said. "Although my husband Canaobo the Fierce hath not circles and crosses implanted in his skin to show that he hath taken a *bohutio* test, I feel that in this respect, my father hath cheated him. I wish to give you both this honor."

Mateo gasped, and in panic, he jumped up from the floor.

"Nay! Nay! Don't tattoo me!"

The servants and *bohutio* looked at each other. When they turned to Neef, he obediently pulled himself up with his crutches and hobbled up to them. The servants encircled him, tossed some cushions upon the ground, and coaxed him to lie down. As Neef lay upon the cushions, he felt the Naborians holding him firmly, as they spoke soothingly to put him at ease. Neef took deep breaths and looked away from the people standing above him, focusing upon the dark silhouettes of *guayacan* beams that stood at angles below the thatched ceiling. He felt a pointed stick begin to etch into his forehead. The jabbing caused his body to tense, but then, he forced himself to relax again. He could feel snakelike paths being carved into him, as the sticks moved down to his nose, his cheeks, and then, his chin. The *bohutio* extended the designs to his neck, probing and probing. Neef thought of Basamanaco and Lida, both whom he would soon be seeing again. He even thought of his sister, Sabila, whom he would never see again. And last, he thought of his vision in the wilderness.

Neef wondered what colors the tattooer was using, for the room was too dark for him to discern the various hues and shades on the sticks. The servants flipped him on to his front, so the tattooer could engrave his back and buttocks. Although his concentration was intense, Neef could still feel sharp pains as the instrument traveled with artistic flows with each incision. The servants flipped him again and turned to his arms. When the tattooer moved to his chest, Neef forced himself to ponder upon his experiences with Mateo, as they both sat with the Admiral's Bible in the wilderness and discussed its stories and philosophies. As the stinging spread throughout his entire body, he thought of some of the verses in the Bible that he had memorized. Mateo was always amazed at how quickly he could learn large sections of the Bible verbatim, whether or not he understood their meanings. To Neef, they were no harder than memorizing an *areita*. Neef concentrated on a passage from Isaiah that went,

> ...concerning the king of Assyria, He shall not come into this city, nor shoot an arrow there, nor come before it with shields, nor cast a bank against it...I will defend this city to save it for mine own sake...

The stinging continued. The priest reached Neef's waist, then moved below his naval, to his hips. But when he reached his legs, he stopped. Neef felt the man's eyes studying his legs, and he perceived that because they were shriveled, the *bohutio* did not wish to touch them.

"Hui, my son," the tattooer said. "It is finished. Now all the world will see thine accomplishments."

When it became Mateo's turn, he panicked again and backed away, but the servants reached him and held him firmly, so that he could not escape.

"Please...I need no tattoos."

"But thou must. They are the greatest honors thou canst receive."

"Nay, nay. Please, please do not tattoo my skin! Especially not my face. I cannot go back to Castile, with tattoos upon my face."

The *bohutio* and servants exchanged glances, and then they looked over to the queen. When Anacoana spoke from her hammock, her voice was surprisingly soothing and patient.

"Mateo, the world must know of thy vision."

"In Europe, they would never understand it."

"Would it please thee, if we placed only a small mark upon thine arm? Perhaps a beautiful design, which will be covered by thy clothes?"

Mateo tried to pull away from the servants, and when the queen spoke again, she sounded as though she were close to tears.

"My son, my son, thy tattoo will be the last one our school shall ever perform. Thy people have ruled these practices unlawful."

Mateo finally relented.

"As you wish, your majesty. But only a small one on my arm, where no one will know."

And then Mateo bit his lips, as the instrument probed into his skin.

When Basamanaco arrived, he was jittery. He no longer had his large canoe with him, but instead, he used a medium-sized one, which he had borrowed from a friend.

Both boys placed their small packs, which held their few belongings, into the canoe. As they began their trip home, Basamanaco did not hum his *areitas*, as he usually did when he traveled, and while he paddled in silence, he constantly turned his head in all directions, as if he were on the lookout for any Spaniards, who could be lurking close by.

"I don't want to be caught," he said. "If the foreigners should find me not working in the cotton fields at this time of the day, they might punish me."

As the small group traveled north, occasionally they heard dogs barking in the distance, which sent sweat trickling down Basamanaco's back. And when the barking ceased, he breathed easier again.

"The foreigners have brought those beasts from Spain," Basamanaco explained. "They are extremely large and vicious, and they are trained to attack our people and to track us down, should any of us try to run away. The small dogs of Quisqueya, which we raise for food, cannot bark as those animals can, nor would they ever turn upon us, like those savage animals."

Because Basamanaco was so nervous, Neef and Mateo paddled in silence. Neef thought back to when he and Mateo had walked through the Mother Kingdom, while they were waiting for Basamanaco to arrive to take them home. He was alarmed at the extreme changes that took place in this land. Fear and uncertainty emanated from the prince and princesses' eyes, whenever he passed them. He recognized his former classmates, who now worked in fields. Instead of reciting poetry and laughing, as students usually did, their mood greatly contrasted from the time he and Mateo left for the wilderness, or even from when he first came to this kingdom at the age of five, for Queen Anacoana's wedding. Neef recalled the beautiful singing that once floated from the large *bohios* of The School. He thought of the joy and exhilaration that also prevailed in the courts, as the princesses and princes chatted in their separate groups. And he wished that he could bring those times back and erase the deep oppression that now dominated the Mother Kingdom.

Now women pulled cotton balls off plants along the hillsides, while men worked close by, gathering the cotton into bunches, and rolling them into large bales. As Neef saw his former classmates laboring alongside commoners, he felt twinges of pain, for this work used to be reserved only for *Naborian* servants. True to what he saw in his vision, he also recognized *undercaciques*, *Nytainos*, *bohutios*, princes, and princesses performing this work. As everyone labored together, they appeared as if they had always been born of equal status. And Neef also saw Spanish men with whips among them, who yelled constantly at these people. He perceived lust in their eyes, as they followed the princesses around, who worked under them. Even those men recognized that the princesses of this kingdom were among the best looking women on the island. Although everyone was treated equally as slaves, these young women still stood out in any crowd, for the simple clothes and brass tokens that they now wore, could not hide their beautiful faces.

As Neef watched the people bent over the cotton, *repartimienderos* often turned toward him, because he was a new Indian in town, but they quickly glanced away, as soon as they saw his crutches and shriveled legs. They did not even bother to check whether he wore a brass token.

Before the canoe reached Guarica, Basamanaco turned up an inland stream and found a way to inconspicuously approach the town, so they would not be discovered. When they finally banked in Guarica, Basamanaco concealed the vessel in some brushes.

"Basamanaco, I want to be with you, just a little longer, before I start looking for Admiral Colón," said Mateo.

So Basamanaco remained hidden in the bushes with Mateo, as they spoke soft farewells to each other. But Neef could not wait to see Lida again. He flung his pack over his shoulder and began to leave.

"Neef?" he heard Mateo call behind him.

Neef swung around and saw that Mateo was holding out the Admiral's Bible to him.

"Here, my brother. Take this as a gift to remember me, when I am gone."

Neef took the Bible gingerly, for he knew how much Mateo cherished this book. Then he removed his *zemie* from his neck and placed it upon Mateo. And they embraced.

Soon thereafter, Neef found the familiar paths to his home. As he hobbled toward the *bohío* that served as his home for many years, he noticed the silence that dominated the village. He passed huts and peered through their open doorways, but saw not a single soul within any of them. Nor were there people lingering in the plazas. And there were no women sitting beneath trees to gossip or sing, as they scraped manioc tubules.

When Neef reached Basamanaco's *bohío*, he stood at the doorway of this beloved home and absorbed the sight of the loom in a corner, where Lida often sat weaving cloth and sang. He walked over to some hava baskets that Lida had woven, which were stacked neatly against the wall, and then he made his way to each of the hammocks that were tied against their posts. They appeared just as he remembered them. His hammock still remained tied in its place, as if he had never left, and the one that Basamanaco later obtained for Mateo, was also tied to its post, in its part of the room. And then, he heard someone moving behind him.

There at the doorway, Lida stood, with a horrified expression, as if she was seeing an apparition.

"Hui, is that you, Neef? Is that you beneath all of those tattoos?"

"I passed my test, Lida. I passed a big test."

Neef could not understand the look on Lida's face. He thought that she would have been happy to see him.

"Oh, Neef, my son, my son. Is it really you? All this time, I thought both you and Mateo were dead. Hui, you have come home at last. We received word that both of you were lost in the wilderness, and you both had probably starved. And when Basamanaco was recently called to the Mother Kingdom, he didn't tell me that he was going to pick you up."

"Mateo came home, too, Lida. He'll be arriving soon. Where are all the people of our town? I don't see anybody, anywhere."

"They are all working in the fields, my son. They must pick cotton for the Christians."

"Everybody?"

"Everybody, Neef."

Her lips trembled, as she held a gourd of water to her body. Then Lida began to weep. It was, not at all, like her to weep openly. She brought her arms up toward her face, to wipe away her tears, but as she did, she revealed two stumps, with no hands at the wrists.

Neef gasped.

"Lida! Where are your hands?"

Lida did not answer, but placed the gourd upon the ground, ran to Neef, and gathered him into her arms.

"You are still alive. I am so glad you are alive."

"Your hands, Lida. What happened to them?"

And when Lida finally comprehended what Neef was saying to her, she withdrew from him, and quickly hid her stumps behind her back.

Then quietly, she said, "I became sick and could not pick enough cotton for the foreigners, so they punished me by cutting off my hands, and now I cannot work for them, anymore."

Anger gushed through Neef, and he could no longer contain himself.

"I have heard and seen enough of the cruelty those foreigners inflicted upon us!" he said. "If they had never come, Sabila would still be alive today. And you, Lida, if they never came, you would still have your hands. Even Basamanaco — he can't even be a trader anymore, but now he must pick cotton and form them into bales. Why should he be forced to do work he was never cut out for?

"I have also seen *undercaciques*, princes, princesses, who have lost their dignity and must work as servants, because of those foreigners."

In anger, Neef released a wail of frustration. Then he reached into his pack and withdrew the Admiral's Bible. With shivering hands, he flung it with all his might across the room.

"I will have nothing to do with any foreigner again! How can I ever be baptized and become a member of a religion that hates and destroys my people?"

As he turned abruptly to leave the hut, he lost his balance, fell with his crutches, and landed as a sobbing heap upon the floor. As he wept, a shadow fell across the doorway, and when he lifted his eyes to see who had come, he beheld Mateo standing before him, silently watching him. And then he was sorry for his outburst, for Mateo must have heard every word he said.

"Mateo, I'm sorry. I didn't mean exactly what I just said. It wasn't directed at you...I didn't mean you...I..."

But Mateo acted as if he had not heard Neef and came over to him. He had a smile on his face and excitement in his eyes.

"I couldn't find the Admiral, Neef, but I've learned that there is a ship that will be leaving for Spain early tomorrow. I'm going with it. I'm finally going home!"

"Oh, Mateo. Don't go. I want you to stay. We need you here with us. But if you must go, please come back, as soon as you can."

"I will, I will. How can I not return, when I have learned from my vision that we are brothers, and we both have a purpose together? Besides, when I return, I will bring you many more books."

As Mateo turned to Lida to repeat this news to her, his jaw suddenly dropped open, and he gasped in horror.

"Lida! Oh, Lida!"

Book Four

32

As a fleet from Spain approached the docks of Caracol Bay, Neef stood waiting, as always. It had been eleven years, since such vessels first arrived in Cuba under the direction of the Admiral. Back in those days when Neef was twelve years old, he stood on a beach among the townsfolk of Jururú in absolute awe, for he had believed that those giant birds had come from heaven. And since that time, many such ships — even larger than those first two caravels — arrived in Guarica, where he lived on Quisqueya. Because the foreigners here missed the food and luxuries of their mother country and demanded that they be imported, these ships came with supplies from Castile. These items no longer looked odd to Neef, as he saw them unloading from the ships. There were crates of wine, furniture of polished wood, urns that carried olives, and boxes of fine clothing. Often he watched as giant animals, such as cows, horses, and pigs, were coaxed down gangplanks. Even chickens had become a common sight in Quisqueya, although Neef never thought that they were as delicious as iguanas. And when these vessels left to return to Spain, they were always loaded with the treasures of Quisqueya, such as gold, silver, slaves, tobacco, and parrots. Years back when the Admiral left on his first ship for home, he took with him much flora and a variety of seeds that did not grow in his land, and Neef had heard that across the ocean, plants, such as tomatoes and corn now thrived.

As one of the ships, *El Adventurero,* neared the docks, Neef watched its sailor toss a rope to shore. He had often noticed this man arrive on this vessel, for his scar across his cheek and missing front teeth distinguished him from the other sailors. And soon after *El Adventurero* was secured, its passengers began filing down its gangplank, lugging their belongings. Neef recognized a few of them, for some were returning to Quisqueya, but most of them had never been to this island. Neef had heard that they often came here for land and adventure. The people who were here for the first time gawked at the surroundings and occasionally pointed out landmarks and vegetation to each other, which probably were unlike anything in Castile.

Neef approached one of the passengers.

"*Perdone señor.* Do ye know if Mateo Gonzalez is on board?"

The stranger stared at him, surprised that an Indian spoke Spanish so well, and after looking him up and down, particularly at his loincloth, he stepped slightly back.

"Never heard of th' man, but perhaps someone else would know him."

Then he walked briskly away.

Neef walked up to the next passenger and asked him that same question, and again he received a similar reply. Mateo had been gone nine years now, and ever since his departure, Neef had always been here at the docks to greet him if he returned, but he was never on board any of the ships. As Neef leaned against a post and watched the passengers go by, none of them resembled his foreign brother. Many of them had beards, which were something his people could never grow. Perhaps Mateo had grown a beard or had allowed himself to grow fat, so Neef wouldn't recognize him. Since Mateo was his age, Neef studied every young man who looked about twenty-three years old.

After the last passengers had left the harbor, Neef stood alone, listening to the shouts coming from the sailors upon the ships. Several grantees rode up with their men to claim some farm animals, which were shipped from Spain. As they guided their herds off the boats, their gruff voices rang through the harbor. Then Neef saw a group of black slaves among those animals, clamoring down the gangplank with chains connecting their ankles and wrists. Among them, the men kept stoic expressions, while the women wept.

The sailor with a long scar across his cheek, climbed upon the railing of his caravel. Shirtless, with tattered pants and unkempt hair that fell below his shoulders, he kept perfect balance as he urinated into the sea. After he had completed his function, he waved to Neef.

"*Oye*, crippled Indian!" he said. "Ye lookin' for yer *amigo* again?"

"*Sí, sí*. Is he here?"

"*No, no est*. But I think I've seen him in Spain in Palos, because I heard someone callin' his name. Th' day before we left, he was askin' about when th' next ship was comin' over to th' Indies. His *nombre* is Mateo Gonzalez, *no*?"

"*Sí, sí.*"

"*El* is a tall young *muchacho* about this high, eh?"

The sailor raised his hand about six inches above his head, which amazed Neef, for he remembered Mateo to be an unusually small person.

"When does th' next ship arrive, *por favor*?"

"*Tal vez* two, three months. Who knows?"

From where the man stood, Neef could see his partially toothless gums as he smiled, and his left arm bore a gaping sore, which told that he had contracted *yaya* and was doomed to die, for the herbs could never cure foreigners from syphilis.

"*Gracias, señor, gracias.*"

As Neef started back to his *bohío*, he took his familiar route from the harbor and hobbled through the European section of town. The Spaniards here had grown so accustomed to seeing him in this area that they assumed that every time a ship came in, he would appear. No one stopped him for not being in the fields or for not having a brass token around his neck, and since the grantees did not care for a crippled slave, Neef was free to travel, wherever and whenever he pleased.

Eight years before when he had come back home with Mateo from the Mother Kingdom, he was shocked when he saw the abrupt changes that had occurred during his absence. Instead of one-roomed grass huts, simple plazas, and windy paths that were a little wider than the width of a single man, the Spaniards had already erected huge homes and buildings of wood and stone near his village. They contained many rooms, and some were even two or more stories high. By now, Neef had grown used to these dwellings, and as he walked past the European structures, he was aware that some of them contained books — many books — the kind that Mateo had promised to bring him, when he returned. Throughout this part of town, were many streets the breadth of ten men, and there were plazas so spacious that they covered the area of a small village. At first, Neef was impressed that the Spanish found no need to live along the side of rivers, as his people did, because like the people of the Mother Kingdom, they created canals and channeled in fresh water to provide power for their gristmills and drink for their crops. Melons, onions, lettuce, cabbages, cauliflower, and chickpeas, which were once imported from lands across the sea, now thrived throughout the countryside, as Neef's people worked all day to cultivate them to provide food for their masters. Fields of wheat and sugar cane also flourished where forests once existed. Even cotton plants that once grew wild along the hills and countryside had become domesticated. And farm animals whose predecessors had originated in Europe, now grazed in fields and pastures. Before the Europeans ever arrived, Neef had never imagined that such a world could ever exist. And once the Europeans started coming, it seemed as if they would never stop.

Neef had heard that east of Guarica, where the River Yaqui emptied into the sea, the Admiral had established another settlement called *Fort Isabela* that was far more populated with Christians than Fort Navidad ever was. In fact, three other forts now thrived on this island, and Santo Domingo, in the southeast, was one of them. He heard many Christians saying that they greatly favored Santo Domingo, because its deep harbor well tolerated the hulls of European ships.

And within the vicinity of Guarica, as foreigners moved out of forts and founded towns, King Guacanagarí extended his friendship and welcomed all of them.

As Neef approached his home, he turned toward the nearby forest, where he grew cassavas in monotones, and after he saw that those plants were doing well, he returned to his hut and extracted weeds from his small garden. On days when he caught fish, he shared what he and Basamanaco didn't need with the rest of the villagers, because his people had not enough to eat, anymore.

When he finally entered his home, it was empty, as usual. The familiar loom stood in its corner, just as it had the day he returned from the Mother Kingdom, but now, it sat unused for five years since Lida's death, when smallpox swept the area and had killed three-fourths of the town. He thought with amazement of how, even after Lida had lost her hands, she had managed to work the shuttle of her loom with her stumps. Now their *bohío* was never as tidy as when she was here.

Close to Lida's loom, Neef saw his papers stacked in neat piles. By now, he had invented his own method of making paper, but he much preferred the ones the foreigners used, for they were smoother and whiter than his, and when he was lucky, he occasionally begged some off the grantees. Upon these sheets, he had recorded the *areitas* of his people, with the alphabet that he had developed in the mountains, when he was with Mateo. He also had recorded his family's history and genealogy, Basamanaco's stories of Guanine, and parts of the Bible he had translated. But sometimes, he didn't always know the words the Bible used, nor did he always understand its concepts, so he left blank spaces and saved them for Mateo to fill in, when he returned.

Neef did not know why he was doing this writing, save only that his Grandfather Cahoba had instructed him to do so in his vision. Many times he had attempted to teach his people his alphabet and how to read it, but they scoffed and said, "What would you, a crippled man, know? How can you possibly believe that such records can save us?" And they refused to have anything to do with him. But Neef couldn't help noticing fear in their eyes and sensed that maybe they felt that he had developed something similar to the foreigner's magic.

At first he was surprised that, even Basamanaco did not show any interest in his work, for Basamanaco viewed what he was doing to be a result of the *bohutio* test, and he never felt that he and Mateo should have taken that test. And now, Basamanaco had grown feeble, and the robustness in his spirit was no longer present. He had grown resigned to his fate as a slave, after a succession of tragedies had struck Guarica. Since the death of Lida, Basamanaco began to withdraw into an inner world. Much of his energy was sapped, as he returned from work each day. And he came home with stories, about how he had seen the Spaniards punishing the traders whom he once traveled with, when they had done no wrong; how the people's *zemies* were smashed, when they were discovered; and how the *bohutios* were forbidden to practice their sacred rituals. And everyday, as soon as the sun was up, Neef watched Basamanaco walk to the cotton fields to perform his labors with hopelessness in his face, with his skin becoming even tougher under the sun than when he was a trader, while his shoulders drooped over his now prominent ribs. Like many others, Basamanaco had turned gray, with only two goals to fill, day in and day out: *I must accumulate twenty-five pounds of cotton every three months, so I won't be punished;* and *I must produce enough food for the foreigners, or be punished.* And he left Neef alone, to do as he wished with his papers.

As Neef pondered over who would give him support for his work, one day he thought of someone whom he had never considered before: *his father, King Guarionex.* He had not heard from him in a long time. He hoped that by now, the problems that his father faced with his uncle had fizzled out, especially since the Spanish had arrived. So he gathered a few of his records together and set out for the Fertile Kingdom.

When Neef arrived in the Fertile Kingdom to see his father, he brought with him a stack of papers from his records. Guarionex received him warmly and wept freely, for it had been many years. He then told Neef of how much he yearned for another yearly vision from the *zemies,* because he needed guidance for his people, but the Fertile Valley was no longer safe, for the Spaniards lurked everywhere on the island. If their people were not where the foreigners said they should be, the foreigners often sent hounds to track them down. And as Neef listened to King Guarionex, he saw in his father's eyes, a hatred for the Spanish dominion, as he kept repeating that now that Canaobo the Fierce was gone, it was no longer an issue of keeping the foreigners *under control,* because those foreigners had become *out of control* and were constantly seeking to keep all of their people *in control.*

As Neef showed his father his pages of writing, he also explained to him that he was translating the Admiral's Bible. But it did not take long before he noticed that Guarionex's face had turned intensely cold.

"What do you think you are doing?"

"I created them, just for our people, Father."

"But these objects resemble the works of the Spanish."

"But the symbols are different, for they represent the language of our people."

"How did you arrive at such ideas?"

"When I learned to read and write in Spanish, I decided to create a writing system, just for us." When Neef perceived a puzzled expression on the king's face, he added, "My Spanish brother taught me to read, Father."

Guarionex backed away.

"Your what?"

"My brother and I...we took our *bohutio* test together in the mountains."

For a moment, Guarionex's countenance went blank, as if he was trying to recall into his past, and then he finally said, "Oh, *that* boy — the one, whom the other *caciques* called the *Yocahu Boy.* I didn't think you would both make it out of the wilderness alive. I thought it was a foolish notion that Queen Anacoana had devised, anyway. So, that boy had actually passed his *bohutio* test, eh?"

"We both did."

"At that time, were you aware of the dangers you faced, when you associated with him? Why didn't you stab him while he slept?"

"What?"

Neef then explained to Guarionex about both his and Mateo's visions.

"Nay, it could not have been my father Cahoba, whom you saw in that vision, but a *mapoya* in disguise. Father would never appear in a vision to any foreigner."

"But don't you see? My work is only for the good of our people. It can give them strength, so they can preserve themselves, as well as raise themselves up, to prepare themselves for the greater knowledge Yocahu will someday bring to us."

Guarionex stared at the records Neef had spread out before him. Suddenly he snatched up some of the sheets and ripped them to pieces.

"Son, you must have nothing to do with any works of those devils!"

Neef stood dumbfounded, not sure of what he saw or heard. This was not the same father he remembered leaving years before, for this man was full of bitterness.

"In what way, can reading and writing help raise us up, Neef? Is it not enough to merely sing our *areitas*?"

"These writings are like the codices in..."

"They are imitations of a foreigner's thinking and the works of a traitor!"

Guarionex suddenly gathered the rest of the records, and with all of his strength, he tore them to shreds. In shock, Neef watched as *uinals* upon *uinals* of hard work, performed with love and hope, were destroyed before his eyes. And before he could think of anything in his defense, he felt servants taking him by the arms and leading him out of the court. As he looked back at his father, he suddenly found himself filled with rage.

"You never wanted me around, did you, Father? Why didn't you ever send for Sabila and me? We've waited and hoped for years, for you to call us back home. I don't believe that those rebellions were dangerous enough to keep us away that long."

Guarionex looked as if his face had turned to stone, and he turned his back toward Neef and said nothing. And as some of the servants gathered up the pieces of Neef's work, while others dragged him away, Neef yelled again, "Don't you see what you are doing? You're rejecting our only hope."

After Neef was tossed down the side of the hill below the royal *bohío*, he quickly began picking up the scattered pieces of his manuscript. Fortunately, he could remember every single word he had written, so all he would need to do was reconstruct his records again. As he looked up the hill toward his father's home, he saw the servants returning to the *bohío*. He also saw a young man, who was holding something wrapped in a piece of cloth, walking up to the servants.

"Is Father at home?" the young man said.

"Be careful when you approach him. He's quite upset, right now."

"Is he angry at the Spaniards again?"

"It was something else this time."

The young man then turned, and without waiting to be invited in, he entered the *bohío*. He held up what he was carrying toward Guarionex.

"Look what I found, Father."

Neef gazed after that young man and realized that during the years that he was gone from his home, he had a younger brother who was born, and he had never known about him. He saw his father's face suddenly soften and light up. And when the young man allowed the cloth to fall away from what he was carrying, Neef saw that he held several weapons that belonged to the foreigners.

"Good work, son," he heard Guarionex say. There was pride in his voice.

As Neef continued to gape into the *bohio* from the side of the hill, he noticed that the servants, who had thrown him out, had turned back toward him. So he quickly gathered the rest of the pieces of his records, took his crutches, and left.

As Neef hobbled down the hill, he could not get his brother out of his mind. His father had spoken to that boy in kinder tones than he had ever used with him.

Neef finally reached the major part of the town and began to head toward its palisade gates, so he could return to the docks.

"Aren't you new around here?" someone said from behind.

Neef spun around to see an elderly woman facing him. Yet he was not certain whether she was actually elderly, for nowadays, many of his people were gray, whether or not they were old.

"I used to live here long ago."

"So, why have you returned to this troubled place?"

As Neef gazed at that woman, she looked vaguely familiar.

"I came to visit my father, but I'm leaving now."

"Do I know you? What's your name?"

"It doesn't matter who I am, anymore."

Neef again started toward the docks, but just then, he recalled whom that woman was. He turned and faced her.

"Don't you make fishnets, and doesn't your husband carve wooden items to trade?"

"My husband is gone now, but we used to produce those items for our business, before we were required to pick cotton in the fields after the foreigners arrived."

She stared at him curiously, and then she looked down at his crutches.

"No...you can't be! Are you really the son of our King Guarionex?"

"I used to travel throughout our kingdom with my father, when I was a boy."

"Why, you're that little boy who disappeared with his sister, soon after your father became king. Everybody was wondering what had happened to both of you. I remember that you used to be the pride and joy of your grandfather."

"I've been away for a long time. I just learned that I now have a younger brother."

"You never knew about him?"

"I've heard very little news from home."

The woman didn't answer, but instead, glanced cautiously around her.

"Shhh," she said. "I think we'll need to talk. Come with me to my *bohio*."

When Meyona led Neef into her home, Neef held his sack of torn records tightly under his arm, determined to never tell anyone what had transpired between him and his father. Fortunately, Meyona never questioned him about this visit, but instead, she told him about the many rebellions that had occurred in the Fertile Kingdom, since he had left. She told him that once his younger brother was born, his father had begun to change his ways and had started a program to reject *the love*. He soon formed armies to protect himself, his family, and his kingdom. From then on, the kingdom began to grow stronger, and Eldest-Son-of-My-First-Wife was pushed out of the land.

212

When he heard this news about his uncle, Neef sat straight up.

"Wait a moment. If Eldest-Son-of-My-Father's-First-Wife was gone and our kingdom had then become safe, why didn't Father call my sister and me home?"

"Should we call your brother to ask him?" Meyona said. "We can send a messenger, who will tell him to remain quiet about this meeting."

It was in the middle of the night when Neef's brother finally appeared. His face was bewildered, as if he was wondering why he was being called.

As soon as he entered Meyona's hut, he said, "Do you have news of the rebellion?"

But Meyona ignored his question and turned to Neef, instead.

"Prince Neef, this is Prince Lampulla."

Neef looked at his brother. He looked about the age he was, when he went out into the wilderness with Mateo for his *bohutio* test, but then, he learned that Lampulla was younger than that, and was only twelve years old, the age he was when he went to Cuba with Basamanaco and his traders.

And when Meyona explained to Prince Lampulla the story about how Neef and Sabila had mysteriously disappeared about five years before he was born, and how no one had ever seen them again, the prince stared into his lap, but did not respond. Finally after a long silence, he looked up toward Neef, and then at Meyona.

"My father tells me often that I had both a brother and a sister, but they had died before I was born. He said that my brother was not fit to become king, nor was my sister fit to become queen. He said that I was the best child he ever had, for I was the only one strong enough to lead our people, if any menacing foreigners arrived."

"And our mother?" said Neef. "How is she?"

"She is doing well, but she does not like working in the fields every day."

Meyona interrupted.

"Nay, Prince Lampulla, you and your brother do not have the same mother. Your father got rid of Neef's mother shortly after Neef and his sister disappeared, and he replaced her with your mother and made her his first and legal wife. Neef's mother was taken away somewhere, and we heard that she had died shortly after you were born. We heard that she was totally disgraced, because your father had said that she had not borne him any children worthy enough to rule the kingdom."

"You mean, Father had sent Sabila and me away, not only to keep us safe from Eldest-Son-of-My-Father's-First-Wife, but because he also wanted to get rid of us, so he could sire another child to be the heir of his throne?"

Meyona did not reply, but only stared at him, as if she did not know the answer.

"But why wasn't Sabila fit enough for the throne? She wasn't crippled."

"Father said that she was rather scatter-brained, and a queen needs to have an understanding for deep and great things," said Lampulla. "He told me that he was glad that she had died, because then, she didn't have to take over the kingdom."

Neef could not believe what he heard.

"So you were born about the time I took my solo," he said.

"It was two years before the Spanish arrived," said Lampulla. "As long as I remember, Father hated those foreigners. I heard that at one time, Father ruled over this entire island, but now our people must work in the fields and he has no more subjects; but the Spanish allow him to remain king, as long as he does not rule over anyone, or anything to speak of."

"But what about the armies you said Father has formed?"

"They work underground. I am assigned to look for weapons the Spanish own, and we are collecting them, so we can someday have a huge rebellion."

"Where's our uncle, Eldest-Son-of-My-Father's-First Wife?"

"After he was banned from our land, he went into hiding, but once the Spaniards found him, they forced him to work in the fields, as the other people."

"Then I have no reason to come home," said Neef.

He arose. Since it was dark outside, he had no idea where he would spend the night. Just as he reached the doorway, Lampulla came and grabbed him by the arm.

"Don't go, my brother. I never knew about you before, and all this time, I had no idea that you were alive. And my sister? Where is she?"

"She is dead."

"Dead? Oh, I'm very sorry to hear that. Well then, I would like to visit you."

"As long as you don't tell Father that you know about me, and you must be careful whenever you come, because sometimes, it's not safe for a healthy young man, like you, to be wandering about in my homeland."

"But I am not yet fourteen years old, so I don't need to wear a brass token."

"You must still be careful, for you look much older than your age."

Then Neef and Lampulla devised a system of parrot calls that Lampulla should use to notify Neef, when he arrived on the beach in Guarica. Meyona also invited Neef to spend the night and prepared a bed for him.

When Neef was again in the Kingdom of Marién, while Basamanaco worked in the fields, he once more sat alone in his hut, bent over his records. As images of Lampulla flashed through his mind, he finally had to push out all thoughts of his brother, so he could concentrate on reconstructing the records that his father had destroyed. As Neef thus struggled over his work, he felt that he had failed his people, for instead of generating a new interest throughout Quisqueya that promoted hope and a desire to acquire a knowledge that lifted everyone's morale, he had caused his people to view him to be their enemy. Frustrated, Neef looked up from his work and spoke into the air.

"Grandfather Cahoba, why? Why have you told me to do the impossible, when our people do not even care for my work?"

But Neef continued in his work, anyway. And soon he became deeply engrossed in the many events of Quisqueya. He found himself writing that the *caciques* were deeply troubled. And even King Guacanagarí was disturbed, despite his broad smiles around the Spaniards and the allegiances he pledged to the Admiral. Neef said that he could not be fooled, for he knew that Guacanagarí's loyalty to the foreigners was mainly out of fear for his own safety.

Neef even recorded the secret deeds and superstitions of the *caciques*. Because his people thought symbolically, they often believed certain rituals could determine the future, and he wrote that after the men at Navidad were killed and before the Admiral had returned, a certain *cacique* from a lesser kingdom had created a ritual that he believed would cause the Spaniards to remain off the island forever.

"If we kill the foreigners' god, they won't be able to return," he said.

So he and his priests filled many bags with gold dust, traveled to the shore, and emptied the gold into the sea. Because they thought that the foreigners' god was now dead, the people who worshipped it could never come back. To celebrate this victory, the king and his priests danced and sang far into the night, with exhilaration in their eyes. But in time, the foreigners reappeared, nonetheless.

214

Neef also wrote about the many ways his people resisted the Spanish dominion. As the *repartimienderos* forced his people into slavery in exchange for the teaching of Christianity, food, clothing, and other needs, pregnant women ate dirt or took herbs to abort their babies, because they did not want them to be born into slavery. Despite their efforts, children continued to be born, anyway, and many of them even had Spaniards for fathers. Neef also wrote that he had heard that the Queen of Spain was now encouraging the Spaniards to intermarry with the royalty on this island, as well as in the surrounding lands, for it would help Spain achieve greater political power everywhere. And Neef noted that if this had happened when Sabila was still alive, she would never have been killed.

As Neef thus continued writing until late into the night, sometimes these stories caused him to weep.

33

When Canaobo the Fierce was defeated years before, the Spaniards divided up his Kingdom of the Mines, and Tomas Mendoza was reassigned to oversee a *repartimiento* in the Cibao Valley. Overnight, he became the envy of the other grantees, for his property had everything they thought would make a man happy — fertile soils and the best mines of copper, silver, and gold the island had to offer. Little did the others know that over the years, Tomas had turned restless, and he often lay awake at nights, weary of his position as grantee. He had long withdrawn from his dreams of finding adventure and becoming rich and conquering the heathens.

Every day as Tomas watched his Indians being lowered into the black shafts of his mines to spend endless hours, chipping away at the bowels of the mountain for gold, their hacking cough from their asthma haunted him. He was well aware that before they were compelled to gather gold dust, they were a healthy people. And when their companions and loved ones collapsed or died on the job, he could never block out the sadness in his workers' eyes, as they carried their dead out into the daylight. Each day Tomas yearned to abandon his work of ten years, for he had learned that he was not like the rest of the Spaniards, as long as the strong Indian drink was not influencing him. In fact, he was actually a man, who possessed a compassion for people, no matter who they were, whether Indian or Spaniard.

For years now, Tomas had abandoned the wild escapades with Hojeda and his men to pacify the island. He was weary of such displays of Spanish superiority. He saw no sense in riding through Indian villages, hooting one's head off, while setting fire to grass huts and slashing at natives with swords, to keep them subservient, and calling, *Take that, ye dirty dog! That'll show ye obedience!*

In fact, such terrorizing caused him to cringe. For too long, he had watched his colleagues swiping at the abdomens of pregnant women with knives or swords, to cause their infants to tumble out of their open bellies, with their umbilical cords still attached. He could no longer bear to hear the thin infant wails that followed, as they were smothered beneath their mother's gushing blood. He also could never be like his colleagues, who snatched up two- and three-year-old children by the ankles, to bash their heads against large stones, and then while laughing, they would throw them into a river and yell at them to swim, while they watched the ripples above their little heads grow pink.

Even the *padres* supported the idea of European superiority, for they said that the Europeans were from a first creation, and the Indians and other non-Europeans were from a *second and inferior creation*; but something within Tomas told him that these Indians were just as good as he was, for they were human beings — with feelings, needs, and even, a fine culture of which he was ignorant.

But he had to live with whatever occurred on this island, whether he liked it or not. Only last year in 1502 after the Admiral was sent back to Spain in chains, because of all the turmoil in Española, the new governor, Ovando, was put in his place and began refining the *repartimiento* system. He created new rules, and supposedly, new improvements. The parcels of land then became known as *encomiendas,* and similar to the previous system, in exchange for Indian labor, the *encomenderos* were held responsible for the teaching of Christianity to the Indians, as well as for giving them food, clothing, and protection. Tomas could not tell what those improvements were, because his system still resembled the old one. And there were no changes or improvements in the Spaniard behavior.

Yet Tomas noticed that when the Indians actually did become Christians, they were far more Christian-like, than any of the Spaniards on this island. But even when they faithfully wore their crosses and trinkets of the Virgin, their *encomenderos* still coerced them. Sometimes for amusement, their *encomenderos* would cut their hands off and would leave only small pieces of flesh attached at the wrists, so that their hands would dangle.

As the Indians wept from this brutality, their masters heartlessly yelled, "There, now. Go show yerselves to yer friends, 'n spread th' gospel!"

But the Indians responded with meekness, as they wept, "Master, master, do not kill us. Can't ye see that we're children of God?"

And their cries haunted Tomas for months.

Tomas had heard that back in Spain, although Queen Isabella wished for this island to be pacified, she was also greatly opposed to the practice of slavery and any form of terrorism. Before the Admiral was sent back to Castile in chains, she had pled with him to set these Indians free, for she only wanted them to be converted to Christianity. Sometimes occasional friars also spewed fire and brimstone, as they condemned the *encomenderos* for destroying the tranquility and paradise that once prevailed throughout this island. But the slave business was too lucrative to end, so the Indians continued to be gathered and sold. And terror prevailed.

Weary from it all, Tomas longed for the peace of Spain. He heard that his father back home was boasting about him and was telling everyone that he, his second son, was extremely successful in these Indies. So Tomas remained on Española amongst the chaos to please his father, even if most of the people, who had sailed with him to this island — including his father — had returned to Castile years before, leaving him behind with the tough and hardened, who constantly bickered and warred.

As Tomas dwelled in his dissatisfactions, one day Ricardo came to him again.

"There's been a mass suicide in my *encomienda, mi amigo,*" he said. "Could ye come with me 'n some of my friends to investigate that village?"

"Oh, Ricardo, please. I get depressed whenever I see these tragedies, 'n I can't help but think we are th' cause of them all."

"It's not pleasant for any of us, ye know, 'n I really need ye to come with me for moral support."

So Tomas went along with Ricardo, since he was a longtime friend. As Tomas, Ricardo and several other men rode on their horses through one of Ricardo's villages, avoiding the corpses that lay across the paths, the smell of death lingered in the air. While the noise from the horse hooves riveted off the cobbled paths, flies coursed through the ghostlike huts, and sometimes lighted upon the Spaniards' arms and shoulders, or bumped into their faces.

As Ricardo rode next to Tomas, he grew angrier and angrier.

"*Córcholis!* How can an entire village kill itself in a mere night? These *cretinos* were alive, only yesterday. They're causin' me to lose a lot of money."

"These dirty dogs aren't adjustin' to their pacification very well," someone from behind Tomas said.

Tomas looked down at his saddle and wished to be away from this group of men, so he lagged far behind and finally steered his horse to the right. No one noticed him leaving. As Tomas wound through the huts alone, his eyes scrutinized the area as he hoped to find at least a single sign of life, for he had known some of these people in this village. He came to a shack and paused in front of it. Inside, he saw a man and a woman lying together in a hammock, with their arms locked around each other in a death grasp. Their children lay sprawled across the floor.

He dismounted and entered the hut. The odor of manioc poison lingered in the room, and within minutes, he located the wooden dish, where the family had mixed the potion that had killed them. It lay near a half opened sack that held the powder.

Tomas turned, walked cautiously out of the hut, approached the next home, and entered. No one was alive there, either. Although this family had belonged to Ricardo, he recognized each of its members, because he had known them well when they were alive. The father had died last year, when he was beaten for what Ricardo said was insubordination. Tomas saw his widow lying facedown upon the floor, with her gray hair spread over her shoulders. He also saw her two unmarried daughters, as they lay side-by-side upon mats on the ground nearby. They, too, were dead.

Tomas walked over to the older girl, who lay with her mouth slightly parted. She looked as though she was at peace. Then his eyes traveled to the younger girl, lying next to her. She had her covers drawn up to her chin. Her black hair fell gently from her face over her pillow. He thought of how he had come to especially know her. He had discovered her one day, as she came to a nearby stream to fill gourds

217

with water. She had the cutest face. She responded to him with smiles, and he found that she was always there at the same time each day. From the start, they both were extremely attracted to each other. Eventually, she allowed him to hold her close and even to caress her. He never knew how old she was, but she appeared to be around fifteen years, or so. Tomas' hands trembled as he brushed back a lock of her hair from her face. Then he partially pulled back her covers and saw the body he once knew, laying beneath it. Because she was not married and was younger than eighteen years old, she wore only a loincloth. He had not seen her for a few months, and he was surprised now that her belly was swollen. It made him wonder if she had been carrying his child. He replaced her covers, and impulsively, he leaned over and kissed her forehead.

"*Mí amante, mí amante, adios*. Ye are so beautiful."

And after he drew her covers completely over her head, he walked to the doorway. Once more, he glanced back at the covered figure of his past lover. As he stared at this house of death, he thought of how the Christianity that the Spaniards had brought to this island had failed to bring these people greater happiness, and he questioned whether it actually saved their souls from Eternal Hell. Even while the mantillas and rosaries increased throughout the island, the people here were dying for more reasons than smallpox, measles, starvation, or overwork.

As he set out to return to the posse, he recalled how last year, a certain group of Ricardo's slaves had once gathered together to hang themselves. But when Ricardo heard about it, he charged up to them in a rage with a piece of rope in his hands, because their death would mean monetary losses to him.

"If ye kill yerselves, then I'll kill myself, right along with ye."

When Ricardo's Indians heard what he had threatened to do, they became so frightened, that they ran away and abandoned their plans of suicide, because to them, it would be worse than Hell to go to the next world with their *encomendero*.

As Tomas mounted his horse to rejoin Ricardo and his fellows, he yearned more than anything else to abandon his position here in the Cibao Valley, for the beauty of this land no longer appealed to him. He had heard of an opening in the Kingdom of Marién for someone to manage an *encomienda*, because the grantee in charge had died of syphilis, and he had no family members to take over that land.

I must leave this place forever, Tomas thought. *As soon as I get back home, I will apply for that position in the Kingdom of Marién.*

He had heard that that *encomienda* was located close to the ocean, and at least the ocean would be away from the mineshafts, and by now, he had grown to despise the sight of gold.

Quisqueya
(Hispaniola)

34

A shrill cry of a parrot pierced the night and startled Neef out of his writing. After a silence, Neef heard it again. As he glanced around his hut and saw Basamanaco sleeping in his hammock, undisturbed by it, he turned back to his quill. But when the shriek came a third time, it suddenly brought only one word to his mind: *Lampulla!*

Neef arose, blew out his wax lamp, and gathered up his crutches to leave his *bohío*. Once outside, he felt his way down a moonlit path that led to the beach. He could hear hounds barking in the distance, probably in pursuit of a runaway slave, or maybe they were yelping after a canoe filled with people, who were escaping from the island. Even if those dogs would not be commanded to chase after him, since he was a cripple and was not required to work (so would not be considered to be a runaway), their yelps caused him to break out in sweat, anyway.

When Neef reached the beach, he saw nothing significant, but the usual waves ebbing back and forth and shimmering in the moonlight, before sinking into the sand. As a light breeze overhead caused palm fronds to gently bob in the night air, he noticed the cluster of trees, where back in the old days, Lida used to stand, as she watched Basamanaco arrive with his traders. Neef almost could hear the children singing their c*ome sit a welcomes*. But nowadays, people did not dare to come out of their homes at this hour, nor had anyone been sitting welcomes, even in broad daylight.

Neef cupped his hands to his mouth and projected a parrot call. Then he waited. Finally out of nowhere, he saw two figures approaching. One was much taller than the other.

"Neef!"

It was Lampulla's voice.

As Neef watched the figures approach, he saw that the shorter one was about the size of Lampulla, and as the moonlight reflected off the hair of the taller one, he saw that it held something in its arms. The dogs began to bark again.

"Let's hurry to my *bohío*," Neef whispered. "I don't like the sounds of those dogs."

He motioned Lampulla and his friend to follow him.

When the three of them entered the hut, Neef lit the wax lamp again. It took awhile to get its fire going, and when it was finally flickering, he looked up and saw

219

that Lampulla and his friend were standing across the hut in the shadows as they stared down at Basamanaco, while he slept. Lampulla's friend no longer carried the object he was holding. Just then, Basamanaco awoke and saw the two people looking down at him. He suddenly jumped up.

"A white man!"

Neef glanced at Lampulla's friend. He had been so intent upon getting everybody into his home, away from the danger of the dogs, that he had not even bothered to notice the person whom Lampulla had brought. Besides, it was too dark to discern anything. He now saw that the stranger was tall and thin, with a bushy beard that appeared silvery in the moonlight.

"Basamanaco, don't you recognize me? I'm Mateo."

Neef could not believe his ears. He walked over to the stranger.

"Mateo? It can't be you. I've been going to the docks every time ships came in. How could I have missed you?"

"I've arrived last week in the Fertile Kingdom. I took the only ship that was leaving Palos, Spain that had enough room for me. And once I reached the Fertile Kingdom, I began asking around to see how I could get here, and someone referred me to your brother, Lampulla."

Basamanaco began to weep.

"Mateo, Lida's no longer here. And everyone must work out in the fields."

Basamanaco paused and reached toward a wooden bowl on the floor to spit out some phlegm. Mateo came over to him and put his arm around him, but he was too polite to say that Basamanaco now looked much older and was hunched and gray.

"It's good to see you again, fellow."

"Why did you take so long to return to us?" Neef said

"The people back home prevented me from returning. My Papa and the monks in the monastery, where I lived, were extremely distressed when I did not return to Castille, when the Admiral first returned. And later on, when further news reached them that everyone at Fort Navidad was killed, they went into mourning. So when I finally made it back home in 1494 when I was 14 years old, they would not allow me to leave again."

"Then why did you come here, if the people back in Spain are so worried about you?"

"I'm a grown man now, and I'm old enough to decide for myself, Mateo. I could never forget the work that I must do with you, and that in my vision, I was told to help your people."

"So what are your queen and king in Spain doing, to help our people here?"

"I do not think that they have the power to change the ways of the Spaniards in this land."

"Why not?"

"From what I can see, the Spaniards here are much too unmanageable."

" How much does your queen know about the conditions of Quisqueya?"

"She does not know enough. Even I did not know what has happening here, until I reached The Fertile Kingdom." Mateo stopped and buried his face into his hands. "Why? Why did God allow such terrible things to happen?"

Basamanaco went into a fit of coughing and spat into the bowl again. Mateo looked over at him with pity in his eyes. He walked over to a gourd of water and brought it back to Basamanaco, and then held it up to his lips. After Basamanaco sipped noisily, he finally looked up and smiled. His gums were now toothless, but his dark eyes emanated gratefulness for Mateo's kindness, and he slowly leaned back in his hammock again.

Mateo placed the gourd of water on the ground, walked to the doorway, and stared out at the dark village.

"All the time I was in Castille, whenever ships arrived from the Indies, I saw your people disembarking in chains. Those scenes told me that conditions were growing worse, as men, women, and even small children — who were prisoners and slaves — were being carted off as farm animals and punished for nothing they had ever done. Year after year as I watched them, I realized that your people were *my* people, and I knew I had to return."

Again Mateo buried his face into his hands.

"My, God. My God. I never dreamed conditions would develop into this."

Basamanaco arose and slowly walked over to Mateo. He no longer looked like a giant next to him, but was still half a head taller, even if his back was now bent forward.

"Mateo, not only are we your people, but you are still my son."

Then Basamanaco went into a fit of coughing again, and Mateo leaned over and rubbed his back. Mateo turned abruptly to Neef and Lampulla.

"Look at him! Basamanaco is younger than my Papa back home, but the work that he is forced to do has quickly added years to him and has practically destroyed him." Then he turned back to Basamanaco. "Tomorrow morning, may I go to the cotton fields to do your work for you?"

Mateo then attempted to remove the brass token from Basamanaco's neck, but Basamanaco clung to it, as if his life depended upon it.

"Nay...nay...nay."

"Please, let me wear it, so you can rest for a day."

"Nay...nay...nay..."

Basamanaco hung on to his token with amazing strength.

"Twenty-five pounds of cotton. I must pick twenty-five pounds of cotton for this quarter, Mateo. My body yearns to rest, but the Spaniards will kill me, if I don't. Or maybe they will cut off my hands, as they did with Lida."

Mateo threw his hands up in the air.

"What have my people done to you? Oh, what can I do for you? You were never afraid of anyone, or anything before. Why, they've broken your spirit.

"I can't believe how few people remain on this island! At this rate, in a few years, there will be none of them around. I cannot see how it is possible to bring your people back to their original state, for their numbers have dwindled drastically. Do you realize that as your people age beneath their burdens, their young ones are growing up to know only bitterness and anger? These younger folk cannot even comprehend *the love*, which once embraced their fathers."

"But I remember *the love*," said Basamanaco. "Neef also remembers *the love*." Then he turned to Lampulla. "Do you remember *the love*?"

"The what?"

Lampulla appeared to be puzzled.

"There are ten years difference in age between Lampulla and I," Neef explained to Basamanaco. "He does not even know about The School. And when he was very little, *the love* was abandoned in his kingdom."

"What is this love, anyway?" said Lampulla.

Neef explained to him about the love of Yocahu, and how for many generations the people of Quisqueya had preserved it, so when Yocahu returned someday, he would find them worthy enough to become the greatest people on earth.

"I hear that many people are escaping on canoes," said Lampulla. "I think those, who want to preserve their old culture, should also leave on canoes. They should go far away, where they can establish what they have lost."

"Oh, but your people cannot run away forever," said Mateo. "You have no idea how the minds of the Spanish work. While I was crossing the Western Ocean on ship, I've heard them discussing plans of how they were going to track down every person on all the islands around to make them slaves. They know the ways of your people more than you realize. Not only do they plan to use their giant war dogs to find you, but also, they have trained themselves to look for signs your people do not realize they are leaving behind. They look for remains of your fires. They look for your shell heaps, your fish bones — everything. Although some of your people think they can reach safety when they escape on canoes, they are only fooling themselves. The Spaniards are talking of searching for your people, night and day, because as slaves, your people can make them rich."

"But they wouldn't be able to find us, if we went to Guanine," said Basamanaco. "It is much too vast, out there."

"You never know, Basamanaco. Besides, I think Neef and I must find a way to help our people *right here*. I hope it is not too late. Do you realize how much the kindness of the Quisqueyans has worked against them? Upon some of the other islands, where the more ferocious inhabitants live, I hear that many of them still retain their cultures, because from the beginning, they have fought off the Europeans to keep them away. People tell me that the Caribs are still a strong people. So are the Lucanyans."

Suddenly Mateo's voice took on an urgent tone.

"I do not know how much longer their luck will hold out, though. But that's not the purpose of my vision. In my vision, I've learned that I must find a solution to help your people *now*. But what can be done to make conditions safe for them here, so they won't feel that they must run to other places?"

Mateo turned to Neef, then to Basamanco, and last, Lampulla.

"You are my family," he said. "I must help my family all I can."

He pressed his forehead against a doorpost, as if he were thinking. Suddenly he snapped his fingers.

"Wait. Queen Anacoana wanted me to be a prince, right? And she wanted me to be a mediator between your people and mine, remember? She was right in her perceptions, because to be effective, I must become a person with power. Even if I never became that prince, who she had aspired for me to become, I can still be that mediator. While I was on the ship that crossed the ocean, I came to know some of the grantees, who travel back and forth between here and Spain. I think I can find a way to appeal to them, to turn their hearts around."

He then turned to Neef.

"And you...you can help me, my brother."

"I need to help, too." Lampulla said.

"We'll deal with you later, Lampulla. But first, I must deal with Neef."

Neef arose.

"Let me show you what I have done to help our people, while you were gone," he said.

He quickly hobbled across the hut and got out his records to bring to Mateo. After Mateo studied them, he returned the papers to Neef and paced the *bohío*.

Finally he said, "Neef, you are doing an excellent job with keeping records, but it will get us nowhere. Just like all the other actions of your people, keeping records is far too peaceful a means to obtain the results we want. You and the rest of your people must change. To help your people in significant ways, we need more action."

As Mateo stood at the doorway, with the moonlight reflecting off his clothes, he suddenly stripped his shirt off, revealing the tattoo he bore on his upper arm, which he had once received in the Mother Kingdom. It signified strength, bravery and courage. Even if it was dark, as he turned toward the people in the hut, Neef could see fire projecting from his eyes.

"I am no longer that boy who had left this island," he said. "As a man, I am now unafraid to do the important work I need to do. From now on, I am going to represent your people, and I will start by dressing like them."

"And I will support your cause," said Lampulla, as he walked over to him.

Just then, a child began to wail from the corner of the hut.

"Eh?" said Basamanaco. "What's that?"

Mateo turned and ran to that cry. Then he returned with the bundle that he had been carrying, when he had entered the hut. He walked over to Basamanaco.

"Basamanaco, this is Joaquín," he said. "Joaquín is my son. I'm married now, but my wife refused to come with me to the Indies. She insisted that I bring our child with me, because she said that if I did, I would feel obligated to bring Joaquín back to Spain. She said that if I came to Quisqueya alone, I might never want to return."

As the covering fell away from the object in Mateo's arms, a little boy, about a year and a half old, yawned and sleepily looked back at the people in the hut. In the moonlight, he appeared blonder than Mateo ever was, and his eyes were even bluer.

With pride in his eyes, Mateo spoke to the little boy.

"Go ahead. Tell these people the word I taught you how to say."

The little boy looked at Basamanaco, then Lampulla, and finally Neef. Then he said only one word.

"Tayno."

Then Mateo reached into the covering in which Joaquín was wrapped and pulled out two books.

"For you," he said and handed them to Neef. "I have more coming in a trunk that will soon be shipped here."

35

The move to the Kingdom of Marién was a disappointment for Tomas Mendoza, for he had thought that its outdoor environment would produce much more healthful working conditions for the Indians, than the mines ever had. But he still saw living skeletons moving about, as they gathered and baled cotton under the hot sun. He could not understand why these people were so thin, because it meant that there was a shortage of food, but these people were definitely producing plenty for him and the other Spaniards to eat.

"I think that God wants to punish those dirty dogs," another *encomendero* said one day. "Perhaps that is why they are just skin 'n bones."

But Tomas remained silent and did not respond.

Along the beaches in the *encomiendas* neighboring his, the grantees had their Indians dive into the ocean for pearls, from morning to dusk. Tomas often watched their emaciated bodies disappearing into the waves, and when they surfaced to place oysters into floating baskets, their bodies often wrenched and gagged, until they vomited blood.

And he often overheard many of them crying out, "Let me die. Please, let me die!"

As Tomas rode daily throughout his *encomienda*, there were always Indians, usually outcasts, following him closely within the villages. He was too new in the Kingdom of Marién, for anyone to know about his reputation for extreme cruelty, so these outcasts did not fear him. These people were often elderly, but some of them had lost their hands from being punished, or maybe they were crippled from birth. Often they reached out to him with their bony limbs and begged.

"Hungry. Hungry. Hungry."

There was always a crippled man among them, who hobbled with crutches. At first glance, Tomas thought that he was about thirty or forty years old, because his hair was streaked with gray, but he had long known to never judge the ages of the slaves by appearances, for he heard that they tended to grow old early. After awhile, he noticed that this crippled Indian's facial features were actually youthful looking, and perhaps he was only in his early twenties. Further, he appeared to be different from the rest of the beggars, for he did not say *hungry, hungry*, but instead, he spoke perfect Spanish and had a dignity that Tomas did not usually see on this island.

"*Señor*, could ye spare a few pieces of paper? I can do any kind of work for ye, for a few pieces of paper 'n a bottle of ink."

At first Tomas did not believe his ears, and he waved this man away. But after weeks went by, he heard the other grantees speaking about him.

"That Indian's always beggin' for paper every day."

"I think that he belongs to one of yer villages, Mendoza," an *encomendero* said nudging Tomas. "I've heard th' Indians callin' him *Neef.*"

"Why does he need paper?"

The other grantee shrugged.

"Maybe he eats it, eh?"

The next day as Tomas traveled through his Indian towns upon his horse, he searched for the crippled Indian, and when he saw him, he stopped his horse right in front of him. He reached into his pack, withdrew a thin stack of paper and a small bottle of ink, and then he handed them over to the Indian. As soon as the Indian saw those items, a light spread across his face.

"*Gracias, gracias, señor.* Now, what kind of work can I do for ye for these items? May I cook for ye or groom yer horses?"

Tomas looked Neef up and down and wondered what kind of limitations his handicap presented.

"Come to my house this evenin'," he said.

And then he turned his horse and galloped away.

As Tomas rode past the slaves in the fields, he observed children, whose heads reached no higher than their mother's waistlines, as they worked among adults. The

224

children weren't required to be out working, but they did, anyway. Spanish blood obviously flowed through their veins, and Tomas knew that many of them were bastards, who had never known who had fathered them. He, himself, had done his share of populating those *mestizos* in this land.

That evening, when Neef arrived at Tomas' home, he handed a bunch of flowers that he had picked to the grantee.

"For yer *señora*," he said.

"I have no wife."

"Then they are for ye, *señor*."

Tomas held the flowers awkwardly, as the crippled Indian looked up in awe at his home, quietly shifting his eyes, as if he had never before been in a house of a grantee. He gaped at the staircase, the chandeliers, the shiny floors, the carpets, and the mirror in the foyer.

Tomas finally motioned to Neef.

"Come into my study."

As Tomas led the way, the Indian's crutches thumped upon the floor, as he walked. As soon as they entered the study, he heard the Indian gasp behind him, and when he turned to glance at him, he saw that the Indian had turned trance-like, as he gawked at the rows and rows of books.

"Won't ye sit down?" Tomas said.

The Indian did not hear him, but continued to gape at the shelves, but finally he withdrew from his stupor, as if he realized what he was doing. He then turned toward Tomas and smiled.

"*Perdone,* for my rudeness, *señor.*"

"Tell me yer name."

"It's Neef, *señor.*"

"It's not a usual Indian name, is it?" Tomas said.

"My grandfather chose that name for me when I was born, but nobody knows why."

"It's short and easy to remember."

"*Sí,* it is." Then Neef pointed to a shelf. "I've never seen so many books before. My good friend came with books like these. His name is Mateo Gonzalez. Do ye know him?"

Tomas shook his head.

"I believe not."

"He came on one of th' Admiral's original ships, but then he returned to Castile for a number of years. When he came back, he brought many books with him. My people do not have such things, nor do they see their value."

"So ye love books, eh? Can ye read?"

"I read all th' time. Before Mateo went back to Castile, he gave his Bible to me. All th' time he was gone, I studied it over 'n over, 'n I even translated many parts of it into th' language of my people. It is difficult work. That book leaves me with many questions."

"Ye said that he left his *Bible* with ye? Does that mean that ye can read Latin?"

"What is Latin?"

"That's th' language Bibles are written in. There are no Bibles written in Spanish. They are only written in Latin or Greek."

"I don't understand. Th' Bible Mateo gave me is written in Spanish. 'N it causes me to wonder." Neef paused for a moment. "Sometimes it makes me think that both yer people 'n my people are alike. After I learned about the story of Adam 'n Eve, I now am certain that ye 'n I are brothers."

Tomas was startled by Neef's words, but then he shook his head.

"That cannot be so. We could never be related. Even th' *padres* say that there were two different creations. During th' first creation, God made men like me 'n th' rest of th' Europeans, who came from Adam 'n Eve. 'N during th' second creation, he made th' other kind of people, like th' Indians 'n th' other races; 'n from th' beginnin', God made them to serve th' Europeans."

Tomas saw a determination grow in Neef's eyes.

"That cannot be correct, *señor*. That is not what th' Bible says."

"Then ye must ask th' *padres*, to see if I'm right."

"Why must I ask them, when I can already have th' book of yer people's religion, any time I reach for it?"

"But yer people are so heathen and base that we can't possibly be related. I've seen yer marriages. They are very barbaric. Our woman keep their virtue, but in yer marriages, yer bride goes into a hut with many different men and make love to each of them."

"What are ye sayin'? Are ye talkin' about *th' struggle?*"

"Yer women have no morals. They give themselves so freely to th' Christians. They are not at all like th' virtuous women of Spain."

"*Señor*, that is not how it used to be, before yer people came. Anyway, yer Bible tells that ye 'n I have originated from th' same set of parents."

"No, no. *Es imposible.*"

Neef ignored Tomas's last comment.

"I am impressed with th' great teacher, Jesus Christ, 'n how he went up into th' heavens after he was resurrected. My people also believe in Yocahu, but he did th' opposite of what Jesus did, because he came down from th' heavens, instead."

"Hmmmm."

"I sometimes think...could they be both th' same god? Perhaps yer god went up into th' heavens in yer people's land, 'n then, he came down afterwards, to visit our people."

Tomas laughed and shook his head.

"No, no, *es imposible!* There can be no connection."

"If yer god is a Father to all of us, why should he favor only th' Jews 'n yer people, 'n forget mine?"

Tomas continued to shake his head.

"No connection...yer people 'n my people have no connection. What other books besides th' *Biblia* do ye own?"

"My friend brought his histories, stories, poetry..."

"When I was in th' Cibao Valley, I used to know an Indian, who could read. He was very bright, 'n learned quickly, but th' Christians killed him, when they were pacifyin' his town."

"*Pacify?* I've heard th' Spaniards use that word often. That means to cause a lot noise 'n trouble, doesn't it?"

"Oh, no. *Pacify* means to make things peaceful. It means that th' Christians are tryin' to teach obedience to yer people."

"I don't understand. Are my people disobedient?"

Mendoza drummed his fingers upon his desk and thought for a second.

"No."

"Then why must ye pacify us?"

Greatly uncomfortable, Tomas arose and pulled out a thin book from his shelf and handed it to Neef.

"Here. Bring this back to me, when ye're finished with it. I read this often when I was a boy."

Neef gingerly took the book, then looked up.

"Señor Mendoza, but why must yer people pacify us?"

Mendoza still did not know how to answer him. He was relieved, when Neef finally changed the subject.

"What can I do for ye to pay for th' ink 'n paper ye gave me?"

"Well, I've been thinkin', Neef. Ye speak Spanish very well, 'n ye have polite manners. I need someone to greet my guests at th' door of my home. Could ye be my doorman?"

Mendoza saw panic grow in Neef's face.

"Ye mean, I must work for ye every day? Oh, no, *señor*. Although I wish to pay for yer paper, I do not want a job that goes on every day."

"Ye can have all th' paper that ye need, if ye serve as my doorman."

When Neef spoke again, his voice was soft and controlled.

"If I work for ye every day, will I need to wear a brass token around my neck?"

Tomas studied Neef's face. It was troubled.

"Ye must understand, *señor*," Neef continued. "A brass token means that I am a slave to ye, but I have a special work to do for my people that is far more important than all th' cotton 'n gold of this island. I need to be free, so I can write my people's records 'n histories. It will require that I be left alone 'n not be interrupted."

Tomas looked down at Neef's crippled legs, his bent body, and then he looked up at his humble eyes. He shrugged.

"Then groom my horses for just a couple of days instead, *mi amigo*."

And then he left the room and returned with a metal box.

"Here, take this also. This will provide a safe place for yer papers."

After Neef thanked him and turned to leave, Tomas called after him.

"Will ye bring yer *Bible* with ye tomorrow? I've never seen a Bible written in Spanish before."

As Neef hobbled outside, Tomas watched after him through a window. Neef had tucked the metal box between one of his crutches and his body, as he headed in the direction of the Indian village. Tomas still felt the impact of the conversation that he had just had with him. It was an equal exchange of ideas, and it went beyond his giving gruff orders. And he couldn't get Neef's eyes out of his head, either, for they emanated such intelligence, sincerity, and humility, with a love that he rarely saw in any of his Spanish colleagues. And he was also impressed that Neef did not seem to fear him, as the other Indians did. Tomas made up his mind that as long as he was Neef's *encomendero*, he would make sure that there was no token around his neck, so he could always be a free man. Tomas was not certain, though, how much longer he could offer Neef this kind of protection, for the new governor, Ovando — the man whom Queen Isabella had sent to these Indies to replace the Admiral — was proving to be far more ruthless than the Admiral and his brothers ever were. Ever since

Ovando took over the Indies, the Indian massacres had greatly increased, and one by one, he was killing the *caciques*.

36

When Queen Anacoana appeared in the plaza, with her wrists tied behind her back, she forced herself to smile and stared straight ahead. As she passed her people, the Spaniards held them back with ropes so they wouldn't get too close, and if they pushed too hard, they threatened them with swords. As she looked ahead, she saw that most of her people had gathered in front of the gallows, from which a lone noose dangled. Her people were so few in number now, and she no longer could distinguish the rich from the poor among them, for they all dressed alike. She saw no *Nytainos* or *undercaciques* with elaborate hairstyles, and everyone was now required to wear the clothes of the foreigners. Occasionally, though, she saw a woman dressed in a simple *nagua* standing within the crowd.

She saw tears streaming down her people's cheeks, and Nila, her faithful *Naborian* and nurse, stood among them. Nila was reaching out toward her, but the crowd held her back, out of fear that she might upset the Spaniards, who would then punish her.

"Oh, my princess...my princess."

Anacoana looked away from Nila, afraid that she would lose her composure. And as she did, she saw Velásquez standing before her. He had suddenly stepped out of the crowd, and now without his helmet and with his armor flashing in the sun, he looked extremely handsome. But she stiffened and looked beyond him. As she attempted to step around him, he grabbed her by the arm, and in front of the onlookers, he kissed her hard on the mouth. She yanked free, with tears smarting her eyes.

"Am I just another dirty dog to ye?"

Her words came as a shout, and she saw him wince, when she mentioned *dirty dog*, for she knew that his queen in Spain had lately declared that term illegal, because the Spaniards had used it too often as they addressed the Quisqueyans.

Anacoana continued her trek toward the gallows, leaving Velásquez behind, as her ears burned. Only two days before, she had given herself and heart to him, after she had entertained him and his men elaborately in her courts. That night, she had demonstrated to him the ancient arts of loving deeply and passionately, as she always did when he came to her kingdom, and he even told her that no woman in Spain could express lovemaking, as well as she did. And when he fell asleep exhausted in her arms, she arose after kissing him on both cheeks, to tend to her duties as a queen — with his gentlemanly manners, beautiful face, and fair eyes still in her mind. Eight years before when he had first arrived in the Mother Kingdom, he came up to her and pressed his lips to her hand, calling her *my lovely queen*. And when he came to visit again two days before, he took her hand and addressed her in that same manner.

"My lovely, queen," he had said. "My soldiers 'n I wish to salute ye 'n yer people at a demonstration in yer plaza tomorrow."

She blushed at his smooth voice and suave behavior, because, unlike Ricardo, who never showed any respect for her, he always made her feel deeply honored and aroused a yearning to share another night with him. And then yesterday, after her people had gathered to witness the display of military grandeur that Velásquez had promised, everyone sat at awe, as three hundred Spanish soldiers marched to the tune of trumpets, with swords glistening in the sun. But suddenly the rhythm of the music changed in the middle of this grand display, and the performance was abruptly interrupted. Before she and her people could think much about it, all three hundred Spaniards were charging into them, slashing at and slaughtering everyone. Among this chaos, someone came and dragged Anacoana from her *dohu* and tied her with ropes to a tree. Thus bound, she witnessed her lover, Velásquez, as well as other Spaniards, committing an endless sequence of murders upon her people. Her handsome Velásquez was showing no regard to how much the surrounding lands revered her country — the Mother Kingdom — to be the greatest of all kingdoms on earth. It was then that she realized that she had lost all love for him.

As Anacoana walked toward the gallows, the soldier behind nudged her to quicken her pace, but she ignored him and continued at her present rate, allowing reflections of the recent events on the island to saturate her mind. As long as she was alive, she was going to record the truth in her brain about what had happened on this island, for she knew that in time, it would be forgotten. She began to visualize each of the executions of the *caciques* on Quisqueya. Under the orders of that man, Ovando, the so-called governor of the Indies, most of the *caciques* were now dead. They were hung at gallows or from trees, or burned at stakes. Although the execution of Queen Higuanamá had occurred before Ovando arrived, she saw this aged queen of the Kingdom of the Great Old Lady, approaching her place of hanging, just as she, Anacoana, was now doing. Then, Anacoana saw this queen's frail and wrinkled body, dangling in midair, with her neck broken and bent, as many of her descendants — whom she, Anacoana, had known at The School of the Princes — wailed around her.

She then thought of King Guarionex of the Fertile Kingdom. If the foreigners had never come, he would be still ruling over all of Quisqueya. But this *cacique* — the highest *cacique* of Quisqueya — was recently burned at the stake. Anacoana also could hear his screams echoing in her mind, haunting those who stood in his town plaza. Those screams also brought to her brain the cries of her own brother Beheccio, which still remained fresh in her mind. Two months before, the Spaniards had given him a slow burning. She had heard them saying that because a slow burning involved just a small fire, it was much more tortuous than a large one, for it stretched out the execution over a longer time period. Even King Guacanagarí of the Kingdom of Marién was thus burned, for reasons she could never understand, for until the end of his life, he had always remained a faithful friend to the Admiral and the Spaniards — even at the expense of turning against her and the other *caciques*. And finally, she thought of her husband, Canaobo the Fierce, who had died at sea years before. He was a rascal, with an immense lust for women. But he was brave, indeed. None of the other *caciques* could ever be as mighty as he was, and even the Spaniards could never match his bravery. And now, Anacoana reminded herself that soon, she would be joining him in the land of *Coaibai*.

Anacoana finally reached the gallows and looked up its stairs. She felt tears welling up in her eyes again, but she blinked them back and forced a smile. Panic immediately began to burst from her, but she also quickly suppressed it.

I must be brave, she told herself.

She raised her head high and straightened her shoulders, proud to be among the last of the *caciques* remaining on Quisqueya. As she mounted the stairs, she forced herself to think upon what she stood for. She saw herself as a small child again, riding in a litter carried by *Naborians*. The crowd stood thick before her, as people gathered along the paths and cheered. She waved back, thinking of her mother's words: *someday thou shalt rule over them.*

And then she remembered the day when her father, the king, called her and her brother Beheccio to him. She still could see his well-proportioned face in her mind, with its high nose and broad cheekbones, adorned with tattoos. She must have stood no taller than the top of his loincloth, in those days. And her braids fell past her shoulders. This time, Father did not teach her and her brother a new *areita*. Instead, he had something else to tell them, and his eyes were sad.

"Last night, a messenger came," he said. "He hath come all the way from the Fertile Kingdom. King Cahoba the Great, who ruleth over the entire island, wanted to tell me that Yocahu visited him in a vision. Yocahu warned him that strangers from the East would arrive someday, to kill the people of Quisqueya. It will happen during the reign of his son. If what he saith is true, then it meaneth that it will occur at the time both of you are ruling our kingdom."

As Anacoana looked up at her father, she began to shiver. She shot a glance at her brother, who peeked back at her with wide eyes.

Then Father encircled both of them in his arms and said, "No matter what happeneth, always remember who thou art."

When Anacoana reached the top of the stairs of the gallows, she knew well who she was, as her years of study at the School of the Princes flew before her, of how to act, how to think, how to behave as a queen, and that she was preparing to someday rule the finest kingdom in the world. She glanced at the crowd again and saw the Spaniards among them in their shining armor. She knew that those men did not know who she was. In fact, she could tell from their smiles that they were enjoying this scene of her execution, as if it were a game. But then, she saw her lover, Velásquez. Unlike the other Spaniards, he was weeping.

Doth he actually love me? Then why did he betray my people and me?

She looked away. How could she have ever believed that the Spaniards were Yocahu and his angels, who had come to save her people from a terrible fate? It was too late now to change her mind, for those foreigners already dominated the entire island.

And then she thought of the Yocahu boy, Mateo, who always had a love of a *zemie* in his eyes. If only more of the Spaniards were like him! She had heard that he had returned to Quisqueya to fulfill his vision, but could he also be too late?

"Come on. Git goin'."

The man behind Anacoana gave her a shove, and she felt the muzzle of his blunderbuss dig into her back. As she stepped forward, she soon saw the noose hanging before her. She closed her eyes, while rough hands guided her by the shoulders to turn around and face her people. She felt the noose slip over her head and rest upon her shoulders. Panic swept through her again, but there was no Nila. To be truly brave, she knew she had to bear this torture alone. Yet she could hear Nila crying above the crowd...*my princess, oh, my princes.* And then, she felt the presence of Father. She couldn't see him, but she knew he was there. He must have come to bring her to *Coaibai* with him. Instinctively, she reached out to take his hand, just as she did, when she was small.

"Father?"

She felt nothing. But she could hear him now. He was repeating what he had constantly taught her as a child. His voice first came as a hum, and then it rose above the noise of the crowd, louder and louder. *Thou must be brave. Thou must defy human suffering. Thou art of the elite, whose ancestors came out of the Cave Cacibagiuagua in the Canta Mountains. Thou art of the choicest born upon this earth. Remember who thou art. Remember who thou art. Remember who....*

The executioner tightened the noose around her neck. She grit her teeth and forced herself to think of her genealogy that she had learned to perfection, of her mother, her father, her grandfather, and all her ancestors from the time they had left the original cave. She thought of the *caciques*, both ancient and those of her time. More than ever now, she knew that they were the greatest people who had walked the earth. Many of their bones still hung in baskets from the ceilings of royal *bohíos* throughout the villages, but because of the changing circumstances, her bones would never be there. Sweat oozed from her face, shoulders, torso, and even feet, but she kept a smile across her face. She wanted to scream, but she clenched her teeth to keep it from escaping.

A drum began to roll, but she ignored it.

She began telling herself, *I am from the elite, of the best in this entire world. For years princes and kings of all the land pursued me. And throughout my wedding day, I fought against the choicest of them, and when I finally stood in front of my royal bohío, I shouted, "I have overcome! The most desirable men of this land have tempted me, but I have resisted them all! I have overcome!*

And then she felt the floor give away from beneath her.

37

As the news of the death of Anacoana swept across the island, the Quisqueyans went into shock, even if at this point, many of them were expecting this event to happen. And when the people of the Kingdom of Marién heard about it, the entire town of Guarica plunged into mourning, for the Guaricans had still not yet recovered from the horror of the execution of their own king, Guacanagarí, when he was burned at the stake in their town square. As the fear of the governor, Ovando, increased, scores of people continued to escape their island by canoeloads.

231

The Guaricans well remembered the grand conference held in their town prior to the Admiral's first return from Castile, when all the major *caciques* of the island, including Queen Anacoana, arrived. But now that the eighty *caciques* of Quisqueya were killed, no such meeting would ever be possible again.

Many of the *mestizo* children, who were babes at the time of the conference, would in a few years be entering adolescence, and they were growing up never knowing of the richness of the culture that once flourished on this island, which the surrounding world once admired. They also never knew a single *areita* their mothers sang, or used to sing, nor did they have fathers to teach them about their genealogies and histories. In fact, often they knew nothing about their fathers, save that they were probably one of those men who rode upon horses with whips, who had used their mothers to fill their base desires. Sometimes, though, these men married into royalty, and their children were part Taino. But the children of this newer generation did not realize that at one time, extreme chastity was the norm among most of the people, and any deviation from it, was not tolerated. And among them, an even newer breed of children was emerging: the *zambos*, or those who were part black. Because the Tainos on the island were dying so quickly, the Spaniards were beginning to import natives from Africa to Quisqueya to replace the Indians they were losing, and these new slaves were also marrying and mating with the Quisqueyans. And to further fill the needs of their diminishing labor force, the Spaniards were scanning the surrounding seas and searching the other islands, day in and day out, to bring slaves to this island and Europe. So the Tainos of Quisqueya were slipping away. Upon this island, only few of them remained, and they were usually the middle aged and older ones, and the people knew that in time, they too, would die.

One day, with his mind filled with the concerns of his adopted people, Mateo entered the *bohio* of Basamanaco. For the first time in a long while, he was in great spirits.

"Basamanaco! I've found a solution to help our people! I just went to your *encomendero*, Señor Mendoza, and he made me his chief helper over this part of Guarica. He said that I could run the property that he's assigned to me any way I please, as long as I meet my goals in production."

When Basamanaco heard this news, his face clouded.

"You? A helper to an *encomendero*? What are you doing, Mateo? You should have nothing to do with any *encomendero*."

Despite Basamanaco's doubts, Mateo smiled.

"Do not be afraid, my friend. I am *not* going to be the kind of *encomendero* helper you know. My land will be different, from all the others. It shall be an example for all the Spaniards to follow, for I will show them that an *encomienda* can function just as well, or even better, if the people are treated with love and kindness, just the way the people here used to live. The first thing I shall establish is a school, like the School of the Princes. Not only will the descendants of royalty be educated here, but also everyone else will have the same privilege to be taught to read and write, both in Spanish and Tainan. In this way, Neef will be able to teach the written Tainan language that he has developed. Christianity will also be taught, along with the *areitas* of the histories and genealogies of this island and Guanine. And most important, we will teach our students about *the love.*"

"But how can you run such a school, if everyone must work in the fields?" Neef said.

"The people shall learn and work in shifts. And Basamanaco, I will make you a teacher of the *areitas* and histories for my school. As I said before, Neef can teach reading and writing, and I will assign other people to teach the specialties, in which they are well qualified. In fact, I am thinking of sending away for Meyona, who lives in the Fertile Kingdom, so she can come here and teach the art of making fishnets. I believe she even knows enough about carving to teach it. I think I will also hire her to take care of my son, Joaquín."

When Basamanaco heard Joaquín's name mentioned, his face lit up. Ever since Joaquín had arrived, he had quickly become attached to him, and the boy's presence had immediately drawn him out of a world to which he had once escaped.

"And how about my brother, Lampulla?" said Neef. "Will you send for him, as you will Meyona?"

"Of course. I might even use him to find ways to recruit students to come to Guarica, if we can get away with it."

"And if we do not attain our twenty-five pounds of cotton?" Basamanaco said.

"That goal will not be my greatest concern. Education will come first in importance, and next, will be that enough food is raised for our people to eat."

"But what will the grantee say to all of this?"

"When he sees our results, he will love it."

It took Mateo and Neef many months to establish a school, which they called The Grand College of Quisqueya. Surprisingly, there was no resistance to it. So finally, Neef could teach his alphabet and reading system to the people, for a Spaniard who was working under an *encomendero* had commanded them to learn, and learn they did, particularly the younger people, who were quick to retain symbols and words. Soon, their eyes skimmed across the sheets of manuscript that Neef had so carefully prepared. They even copied Spanish words out of the Bible. And they began to also write stories that they had created themselves. Some of them even wrote about the two caves, while others, wrote about the ancient family that crossed the ocean in a boat. And of course, some created their own *areitas*, and if their songs were of outstanding quality, they were taught to the rest of the people. And once more in parts of Guarica, the music of the ancient fathers rang through the countryside. However, the old philosophies were often difficult for the younger generation to comprehend, for unlike their mothers, the philosophies in the older *areitas* were not taught to them from birth, so the ideas in them came across as being rather strange. And the Tainan language, too, presented problems, for these children were growing up during a time when the island was experiencing tremendous change, when the people were moving away from speaking the pure Tainan tongue, particularly its mother tongue. The language throughout the island was becoming a mixture of Taino, the dialects of the other islands, Spanish, even French, and words of the black slaves. Nevertheless, as Mateo ran his school, the *bohios* he used remained simple and never were as elaborate as those in the Mother Kingdom. And most important of all, the oppression that once hovered in this area, began to dissipate.

There was one *areita* that became particularly popular in Guarica. It told of an ancient philosophy concerning an event that had happened somewhere in this universe before the world was created. It was about twin brothers — Yocahu and Guaca — who had fought in a war over the fate of humankind. And within the cotton fields, the slaves often could be heard singing this *areita*, but somehow, its words did not sound quite right to the older people, for the younger generation could not help but add the influence of Catholicism into it, as they sang,

> Saint Yocahu saved the fate of mortals
> In his struggle with dark Guaca
> Brooding Guaca waits revengeful
> Forever angry with Saint Yocahu
> Always angry with Saint Yocahu
> Always angry with Saint Yocahu.

The older people often clicked their tongues in dismay, as they listened to the younger folk singing corrupt forms of their ancient songs, especially when the younger ones pronounced their Tainan words with heavy accents. Despite it all, these older folk were glad to hear their *areitas* again.

Among these slaves, was a new worker who had escaped from the Fertile Kingdom. He had heard all about this *encomienda* that functioned under Señor Tomas Mendoza and wished to be here. Nobody knew what his real name was, because he told everyone to call him Eldest-Son-of-My-Father's-First-Wife. As Eldest-Son-of-My-Father's-First-Wife listened to the younger generation singing, he did not approve of these changes and remained suspicious of Mateo's intentions. But it was much more pleasant to be here, than to be working under his former taskmaster, who was extremely cruel. As he baled cotton alongside the others, he often grumbled to the person next to him.

"What kind of school is this? That Spaniard is only teaching us how to live like foreigners, for he does not understand our traditions. The younger people are not learning the ancient *areitas*, but they are mixing them up with Christian philosophies and stories. Even our histories are scrambled."

But the other workers good-naturedly laughed, slapped him on the back, and said, "Oh, but this is marvelous. You should have been here, when the old *encomendero* was in charge. No one smiled. Now we have laughter; we have more to eat; and we even have a bit of the old culture back."

"Just because that helper Señor Mateo Gonzalez does not whip us, does not mean he is being any better than the other Spaniards," Eldest-Son-of-My-Father's-First-Wife grumbled.

Often some of the older folk, who knew the original histories and *areitas*, agreed with him. However, they did not notice that whenever Mateo passed by with his crippled friend who walked with crutches, Eldest-Son-of-My-Father's-First-Wife often watched them intensely.

As Señor Tomas Mendoza rode through the cotton fields, he noticed that the people working for Mateo seemed much happier than the others in his *encomienda*, and although they were not pressured to work as hard as in the other areas, they even exceeded their quotas, for they often helped each other out. If a person fell short one day, there were always others willing to band together to fill in what he didn't produce. Tomas did not mind this kind of cooperation, as long as they met their quotas. Besides, in this place, there prevailed a feeling of great love and tranquility. The Indians even looked much healthier and stronger, than any others on this island. Although throughout the years, Tomas had picked up several of the Indian dialects, he found that he could never understand the *areitas* that were now being sung. Even if the tunes were catchy, the subjects that the people sang about never made any sense to him. But he did not realize that they also did not make sense to many of the younger slaves, either.

Tomas also noted that throughout the other parts of his *encomienda*, the Indians were aware that Mateo was their friend, and they often came to him and pleaded to be allowed to work under Mateo's direction and protection. Tomas knew of other *encomenderos* on this island who did not deal harshly with their slaves, and the Indians in those surrounding areas also were greatly attracted to them. He did not know exactly what was happening in Mateo's area, only that the people here were always singing as they worked, and much laughter prevailed. Neither was he aware of the school that had been established. However, he was well aware that Neef, the crippled Indian who often visited him, was close friends with Mateo. Yet he still couldn't believe what Neef had told him about Mateo, that he was from the group of men whom the Admiral had left here on this island during his first journey, for everyone knew that all of those men were killed.

As Tomas rode through his cotton fields, he found that he thoroughly enjoyed being in the land that Mateo managed, for while he was here, he finally began to love this island. He even felt his restlessness and yearning for the peace of Spain ebbing away. And within Mateo's realm, he found all that he had hoped to find in an *encomienda*, when he had left the gold mines of the Cibao Valley.

38

Off the shore of Jamaica

*M*onday, *8 January 1504*

I am now in the Indies for the fourth time, and I realize that I can no longer endure the problems these trips present, for gout plagues my body, excruciating pains emanate from my joints, and I can barely move.

We have been marooned off the coast of Jamaica for six months, and last July as soon as this mishap occurred, I sent my two most able men, Mendez and Fieschi, on two canoes to Española for help. I sent twenty other Christians with them, as well as nine of our best Indian paddlers. Thus far, they have not returned. In the worst of winds, their canoes should have traveled a minimum of ten leagues a day, and since Española is a hundred leagues from here, they would have reached their destination in just ten days. No doubt, the sea must have swallowed them up. Or maybe, once they reached Española, Governor Ovando detained them, because he hates my brothers and I. And I wouldn't put it past him to deliberately leave us stranded here to perish.

For months I pleaded with God for help, and still no one came to our rescue. Our ships can no longer remain afloat; the sea has been up to our decks for many weeks; our pumps are exhausted from continual use and are in need of repair; and thousands of woodworms tunnel through the hulls of our vessels.

Six months in this condition is far too long for anyone to wait to be saved. My crew has been restless for a long time, and mutiny is in the air. Although the Indians here are gentle and constantly bring us food and drink in exchange for beads, hawk's bells, and an occasional pair of scissors, my Christians are sick of Indian food. Instead, they wish for the food of Española, freedom, and women.

It has become impossible to order my men to remain on board at all times, and I fear that if they were allowed to go ashore, they would cause mischief in the Indian villages, especially among the women.

As the Admiral hunched over his desk, he blotted the ink on the page of his journal and closed it. Painfully, he inched his way to his bed. As he pulled his covers up to his chin and rested his head on his pillow, he could hear the voices of some of his crew coming from outside.

"Do ye think Mendez 'n Fieschi actually perished at sea?"

"Naw...they couldn't have. Española is only 10 days from here. Ye know what I really think? I think th' Admiral actually sent them back to Spain."

"Ye don't say. What for?"

"Ye see, th' Admiral's a man of many secrets 'n doesn't tell us everythin'. I think he was actually sendin' them home, because our king 'n queen had actually banished him from Spain, 'n he's spendin' his exile here, 'n that's why we are all confined to these ships, because we were chosen to protect him."

"Yeah, what ye're sayin' makes a lot of sense. Our king 'n queen are not happy with him, all right. That's why three years ago, they chained him up, sent him back home, 'n put Ovando in his place."

"So what are we goin' to do about it? Remain here with him until he dies?"

"It's not necessary, is it? Look, th' Indians around here are peaceful, so they won't hurt him, if we left him here by himself. He's goin' to be all right, because these three ships are safe 'n secure, since we've fixed them so solidly together, that they can't even budge."

As the Admiral lay listening to this conversation, it sounded no different from his other experiences at sea. By now, he had grown calloused to such talk. So when the voices grew low and he could no longer hear anybody, he drifted off to sleep.

Suddenly the Admiral awoke with an eerie feeling. With caution, his eyes shifted from the ceiling to the side of his bed, and there before him, he saw that his cabin was filled with angry faces, as his crew pressed close-by. He beheld their weapons. And his most trusted man, Captain Francisco de Porras, was standing in front of everybody, gripping both a musket and a sword. Porras was breathing heavily, with his hair falling past his nose. Still half asleep, the Admiral reached toward the friend he trusted, but Porras retracted from him. Although Porras was usually a man of much control, the Admiral now saw craziness reeling in his eyes.

"*Señor*, ye want us all to perish here, don't ye?" Porras growled.

Painfully, Colón shifted his body into sitting position, calmly reminding himself that this rebellion was only one of many in his lifetime, and he had survived them all, for God was with him. As he ignored the gout that tormented his body, he grit his teeth as he rose to his feet, pretending to experience no pain.

"I wish for nothin' of th' sort, gentlemen."

236

"Then why aren't ye takin' us back to Castile?"

"My good men, ye all know that our ships are now defunct, and we need to be rescued. If any of ye can propose another plan, I beg that ye kindly submit it to th' council of captains 'n other officers for discussion."

Porras fired his musket into the ceiling, spat, swung around, and faced the others.

"I say, let's git back to Castile! Who agrees with me?"

"I do!"

"Then back to Castile, men! To Castile!"

As the Christians waved their weapons, they pushed their way out of the cabin, and Colón heard them splashing across the sloshy deck outside. A battle soon ensued, with shouts from the rebels overpowering all other sounds, as they took away from the Admiral's faithful men the round tops, mainmasts and castles.

"To Castile!"

"Death to those who oppose us!"

But the Admiral sat helplessly at the edge of his bed, as swords crashed and muskets exploded. He arose, staggered to a window, and saw his few, faithful men defending their positions. Then he saw his brother Bartholomew, who was once the governor of the Indies, positioned with a lance in hand. Suddenly a sword crashed down upon his weapon, sending it clattering across the deck. Bartholomew turned and sped away, and soon, the Admiral heard him entering his cabin, slamming the door shut, and bolting it. The Admiral slowly made his way over to him, and together, they pressed their ears against the door.

Porras' voice could be heard above everyone's.

"Okay, men, now that we've killed them all, let's go 'n kill th' Admiral!"

But his shout caused the men to turn silent.

"No, Señor Porras, we must never kill th' Admiral. If we are caught, we will never be allowed back into Spain, 'n that crime will bring severe punishment upon us all."

After a long silence, the Admiral finally heard footsteps that sounded as if the Christians were clearing the decks. Then all turned quiet.

When the Admiral and Bartholomew finally went out into the open, they saw the bodies of their faithful Christians scattered across the deck. Less than twenty men remained uninjured. The Admiral then made his way to a man covered with lacerations, who was moaning on deck.

"What a cursed lot we all are!" the man said. "As long as we are stranded here, we are all doomed to die."

The Admiral saw that he was seriously wounded and would not live much longer. And then, Bartholomew pointed into the distance.

"Look! There they go."

The Admiral looked up and saw the Christians leaving on ten canoes. They had taken eighteen Indians with them to serve as paddlers. He, himself, had instructed his men to take possession of those canoes from the Indians, as soon as they arrived here in Jamaica, to limit those people's mobility and prevent them from attacking. And now, he and his brother watched helplessly after the Christians as they grew farther away in those canoes and headed toward the east end of Jamaica, in the same direction that Fieschi and Mendez went with their men six months before.

The Admiral turned toward his few loyal ones, who remained on board. He perceived that their faith in him was now sapped. And he sensed that if those who were injured and groaning were well, they would have also joined the Christians who had just left. As he dismissed those perceptions from his mind, a great love overpowered him, and soon, he found himself speaking to his remaining crew in a soft, kind voice.

"My good men, God will take care of us, do not fear."

With all his energy, he expounded encouragements until his men's spirits were finally lifted. And when he was done with his speech, his brother Bartholomew helped him back into the cabin to his bed.

Wednesday 7 February 1504

Why has God deserted me? From the time I was a boy, I served Him with all my might. As soon as I learned how to read Latin, I searched the Bible for greater wisdom and understanding that went beyond this world. Even as a boy, as I stood upon the docks of Genoa, watching the ships come and go, I felt a closeness to my Maker. I believed that somewhere, sometime, I had made promises in a world that is now invisible to me. I have always remained faithful to my knowledge that I was a man of destiny, that I was a chosen vessel to bring the true religion of the one and only God and of Jesus Christ to the heathen nations.

As the Admiral closed his journal, he shed tears that only a man of remarkable strength could shed. In great pain, he hobbled from his desk to his bed, slid to his knees to offer his usual thanks to his Maker, and poured out his heart for forgiveness for his impatience.

As he uttered his troubles heavenward, something suddenly rushed to his heart and mind, and said,

O fool and slow to believe and to serve thy God, the God of every man! What more did He do for Moses or for David His servant than for thee? From thy birth He hath ever held thee in special charge.

Peace suddenly flooded the Admiral, and when he finally climbed into bed, his eyes were no longer moist, for he was filled with indescribable joy. And again, he felt like that little boy of long ago in Genoa, who, while watching ships come and go, always knew that he was a man of destiny.

Friday, March 8, 1505

Today Garcia returned alone. He said that he made it back here with the help of Indians. As soon as he reached us, he begged for forgiveness for his rebellion, and I gladly gave it to him. He said that in his heart, he had always been loyal to me, but he left with the rest of the Christians, because he was afraid that he would spend the rest of his life here on these ships. Then he proceeded to tell Bartholomew and me what happened to the Christians, after they departed, and he said that those experiences made him realize that God was with me; and for that reason, he came back, even when the others did not.

Garcia said that after he and the Christians left for Española on the canoes, they reached about four leagues out into the sea, when contrary winds hit them, as if

demons suddenly descended upon them. As they were tossed about, the gusts blasted so loudly that the men could barely hear above their shouts. And all of them became afraid that their canoes would sink.

"We've got to lighten our load!" the Christians shouted. "We must throw out everthin' we own, even our food!"

In desperation, the Christians tossed out all of their possessions, but not their weapons. And when the winds did not cease and the load was still not light enough, the men looked at each other with understanding of what the next step should be. Suddenly Porras removed his knife from its sheath and stabbed the Indian sitting next to him. Then he threw him overboard. Immediately other Christians joined in with this slaughter. When the Indians who were still alive realized what was happening, they dove overboard and swam as far as they could, but since there was no land nearby, when they grew tired, they returned to the canoes and hung on to the gunwales.

"They're weighin' us down!" Porras yelled. "They're goin' to kill us all!"

So the Christians grabbed their hatchets and hacked off the Indians' hands. And soon, all eighteen of the Indians were dead.

Because of adverse conditions, the Christians were forced to find land. Since the Indians on the nearest island did not know that the men had recently slaughtered their own people, they sympathized with them, brought them provisions, and invited them to stay in their villages. As the storm increased by the day, the Christians helped themselves to the possessions the Indians owned and took their women.

When the weather grew calm again, they resumed toward Española, but as soon as they did, the winds returned, so they had to return to land. They attempted this journey when the weather grew calm at least two more times, but always, the frightening winds reappeared. And each time, they were forced back to land. At this point, Garcia approached some Indians in secret and asked to be brought to us, here in Jamaica, because he said that he realized that the winds that kept reoccurring were from God, who was punishing the Christians for their rebellion.

Saturday, June 29, 1504

Today we were rescued! After a year of being marooned off the shore of Jamaica, Mendez finally arrived on a small caravel. He brought some wine and a slab of salt pork. Although this ship was not large enough to take the entire crew, its captain promised that another one would soon be coming.

As I rode away with Mendez, he told me that once he and Fieschi reached Española, as I suspected, when Governor Ovando learned that they were my men and more of us were marooned here in Jamaica, he detained them in the Mother Kingdom. Soon after Mendez was released, though, he traveled to Santo Domingo and purchased a small caravel, so he could finally rescue us.

Later, as soon as I was alone, I fell to my knees and thanked my God for again having a hand in my affairs.

Cuba

Windward Pass

Atlantic Ocean

Kingdom
of Marién

Fertile
Kingdom

Kingdom
of the Mines

Kingdom of the
Great Old Lady

Guayacarima

Mother Kingdom

Santo
Domingo

Borinquen
(Puerto Rico)

Quisqueya
(Hispaniola)

Guanine

Caribbean Sea

39

Lately the crippled Indian appeared frequently at Tomas' front door. Besides working for paper and ink, he earned two more metal boxes to store his records. Although paper was not abundant on this island, Tomas was always willing to give him what he could, and Neef insisted on paying him for these materials in the form of work. Sometimes he even paid Tomas with food, such as a fish that he caught that morning. And Tomas never grew weary of Neef's humble eyes as he stood at the doorway and politely said, *Señor, I need more paper, por favor*, to which Tomas always swung his door wide open for Neef to enter, so they could spend an hour or two together in his study, in deep discussion.

Ever since Neef had shown him a Bible that was written in Spanish, Tomas began to understand a book he never knew. Not only could he now read it, because it was in a language he spoke, but Neef posed questions concerning perceptions Tomas had never considered, thus drawing both of them into new dimensions. What impressed Tomas was that Neef combined the concepts of the Bible with his Indian spirituality that the *padres* could never do. However, Tomas knew that if any Christian were to find out about that Bible, he and Neef would both be punished as heretics, and that book would be burned.

Because Neef was working closely with the Bible, their discussions were often related to Christianity, but Tomas knew that if Neef were studying a book of history or astronomy, their discussions would revolve around those subjects. Although he, himself, was not a religious person, Tomas was surprised that Neef could get him involved into religious thinking. He did not feel that Neef was at all interested in becoming baptized; nor did he feel that Neef even wished to become a Christian, the way the *padres* wanted him to be. But he perceived that Neef wondered about Christianity, because he had a mind and heart that thought deeply upon everything he studied. In fact, as far as Tomas knew, Neef still worshipped his *zemies*.

Neef intrigued him, for he was not afraid to venture into areas where he, Tomas, was taught as a boy to never question. He was touched by Neef's confidence in him, as if he were a person capable of understanding great mysteries. At first Neef began with basic questions about Christianity, such as, *what is the Holy Ghost*, and *what is its purpose? Why does the Bible say that God is a just god, when He favored the Jews and said that they were His chosen people?* Neef pointed out that it was not fair to favor one type of people over another. And one day he asked, *for many*

240

generations we Tainos of Quisqueya also felt that we were a chosen people, so why does the God of Abraham not favor us?

Tomas liked Neef's straightforward, simple questions, because unlike those that the religious people he knew posed, they were not the kind that caused a person to wander about in circles. Neef's questions made him realize that as a grantee, while Spain held him responsible for converting his Indians to Christianity, which he ignored, Neef — an Indian — was converting him.

Once during their discussions, Tomas threw up his arms and said, "Why do ye ask me? Ye should ask a *padre*, instead!"

"I have. They are not interested in my questions. They loathe the way I think. They only wish for me to be baptized, with no questions asked, especially if I pay them for it."

"But why do ye come to me, when ye know that I am a wicked man?"

Neef looked him straight in the eyes.

"Ye? Wicked? I see much good in ye, *señor*."

"Ye don't know of all that I have done in this life. There's no hope for me. It is already determined that I will burn in Hell. Even th' *padres* do not allow people, like me, to confess their sins to them."

"But there is still much good in ye, *señor*. I can see it. It fills yer body."

"Eh?"

Just then, Neef arose to leave, as he held his supply of paper and ink that he had just earned.

"*Gracias*, Señor Mendoza. We had another good visit again." He then patted Tomas on the shoulder and added, "Ye're a good man."

"Wait. Don't go."

Neef paused politely.

"Do ye realize what ye do to me every time ye come here? Ye always leave me with so much to think about, 'n those ideas won't leave my head for days. I never had this kind of friendship with any Indian before, or with anyone else, for that matter, not even with th' people of my own family, back home. Why is it that ye can see somethin' in me that nobody else ever sees — not even myself?"

After Neef thought for a while, he said, "Maybe it is because I understand somethin' few people ever can."

"What is that?"

"I know *the love* of Yocahu 'n I have often reached my *ayiti*. These are concepts my people have taught for generations, but sometimes, not even my people know what they are."

Later that day as Tomas took his daily ride to oversee his slaves, he still was deeply touched by the love he felt emanating from Neef. As he rode through Mateo's section, he felt the same kind of peace that Neef always brought with him, permeating the air. He could even feel his horse beneath him relax considerably. Far away, he heard people singing. Those sounds, too, always made him happy. As Tomas rode in the direction of the singing, his eyes fell upon Mateo in the distance. He was working among a group of Indians. He was stripped to his waist beneath the hot sun, and his long, blond hair was tied behind his neck, as if he, himself, was an Indian slave. As women and children brought their *hava* baskets filled with cotton balls over to him, Mateo baled cotton with the men, and Tomas could see that he was sweating, just as much as the Indians around him.

As Tomas drew closer, Mateo looked up from his work and wiped his brow with the back of his palm. However, when the Indians saw Tomas approaching, their singing suddenly stopped.

"*Tayno*!" Mateo said as he grinned.

Just then, Tomas noticed the tattoo upon Mateo's arm. He saw its snakelike designs, its curves, and its various colors. It was an Indian type of tattoo.

"What, th' devil? What's that on ye?"

"This tattoo, *señor*? It means that I am officially a *bohutio*, or a priest of th' highest level. I earned this position, when I started my education in th' wilderness of th' Mother Kingdom at th' age of thirteen that lasted for a year-'n-a-half."

Tomas brought his horse forward, so he could have a better look at the tattoo.

Perhaps this man is actually an Indian with a fair skin, he thought. But he dismissed that idea, for Mateo's features were too European to be Taino. And he spoke Spanish too perfectly. When Mateo turned to the people, who stood gaping from behind him, he told them in their tongue to continue with their work. Tomas noticed that he spoke their language, just as well as he spoke Spanish.

"Who are ye, anyway?"

Mateo smiled and swung his arms in the direction of the Indians.

"I am their brother."

This response came as a shock to Tomas, and not knowing what to say, he swung his horse around. As he rode away, he wondered how Mateo had formed his heretic view of being a brother to the Indians, for everyone knew about the two creations. The first was when God made real men; and the second was when He created the Indians and the heathens to serve the real men. That was what the *padres* said, anyway. Yet Mateo, whom he had hired, seemed extremely content among these Indians, as if he actually believed that he and the Indians *were* brothers. And deep, down inside of him, Tomas wished that he could also develop similar friendships with *all* of his Indians, for he couldn't forget the satisfaction he received from the closeness with Neef. But every time he came near his workers, they cowered in fear from him.

He also wished that he could develop close friendships with the other Spaniards, and even his father, but because he was not like any of them, he felt that thick walls were now built between him and all of them. Only four months before, he received a letter from home, and his father had said that he was greatly pleased with his success in the Indies, but Tomas felt that he only wanted him to make a lot of money, and he saw no value in the Indians as human beings. In his letter, his father also mentioned that Queen Isabella had died recently. It was dated in 1504, but by the time it arrived in Española, it was already 1505.

As Tomas rode farther away, he saw another rider approaching in the distance. His horse was kicking up much dust in the road. And then he recognized that it was his old acquaintance, Ricardo.

"Damn! What is he doin' here in th' Kingdom of Marién? I thought I got rid of him forever, when I moved out here."

As before, Ricardo's appearance repulsed him, for it brought back a flood of memories of everything that Hojeda had assigned him to do. Tomas immediately turned his horse around and hoped that Ricardo did not see him. He was in no mood for Hojeda today, or any other day.

He headed toward a river and rode along its bank for several hours, until long after it turned dark. And then he stopped at a tree that looked good enough to spend the night beneath, figuring that by morning, Ricardo would have left the area, especially after learning that he was not at home.

The next morning when Tomas returned to his home, as soon as he entered his living room, he discovered that his servants had invited Ricardo in, and now he was asleep on a couch in his parlor. At that point, Tomas knew that he had no choice but to find out the purpose of Ricardo's visit.

Ricardo had hardly opened his eyes, when Tomas yelled at him from across the room, "I'm not doin' anythin' more for Hojeda, ye hear?"

But all Ricardo did was lean back on the couch and laugh.

"I have not heard from Hojeda in a long time, *mi amigo*."

"I don't believe ye. Then why are ye here?"

Ricardo cleared his throat.

"Ye don't understand, Mendoza. I came here to bring ye presents from yer father."

"My father? Presents? Why couldn't he send them directly to me?"

Ricardo reached into a bag and produced several bottles of wine.

"See? Th' finest Spain has to offer. Yer father still remembers me, from when he met me here in th' Indies, 'n he wanted to send me some of these for my birthday. So when he sent me these bottles, he included a note to bring a few over to ye as a surprise."

"Don't lie to me, Ricardo," said Tomas pushing the bottles away. "I've not touched any of these things in years. Once I moved to th' Kingdom of Marién, I've become a new man."

"Ye know what th' trouble is with ye, Mendoza? Ye're lonely. How long has it been since ye've had a woman? Years, I bet. Ye've no more excitement in life."

Ricardo arose, went to the next room, and returned with two glasses.

"*Dios*, Ricardo. Ye still look at me, as if I'm th' same *imbécil* I was four years ago. I've changed, since then. I'm even interested in religion, ye know."

"Ye? Religion?"

Ricardo guffawed.

"Ricardo, I am tellin' ye th' truth. Have ye ever wondered why Jesus Christ doesn't know anythin' about these Tainos, when these people always felt that they were a chosen people of a great god in th' heavens?"

"*Amigo, amigo*. Let's have a good visit. Let's share a drink together today, just for old times' sake, *eh*? What do ye say?"

Tomas backed away.

"To hell with ye, Ricardo. I'm tired of that old life. There was no meanin' to anythin', back then." Tomas groped quickly for any excuse to make Ricardo go away. "I can't do anythin' more for Hojeda, because I'm...I'm...I'm thinkin' that I should...I should... ah, enter th' priesthood 'n become a *padre*...that's right, a *padre*! I want, I want to answer th' questions th' Indians may have about Christianity. Yes...yes, I'd really like to do that. I would never stifle anythin' they asked. Ye know how we are told that we must spread the gosp..."

"Wait. Did I hear ye say that ye want to become a priest?"

Ricardo flung his head back and guffawed again.

As he wiped his eyes, he said, "Ye could never be a priest."

243

He poured two drinks.

"I'll only talk with ye, Ricardo, but I won't drink anythin'. Ye must drink alone."

"*Amigo, amigo*...just one drink before breakfast?"

"No...all right, only one drink. 'N then ye must go."

Tomas feebly took the glass and downed his drink. It didn't taste like wine, nor did it look like wine. It wasn't the right color, and it had so many bubbles in it that it foamed when it was poured. Somehow, it felt familiar in his throat. Even with that one glass, he felt his sensitivities beginning to ebb away, but by then, it was too late.

"Ye bastard! That was not wine from Spain. That was...that was...*chicha* that ye poured into that bottle. 'N ye put some colorin' in it, to make it look like wine. Ye have always known that *chicha* makes me lose control of myself 'n act crazy. Why have ye done this to me? Whenever I drink that stuff, it makes me hate myself for months."

Now Tomas could feel the *chicha* affecting him, the way it always used to. He pushed the glass in front of him away, but Ricardo filled it again.

"*Mi amigo*, only one more won't hurt ye."

"No! I said, no!"

But finally after much urging, Tomas took that drink also, with Ricardo filling glass after glass for him, until in anger, Tomas threw his glass across the room.

"Damn ye to Hell! What does Hojeda want from me, now?"

"Nothin', I told ye, nothin'."

"Then what do *ye* want from me?"

"Absolutely nothin', *mi amigo*. But another man, Valésquez, has sent me to ye this time. Valésquez has asked me to round up th' best men on this island to help him."

Tomas tried to rise, but the room spun before him.

"Ye son-of-a-bitch!"

"Valésquez needs ye to help pacify Cuba."

Enraged, Tomas picked up a chair and threw it at Ricardo, but Ricardo dodged out of the way.

"Come with me, *amigo*. Th' ships leave for Cuba in th' mornin', 'n we have a long way to go to git to them."

As he staggered away from Ricardo, Tomas roared at him across the room.

"What price is Valésquez payin' ye to get me, now?"

Ricardo laughed and urged Tomas toward the door. And with his head whirling in circles, Tomas felt anger well up in him — not at Ricardo, and not even at Valésquez — but at himself, for being a person of so little strength, for he was always bending to the will of others, whether they were his father or his ruthless Spaniard associates. In his drunken state, he yearned to gain an inner stamina, so that he could stand up for his own convictions, just as Neef and Mateo could.

"*Bien lo sabe Dios!*" he yelled.

40

Thousands of screams surrounded Tomas Santiago Mendoza.

"Go away! Leave me alone!"

As he yelled, the cries in his head increased in magnitude. He saw himself riding upon his horse in Cuba, with other *conquistadors*. Because he was numb with *chicha*, he could tear into crowds of Indians with no feeling for them. As he lashed at them with his sword and produced rapid bloodshed, he saw dozens of human lives ebbing away before his eyes. He could care less, even if he understood their native tongue well enough to know that these people were pleading for justice, for mercy, to be recognized as a good and important people, and for their gods to come to save them. And then, above all of those screams, he heard high-pitched ones that came from Indian children, as they were slaughtered *en masse*.

Tomas bolted upright, tearing at his hair.

"Stooooop!"

As the nightmare dissipated, he realized that he was no longer in Cuba, but was now in his bedroom. He groped for his candle and made his way to the fireplace in his room, where he found a piece of coal, glowing in the dark. He lifted it with tongs to light the wick. When the candle was finally lit, he edged his way to his bedroom door, stepped out carefully into the hallway, and made his way down the stairs.

"*Señor*, ye yell all night in yer room," a servant called in broken Spanish from downstairs. "What wrong?"

"Nothin', nothin', *señora*. Go back to yer bed."

After Tomas went down to his study, he found a wine bottle on a shelf. He recognized it to be one of the containers Ricardo had filled with *chicha*. A servant must have placed it there, after he and Ricardo had left for Cuba. Ever since that time, it had remained untouched. Tomas picked up that bottle, drew open a window, and hurled it outside. He watched after its silhouette as it spun, nonstop, into nothingness, and then he heard it shatter far away.

"*Señor?*" the servant called.

"Go back to sleep, I said."

He built up a flame in the fireplace in his study and tried to read by its light, but the screams in his head returned. Finally he threw his book down and slunk to the floor.

Help me. Somebody, please...help me. I need to erase my sins.

Then he heard a single word course through his mind: *Confess!*

In a split second, he was on his feet.

That's it! Confession! I must see a padre.

The next thing Tomas knew, he was out in the night, stumbling across the cobblestoned path that led to his stables, and then he was riding madly toward town, as he, a grown man, bawled like a babe. He needed to talk to someone — someone who would listen to him and could help him.

As Tomas rode along, he saw himself in Cuba again among other Christians, whom Ricardo had also recruited to pacify that island. And when he encountered the Indians of Cuba, he was surprised at what good fighters they were, for their skills were beyond anything he ever saw on Española. Both men and women shot their arrows from places he never expected and caused Christians on either side of him to fall from their horses. But he, Tomas, remained unhurt and surged ahead. As arrows whizzed in scores, even Ricardo became hurt. Yet Tomas warded the arrows off with his shield, although one managed to singe his arm.

The war dogs that he and his men set after the Cubans, fought fiercely, but the Cubans dodged them and even killed many of them. The farther inland the Christians pushed, the more thickly the arrows came, but it made Tomas even more determined to defeat those heathens, so peace would prevail in that land. Under the influence of *chicha,* he found himself becoming increasingly enraged at his attackers, and he swung harder with his weapon. He saw his victims falling faster. As Ricardo fought close to him, he was bleeding badly. And the Christians, who battled with them, also were bleeding. They consisted not only of Spaniards, but also Italians, Englishmen, and even Moors and Jews, who were converted to Christianity. All of them were in these Indies for adventure, and under the direction of Valásquez, they were experiencing plenty of it. And as they traveled from village to village, they defeated men and women, who were unafraid to defend themselves.

"Freedom!" he heard the Cubans yell. "We must save ourselves and families!"

Soon Tomas and the men reached a forest. Just as they were about to turn right to find the next village, one of the Christians said, "Let's ride through those trees, to see if we can find any of those *cretinos* hidin' among them."

As the Christians crashed through the thick foliage, they soon discovered that this forest was where the Cubans had hidden their children. The Indians must have thought that they would be safe here, while they fought in their villages, because it appeared as if villages had consolidated to hide their children in these woods; for there were hundreds of little ones — perhaps even a thousand of them — concealed among the trees. Many were so young that they could only sit or crawl; and there were others, who were no older than eight or nine years of age, who were given responsibility for two, three, or sometimes even four tiny ones. And those older children clutched as many of the babies in their arms as they could. There were also older boys, who were perhaps twelve years old, whom the Indians assigned to protect these children, and Tomas was amazed at how well they shot at the Christians, with the same ferociousness as the adults. But most of the children there had no weapons, and they were defenseless.

As soon as Tomas and his men appeared, many of the little ones panicked, and even the babies screamed. They ran hollering in every direction among the trees, as they stumbled over rocks and bushes, with some of them still holding littler ones. Some of the older children were so frightened that they dropped babies and ran to save themselves, leaving their siblings, or whomever they carried, bawling on the ground.

As Tomas and his companions — the Spaniards, Italians, Englishmen, Moors and Jews — charged into the crowd of children with their horses, he heard hundreds of children's voices shrieking. He and his men whipped at them with their swords. And when they were through with them, their little bodies lay mangled and covered with blood among the trees, with the brave, twelve-year-old boys among them. The forest had become suddenly still, as if even the animals understood what had just occurred, for not a single bird chirped.

As his colleagues rode off to the next village, Tomas remained behind. Even if he was filled with *chicha,* he found that he was not actually beyond feeling, as he thought he was, and he sat petrified upon his horse. He could not stop staring at the scene that he and the others had just created. So many children. Dead. And then he saw Ricardo lying among them, with an arrow penetrated through his chest. Most likely, he was shot by one of the twelve-year-old boys.

Tomas began to weep, not for Ricardo or himself, but for the children. And all he could say was, "Oh, my God, oh my God!" And as he looked heavenward through the treetops into the clouds, he muttered to himself repeatedly. "*Dios, mió,* forgive me."

As the horse now carried Tomas into town, the moonlight reflected off wooden walls, stone edifices, and ornate fences. Even while a hound bayed into the night, the people slept despite its noise. Tomas steered his horse toward the building, where the *padres* lived, and approached its two large, metal gates. This was one place that he always avoided, because he was never needed here. He found a bell to the side of one of the gates and pulled its string. Its clang left a ringing in his ears. When no one stirred, he rang again.

"*Quién es*? Why in th' world are ye ringin' my bell at this time of th' night?"

Tomas swallowed and kept his voice steady, so that the *padre* would not suspect that he was been crying.

"I need to see a *padre*."

"Which one? There are six of us here."

"I don't care who. Father Sanchez, Father Rodriquez, Father Franco, anyone."

"I'm Father Franco. How can I help ye, my son?"

"I need to confess, Father."

"At this time of th' night? Please come back in th' mornin'."

"No, it must be now. I cannot sleep. I've been haunted all night. In fact, I've been haunted for weeks."

"It can wait, my son."

"But it does not leave my head. Those thousands of screams..."

His voice broke into sobs.

"I see that ye are deeply troubled, my son."

"I-I-I came back from Cuba a few weeks ago. I was told that that island needed to be pacified. There were terrible battles against both men 'n women, but we finally overpowered them 'n took many prisoners."

Tomas broke down again.

"Get hold of yerself, son. Ye're cryin' so hard that I can't understand ye."

"Please let me go into th' chapel to confess."

"Son, ye must calm down."

"Ye must realize that it's not those Cubans we fought that bother me so much, Father. It's those babies...we killed them...all of them!"

"*Un momento*! Are ye an *encomendero*?"

"What does it matter to ye, if I am?"

"To whom am I speaking?"

"Tomas Mendoza, *señor*."

"I've heard of ye. I'm sorry, but ye must go home. I never deal with any *encomenderos*."

"But I must confess, *por favor*."

"No, no. Be off with ye. Good night."

"But those children...I must talk...Father."

Mendoza heard a door slam shut.

And then he fell to the ground, sobbing and babbling as though he were a madman.

As he pounded the ground with his fists, he cried, "Neef! Neef! Ye're wrong! There is no good in me! Can't ye see? I was meant to always go to Hell, from th' day I was born. I am bad, bad, bad!"

41

Another *encomendero* had gone insane in Guarica, but this time, it was not from the final stages of *yaya*, as it was with the former *encomendero* Señor Rodriquez, and no one knew the cause of his madness. His name was Tomas Santiago Mendoza, and like the last grantee, he had no family in Quisqueya to take his place. His slaves were told that he would soon be replaced. Throughout Guarica, the people urged Mateo to apply for this position, for they all wished for him to be completely in charge over them. But when Mateo inquired, he learned that this position of grantee was already assigned to another, and he was told that the new *encomendero*, Señor Gomez, was coming the following week.

Mateo was also told that the *encomendero* over him, Tomas Mendoza, would be leaving the following morning. So early the next day, he and Neef started out to see if they could catch their grantee before he left. When they reached his home, they saw a carriage parked in front of the mansion. The servants were busy with the final packing for their master. A few Spaniards, who were friends of the new grantee Gomez, were giving the servants orders.

When Mateo inquired about the whereabouts of their beloved *señor*, one of the Spaniards snapped, "Why bother?"

"We'd like to see him."

"Why should ye? That man's crazy."

"He is our friend. Where are ye takin' him?"

"It is no business of yers. Most likely he'll go to Santo Domingo, to a special home, where he'll get some rest. His work was too stressful. He had no wife, ye know, so it must have made his work harder to bear. Ye must go away, now."

Reluctantly, Neef and Mateo turned back toward the Indian village. They were surprised at the abrupt change of mood in the grantee home, and the harshness that now lingered there disturbed them. They had not gone far, when Neef turned around and saw a small group of people leading Señor Mendoza out of the front door to the carriage. The *señor* appeared to be in a world of his own, while he muttered to himself and clutched at his head, as if he were trying to get something out of it.

Neef swung around and hobbled with his crutches with such speed, that Mateo had to run to catch up with him. Soon they were both in front of the grantee. Señor Mendoza walked past them, still muttering, oblivious of their presence. The small group that surrounded him consisted of mostly Taino servants, but there was a Negro slave and two Spaniards with them.

"*Adios, señor,*" Neef said.

"I thought we told ye both to go away," one of the Spaniards said.

Señor Mendoza paused, then turned toward the two men, who came to see him. He appeared to recognize Neef, and he smiled weakly. He extended his hand toward him and feebly mouthed his words.

"*Buenos dios, amigo...*"

Neef clasped his hand. Then he boldly flung his arms around him, Tainan style, and kissed both of his cheeks.

"*Señor, señor...*" Neef said. "Th' best of luck to ye, 'n may ye regain yer health soon. 'N remember...I know that ye are a good man, a very good man. Ye have shown me many times that ye are a very special person."

The Spaniards pulled Tomas away and began to nudge him toward the carriage.

248

"*Tayno, señor, tayno.* I will always love thee, just as Yocahu loved my people."

The small group ignored Neef, but Tomas looked back at him, as if he comprehended what Neef meant, and his eyes filled with tears, while he tried to extend his hand toward Neef again, but the others pushed him into the carriage.

When the new grantee Señor Gomez arrived, he was not happy with Mateo's section of his *encomienda,* for as far as he was concerned, the Indians here were too much at ease, and because they did not cower from Mateo, he said that Mateo allowed them to be too bold. He said that they were in great need of pacification, for in the past, he had worked extensively with Hojeda, and he felt that he knew all about how an *encomienda* should function.

When he saw Mateo working among the slaves one day, he charged upon his horse until he stood in front of him.

"*Por Dios*! Don't ye know what ye are doin'? Ye are encouragin' rebellion among these Indians! When ye put them up so high, they will soon demand to be put at yer level, or even be placed above ye. Before ye know it, they'll be runnin' the entire Indies. Always put them in their proper places, 'n show them yer superiority."

Mateo smiled and calmly said, "But these are my brothers, *señor,* 'n we are friends. There are no distinctions among us."

"I must insist that my land be properly managed. I will have no such nonsense in my *encomienda.* If ye don't change yer ways, ye will no longer be workin' for me. If I can help it, I will even have ye sent back to Spain."

When Mateo entered Basamanaco's *bohío* that evening, he found Neef bent over his translations, and since Basamanaco and Meyona were out on a walk with Joaquín, he was alone.

Neef looked up from his work and said, "Perhaps it was wrong of me to begin translating the Bible. When we were both in the wilderness for our test, you said that only men who were called of God could write the Bible. If no one from heaven commissioned me to do this work, I have no right to do any of it. I would have been better off serving as a butler for Señor Mendoza, instead. Somehow, I feel that if I were a closer friend to him, I could have prevented his going mad."

Mateo sighed and said, "Perhaps we both should have never started our work, and perhaps we should have ignored our visions, because in them, we were asked to accomplish the impossible."

Then he turned and walked to his trunk that held his belongings. After he rummaged through its contents, he returned with a thin book.

"I have kept this from you, because I was saving it for a time like this."

Mateo then handed the book to Neef. As Neef examined its contents, he saw that it did not contain any history or stories, but rather, there were drawings in it that he did not recognize.

"What kind of book is this?"

"You've never seen anything like it before, have you?"

"Its pictures puzzle me."

"They are pictures of weapons of my people, Neef. This book tells how to make them."

Mateo leaned over and flipped through the pages, until he came to the back of the book.

"This section describes the weapons of the Moors. I've never told you about those people, but the Christians call them infidels, and they lived in my land until they lost a war, and then they were expelled from Spain — unless they became Christians."

Neef studied the drawing of a cannon. As he thumbed through the pages, he stared at a crossbow, then two types of daggers. He handed the book back to his brother.

"These are curious objects, indeed."

"Neef, listen to me. I know that I have said that I shouldn't have begun my work here, but as long as I have started it, I intend to finish it. I came here to win a battle. I came here to fight for our people, to re-establish what they have lost. At first I thought this battle was going to be peaceful, but now I realize that I was being too unrealistic. Tomorrow I shall begin to teach our people how to make some of these weapons. And as soon as possible, I am going to teach them how to fight. And your brother, Lampulla, has consented to help me, once I get him over here to Guarica, I've discussed this issue with him many times. And he says that he is ready to start preparations for a rebellion, whenever I give him permission to do so. He even told me that whenever I need it, he would be willing to bring over the weapons that he had gathered in the Fertile Kingdom. He says that there are many people in his kingdom also prepared for a rebellion, and they are willing to come here, to help us."

Neef's jaw fell open, and for a long time, he could not take his eyes away from Mateo.

"Nay...."

He arose and pulled himself up high with his crutches.

"It should never happen in Guarica, or in any other part of the Kingdom of Marién. Nor should it ever occur on this island."

"Neef, please, you must understand. Even the Christians in Europe, from time to time, conducted Crusades that fought wars to fight for their cause."

"But what did they know about *the love*? We cannot be as they are, for we are Tainos. We cannot be as those in the Kingdom of the Mines or the Fertile Kingdom, for the people there have resorted to fighting the Europeans and have forgotten the teachings of the fathers. We must always retain *the love*, for we are Yocahu's special people, who await his return some day. We shall never fight."

"The *caciques* are dead, Neef. Even your father Guarionex is dead. And Guacanagarí is also dead, because he was foolish and tried to placate the Spaniards, and despite his efforts and kindness, the very people to whom he remained loyal, burned him to death. We cannot have that happen to any more of our people."

Mateo began to pace the floor, and occasionally he glanced over at Neef, who stood staring back at him. Finally he spoke again.

"Neef, today Señor Gomez ordered me to change the way I am treating our people. He wants me to become a cruel taskmaster, to keep our people submissive. I can never do this! The Tainos are my brothers. And I must always remember that my mission here is to help them in every way I can, and right now, they are facing extinction. Fighting with weapons to preserve them and their culture, is the only logical way I know how to accomplish this goal."

"Nay, Mateo. Nay. If we fight, we are no longer Tainos. Don't you understand what your great teacher in your Bible meant when he said, *Father, forgive them, for they know not what they do?*'"

"Neef, do not misinterpret that passage or take it out of context. At the time He said those words, He was being crucified, and people were standing around him and mocking him. They did not understand His purpose here on earth."

Neef's eyes were ablaze.

"I understand! I understand those words!"

"Neef, you must remember it was a totally different situation from the one we now face."

"I understand, I tell you. Your Master was speaking, not only for that particular moment at his death, but He was also pointing out a common weakness in humankind that happens often, in all ages. Those people around him did not understand how they were treating Him, nor did they understand who He was. The Caribs do not understand how they treat people on the various islands, nor do they know who they are. The people of Guanine never understand what they are doing, when they go to war. Even my people sometimes do not understand what they are doing. They all do not understand that, whenever someone tramples another, they are breaking sacred laws that Yocahu has taught, which exist in this universe. But I, Neef, understand those words of your Master, and with the *ayiti* that I have gained, I understand them more than ever before."

"Neef..."

"If all men are brothers, then whatever they do to each other, whether good or bad, they are affecting their own kin. Mateo, remember the *areita* about Yocahu and his twin brother? His brother's name was Guaca, and he was angry with Yocahu. That *areita* tells that at one time, we all existed in the heavens as one, large family. Many of us were best of friends.

"What this means is that when we mistreat anyone in any way, we could be actually destroying someone whom we were once close to in the heavens. That someone is our brother, whom we once loved dearly. We, as human beings, have no idea which people could have loved us back deeply, if we allowed the same relationships we once had in the heavens to develop on earth."

"Wait a moment, Neef. Regardless of whether at one time the Spaniards and our people loved each other, we can't let the Spaniards destroy the people of our island, anymore."

"My people, the Tainos of Quisqueya, are Yocahu's chosen people. They should never resort to the base behavior of others, who know not what they do."

"You mean, you will allow men like Hojeda to come upon you at night, burn your home, and keep you bending to his will? *Dios*, Neef! Our people are almost gone!"

Neef stood as tall as he could and said, "Did your great teacher fight back?"

"He stood up for himself."

"But he let others kill him."

"You blasted Indian!"

Mateo snatched up the book of weapons and threw it across the *bohío*.

"We would rather be killed, than fight," Neef said, still standing high.

Mateo tromped over to him, and when he looked into his face and saw determination emanating from his eyes, he yelled, "How stupid can you be? Everything I just said, is to no avail! We can't let the Spaniards kill our people, you hear? We must defend ourselves, so we can show them what our people represent; that we have a vast knowledge of herbs that heals infections, broken bones, and illnesses — faster than any of their medicines can. Those foreigners have no idea that our people know the stars better than they do, that entrenched in our culture is an advanced method of weaving baskets that can even hold water; and our fishing with remoras is far more efficient that their flimsy metal hooks. If our people develop the strength to fight those foreigners off, it will enable them to continue memorizing their genealogies and histories to perfection that extend back to the caves, or maybe, even back to a first family; they can again sing their *areitas* freely and exercise their deep, spiritual ties with their ancestors that the Europeans cannot even begin to understand; they can also live the strict, moral code that was robbed from them; and most important, if we can get the foreigners to leave, the love and peace of Yocahu can once more flow through this land. Where else in this world, could you find people with hearts, such as Basamanaco and Lida's, who would adopt someone, like me, and love him as their very own son — after his people had abused everything they cherished?"

"Put your book back with your other possessions, Mateo."

In fury, Mateo grabbed Neef by the shoulders and shook him with all his might. "You won't change!"

As Neef was being shaken, although he appeared to be calm, his eyes continued to show a great stubbornness. After Mateo finally released him, he staggered backwards to keep his balance, and as he braced himself with his crutches to keep from falling, he said in Spanish, *Comó! I see that ye are also inflictin' th' violence of yer people upon me.*

His words were more than Mateo could handle. In frustration, Mateo lifted an arm and took a slug at him. As Neef went sprawling across the floor, with his crutches clattering and sliding in opposite directions, his body came to a halt, when his face slammed into a *guayacan* post. While he lay stunned upon the ground, Mateo came and bent over him, too proud to help his crippled brother up, but instead, as anger spewed from him, he clenched both fists and shook one of them.

"Don't you care that if you do not protect whatever you have left, your wonderful and grand culture that once spread across this island will disappear? In a short time, all of you and all that you stand for, will be gone, Neef — gone!"

Neef stared up at Mateo, calmly wiping blood that streamed from his mouth, but he still did nothing to defend himself. And with his dark eyes staring steadily at Mateo, he quietly answered.

"Nay, just because we may soon be dead, does not mean that we will be gone. Our *opias* will still live, and when they are not resting in *Coaibai*, they will wander throughout this earth, teaching the good we know to those who are living, whether they realize it or not."

Mateo threw up his hands, turned, walked across the hut, picked up his book of weapons, and left.

Soon afterwards when Basamanaco, Joaquín and Meyona returned from their walk, they found Neef sitting alone upon a mat. He had put away all of his papers, records, and translations into the metal boxes that Señor Mendoza gave him. And he sat staring into space, deep in thought.

"Where is Mateo?" Basamanaco asked. But Neef only shrugged.

The next day when Mateo began to give the people instructions about weapons, mostly the younger folk were receptive to what he had to say, excepting for an older man, who called himself Eldest-Son-of-My-Father's-First-Wife. Mateo could not help but notice a glee in that man's face, and he could tell that something was stirring inside of him. When that man asked to see the book Mateo held, he thumbed through it for a long time and closely examined each illustration. He asked questions about how to acquire metals and how to create alloys, but Mateo could answer him only briefly, concerning those subjects.

"Our people had many metals in our mountains in the Kingdom of the Mines," he said. "But the Spaniards took them away from us."

"We can only make a limited amount of these weapons," Mateo said. "But anything more than what we already have will greatly help us."

When Eldest-Son-of-My-Father's-First-Wife extended a hand of friendship toward Mateo, as Mateo grasped it, he noticed that it was extremely large and rough. Not once did he realize that this man was Neef's uncle. Nor did he realize that years before, he was the stranger, who had once stood on the beach and had shot an arrow at him and the Admiral, as they rowed to the Santa Maria.

As Mateo slept alone beneath the stars that night, too proud to return to Basamanaco's *bohío*, he could see that there was a wax light flickering in one of the huts. It was coming from the home where Eldest-Son-of-My-Father's-First-Wife lived, and from it, he could hear someone chipping away at some wood with a stone instrument, as if that person was creating an item of importance. As Mateo listened to that person working, he thought of his son, Joaquín, who was sleeping in Basamanaco's home. He was now growing up and chattering in both Spanish and Taino. Neef had told him that ever since Joaquín had come here, he brought back hope and joy into Basamanaco's life, and as Basamanaco grew to know and love Joaquín deeply, he quickly regained his old personality. But now, Joaquín was already five years old and must soon return to Spain, for he needed his mother and would also need to start school. But he, Mateo, was not ready to return, for his mission with these people was not yet fulfilled.

Then Mateo thought with tender feelings of his wife, Adelina, whom he had left behind. He promised her that he would return as soon as he could, but it was already nearing the end of 1506, and time was slipping quickly away. The other day he even heard that Admiral Captain Colón had passed away in Valladolid, Spain. And the very thought of Captain Colón's death made Mateo realize that he couldn't wait much longer, that the time to fill his mission on this island was now, so he could finally return to Spain to be with Adelina.

42

W inds howled and tore at the grass walls of the huts, and an occasional frond snapped off a palm tree and crashed to the ground. As Neef lay in his hammock, listening to the ghostlike wails outside, he wondered where Mateo was spending the night. He glanced over at Joaquín's hammock, and he saw the little boy's silhouette slip out of bed and edge its way in the dark toward him.

"I want Papa."

As another frond broke away from a tree and clattered down its trunk outside, Neef gathered the little boy into his arms and drew him into his hammock.

"Why doesn't Papa come home, anymore? Is it safe for him to be outside, right now?"

Neef heard that Mateo slept in the forest at night, and he quickly thought of an appropriate answer to give a five-year-old boy.

"Your Papa is safe, Joaquín. He stays away, because he has some very important work to do. I am sure we will see him again in the morning."

Although Mateo had been gone for several *uinals* now, every morning before he went out into the fields to work with the slaves, Neef saw him in the village with a crowd of people around him. Many of them were younger folk, who were not much older than children, whose fathers were often Spaniards. They often never knew who had sired them. They now listened eagerly to Mateo as he taught them about weaponry and warfare. Lampulla also helped with the instructions, particularly on how to use the weapons that he had taken from the Europeans, which he smuggled from the Fertile Kingdom. As Neef observed Mateo and his group from a distance, he was amazed at the adeptness they developed with the bow and arrow, and he was also at awe at the devices they created, such as large catapults, which flung huge stones with almost as much force as the Lombards the Europeans used. And always, he saw his uncle, Eldest-Son-of-My-Father's-First-Wife, among them.

"Why don't you fight, like Papa?" Joaquín said in Neef's ear. "Even Basamanaco is training to fight with Papa and his people, and he is now giving lessons on wrestling. He said that he used to fight off cannibals long ago, when he was a trader."

Neef did not say anything for a while, for he did not know how to reply to Joaquín's comments. Finally he said, "I do fight, Joaquín, but I fight in another way. I fight with love."

"But that's not fighting. Papa said that when the fighting is over soon, he'll take me back to Spain, so we can be with my mother. But I want us to stay here forever, so we can always be with you, Basamanaco and Meyona."

Joaquín was so young when he came to Quisqueya, that he did not remember his mother, and Neef could not tell him that his father stayed away, because he was angry. But he knew that Mateo loved and missed Joaquín, because in the mornings while he trained his followers, when Joaquín went up to him, he always held him in his arms. Because Mateo was also spending so much time teaching warfare, as well as was laboring in the fields with his slaves, the lessons on history and genealogy had come to a halt; the *areitas*, too, which once gave people hope, were rarely sung. And Mateo's part of Guarica suddenly plunged into depression. In addition, Mateo became irritable under the added stress, so whenever Señor Gomez came by and saw him snapping at someone, he interpreted this behavior to be an improvement over the past and thought that Mateo was putting the slaves in their proper places. But Basamanaco and the rest of the workers understood Mateo's predicament, and they tolerated his short temper and even continued to support his cause, by attending additional meetings in the evening each day, for further training.

As Joaquín snuggled up to Neef, Neef lay back and thought of what he often overheard Mateo telling his followers.

"Our need to fight and protect ourselves will only be temporary. It is necessary for us to learn how to stand up for ourselves, so if the Christians should ever descend upon us, we will show them that we will not stand to be treated with violence. When they see how well we can resist them, and that we are actually a strong people, then they will leave us alone and will allow us to live as we please."

"Mateo, when we win our victory, will the Grand College of Quisqueya resume?" Neef often heard people ask.

"Of course. That is my promise."

As the wind continued to whistle outside, large pieces of debris tumbled across the ground. Joaquín then put his mouth to Neef's ear and said, "Does Papa still love me?"

"Yes, Joaquín. Very much."

When he heard this answer, Joaquín curled up, as if he were feeling secure and content. And soon, he was fast asleep.

As Neef stared into the dark, he thought of the recent unfortunate conditions that began to develop in the *encomienda*. Since Mateo started his military program and began training people, the food supplies had grown lean, just as it was in the other *encomiendas*. The quotas of cotton were now harder to achieve, for everyone was left with less time to help each other. The oppression that once prevailed in this part of Guarica before Mateo came had now returned. And Señor Gomez was now alarmed over the drop in production among Mateo's Indians and constantly nagged him.

"Use yer whip on them, I tell ye. Cut off their hands, to set them straight with their goals 'n to keep them pacified."

But Mateo ignored him. And despite Mateo's instructions to his people concerning warfare, he did not encourage them to be aggressive. Instead, he advised that their weapons were to be used only when under attack, for the sake of preserving themselves. As Mateo continued to lead his people with kindness, Señor Gomez pressured him constantly to improve the production in his *encomienda*, until one day, with much reservations, Mateo announced to his people that it was necessary to create a new program to increase yields.

"From now on, every human being in this section of the *encomienda* must work in the fields," Mateo said. "This includes those who are younger than the age of 14, those who were once considered too old to work, as well as, those with physical handicaps."

So that meant that Neef, although he was crippled, all outcasts who were once considered un-useable, and those who were ill were required to begin laboring on the cotton grounds with brass tokens around their necks. Even Meyona, whom Neef hired to care for Joaquín, was no longer exempt from this work. So Joaquín went along with her to the fields every day and worked with her. And all workers labored from early morning, until the sun went down.

The gusts were getting stronger now, and as Joaquín slept contentedly by Neef's side, Neef arose from his hammock. As he hobbled toward the door of the *bohio* and stared out into the night, he felt Basamanaco come to his side.

"I wish Mateo was not so stubborn and would come back to us," Basamanaco whispered.

"I'm glad that I taught him how to survive in the wilderness, when we were both 13 years old. I would be much more worried over him, if I hadn't."

"Neef, I think Lampulla is right. When you become friends with Mateo again, I think you should consider what Lampulla said about starting a new Quisqueya somewhere else, where the Europeans can't reach you. There is no hope for us, here on this island."

"But didn't Mateo say that someday when the Spaniards learn more about Guanine, that they would eventually start looking for people there, to work for them?"

"That won't happen for an extremely long time, Neef. Guanine is very large."

As both Neef and Basamanaco stared out into the windy night, strange noises came from outside. Then a horse neighed.

"Did you hear that, Basamanaco? Whenever there's a horse, it usually means that a Christian is near."

"What would a Christian be doing here, at this hour of the night?"

Both Basamanaco and Neef listened, and smothered beneath the sounds of the bellowing wind, they heard quiet and slow, clopping from not just one horse, but from many.

"What do you think is happening?" Neef said.

He reached for his crutches, hobbled outside, and scanned into the distance. Although he could not see any horses, he saw numerous flames bobbing far away, as they approached.

"Basamanaco!" He whispered. "I see torches coming."

A trumpet suddenly bore rudely into the night, followed by other blasts. Within minutes, the clatter of gallops approached town, and soon, riders began thrusting torches into the walls of the huts to set them on fire.

"Our village is being pacified! Quick! Take Joaquín and wake up Meyona, while I warn everybody."

Neef sped across the town plaza.

"Wake up, everybody! Señor Gomez is pacifying our town!"

More trumpets blew.

In a short time, Spaniards coursed through the town and began yelling, "Accept Christianity, or be punished, ye heathens!"

Hooves thundered everywhere and surrounded the huts. Homes burst instantly into flames. Within minutes, the entire village was set on fire. People began running and coughing out of their huts, while all around them, their village blazed with intense heat. As they screamed and panicked, Christians whipped at them with their swords.

"So ye're not goin' to accept Christianity, eh?"

Among the burning structures, Neef saw that Mateo and his followers had appeared with their weapons. Soon their arrows sung through the air. They expelled rocks with catapults, aimed with crossbows, and even shot with European guns. Most of the time, they hit their targets. Neef saw them with weapons that he did not recognize, but he recognized the fearlessness of the fighters who used them. And he also saw his uncle, Eldest-Son-of-My-Father's-First-Wife, using his own inventions among them. All of these weapons caused the Spaniards to fall fast from their horses.

"I'm goin' to git more help!" one of the Christians hollered, and then a horse sped away into the darkness.

Neef looked for Basamanaco, but could not find him, Meyona, or even Joaquín. His instincts told him to flee, so quickly, he turned and hobbled as fast as his crutches allowed him to go, away from all the screaming and weeping. The forests were no longer safe places to escape to, as they once were years before, so he turned toward the dark cotton fields, far ahead. As the winds increased in velocity, he bent forward against them and continued to charge ahead. After a while, he glanced once

256

more over his shoulder and saw Mateo and his followers far behind. The flames flickered off their faces, as they put out a hard battle against the swords and muskets. The tempests whipped around them and caused the fire to spread even more rapidly. But Neef turned, looked ahead, and resumed his escape. As other people ran past him to save themselves from the massacre, Neef suddenly stopped.

What am I doing? I am running away from my enemy. I am repeating exactly what my people have done for generations, when under attack. I am being a coward.

Then he heard distant hooves clattering from behind, and they were coming nearer. As he turned to investigate that noise, he saw a new army of Christians approaching. As Mateo and his brave, young followers persisted in battle, unafraid of their enemies, the fresh supply of Christians began to force their way into the crowd. Neef could see that Mateo and his group were at a great disadvantage. Suddenly the words whipped through his mind: *We share the same battle and same cause.* And then he realized that he was deserting his brother, Mateo, as well as his own people. Neef turned abruptly and charged back toward the village.

When he reached the huts, fire roared around him. He came to a *mestizo* child, about twelve years old, who had a bow in her hands. As her beautiful long hair fell across her shoulders, she carefully aimed an arrow into a crowd of Christians. Before she could shoot, a musket cracked, and the child fell backward, with blood spurting from her face. She lay screaming, with her bow beside her, as she clutched at her eye.

Neef took her in his arms, as the girl bawled from her injury.

"That man who shot me. He is my father. My mother pointed him out to me many times. But he doesn't even know I exist. I hate him. I hate him."

Neef tried to comfort her.

"Oh, this pain. I cannot stand this pain. Give me something to make it go away."

And then Neef heard a musket go off again. Within the light of the flames, he saw something whizzing toward him. And then he felt the child in his arms shiver, as a bullet struck her, and she then grew limp. A man rode up to them, with his gun still smoking from its barrel. As he then tucked his weapon into his belt, he removed his sword from its sheath.

"Git away, ye miserable cripple. Let me finish off that brat 'n give her what she deserves. She nearly killed me."

Neef stared directly at the Christian, who held the sword. He was the man whom the child had identified to be her father.

In Spanish he said, "Ye just murdered yer own flesh 'n blood." When the Spaniard looked at him as if he did not comprehend what he said, Neef continued, "Yer own daughter, I tell ye, ye just killed yer own daughter. Ye never knew about her, did ye? All ye've been doin' was cause mischief on this island, 'n never cared about th' children ye peppered across it. There's no tellin' how many other of yer own children ye killed tonight."

The man upon the horse seemed to finally understand what Neef was saying, and then he looked down at the dead child in Neef's arms. His mouth parted slightly.

"What do ye mean, she's my daughter?"

"Can ye blame a child or a people for th' anger 'n hate ye have caused, when they have known only brutality from their very own fathers, who refused to know them, because their lusts came foremost in their lives? If ye allowed it, there could have existed joy, love, bonds 'n close relationships, but instead, ye bred nothin' but hate. Yer own daughter, I tell ye. Ye have killed yer own daughter, not just at this moment, but from th' day she was born."

The Spaniard dismounted his horse and removed his helmet, as he stared down at his child. Then another Spaniard rode up.

"Miguel! What are ye doin'?"

"Only a minute, "Miguel said. "Let me stay here only a minute."

"Leave that brat alone 'n help us get these people under control!"

And then that Spaniard rode away.

As the fire flickered off Miguel's face, Neef could see that his eyes were moist. He then placed a hand upon Neef's shoulder.

"*Gracias*," he said quietly. "I don't even know which woman she came from."

And then he mounted his horse and rode away.

Neef gently placed the girl upon the ground and reached for the bow and arrow, which she once used. He raised the bow, carefully positioned the arrow at a Christian, but repulsion filled him so intensely that he had to put the weapon down, with the realization that he was a pure Quisqueyan Taino to the very core, but Mateo and his young followers were not.

When Mateo and many of the young men and women were discovered to be the main source of resistance in the battle, the Christians surrounded them with their horses. Neef noticed that Eldest-Son-of-My-Father's-First-Wife was not among those who were being encircled. As horses closed in around the various groups, who fought under Mateo, many of the youth screamed in panic, and when some of them attempted to escape, the men hacked them dead. Until tonight, never before had Neef heard the word *hate* mentioned among his people. But before the young people were killed, many of them screamed at the Spaniards, "I hate you! I hate you! I hate you!" The Spaniards often did not understand their language, but if they did, they did not understand why the children were yelling those words at them.

"Here's th' traitor who's th' cause of th' trouble," said one of the Spaniards, as the horses enclosed around Mateo.

Mateo stood straight and tall and looked right at the Spaniards.

"I am no traitor, for I am just as loyal to Spain, as ye are. I happen to also represent these young people, who have grown up to despise their fathers. It was not th' workin's of their mothers that have taught them to hate ye, for their mothers have loved all of ye, who have fathered their children. Th' hate resulted from th' bad examples ye men have set that these children have witnessed all their lives. Because of their fathers, they have no roots to cling to, for th' culture of their mothers has been killed, 'n they never knew th' culture of their fathers. Among them, where there was once pride for a heritage that thrived with their ancestors, there is now a void."

Neef gasped, for behind Mateo, he saw one of the Spaniards raising a club.

"Mateo! Watch out, behind you!"

But Neef's warning came too late, for the club slammed down upon Mateo's head, and Mateo grew limp and slumped to the ground.

"Let's take this traitor in. Who has th' handcuffs?"

"Gomez warned him that trouble would start among these Indians if he continued to be too soft with them."

"See what happened? These people have nearly won him over to their side. This man is crazy."

258

"He absolutely needs to be tried 'n punished. Where's 'th handcuffs, I said?"

"We don't have any with us. Let me go back to get some."

Someone rode off into the night again. As that rider sped away, lightning streaked across the sky, and the wind suddenly increased and whipped mercilessly at the trees, splitting some of them in two and tearing off limbs. Thunder rumbled, and soon it grew so loud, that it shook the ground, as if an earthquake was in full force. When more lightning lit up the sky, the Christians looked upward.

"*Dios mío*! This isn't just any old storm. It's a hurricane! Quick, everybody! Let's get into shelter before it's upon us! Everybody, get back to yer homes!"

Within minutes, all of the Christians had galloped away, leaving Mateo, the wounded, and the dead still upon the ground.

But Neef looked heavenward and thought, *the God of Abraham also remembers the Tainos, for He has saved us tonight.* And then he hobbled over to Mateo, who lay unconscious upon the ground. Basamanaco suddenly appeared, and together, with Neef using only one crutch to walk, they carried Mateo to the communal hut, for it was the only structure that was left unburned. After Mateo was safely in, survivors went out in groups to scan the grounds. As rain soaked their bodies and winds raced around them, they searched for anyone who was still alive, so they could bring them back to the long hut.

"Have you seen Joaquín?" Neef called out to Basamanaco.

Basamanaco had not.

As they pushed against the wind, they heard a child screaming in the distance. Quickly they went to those cries and found Joaquín standing among a pile of rocks, weeping.

"Come, Joaquín, let's get you to safety."

But Joaquín resisted them and shook his head, as he pointed ahead.

"Meyona! Something's wrong with her!"

Neef found Meyona lying across some rocks, with her body mangled by the blade of a sword. Despite her condition, she looked at peace, for she clutched a small child, who was also dead, as if she had been trying to help that child to safety, before she died. Close to her lay another woman, who was one of Lida's good friends. That woman, too, was dead, and several of her grandchildren lay lifeless near her.

Basamanaco and Neef tenderly lifted Meyona's stiff body, as Joaquín ran along side of them, sobbing. They carried her to a spot, where they could leave her until the storm passed, for she and others would need proper burials, so their *opias* could go to *Coaibai* to rest.

"Meyona is the only mother Joaquín remembers," Basamanaco said to Neef.

When they finally returned to the long hut, Neef noticed the Guaricans counting the heads of those who were alive. But he did not see Eldest-Son-of-My-Father's-First-Wife among them. When the people felt that they had located everyone who needed to be in the communal hut, they huddled together in this shelter, listening to the winds beating against the *bohío* walls, as thunder bellowed. For three days, the people remained in this hut, and when the fourth day arrived, a glimmer of sunshine finally peeked through the sky, amongst a gentle rain. And by then, Mateo was up and about with a prominent bruise upon his head.

"I am ready to lead you again," he said to everyone.

When Neef walked out into the rain, he helped the Guaricans gather the bodies of the dead. Since the eye of the hurricane had passed, the winds were now tolerable.

Rain pelted down upon the backs of those who dug deep into the ground, as they carved out graves their loved ones deserved. And while standing among the Guaricans, Neef cast his eyes toward the section of town, where the Europeans lived, and he saw that most of those buildings were now flattened.

"Do you understand what has happened?" Neef said to his younger brother, Lampulla. "Something that we should be proud of has just occurred. See how those grand buildings the Europeans have built are all destroyed? But notice how our communal hut still remains standing, just as strong as the day it was constructed generations before. It is because our fathers knew how to build structures that withstood hurricanes. And if the Christians had not burned our other homes, those *bohíos*, too, would still be standing straight and tall, unharmed by the hurricane."

After Joaquín was left in the care of village folk, Neef, Basamanaco and Mateo returned to the remains of their *bohío*. Among the soggy and blackened residue, Neef found his metal boxes covered with soot, but his records within them were unharmed. He also found that in one of those boxes, the black piece of coral that he kept to remind himself of his Grandfather Cahoba was also unharmed.

Again, Neef looked heavenward and thought, *not only does the God of Abraham also remember the Tainos, but so do our zemies.*

Then Neef called over to Basamanaco and Mateo, who were both rummaging through the debris to see if they could salvage any other belongings.

"Basamanaco, I found my records. They are safe."

When he saw both Basamanaco and Mateo looking in his direction, Neef added, " I think you are right, Basamanaco. We will need to take these records away from here. And we should also bring whoever is willing to come with us to start our new Quisqueya. I think we should go to Guanine. But when I take these people with me, you, Mateo, must go back to Spain with Joaquín."

Mateo came over to him.

"I'm coming with you. As brothers, both of us must work together to establish our new Quisqueya."

And then they both embraced.

43

As the sounds of hammering came from the Christian section of Guarica, Neef saw that Basamanaco was deeply troubled as he paced the floor of the communal hut. Finally he stopped in front of Mateo.

"Mateo, the hurricane was a blessing from the *zemies*, because for a short while, it has diverted the Christians from us, for now they are more concerned over their dead and reconstructing their homes than seeking you out. But this period is only temporary, for once they are done with their repairs, they will start looking for you again to punish you for rebellion. They'll probably imprison you, place you in stocks in the town square, or mostly likely, put you to death. You must take advantage of this time, *right now*, and leave this island to establish our new Quisqueya elsewhere."

"But I'm not even prepared to go," said Mateo. "My followers and I have only begun to build a boat. Although we keep it hidden, its construction will take time, and we are still in need of materials."

"Nay, you must go tonight, my son, for you are in grave danger. Besides, I do not see how you could possibly make it back to Spain on any Christian ship, because the Spaniards are on the lookout for you."

"But how could we possibly leave right away?"

"You can take my canoe. I still have it. After the Europeans began making us slaves and were taking away our valuables and every possession we owned that would enable us to escape, I buried my canoe, so it could never be found. It can hold up to eighty men, plus a heavy load of goods. I hid it in the sand, in front of the cluster of trees, where Lida used to wait for me. As soon as it is dark, you must dig it up, load it with whatever you'll need, and then, you must go quickly."

"Then I'll organize my group right now to gather provisions," said Mateo.

Basamanaco placed his hand on Mateo's shoulder.

"Wait. There is one more thing that I must say."

"We're both willing to listen to whatever you have to tell us," said Neef.

"I cannot go with you to start a new Quisqueya. Someone must remain here with Joaquín."

"But Joaquín is coming with us," Mateo protested. "I won't leave him behind."

"Nay, the journey is far too dangerous for a small boy. Someone must make sure that he's sent back to Spain. To establish a new Quisqueya will take years, and the boy needs his mother. Besides, how are you going to ever return to Spain, if you are wanted by the Spaniards?"

Neef looked over at Joaquín, who was playing with the Taino children, as if he were one of them.

"Who will be going away with you?" he heard Basamanaco say.

"All of my followers, who have survived the battle," said Mateo.

"I'm also coming, and so is Lampulla," said Neef.

"If I cannot return to Spain, who will take Joaquín back?" said Mateo. "I have already alienated the Spaniards, and none of the Tainos would want to go there."

"I know what you can do," said Neef. "Basamanaco, could you take Joaquín to Santo Domingo and find Señor Mendoza there? Maybe the *señor* is well by now, and if he isn't, perhaps one of his friends there will be able to take the boy. I am sure that if Señor Mendoza was given charge of Joaquín, he would take excellent care of him."

"Tell Señor Mendoza to bring Joaquín to the monastery, La Rábida, in Palos, Spain," said Mateo. "Tell him to ask for Juan Perez, who is one of the monks there. If Señor Mendoza told him that Joaquín is my son, he will know where to find my wife, Adelina."

When Neef and his followers unearthed Basamanaco's canoe that night, they found it to be in surprisingly good condition. Quietly, they carried load after load of provisions to it, including four metal boxes, packed with Neef's records. Only a few Tainos knew of this parting, because the group feared that, if the news leaked out, it would eventually reach the Christians, and those people would never understand the reasons for this trip. In fact, they would suspect that another rebellion was brewing.

It was extremely late when the preparations were finally complete, and in the light of the moon, a small group gathered on the beach to bid farewells to those who were leaving. But Joaquín was not told that his Papa was going, for they feared that, should he weep, it would carry over to the Christian part of town and would wake them. Instead, he was put to bed at his usual time. And now, with many wordless tears, the people pushed the vessel into a clearing, while hounds, owned by Christians, bayed far away. Fewer dogs howled tonight, for many of them were killed in the last battle. Nevertheless, their howls sounded lustier than ever.

"Good-bye, my friend," Neef said and flung his arms around Basamanaco.

Basamanaco surprised him, when he bawled as a baby. Then he said, "Neef, I am so sorry that I never brought you back to Cuba, as I promised. I would have, if I could."

When Mateo also embraced him, Basamanaco said, "I'll take good care of Joaquín."

Mateo then dug into his pockets, took out several brass tokens, and gave them to Basamanaco.

"Here. Keep these, in case you lose yours."

As the younger people sat patiently in the canoe, waiting to depart, Neef and Mateo finally turned toward them.

"Let's be off, now."

They had not walked far, when a singing sound whizzed through the air. Then Neef heard a thump. Mateo released a gasp. When Neef turned to see what had happened, he saw Mateo grabbing at his chest, as he staggered backwards across the wet sand and fell to the ground, groaning. In shock, Neef stared at his brother and saw him looking up at him. As the moonlight shown upon Mateo's countenance, it was glassy-eyed with horror frozen upon it. Neef discerned a blackish substance spreading out on the ground beneath his brother, and when he bent to touch it, he realized that it was a pool of blood.

"Mateo, what happened?"

Mateo could only whisper.

"An arrow...someone shot me with an arrow."

"But who?"

Neef looked around and saw no one suspicious. Yet Mateo was bleeding profusely, and there was, indeed, an arrow that had penetrated his chest.

Basamanaco was immediately at Neef's side and was soon tugging at the arrow. Neef recalled how Basamanaco said that he had taken many arrows out of his traders, when they were shot. And many of them had even survived. In a few seconds Basamanaco withdrew the arrow from Mateo's body, and he was cradling Mateo's head in his lap.

"Quick," Basamanaco said. "Someone, bring me a rag to stop his bleeding."

In panic, people silently scampered across the beach, and one of the young followers ran over with a piece of cloth that he found in the canoe. And as that person held it to the wound, Basamanaco stroked Mateo's forehead, with unsteadiness in his voice.

"My son, my son..."

When Mateo spoke, his voice was barely audible.

"Basamanaco, I tried very hard to help our people."

"I know, Mateo. I know, Basamanaco-el."

Neef placed an encouraging hand on his brother's arm.

"You will get well, Mateo. I still remember which herbs Lida used for wounds from arrows, after the Caribs attacked us. They cured many people who were wounded badly. We will get you well, just as she got those people well. We won't leave on our journey, until you have recovered."

Mateo tried to sit up, but winced, and leaned back again.

"Nay, Neef," he whispered. "I think I was not meant to come with you."

"My brother, I said, we will wait for you."

Just then, Mateo seemed to gain a spurt of strength, for he suddenly spoke louder and clearer.

"Don't you see what must happen, Neef? Our ghosts are stronger than we are. While we are alive, people often scoff at our ideas and for what we believe in, if they are different from theirs. But it is only after we die, when people begin to consider what we stood for, and our beliefs begin to haunt those we left behind for generations, and sometimes, they can even influence the entire earth."

"Mateo, you will not die now, but you will live to build our Quisqueya."

Mateo relaxed further in Basamanaco's arms.

"I feel myself slipping away. I see a beautiful garden of greens, oranges, yellows. Such marvelous fruit, here. They are the size of guavas, and they look so soft and sweet. If only I could taste one of them. It's so peaceful here. Oh, my gosh! This isn't Purgatory! Why, it's...it's...*Coaibai*!"

"Mateo, you must believe that you will get well!"

"Neef, I promise, I will not always remain here forever, for I will often leave this beautiful place to roam the earth, so I can teach and inspire people everywhere, how to love all men, especially our people."

"Nay, Mateo, nay."

Mateo sighed.

"Could someone tell Adelina that I love her for me?"

Then he closed his eyes and grew limp.

"Mateo!"

Neef shook Mateo, as if he had gone mad.

"Mateo!"

Basamanaco placed a hand on him and said, "Let him go, Neef."

"But he's the main cause for our leaving this island."

In the distance, one of the younger people who stood by the canoe pointed into the shadows and shouted, "Watch out!"

A figure was coming toward them. None of the people on the beach had any weapons with them, and they froze, as it slunk into the open. Neef discerned that it was a man, who held a bow and arrow. It walked boldly toward them. Even in the darkness, Neef discerned that he was dressed in the traditional Taino attire of an *undercacique*, with a crown of feathers, a loincloth, and a cloak over his shoulders. As the figure stepped into the moonlight, Neef recognized it to be his uncle, Eldest-Son-of-My-Father's-First-Wife and realized that he was the one, who had murdered Mateo. Neef released a hoarse cry. In the meantime, the people on the beach backed away from this man, lest he tried to kill them also, but Eldest-Son-of-My-Father's-First-Wife merely tossed his head back, laughed, and allowed the moonlight to reflect off his body.

"Well, my friends," he said smoothly. "Our people have suffered enough injustices, so now it is time for your foreigner friend to have his turn."

And then he laughed again. Coldly, he looked down at Mateo.

"Is he dead, yet?"

Although Neef's first impulse was to shrink from his uncle, he found that he was no longer afraid of him, as he used to be, even if his uncle was armed. Anger that he never experienced before burst from him. In a rage, he hobbled toward his uncle and lunged, but Eldest-Son-of-My-Father's-First-Wife stepped out of his range.

"Stop, Neef, stop..." Basamanaco called softly. "He is dangerous. We must forgive him, remember? This man does not always know what he is doing."

With anger exploding from within him, Neef moved toward his uncle, who had a smile set upon his lips. As Neef's fury increased, he stepped closer to him, determined to wring every bit of evil out of his body with his bare hands.

"What's wrong, crippled man? Don't you have *the love* of Yocahu, anymore?"

Neef began to yell at the top his lungs, and then he lifted one of his crutches and swung. He felt a smack, as his uncle attempted to dodge from him again.

"Why did you kill our dearest and most helpful friend, who loved our people, more than anyone else ever had? Why didn't you kill an enemy, instead?"

As Neef continued to close in on his uncle, he saw a sudden drop in Eldest-Son-of-My-Father's-First-Wife's face, but it was not because he was coming toward him, but because his uncle was also listening to distant sounds. He, Neef, had made so much noise, that the foreigners' dogs heard him. They were now barking in response to his screams, as if they were crazy, and their yelps were growing more savage by the minute. Finally, Neef heard Spaniards shouting from far away.

"Did ye hear that? There's trouble, somewhere."

Quickly Eldest-Son-of-My-Father's-First-Wife darted away into the darkness.

"Neef, you must leave this island, now!" Basamanaco yelled. "Hurry. The foreigners are coming."

"But I don't want to leave Mateo here."

"I'll see to it that he has a proper burial. But leave!"

Neef hobbled to the canoe, and as soon as he climbed in, the young followers launched the vessel. As they paddled from shore, Neef could see figures fleeing into the brush, to escape the oncoming dogs, which were speedily advancing. He saw that Basamanaco had also left, and the dark form of Mateo lay abandoned upon the ground. Neef groped on the floor of the canoe and found his paddle, and then he plunged it deep into the water, to help the rest of the crew glide the canoe away.

The dogs came closer, and soon Neef saw them in the clearing. They turned and ran toward something in the distant brush. Their barks went crazy, as a man, whom Neef could not see, screamed in panic.

"Get away from me!"

It was Elder's-Son-of-My-Father's-First-Wife's voice. Soon Neef saw him running through the vegetation. He heard twigs snapping, and then his uncle came into the clearing. In a blur, he swept across the beach, as a group of animals bayed and yelped at his heels. His uncle screamed again, as dogs surrounded him, snarling and nipping. One of them leaped at his shoulders, attempting to sink its teeth into his throat. His uncle staggered backwards, but kept his balance. He released a long and loud wail, which carried across the water to the canoe. And then, the Spaniards appeared upon their horses and called off their dogs.

The canoe glided faster now, but still, the echoes from shore carried out to it, as the men calmed the dogs down.

"Heavens! Somebody was killed here. It looks like it was an Indian."

"*Un momento*! He's dressed like an Indian, but he's...he's...*bueno*, isn't he that Christian who was an Indian lover? Ye know, th' one who was rebellin' against us?"

"So, he met his fate. Th' Indians finally turned against him 'n killed him. Guess you can't trust Indians, even if ye become their friend."

"*Sí*, 'n look how they left him out here to rot."

As Neef and the young people retreated even farther from shore, it was too dark for the Christians to see them. The Christians remained unaware that runaways lurked only a few yards from them out in the water, as they searched the beach with their lamps for further evidence of any Indian activities.

"Let's leave th' traitor here. We'll take care of him in th' mornin'."

"Good idea. Rojas, take this Indian, whom we just caught, 'n lock him up. Why in th' world is he dressed up in this crazy outfit, anyway? Aren't these Indians supposed to be dressed in European clothes? We'll make sure he gets his proper punishment. Th' rest of ye, come with me. I thought I heard more of those *cretinos* movin' in that direction."

The horses galloped away, with their dogs running and yelping ahead of them, as they left the body of Mateo alone on the beach.

As Neef and his crew continued to paddle away from Quisqueya, the silhouette of land was no longer visible, and in a few hours, they found themselves enveloped in an abyss, with only the moon and stars to direct them.

"Where do we go, now?" someone asked.

Neef looked into the darkness.

"West," he said. "There are parts of Guanine, where people can read and write. I want to be among them, so I can learn from them. I want to see and feel their codices of bark. Or maybe, they might even have plates of metal, in which they have engraved their histories and *areitas*."

Neef cast his eyes heavenward, read the stars, and pointed westward. But soon, they sailed beneath clouds, which hid the moon and stars, and he found that he had lost all sense of direction. If the School of the Princes had not closed by the time he returned from his *bohutio* test, he would have acquired a vast knowledge of astronomy by now, with even the ability to predict weather from it. And in addition, he would have learned how to navigate without stars. But now beneath the cloud-skinned heavens, he had no sense of which way was east, west, north, or south.

"Perhaps in the morning we can re-orient ourselves," he said.

Then he yawned and lay down on the floor of the canoe to rest, while the other people also curled up on the floor and went to sleep.

The days and nights continued endlessly, with no sight of land. For some reason, Neef and his group were not reaching any shore. Yet Neef was too proud to admit that they were lost, and he advised his crew to distribute the food supplies sparingly. Sometimes they caught fish, and on rare occasions when they got hold of a turtle, they first drank its blood to quench their thirst, and then they feasted upon its raw flesh and organs. And Neef warned them to dare not weep, for the loss of tears would drain fluids from their bodies.

Upon this vessel, Neef encouraged everyone to sing *areitas,* as well as recite chants. It was not only for the sake of restoring their tradition, but to keep everyone from going insane. And after the crew sang all the *areitas* they knew many times, Neef often opened the Admiral's Bible and read to the crew out of it, as well as taught them to memorize its passages, as if they were also *areitas*. Soon the crew began to create singsong rhythms of Biblical verses, as if they were originally created for their people.

"Blessed, blessed, blessed are the meek, meek, meek, for they shall..."

The young people began to compose songs of their own, as they sang about the six days of creation, David and Goliath, Abraham, the beatitudes of Christ, the verses of the Psalms, and the commandments. Their chants kept them from thinking that their escape to create a new Quisqueya was insane; that the chance of their surviving in the open sea on a lone canoe was slim, especially when they did not know where they were heading. Neef never mentioned that their cause to preserve Quisqueya was merely a dream, which each of them could not let go of.

They lived in fear that the canoe would overturn. They counted the waves and classed them into categories — the ones that looked like mountains, the ones that looked like dogs, and the ones that resembled *zemies*. To all of them, the surrounding water transformed into figures that sometimes laughed hysterically. But Neef also saw additional figures, such as Mateo, Basamanaco, and Lida, who now had her hands back. And they disappeared, when he reached out to them.

Sometimes Neef withdrew into his thoughts, often looking heavenward, as he tottered back and forth between Christian ideas and the philosophy of his own people. *Why are my people out of favor with the zemies? Why cannot the Christian God help us, like he did the Israelites?*

And one day, without realizing what he was doing, Neef pulled himself up with his crutches and violently rocked the canoe, as he yelled heavenward, "Makanaima, is it our *zemies*? Is it our *zemies* that anger you, because they are what the Christians call idols? Is that why our people were destroyed?"

Neef felt the others grabbing his arms to calm him down, to pull him back. He saw the horror in their faces.

"Neef, Neef, do not offend the *Zemie of the Heavens*. You might cause lightning to strike us."

But Neef was reluctant to be seated, as he cocked his head upward and listened for a response from heaven, or if his creator, Makanaima, or the God of Abraham and Moses — or whoever was up there — would speak to him. But all he heard were the sounds of the sea. He waited for answers, anyway, as a child expects a miracle.

"Makanaima, we have waited for Yocahu, for too long. Are we not faithful enough? "

Dark clouds suddenly formed. Soon lightning streaked across the sky, followed by thunder. And the others on board began to weep.

"Neef, please. You are angering the heavens."

But Neef picked up the Admiral's Bible and waved it into the air and continued.

"Makanaima, why were my people not called to write sacred records, such as these?"

Huge drops pelted down on the canoe and drenched Neef's hair, cape, and the rest of the crew. The rain caused Neef to burst into laughter.

He turned to the crew, with wildness in his eyes, and said, "See what I did? Makanaima has heard me. He knew that we are thirsty, so he is now sending us water, so we can drink! See? It's like manna. Look, Makanaima sent us waterrrrr."

Neef cupped his hands to catch the rain and gluttonously gulped it down. His followers also drank their fill, and many of them clamored to fill gourds. As the rain continued, they even had to bale water out of the canoe.

When Neef looked heavenward, he thought he could feel the presence of an *opia*.

"Mateo?" he said. "Did you leave *Coaibai* to help us find our new Quisqueya?"

With his body refreshed from the rain, Neef continued to call up to the heavens. "Yocahuuuuu! Come down and save us! My people need youuuuuu!"

Then Neef clutched the edge of the canoe and screamed out an *areita* that he had known, since he was a boy.

> Yocahu saved the fate of mortals
> In his struggle with dark Guaca
> Brooding Guaca waits revengeful
> Forever angry with Yocahu
> Always angry with Yocahu
> Always angry with Yocahu

Epilogue

It was I, who hath caused the rain to fall upon Neef and his young people, because they needed relief from the heat, for when I saw the sun beating upon their emaciated bodies, I felt pity for them. In ignorance, Neef hath guided them farther north than he realized. After the canoe overturned, and all but Neef were drowned, I buoyed his body up in the water and caused the waves to toss him toward Guanine, until he was safely washed upon the shore of Florida. The next day, I whispered into the ears of Calusan women to run to the beach, where they discovered his body, bloated and belching of sea water, with kelp tangled in his hair. After they carried him to shelter and placed him under covers near a fire, they listened in awe to his strange language, as he babbled and slipped in and out of delirium.

The Calusans assigned a widow of their tribe to nurse Neef back to health. Like Lida, she was an extremely goodly woman, who faithfully fed him herbs, washed his face, prepared his meals, and learned his language. I made certain that she fell deeply in love with him, even if he was a cripple. The Calusans are a large people, similar to those from whom Basamanaco hath descended. Their men are powerful, warlike, and muscular, who average at least seven feet tall. Compared to them, Neef was a runt. But this widow loved him, anyway, for she saith many times that Neef was stronger, braver, and more of a man, than any of the men of her tribe, and she desired to marry him and bear his children.

For years after Neef recovered, I often saw him standing at the shore, as he leaned upon two canes that his wife hath made for him, with a child or two by his side. He even hath taught his children to read and write.

As the ocean swished over their feet, he often pointed southward and spake, "Somewhere out there are my records and a Bible. They are at the bottom of the sea, probably waterlogged, with their ink long washed out of them. And close to them, lies a small piece of black coral that reminds me of my Grandfather Cahoba."

And then one day, Neef and his family were no more among the Calusans. They disappeared, soon after news reached the village that strange ships, manned by Europeans, were seen sailing along the coast. The leader of this fleet was Ponce de Leon, and he was searching for an island called Bimini, where someone hath told him that there was a Fountain of Youth. The family vanished, even before the sore battles occurred with the foreigners, which left Señor Leon seriously injured. Only I know, to where that family hath fled.

Years later, a stranger, a handsome black man, arrived upon a canoe. With gestures, he explained to the Calusans that he hath escaped with many other black slaves from Quisqueya, who were imported from the land of Africa. This man was the only one who hath survived that trip. He spake of several *padres* on Quisqueya, who spent all of their days helping the slaves, particularly the Indians. One of them was named Father de Las Casas. Although Las Casas hath taken many trips to Spain to complain about the treatment of the Indians, his stories were so bizarre, that the people there thought he was insane. And since Las Casas wanted so much to help the Indians, he made a grave error of convincing the sovereigns of Spain to use more black people to replace the Indian slaves, because he said that they had greater stamina and could endure greater physical hardships than the Indians.

269

The black stranger spake of another *padre*, who worked closely with Father de Las Casas, who hath fought just as hard for the slaves. He said his name was Father Tomas Mendoza. Father Mendoza spake often about a crippled Indian, whom he said was responsible for influencing him to turn to the priesthood, for that Indian shewed him how to understand himself. By understanding himself, he learned of his own worth, as well as the worth of each human soul — especially the souls of the Indians.

The Calusans knew not that the crippled Indian, whom the black man mentioned, was the same crippled stranger, whom they once rescued on their beach. They listened in fascination, as the black man spake of how the Quisqueyans became a mixture of many peoples, of whites, of blacks, and of a variety of Indians. Not once did he mention the women of the Mother Kingdom, who were at one time considered to be the most beautiful in the world, because he never knew about them, for they no longer existed. Instead, he said that more black slaves were being imported from Africa unto the land of Quisqueya, and it was quickly being filled with black people, who brought with them their rich culture and deep, religious philosophies. And he recognized that the peace and tranquility that was robbed from the *caciques* years before, was replaced by turmoil that never left that land.

For generations, I have heard the blood of the Quisqueyans and others throughout Guanine constantly crying up unto me, pleading against those, who were merciless, who have exercised dominion and brutality over them. Occasionally my helpers, such as Cahoba the Great, Mateo, Neef, Anacoana, and even Lida, leave *Coaibai* to roam the earth, to open the eyes of many. They teach about *the love* for all humans. But the people on earth remain stubborn and set in their ways; and, just as the words Christ murmured as he hung upon the cross, *they know not what they do.*

So much time hath elapsed since I visited the ancient fathers, that now, those who have awaited my return, can wait no longer, and they beg constantly for justice and equality to be established among all men. But humans still have much to learn, many trials to face, many weaknesses to overcome, and they still have need to understand that they are all truly brothers. They must also raise their intellectual standards, so that they can grasp the new knowledge that I intend to bring unto them. And when the time is ripe, I will show myself again unto them, as I did with their fathers, to bring a level of learning and love that is even greater than their fathers ever knew. Then and only then, shall my followers realize, that it is through their faithfulness, their tribulations and hardships, and how they overcome their trials, that will make them the choicest people on the earth. And when these come to past, the *ayiti* that shall flow through my people throughout the lands, will far surpass the beauty of any *areita* that hath yet been written.

Acknowledgements

A thousand thanks to the following people: The two young brothers, Paul and Samuel Schneider, who posed as models for my front cover in more ways than one can imagine; Dr. Lynne Guitar, coeditor of the *Caribbean Ameridian Centrelink* and Resident Director of the CIEE program in Spanish and Caribbean Studies at PUCMM, Santiago de los Cabelleros, Dominican Republic for the photograph of the Cueva Peñon Gordo, which she took in the East National Park in the Dominican Republic; Wayne Melander, for translating from Spanish to English the works of the 15th century *padre*, Bartholomé de Las Casas; Dr. Phillip Koldewyn, professor of Latin America studies at Claremont McKenna College, for explaining the *repartimiento* and *encomienda* systems and translating many sentences into Spanish. I apologize that I could not use most of his sentences, because readers who did not understand Spanish reacted to them; Dr. Kendall Brown and Dr. Ray Matheny of Brigham Young University in Provo, Utah, who transformed the history and cultures of Latin America into compelling adventures in their classes; Dr. John Bennion, professor of novel writing at Brigham Young University in Provo, Utah, who saw potential in my work; and the various people from the Caribbean who shared with me how it is to live in this area.

I also wish to thank: My own three daughters, Katherine Bowman, Heidi Bond, and Tami Bond; Katherine, for the word arrangements on the cover of this book; Heidi, for the blurb on the cover, as well as for her other suggestions; and Tami, for the stanzas of free verse that made the *areitas* come to life. Thanks also to Phillip Pardi, who assured me that I could also write poetry, when Tami no longer could create stanzas, because she had become too busy; Professor Rose L. Tse, M.D., who provided the means to have this book and other creations to be published; Oakley Hall, who volunteered his expertise beyond the Squaw Valley Community of Writers Conference, when I didn't even ask for it; Tom Jenks, retired editor of *Esquire* and other magazines, to whom Oakley had referred me, to help further refine my writing skills; the late Carolyn Doty, director of Squaw Valley Community of Writers, who was so impressed with my work that she referred me to her own personal agent. Although this effort did not work out, Carolyn's faith in my abilities affected me permanently.

I must also remember to thank the first person in my life who ever had faith in me, the late Dr. Alfred A. Levy, of Indiana University and the University of Hawaii, who told me often whenever he read my papers when I first entered college, "Wait until you mature! You'll really be something else!" Because of him, I am still looking forward to that day.

And of course, I must thank my dear husband, for his support during my struggle to become the person that I should have been years before.

Gloria Bond lives with her husband in both Germany and the Pacific Northwest. She is presently working on the prequel to *Sons of Yocahu: A Saga of the Taino's Devastation on Hispaniola* and will eventually create a third book to complete this trilogy.

Printed in the United States
96487LV00001B/284/A